Philip H. Stanhope

Life of the Right Honourable William Pitt

Volume 1

Philip H. Stanhope

Life of the Right Honourable William Pitt
Volume 1

ISBN/EAN: 9783337189969

Printed in Europe, USA, Canada, Australia, Japan

Cover: Foto ©Raphael Reischuk / pixelio.de

More available books at **www.hansebooks.com**

LIFE

OF

THE RIGHT HONOURABLE

WILLIAM PITT.

.

BY EARL STANHOPE.

IN FOUR VOLUMES.—VOL. I.

THIRD EDITION.

LONDON:

JOHN MURRAY, ALBEMARLE STREET.

1867.

LONDON: PRINTED BY W. CLOWES AND SONS, STAMFORD STREET,
AND CHARING CROSS.

PREFACE TO THE THIRD EDITION.

In my small volume of 'Miscellanies' (the Second Edition of which appeared in 1863) will be found various additional Letters from Mr. Pitt—as to the Duke of Rutland, the Earl of Harrowby, and Sir Walter Farquhar—many of which did not come into my hands until after my account of his Life was completed and published. I have not attempted to embody these Letters with my present edition, first because they are none of them essential to the narrative ; and secondly, because in regard to books of large compass I think it unjust to the purchasers of the earlier copies to make any important changes in the later, except only in correction, if need be, of proved and admitted errors.

S.

January, 1867.

PREFACE.

According to the desire expressed on his death-bed by Mr. Pitt, the papers which he left were in the first instance delivered to his early friend Dr. Tomline, Bishop of Lincoln. After the decease of the Bishop and of the last Lord Chatham, these MSS. devolved to my cousin, William Stanhope Taylor, Esq., grand nephew of Mr. Pitt. When Mr. Taylor also died, the papers came into the possession of another grand nephew of Mr. Pitt through his younger sister—Colonel John Pringle, who has in the kindest manner and without the smallest reserve placed them in my hands.

The Bishop of Lincoln, in his examination of these MSS. and in pursuance of the discretion assigned him, appears to have destroyed nearly all the letters addressed to Mr. Pitt by members of Mr. Pitt's family. Among those that now remain in the collection there is not one from his mother, from either of his sisters, or from either of his brothers, until the time when his eldest brother became his Cabinet colleague. The letters addressed to him by the Bishop himself, and by several other personal friends, have also been removed.

On the other hand, there still exists the series of letters which Mr. Pitt wrote to his mother. These from the first she appears to have carefully preserved, and they were, I presume, returned to him after her death. A few blanks in the series may, indeed, here and there be traced, and some accident appears to have befallen the concluding portion. Since October, 1799, only one letter to Lady Chatham is left, bearing the date of January 5, 1802, besides another of September 17 following, to her companion, Mrs. Stapleton. There are also very confidential letters addressed by Mr. Pitt to his brother, Lord Chatham, though some are missing from the series, and though none among them bears an earlier date than 1794. Of these letters, both to his mother and his brother, which will be wholly new to the public, I have inserted the greater portion in my narrative.

I have also largely availed myself of the series

of MS. letters addressed to Mr. Pitt by King George the Third. This is, I believe, quite complete, although on the other hand there are now preserved very few drafts of Mr. Pitt's own communications to the King.

There are in this collection many letters from Mr. Pitt's colleagues and other men of note in politics; and also drafts or copies, although not equally numerous, of his letters to them.

In 1842 my much valued friend the late Duke of Rutland entrusted to me, in the original MSS., the correspondence between his father and Mr. Pitt, and gave me leave to put it into type. The copies, of which the number was fixed at one hundred, were confined to a circle of friends; but I had the Duke's sanction to insert some considerable extracts in the Quarterly Review, No. 140, and in my own collected Essays.

In 1849 I had an opportunity, through the kindness of the late Lord Melville, to examine the papers at Melville Castle, and to take several transcripts. No letter from Mr. Pitt of an earlier date than 1794 is, so far as I saw, there preserved. In 1852 I obtained permission from the present Lord Melville to print for private circulation the most important of these papers in a small volume, which I entitled "Secret Correspondence connected with Mr. Pitt's Return to Office in 1804."

I may observe that the letters of Mr. Pitt to his friend before the peerage begin "Dear Dundas," while on the other side it is always "My dear Sir."

I have also obtained some communications of considerable value through the kindness of the Duke of Bedford, of Lord St. Germans, of Mr. Dundas of Arniston, and of other gentlemen, to whom my warm thanks are due; and I need scarcely advert to the great interest and importance of several published collections, more especially the Malmesbury, the Buckingham, and the Cornwallis Papers, and the biographies of Lord Sidmouth and Mr. Wilberforce.

STANHOPE.

Chevening, January 23, 1861.

CONTENTS OF VOL. I.

Preface ..   Page v

CHAPTER I.

1759 — 1780.

Birth of William Pitt — Early signs of great promise — Feeble health
in boyhood — Education — At seventeen admitted M.A. at Cambridge — Study of elocution — Death of his father — Economical
habits — Entered at Lincoln's Inn — Attends Parliamentary debates
— Introduction to Fox — Called to the Bar — Joins the Western
Circuit — M.P. for Appleby   1

CHAPTER II.

1781 — 1782.

Enters the House of Commons — State of parties — Attaches himself
to Lord Shelburne — Goostree's Club — Pitt's first speech — Congratulated by Fox — Vindication of his father's opinions, and statement of his own, on the American war — On the Western Circuit,
and in the Court of King's Bench — General character at the Bar —
Readiness of debate — Speeches on Parliamentary Reform — Appointed Chancellor of the Exchequer — Letters to his mother.. 49

CHAPTER III.

1782 — 1783.

Acknowledgment of American independence — Proposed cession of
Gibraltar — Preliminary treaties with France and Spain — Conference between Pitt and Fox — Coalition of Fox and North — Defeat
of Lord Shelburne — Pitt's great speech in vindication of the
Peace — Resignation of Lord Shelburne — Pitt refuses the offer of
the Treasury — Resigns office of Chancellor of the Exchequer —
Duke of Portland's Ministry — Pitt in private life — Again brings
forward Parliamentary Reform, but is defeated — Prince of Wales
— Marriage of Lord Chatham   87

CHAPTER IV.

1783.

Pitt's excursion to France — Abbé de Lageard — Return to England — Fox's India Bill — Great speech of Burke — Bill passes the Commons, but is thrown out by the Lords — Dismissal of Fox and North — The Royal Prerogative — Pitt appointed Prime Minister — Resignation of Lord Temple — The new Cabinet .. Page 129

CHAPTER V.

1784.

Difficulties of Pitt's position — His India Bill — His public spirit — Fox's popularity declines — Proceedings of the "Independents" — Party conflicts in the Commons — Address to the King — Pitt attacked in his coach — Revulsion of national feeling — Schemes of Fox — The Great Seal stolen — Dissolution of Parliament .. 169

CHAPTER VI.

1784.

Pitt elected for the University of Cambridge, and Wilberforce for the County of York — Fox's Westminster Contest — Numerous defeats of Fox's friends — New Peerages — Meeting of Parliament — Predominance of Pitt — Disorder of the Finances — Frauds on the Revenue — Pitt's Budget — His India Bill — Westminster Scrutiny — Restoration of Forfeited Estates in Scotland — Letters to Lady Chatham — Promotions in the Peerage — Lord Camden President of the Council 204

CHAPTER VII.

1784 — 1785.

Gibbon's character of Pitt — Pitt's application to business — Parallel between Pitt and Fox — The King's Speech on the opening of Parliament — Westminster Scrutiny — Success of Pitt's Financial Schemes — Reform of Parliament — Commercial intercourse with Ireland — The Eleven Resolutions — Pitt's Speech — Opposed by Fox and North — Petition from Lancashire against the measure — Opposition in the Irish House of Commons — Bill relinquished by the Government — Mortification of Pitt 236

CHAPTER VIII.

1785—1786.

Four-and-a-half Fund — Marriage of Pitt's sister, Lady Harriot — Pitt purchases a Country Seat — Embarrassment of Lady Chatham's and of Pitt's private affairs — The Rolliad — Captain Morris's Songs — Peter Pindar — Pitt's Irish Propositions — Contemplated Treaty of Commerce with France — Proposed Fortifications of Portsmouth and Plymouth — Pitt's Sinking Fund — Impeachment and Trial of Warren Hastings — New Peers.. .. .. Page 276

CHAPTER IX.

1786—1787.

State of the Ministry — William Grenville — Lord Mornington — Henry Dundas — Lord Carmarthen — Death of Frederick the Great — Margaret Nicholson's attempt on the life of George the Third — Death of Pitt's sister, Lady Harriot — Treaty of Commerce with France — State of Ireland — Dr. Pretyman becomes Bishop of Lincoln and Dean of St. Paul's — Parliamentary Debates on French Treaty — Mr. Charles Grey — Proceedings against Hastings resumed — Unanimous testimony to Sheridan's eloquence — Pitt's measures of Financial Reform — The Prince of Wales and Mrs. Fitzherbert — Attempted Repeal of the Test Act — Settlement in Botany Bay 308

CHAPTER X.

1787—1788.

State of parties in Holland — Differences respecting the French trade in India — Prussian troops enter Holland — Death of the Duke of Rutland — France and England disarm — Trial of Hastings — India Declaratory Bill — Budget — Claims of American Loyalists — First Steps in Parliament for the Abolition of the Slave Trade — Exertions of Wilberforce and Clarkson — Pitt's Resolution — Sir W. Dolben's Bill — Horrors of the Middle Passage — Controversies on Slavery 339

CHAPTER XI.

1788.

Official changes and appointments — Treaties of Defensive Alliance
with Holland and Prussia — Mental alienation of the King — Pitt's
measures — Prince of Wales consults Lord Loughborough — Mani-
festation of national sympathy — Objects of Pitt and Thurlow —
Meeting of Parliament — The King's removal to Kew — Fox's
return from Italy ..   .. Page 375

APPENDIX.

Letters and Extracts of Letters from King George the Third to
Mr. Pitt   ..   .. i—xxiii

LIFE

OF

THE RIGHT HONOURABLE

WILLIAM PITT.

CHAPTER I.

1754 — 1780.

Birth of William Pitt — Early signs of great promise — Feeble health in boyhood — Education — At seventeen admitted M.A. at Cambridge — Study of Elocution — Death of his father — Economical habits — Entered at Lincoln's Inn — Attends Parliamentary debates — Introduction to Fox — Called to the Bar — Joins the Western Circuit — M.P. for Appleby.

WILLIAM PITT the elder, best known by his subsequent title as Earl of Chatham, married in 1754 Lady Hester Grenville, only daughter of Hester, in her own right Countess Temple. William Pitt, their second son, was born on the 28th of May, 1759, at Hayes, near Bromley, in Kent.

The house and grounds of Hayes, which had been purchased by Lord Chatham, were disposed of by his eldest son some years after his decease. So far as can be judged at present, the house has been but little altered since his time. The best bedroom is still pointed out as the apartment in which William Pitt was born; it is most probably also the apartment in which his father died.

Besides William, Lord and Lady Chatham had two sons and two daughters. John, the eldest son, was born in 1756, and James Charles, the youngest, in 1761. The daughters were Hester, born in 1755, and Harriot, born in 1758. Lord Chatham designed his eldest son for the army, and his third for the navy, while the second, who had early given signs of great promise, was reserved for the Bar.

The year 1759, in which William Pitt was born, was perhaps the most glorious and eventful in his father's life. The impulse given to the war by that great orator and statesman was apparent in unexampled victories achieved in every quarter of the globe. In Germany we gained the battle of Minden, in North America we gained the battle of Quebec. In Africa we reduced Goree, and in the West Indies Guadaloupe. In the East we beat back the son of the Emperor of Delhi and the chiefs of the Dutch at Chinsura. Off the coast of Brittany we prevailed in the great naval conflict of Quiberon; off the coast of Portugal in the great naval conflict of Lagos. "Indeed,"—so Horace Walpole at the close of this year complains in a letter to Sir Horace Mann—"one is forced to ask every morning what victory there is, for fear of missing one!"

But years rolled on, and fortune changed. In 1761 Mr. Pitt on a difference with his colleagues resigned the Seals. The King on this occasion bestowed on him a pension of 3000*l.* a-year for three lives, and raised Lady Hester to the peerage in her own right as Baroness Chatham.

In the summer of 1765 the retired statesman went

with his family to reside at Burton Pynsent, an estate of 3000*l.* a-year in Somersetshire, which had been most unexpectedly bequeathed to him by an entire stranger, Sir William Pynsent.

On a sudden in July, 1766, Mr. Pitt was called back to office, it may be said almost unanimously, by the public voice. But by a grievous error of his own, he determined to leave the House of Commons. He accepted together with the Privy Seal the title of Earl of Chatham.

At this period his two elder sons, and his daughter Hester, were residing at Weymouth for the benefit of their health, under the charge of their tutor, the Rev. Edward Wilson. That gentleman reports little William as "perfectly happy" in retaining his father's name. Three months before he had said to his tutor in a very serious conversation, and in reference, as it must then have been, to his mother's peerage, " I am glad I am not the eldest son; I want to speak in the House of Commons like Papa."[1]

There is another story, which belongs to almost the same period, but which is of more doubtful authenticity, as depending only on distant recollection. Lord Holland tells us that the Duchess of Leinster once related to him a conversation, at which she was present, between her sister, the first Lady Holland, and her husband, Lord Holland. The lady, in remonstrating with the gentleman on his excessive indulgence to all

---

[1] Letter to the Countess of Chatham, dated August 2, 1766, and printed in the Chatham Correspondence.

his children, and to Charles Fox in particular, added,
"I have been this morning with Lady Hester Pitt
(Lady Chatham), and there is little William Pitt, not
eight years old, and really the cleverest child I ever
saw; and brought up so strictly and so proper in his
behaviour, that, mark my words, that little boy will be
a thorn in Charles's side as long as he lives." [2]

As the "little boy" grew up, he evinced to all
around him many other tokens of his genius and ambition. In April, 1772, during a few days' absence, we
find Lady Chatham write as follows to her husband :—
"The fineness of William's mind makes him enjoy with
the highest pleasure what would be above the reach of
any other creature of his small age. The young Lieutenant may not perhaps go quite so deep." [3] This
young Lieutenant was Lord Pitt, the eldest son, whom
William, though three years the junior, had already
on all points excelled.

To the same effect there is other not more discrimi-
nating, but more disinterested testimony. In the summer of 1773 the two brothers had gone with Mr.
Wilson for the sake of sea-bathing to Lyme. There
Hayley the poet became well acquainted with them.
In his Memoirs he describes William Pitt as "now a
wonderful boy of fourteen, who eclipsed his brother in
conversation." And he adds :—" Hayley often reflected
on the singular pleasure he had derived from his young
acquaintance; regretting, however, that his reserve had

---

[2] Memorials of Fox, by Lord
John Russell, vol. i. p. 25.

[3] See the Chatham Correspondence, vol. iv. p. 207.

prevented his imparting to the wonderful youth the epic poem he had begun."[1] The very youngest critic that ever perhaps any poet chose!

But at this period William Pitt had himself become a poet. He had written a tragedy in five acts, and in blank verse, entitled 'Laurentius, King of Clarinium.' We learn by a note of Lady Chatham that it was represented for the first time at Burton Pynsent, August 22, 1772, and it was acted again in the spring of the ensuing year. There is a prologue, which was "spoken by Mr. Pitt," and of which a copy is signed in his own hand. All the parts were sustained by the five brothers and sisters, and the spectators were only their parents, with Lord and Lady Stanhope, and a very few other family friends. The manuscript of this play is still preserved at Chevening. I showed it to Lord Macaulay in one of the country visits—alas! too soon concluded—which I had the great pleasure to receive from him; and Lord Macaulay speaks of it as follows in his excellent biographical sketch of Mr. Pitt, the last of all his published compositions:—"The tragedy is bad of course, but not worse than the tragedies of Hayley. It is in some respects highly curious. There is no love. The whole plot is political; and it is remarkable that the interest, such as it is, turns on a contest about a Regency. On one side is a faithful servant of the Crown; on the other an ambitious and unprincipled conspirator. At length the King, who had been missing, re-appears, resumes his power, and

---

[4] Memoirs of William Hayley, written by Himself, vol. i. p. 127.

rewards the faithful defender of his rights. A reader who should judge only by internal evidence, would have no hesitation in pronouncing that the play was written by some Pittite poetaster, at the time of the rejoicings for the recovery of George the Third, in 1789."

But while Lord and Lady Chatham watched with no common pleasure the intellectual promise of their second son, they were frequently distressed by his delicate health. "My poor William is still ailing:" such is the constant burthen of his father's letters during his boyhood. There were great fears that so frail a plant would never be reared to full maturity.

It was no doubt on account of his feeble health in boyhood that little William was not sent to any public or private school. He was brought up at home by the tuition of Mr. Wilson, and under his father's eye. Lord Chatham was indeed most careful of the education of his family. Bishop Tomline assures us that " when his Lordship's health would permit, he never suffered a day to pass without giving instruction of some sort to his children; and seldom without reading a chapter of the Bible with them." [5]

Under Mr. Wilson, William Pitt studied the classics in Greek and Latin, and the elements of mathematics. In spite of the frequent interruptions from ill-health he made most rapid progress. He had so peculiar a discrimination in seizing at once the meaning of an author, that as Mr. Wilson once observed, he never seemed to

---

[5] Life of Pitt, vol. i. p. 5.

learn, but only to recollect. At fourteen he was as forward as most lads at seventeen or eighteen, and was considered already ripe for college.

Without any disparagement to Mr. Wilson, it was certainly from Lord Chatham that young William profited most. Lord Chatham was an affectionate father to all his children. He took pleasure, as we have seen, in teaching them all. But he discerned— as who would not ? —the rare abilities of William, and applied himself to unfold them with a never-failing care. From an early age he was wont to select any piece of eloquence he met with and transmit it to his son. Of this I have seen a striking instance in a note from him to Lady Chatham, which is endorsed in pencil " Ma. 1770," and which was thought to have no literary value. It was kindly presented to me in answer to my request for autographs to oblige some collectors among my friends; and it was designed to be cut up into two or three pieces of handwriting. But I found the note conclude with these words : " I send Domitian as a specimen of oratory for William." Now, " Domitian " was one of the subsidiary signatures of the author of ' Junius,' and the letter in question seems to be that of March 5, 1770.[6] The words of Lord Chatham prove what has sometimes been disputed, that the eloquence of the author of ' Junius' was noticed and admired by the best judges, even when his compositions were concealed under another name.

In the same spirit Lord Chatham used to recommend

---

[6] See Woodfall's Junius, vol. iii. p. 249.

to his son the best books as models. Thus he bid him read Barrow's Sermons, which he thought admirably calculated to furnish the *copia verborum*. Thus again he enjoined upon him the earnest study of the greatest Greek historians. Bishop Tomline says:—" It was by Lord Chatham's particular desire that Thucydides was the first Greek book which Mr. Pitt read after he came to college. The only other wish ever expressed by his Lordship relative to Mr. Pitt's studies was, that I would read Polybius with him."

But I have yet to notice what for Lord Chatham's object was his main plan of all. In 1803 my father, then Lord Mahon, had the high privilege, as a relative, of being for several weeks an inmate of Mr. Pitt's house at Walmer Castle. Presuming on that familiar intercourse, he told me that he ventured on one occasion to ask Mr. Pitt by what means he had acquired his admirable readiness of speech—his aptness of finding the right word without pause or hesitation. Mr. Pitt replied that whatever readiness he might be thought to possess in that respect was, he believed, greatly owing to a practice which his father had impressed upon him. Lord Chatham had bid him take up any book in some foreign language with which he was well acquainted, in Latin or Greek especially. Lord Chatham then enjoined him to read out of this work a passage in English, stopping, where he was not sure of the word to be used in English, until the right word came to his mind, and then proceed. Mr. Pitt stated that he had assiduously followed this practice. We may conclude that at first he had often to stop for awhile before he could recollect the proper word, but that he found the difficulties gradually disappear, until what was a toil to him at first became at last an easy and familiar task.[7]

To an orator the charm of voice is of very far more importance than mere readers of speeches would find it easy to believe. I have known some speakers in whom that one advantage seemed almost to supply the place of every other. The tones of William Pitt were by nature sonorous and clear; and the further art how to manage and modulate his voice to the best advantage was instilled into him by his father with exquisite skill. Lord Chatham himself was pre-eminent in that art, as also in the graces of action, insomuch that these accomplishments have been sometimes imputed to him as a fault. In a passage of Horace Walpole, written with the manifest desire to disparage him, we find him compared to Garrick.[8]

To train his son in sonorous elocution Lord Chatham caused him to recite day by day in his presence passages from the best English poets. The two poets most commonly selected for this purpose were Shakespeare and Milton, and Mr. Pitt continued through life familiar with both. There is another fact which Lord Macaulay has recorded from tradition, and which I also remember to have heard :—"The debate in Pandemonium was, as it well deserved to be, one of his favourite passages ; and his early friends used to talk, long after his death,

---

[7] Already related by me in my Aberdeen Address, March 25, 1858. p. 20.

[8] Memoirs of George II., vol. i. p. 479.

of the just emphasis and the melodious cadence with which they had heard him recite the incomparable speech of Belial."

Being at fourteen so forward in his studies, William Pitt was sent to the University of Cambridge. He was entered at Pembroke Hall in the spring of 1773, and commenced his residence in October the same year. Mr. Wilson in the first instance attended him to Cambridge, and resided with him for some weeks in the same apartments, but solely for the care of his health, and without any concern in the direction of his studies. He had been commended to the especial care of the Rev. George Pretyman, one of the two tutors of his college; and it was not long ere that gentleman became both his sole instructor and his familiar friend.

George Pretyman, whom I have already cited and called by anticipation Bishop Tomline, was born at Bury St. Edmunds in 1750. Proceeding to Cambridge he showed not indeed any brilliant ability, but a keen and unflinching application. He made himself an excellent mathematician, as well as an excellent scholar, and in 1772 he was the Senior Wrangler for the year. I shall have occasion to show how in after life the friendship of Mr. Pitt as Minister raised him to high honours in the Church, and above all to the Bishopric of Lincoln. In 1803 he assumed the name of Tomline, on the bequest of a large estate. He was translated to the See of Winchester in 1820, and he died in 1827.

It was Bishop Tomline to whom, as we shall see, Mr. Pitt bequeathed his papers for examination. Some years later the Bishop evinced his attachment to the

memory of his pupil and his patron by undertaking
the Memoirs of his Life. This work he did not live to
finish. The first part, which was published in 1821,
and which now lies before me, in three octavo volumes,
extends only to the close of 1792. Great expectations
had been formed on the appearance of this work. I am
certainly not going beyond the truth if I say that such
expectations of it were much disappointed. It does
indeed impart to us an authentic and important though
rather meagre account of Pitt in his earlier years. It
does indeed contain some, though very few, extracts
from his private correspondence. But nearly the whole
remainder of this biography is a mere compilation.
It gives us for the most part Pitt's measures from the
'Annual Register,' and his speeches from the Parliamentary debates. It was composed, as an Edinburgh
reviewer said at the time, not by the aid of his
Lordship's pen, but rather " by his Lordship's sharp and
faithful scissors!"[9]

At Cambridge William Pitt was still intent on his
main object of oratorical excellence. Immediately after
his arrival we find him attend a course of lectures on
Quintilian.[1] But his health at this period gave cause
for great alarm. From a boy he had shot up far too
rapidly to a tall, lank stripling, with no corresponding
development of breadth and muscle. In the first few
weeks of his college-life he was seized with a most
serious illness. For nearly two months he was confined
to his rooms, and reduced to so weak a state that upon

---

[9] Edinburgh Review, July, 1821, p. 452.

[1] See the Chatham Correspondence, vol. iv. p. 295.

his convalescence he was four days in travelling to London.

Returning under such unfavourable circumstances, his father kept him at home for half a year. During this interval he was placed under the care of the family physician, Dr. Addington. This gentleman recommended early hours, with exercise every day on horseback, and a careful system of diet. But he further prescribed liberal potations of port-wine. It was a remedy which certainly accorded well with the young man's constitution. He took it at this time with manifest advantage, and he adhered to it through life. It was his elixir of strength amidst all his toils and cares, but perhaps in the long run with no good effect. While it must frequently have recruited his energies, it may be suspected of combining with these toils and cares to undermine his constitution.

Alarming as it seemed at the time, the illness of Pitt in the autumn of 1773 proved in truth the turning point of his disorder. By attention to Dr. Addington's rules he much more than recovered his lost ground. In July, 1774, some weeks before the commencement of the autumn term, he was permitted to return to Cambridge—" the evacuated seat of the Muses," as Lord Chatham calls it in his somewhat affected epistolary style.[2] William Pitt renewed at once his study of Quintilian and Thucydides, but did not pursue that study by night. "The Historic Muse"—thus he writes to his father—" captivates extremely, but at the

---

[2] Chatham Correspondence, vol. iv. p. 364.

same time I beg you to be persuaded that neither she nor any of her sisters allure me from the resolution of early hours, which has been stedfastly adhered to, and makes the academic life agree perfectly."[3] Nor did he at this time neglect his daily ride nor yet his daily draughts of port-wine. He had no relapse nor material check, and by slow but sure degrees gained strength. "At the age of eighteen," says his tutor, "he was a healthy man, and he continued so for many years."

In December, 1774, the family circle of Mr. Pitt was agreeably extended. His eldest sister, Lady Hester, became the wife of Charles Lord Mahon. There was already some relationship, since the first Earl Stanhope had married Miss Lucy Pitt, an aunt of Lord Chatham. But besides this tie of kindred the two families had for many years past been on terms of most friendly intercourse ; and in public life Lord Stanhope was one of the few remaining followers of Lord Chatham. The "Great Earl" was on this account much pleased at the alliance, and also as having formed a most favourable opinion of his future son-in-law. In an unpublished letter of this period, dated November 28, 1774, addressed to Mr. James Grenville, he describes Lord Mahon as follows :—

"Though the outside is well, it is by looking within that invaluable treasures appear ; a head to contrive, a heart to conceive, and a hand to execute whatever is good, lovely, and of fair repute. He is as yet very new

---

[3] Chatham Correspondence, vol. iv. p. 358.

to our vile world, indeed quite a traveller in England. I grieve that he has no seat in Parliament, that wickedest and best school for superior natures."

Lord Mahon had been educated at Geneva, where he imbibed an ardent zeal both for liberty and science. Between him and William Pitt there now grew up a warm feeling of friendship. Lord Mahon was about six years the elder, but in their intercourse this difference might be compensated by the superiority of talent in William. Under Lord Chatham's guidance the two young men looked forward to the same course in politics, and there seemed every probability that the confidence between them would through life continue unimpaired.

In the spring of 1776, and at the age of seventeen, Mr. Pitt was admitted to the Degree of Master of Arts at Cambridge, without any examination, according to the unwise privilege which was still at that time conceded to the sons of Peers. His tutor tells us that " while Mr. Pitt was an undergraduate he never omitted attending chapel morning and evening, or dining in the public hall, except when prevented by indisposition. Nor did he pass a single evening out of the college walls. Indeed most of his time was spent with me." [4]

On taking his degree Mr. Pitt did not, according to the common practice, take his leave of college. On the contrary he continued to live for the most part as before at Pembroke Hall until near the period when he came of age. Thus his whole residence at the University

---

[4] Life of Pitt, by Tomline, vol. i. p. 7.

was protracted, although with considerable intervals
of absence, to the unusual length of almost seven years.
"In the course of this time," adds his tutor, "I never
knew him spend an idle day, nor did he ever fail to
attend me at the appointed hour."

It was during these graduate years at Pembroke Hall
that Mr. Pitt laid in his principal stores of knowledge.
They were in many branches very considerable.   In
mathematics, the especial pride of Cambridge, he took
great delight.   He frequently alluded in later life to
the practical advantage which he had derived from
them, and declared that no portion of his time had been
more usefully employed than that which he devoted to
this study.   He was master of everything usually
known by the academic "wranglers," and felt a great
desire — but Mr. Pretyman did not think it right to
indulge the inclination — to fathom still farther the
depths of pure mathematics.   "When," adds Mr. Pretyman, "the connection of tutor and pupil was about to
cease between us, he expressed a hope that he should
find leisure and opportunity to read Newton's Principia
again with me after some summer Circuit."

The general rule of Mr. Pretyman was to read with
his pupil alternately classics and mathematics.   In the
former as in the latter the knowledge of Pitt became
both extensive and profound.   He had never indeed,
according to the fashion at public schools, applied himself to Greek or Latin composition.   He had never
mastered the laborious inutilities of the ancient metres.
But as to the true and vivifying aim of classic study
—the accurate and critical comprehension of the classic

authors—he was certainly in the first rank.   There
was scarce a Greek or a Latin writer of any eminence
among the classics the whole of whose works Pitt and
Pretyman did not read together.   The future statesman was a nice observer of their different styles, and
alive to all their various excellences.   So anxious was
he not to leave even a single Greek poet unexplored,
that at his request Mr. Pretyman went through with
him the obscure rhapsody of Lycophron.   " This," says
his preceptor, " he read with an ease at first sight,
which, if I had not witnessed it, I should have thought
beyond the compass of human intellect."

How well amidst all the cares of office Pitt retained
through life his classic knowledge is shown among
several other testimonies by one which Lord John
Russell has recorded.   Lord Harrowby said that, being
with Mr. Pitt at his country-house, he and Lord Grenville were one day waiting for Mr. Pitt in his library :
they opened a Thucydides, and came to a passage
which they could not make out.   They continued to
puzzle at it till Mr. Pitt, coming in, took the volume
and construed the passage with the greatest ease.[5]

Of the modern languages, French was the only one
that Pitt acquired.   Once and once only in his life, as
we shall find, he passed a few weeks in France.   During

---

[5] Memorials and Correspondence
of Fox, by Lord John Russell, vol.
ii. p. 3.   I have myself heard Lord
Harrowby relate the same story,
with this addition, that the two
gentlemen were waiting to join
Mr. Pitt in an afternoon ride, and
that Mr. Pitt, coming into the
room ready to go out, translated
the passage in a moment, hat in
hand.

this excursion and before it he applied himself to the
language of the country, which he learnt both to speak
and write with ease. In its literature also he was by
no means unversed. My father told me that he had
been present at an animated argument between Lord
Grenville and Mr. Pitt on the merits of Molière.

Besides his primary studies in mathematics and in
ancient languages Pitt gave great attention to the
public lectures in Civil Law, of which he felt the
importance as bearing on his future profession. He also
attended the lectures upon experimental philosophy,
to which he was incited by the zealous example of his
relative at Chevening, and in which, as is said, he took
great pleasure.

Of the English books which he read at Cambridge,
there was none, as Mr. Pretyman records, which gave
Pitt greater satisfaction than 'Locke's Essay on the
Human Understanding.' He drew up for himself a
complete and correct analysis of that important work.
We may further conclude, from the early zeal with
which he espoused the principles of Adam Smith in
the House of Commons, that even at the University
he had been an assiduous reader of the 'Wealth of
Nations.'

Pitt—so Mr. Pretyman tells us—was not an admirer
of Dr. Johnson's style, and still less of Gibbon's. As
writers he much preferred Robertson and Hume. He
was fond of Middleton's 'Life of Cicero,' and fonder still
of Lord Bolingbroke's political works. These last had
no doubt been earnestly commended to him by Lord
Chatham ; for in a letter at an earlier period addressed

to Thomas Pitt we find Lord Chatham praise them in
the highest terms. Of one of them, namely, the ' Remarks on the History of England,' published under the
name of Sir John Oldcastle, he says that they are " to
be studied and almost got by heart for the inimitable
beauty of the style." [6] Pitt appears to have retained
through life an equal admiration of them. At Walmer
Castle my father heard him more than once declare
that there was no loss in literature which he more
lamented than that scarce any trace remained to us of
Bolingbroke's Parliamentary speeches.

But whatever the studies of Pitt, whether in the
ancient languages or in his own, the aim of public
speaking was kept steadily in view. He continued with
Mr. Pretyman the same practice of extemporaneous
translation which with his father he had commenced.
We further learn from his preceptor that " when alone
he dwelt for hours upon striking passages of an orator
or historian, in noticing their turn of expression, and
marking their manner of arranging a narrative. A few
pages sometimes occupied a whole morning. It was a
favourite employment with him to compare opposite
speeches upon the same subject, and to observe how
each speaker managed his own side of the question.
The authors whom he preferred for this purpose were
Livy, Thucydides, and Sallust. Upon these occasions
his observations were not unfrequently committed to
paper, and furnished a topic for conversation with me
at our next meeting. He was also in the habit of copy-

---

[6] To Thomas Pitt, May 4, 1754.

ing any eloquent sentence or any beautiful or forcible expression which occurred in his reading."

We have seen that as an undergraduate Mr. Pitt made few acquaintance, and went into no society. It is probable that at fourteen and fifteen his fellow-collegians might regard him as a boy. But after taking his degree at the age of seventeen he began to mix freely with other young men of his own age at Cambridge. There he laid the foundations of several of the future friendships of his life. His manners at this time are described as gentle and unassuming, and free from all taint of self-conceit. Those who in after years confronted night by night in the House of Commons the haughty and resolute Prime Minister, armed on all points, and ever self-possessed, had great difficulty in believing how far in his social hours he could unbend. Yet the testimony as follows of Mr. Pretyman at Cambridge will be found confirmed by several others a little later, but to the same effect:—" He was always the most lively person in company, abounding in playful wit and quick repartee; but never known to excite pain, or to give just ground of offence."

" But though "—thus Mr. Pretyman proceeds to say —" his society was universally sought, and from the age of seventeen or eighteen he constantly passed his evenings in company, he steadily avoided every species of irregularity." This remark of his preceptor is by no means to be limited to his college years. Then and ever afterwards the strictness of his morals was maintained. Indeed throughout his life it became for want of a better the favourite taunt of his opponents. Whoever looks through the Whig satires or epigrams of that day which proceeded from the wits at Brooks's—some of them remarkable for their talent and spirit—will be surprised at the number of sarcasms on that account aimed in various forms at the "immaculate young Minister." To be of an amorous temper is there assumed as among the most essential qualifications of a statesman!

The residence of Pitt at Cambridge was varied by occasional trips to London; above all, when Lord Chatham brought forward any important motion in the House of Lords. Thus in January, 1775, we find him report as follows on the next day after the debate to Lady Chatham :—

"I can now tell you correctly : my father has slept well, without any burning in the feet or restlessness. He has had no pain, but is lame in one ankle near the instep, from standing so long. No wonder he is lame ; his first speech lasted above an hour, and the second half an hour—surely the two finest speeches that ever were made before, unless by himself ! He will be with you to dinner at four o'clock." [7]

There are also on record two letters to his mother, giving a full report of the great debate, which in like manner he attended in May, 1777.[8]

But chief of all was the scene on the memorable 7th of April, 1778, on the final, and as it has been called the dying, speech of Lord Chatham. His eldest

---

[7] See the Chatham Correspondence, vol. iv. p. 377.
[8] See the Chatham Correspondence, vol. iv. pp. 435, 438.

son and also his youngest were at this time absent
on foreign service.   It devolved on William conjointly
with Lord Mahon to support between them their venerable parent, as with feeble steps but no faltering spirit
he tottered in through the assembled Peers, and raised
for the last time his eloquent voice in his country's
cause.   Need I again relate what I have elsewhere told
—how on rising to reply he fell back in convulsions—
how his son and son-in-law, aided by the Peers around
him, bore him forth to a private chamber—how he was
removed to Hayes—and how on the 11th of May following the great orator and statesman died?

At the death of Lord Chatham all parties, seemingly
at least, combined to do him honour.   The House of
Commons granted 20,000*l.* for the payment of his debts.
An Act of Parliament passed, annexing an annuity of
4000*l.* for ever to his Earldom.   A public funeral and a
monument to his memory were unanimously voted.

The public funeral took place in Westminster Abbey
on Tuesday the 9th of June.   William Pitt, in the
absence of his elder brother, walked as the chief
mourner, supported on one side by Lord Mahon, and on
the other by Thomas Pitt of Boconnoc, the head of the
Pitt family.   Late the same afternoon we find him write
as follows from Lord Mahon's house in Harley Street to
Lady Chatham, who had remained at Hayes :—

                              " Harley Street, June 9, 1778.

" MY DEAR MOTHER,

          " I cannot let the servants return without letting
you know that the sad solemnity has been celebrated so

as to answer every important wish we could form on
the subject. The Court did not honour us with their
countenance, nor did they suffer the procession to be as
magnificent as it ought; but it had notwithstanding
everything essential to the great object, the attendance
being most respectable, and the crowd of interested
spectators immense. The Duke of Gloucester was in
the Abbey. Lord Rockingham, the Duke of Northumberland, and all the minority in town were present.
The pall-bearers were Sir G. Savile, Mr. Townshend,
Dunning, and Burke. The eight assistant mourners
were Lord Abingdon, Lord Cholmondeley, Lord
Harcourt, Lord Effingham, Lord Townshend, Lord
Fortescue, Lord Shelburne, and Lord Camden. All our
relations made their appearance. You will excuse my
not sending you a more particular account, as I think
of being at Hayes to-morrow morning. I will not tell
you what I felt on this occasion, to which no words are
equal; but I know that you will have a satisfaction in
hearing that Lord Mahon as well as myself supported
the trial perfectly well, and have not at all suffered
from the fatigue. The procession did not separate till
four o'clock. Lady Mahon continues much better, and
has had no return of her complaint.

" I hope the additional melancholy of the day will not
have been too overcoming for you, and that I shall
have the comfort of finding you pretty well to-morrow.
I shall be able to give you an account of what is thought
as to our going to Court. And I am ever, my dear
Mother,

       " Your most dutiful and affectionate son,

             " W. PITT."

Shortly afterwards William Pitt accompanied his mother and sister Harriot to Burton Pynsent, where he remained with them during the summer and autumn months. But in October we find him again at Pembroke Hall.

At this time there occurred a transaction chiefly remarkable as the first that brought Mr. Pitt into public notice. Some communications had passed at the beginning of the year between Sir James Wright, a friend of Lord Bute, and Dr. Addington, the friend and physician of Lord Chatham. Acting without authority, they had sought to bring the two statesmen into concert with each other. But after Lord Chatham's death their gossiping interviews gave rise to a bitter controversy. Lord Mountstuart, eldest son of Lord Bute, taking part in this, addressed a letter to the newspapers on the 23rd of October. The second Lord Chatham was still on foreign service, so that the duty of reply devolved on William Pitt. Accordingly he published a letter dated Harley Street, October 29th, going fully through the documents adduced, and showing that his father, so far from courting, had without hesitation rejected every idea of a political union with Lord Bute.[9]

The state of his father's fortune, as bearing on his own, must here also be referred to. Lord Chatham had been himself a younger son of small patrimony. In public life he had been most disinterested. In private

---

[9] All the papers on this no longer interesting subject will be found in the Annual Register for 1778, pp. 244–264. For a fuller account of it I venture to refer to my History of England, vol. vi. p. 321.

life he had been a little unthrifty.   Notwithstanding
the unexpected bequest of Burton Pynsent, he was, as
we have seen, much embarrassed when he died. William
Pitt therefore found it requisite even from his early
years to practise strict economy.   When in 1773 he
began his college-life, he was most amply cared for
on every point of study or of health.   In other respects
he received but a scanty supply.   One of his first
calculations at Cambridge was how most cheaply—
whether on meadow or in stable—he could keep his
horse.[1]

At the death of his father economy became more
than ever requisite for William.   The generosity of
Parliament did indeed enable his eldest brother to
maintain—and no more than maintain—the family
honours.   His mother also was in comfortable circumstances, from the receipt of the pension of 3000*l.*
granted in 1761 for three lives ; although, as appears
from many passages in the Pitt Correspondence, she
was often distressed by the non-payment of arrears.
But William himself could only look forward, on
coming of age, to an income of between 250*l.* and 300*l.*
a year.   Meanwhile, whether at Cambridge or in London,
he does not appear to have received any fixed allowance.   He was wont to write home from time to time,
naming the moderate sum which the payment of his
bills and his other late expenses would require.

Under such circumstances as to fortune there arose
for Pitt the question of the purchase of chambers at

---

[1] See his Letter in the Chatham Papers, vol. iv. p. 355.

Lincoln's Inn; and on that subject we find him write to
Lady Chatham as follows:—

"Pembroke Hall, Nov. 30, 1778.
" My dear Mother,

. . . .

"I am much obliged to you for thinking of my
finances, which are in no urgent want of repair; but if
I should happen to buy a horse they will be soon; and
therefore, if it is not inconvenient to you, I shall be
much obliged to you for a draft of 50*l.*, which I think
will be sufficient for the current expenses of this quarter.

"Another object presents itself, which would require
a more considerable sum, and which I wish to submit to
your consideration. It will very soon be necessary for
me to have rooms at Lincoln's Inn, and upon the whole
I am persuaded the best economy in the end would be
to purchase, though I do not know what means there
may be of advancing the sum necessary for that purpose. While I was in town I saw a set which are to be
disposed of, and which have no other fault than being
too dear and too good. At the same time I heard of
none at an inferior price, which were not as much too
bad. The whole expense of these will be eleven
hundred pounds, which sounds to me a frightful sum,
although I know that if I do not sink so much out of
my capital, the annual diminution of my income (if I
was to hire) would amount to near the interest of that
sum. The rooms are in an exceeding good situation
in the new buildings, and will be perfectly fit for habi-
tation in about two months. Soon after that time it
will be right for me to begin attending Westminster
Hall during that term, and these chambers will be more
convenient than any other residence. If I should take

these, the sum to be paid immediately is somewhat
more than three hundred, and the remaining eight
about next Easter. I have done no more than to secure
that they may not be engaged to any other person till
I have returned an answer, and I shall be glad to know
your opinion as soon as possible. You will be so good
as to consider how far you approve of the idea, if it be
practicable, and whether there are any means of advancing the money out of my fortune before I am of
age. If in either light you see any objection to the
scheme, I shall without any difficulty lay it aside, and
shall probably at any time hereafter, when it becomes
convenient, be able to suit myself without much trouble,
as there will always be rooms vacant. If, however, you
approve of it, I should be rather inclined to embrace
this opportunity.

" Ever, my dear Mother, &c.,
" W. PITT."

The purchase of the chambers in question was happily
effected. It appears that Earl Temple, Lady Chatham's eldest brother, supplied the money required, as
an advance upon the fortune to which his nephew would
be entitled when he came of age. But it is certainly
striking to find the future Prime Minister, destined in a
few years more to dispense in his country's service tens
of millions of pounds sterling, speak of eleven hundred
as " a frightful sum."

Being duly entered at Lincoln's Inn, Pitt began to
keep his terms. These involved only occasional visits,
of a few days each, to London. But the young lawyer
eagerly availed himself of such opportunities to attend
any remarkable debate that might take place in Parlia-

ment. It is said that on one of these occasions he was introduced, on the steps of the throne in the House of Lords, to Mr. Fox, who was his senior by ten years, and already in the fulness of his fame. Fox used afterwards to relate that, as the discussion proceeded, Pitt repeatedly turned to him and said, "But surely, Mr. Fox, that might be met thus:" or, "Yes, but he lays himself open to retort." What the particular criticisms were, Fox had forgotten ; but he said that he was much struck at the time by the precocity of a lad who through the whole sitting was thinking only how all the speeches on both sides could be answered.[2]

I proceed with some extracts from Pitt's family correspondence :—

"Hotel, King Street, Feb. 11, 1779.

"MY DEAR MOTHER,

"I flatter myself that a letter from me may not be unwelcome, though it cannot have the merit of much news to recommend it, neither of a public nor private sort. To begin with the second, which I believe pretty generally claims precedence, nothing has, I am afraid, yet been obtained on the subject of the arrears. I saw Mr. Coutts on Tuesday, who told me that Mr. Crauford had been ill, which had delayed the presenting of the memorial, but that he now expected to hear of its effect every day. I shall renew my inquiry in a short time, and wish I may receive a favourable account of the seven quarters. . . . . .

"I am to meet my sister at Hayes on the subject of

---

[2] I give this Holland House tradition, which is no doubt quite authentic, in the very words of Lord Macaulay (Biographies, p. 147, ed. 1860).

your commission, as soon as she can find a leisure moment. Her great business is that of secretary to Lord
Mahon, whose ' Electricity ' is almost ready for the press,
and will rank him, I suppose, with Dr. Franklin. I have
just been dining with a brother philosopher of his, Dr.
Priestley, at Shelburne House. His Lordship is very
cordial in his inquiries after you; and if you continue
in the West till next summer, 'will think it his duty to
make them in person at Burton.' He is very obliging
to me. . . .

" You will have the goodness to excuse the haste of a
letter written in my way to the Opera.

" Ever, my dear Mother, &c.,

" W. PITT."

" Nerot's Hotel, Thursday, Feb. 18, 1779.

" At present I hope to set out Sunday or Monday;
and nothing probably can tempt me to any delay except
the prospect of an interesting debate, which, however,
I do not foresee at present.

" If it should happen, I will certainly write to you
next post. I have been for two or three days an auditor at one or other of the Houses, but without any
great entertainment. To-day I had the honour of being
squeezed with the Duke of Cumberland in the gallery
of the House of Commons, and hearing the Speaker
deliver the thanks to Admiral Keppel."

" Nerot's Hotel, Wednesday night (1779).

" I have heard no news of any kind. James is
gone with my sisters to the ball as a professed dancer,
which stands in the place of an invitation; a character
which I do not assume, and have therefore stayed
away."

" Nerot's Hotel, Tuesday, Half-past Two (1779).

" I was just going to mount my horse about an hour ago, when the most violent of all April showers prevented me, and by that means it is now so late that I have no chance of reaching Hayes by dinner. Consequently I must at all events give up the hope of enjoying much of your company this evening; which being the case, the double temptation of a seat in the gallery of the House of Commons, and a ticket for the Duchess of Bolton's in the evening, determined me to defer it till to-morrow morning.

" Nothing less than the concurrence of all these circumstances could have been sufficient to alter my resolution of coming to you to-day; and even now I should be almost afraid that the engagement which called me from Hayes last night, and that which detains me here at present, might completely stamp me for a fine gentleman, if the House of Commons did not come in to support the gravity of my character. I shall certainly be with you to-morrow, at as early an hour as the raking of this evening will permit."

" Nerot's Hotel, June 19, 1779.

" You will easily imagine that the principal subject of conversation here is the Rescript which has been delivered within these few days from Spain; and that subject, I am sure, does not afford matter of agreeable consideration.

" The situation of public affairs is undoubtedly in most respects rendered still more melancholy and deplorable by that event, and all the dangers that have for some time been apprehended are accelerated and increased.

" There seems, however, to be less despondency than

might be expected in such circumstances; and I am willing to flatter myself that it may, in the midst of many evils, be productive of some good effects at home, and that there may still be spirit and resources in the country sufficient to preserve at least the remnant of a great empire. I was very glad to be present at the debate on this subject in the House of Lords, which, though not so good in point of speaking as many I have heard, could not fail of being extremely interesting. My brother, as well as his friend the Duke of Rutland, took their seats on this occasion, and added two to a respectable minority. Lord Shelburne spoke as usual with great ability, and made the roughest invective I ever heard against several of the Ministry, Lord North in particular."

" Pembroke Hall, June 28, 1779.

"I left Lord and Lady Mahon and Harriot in town, not likely, I imagine, to quit it for some time. Unless the Parliament should continue sitting, they will probably have as solitary a vacation there, as I propose to myself here. This place has so many advantages for study, and I have unavoidably lost so much time lately, and can spare so little for the future, that I cannot help wishing to continue here a considerable part of the summer. It is, however, quite indifferent to me whether that part be at the beginning or end; and at all events, if there is any particular time at which you wish to see me at Burton, I shall always be in readiness to obey your summons immediately."

" Pembroke Hall, July 3, 1779.

" Within a short time the scenes of Cambridge are become doubly interesting to me, as I have lately found very good reason to hope that the University

may furnish me with a seat in Parliament possibly at
the General Election. It is a seat of all others the
most desirable, as being free from expense, perfectly
independent, and I think in every respect extremely
honourable. You will not wonder that I am not indifferent to such an object, and my wishes on this occasion will, I trust, coincide with yours for me. You will
perhaps think the idea hastily taken up, when I tell
you that six candidates have declared already; but I
assure you that I shall not flatter myself with any vain
hopes, or stir a step without all the certainty which the
nature of the case admits. Hitherto I have not pursued
my inquiries far enough to form quite a confident
opinion, and till I have, I shall keep the idea a perfect
secret, which is indispensably necessary to its success.
I may probably very soon be enabled to judge, and
may be obliged to declare my intentions; but you shall
undoubtedly hear as soon as possible the further progress
of this business."

The design here communicated as a secret was soon
afterwards publicly announced. Mr. Pitt wrote to
several persons of weight and influence, asking their
support. Amongst others we find him on the 19th of
July address a letter to the Marquis of Rockingham, the
chief, in name at least, of the Opposition at that time.
But his Lordship was cold and ungracious. He left
Mr. Pitt for upwards of a fortnight without any answer
at all; and on the 7th of August he thus replied:—

"I am so circumstanced from the knowledge I have
of several persons who may be candidates, and who
indeed are expected to be so, that it makes it impossible
for me in this instance to show the attention to your

wishes which your own as well as the great merits of your family entitle you to."[3]

In the same month of August Mr. Pitt wrote to Lady Chatham on a wholly different and still more interesting subject:—

"Nerot's Hotel, King Street, Saturday, Aug. 21, 1779.
"MY DEAR MOTHER,

"The accounts which have been received within these few days of the French and Spanish fleets have brought the apprehension of danger nearer to our doors, and rendered the suspense on public affairs still more anxious than ever. While the idea prevailed, which it did for a little while, of a force actually landing at Plymouth, I was also more particularly solicitous, because your neighbourhood to that place, though not such as to expose you at all to anything immediately very serious, might, I feared, be productive of great inconvenience and distress. That report first reached me at Chevening, and I came to town immediately with the intention of setting out for Burton to-day, thinking that it might be more satisfaction to you, and feeling that it would be so to myself, to be near you at such a time. I find, however, to-day that it is understood that the enemy had retired from the coasts without attempting anything, and an engagement with Sir Charles Hardy seems to be the first event which people now expect. I do not learn that any official account has yet been received from him, but fresh intelligence is expected every moment. On the whole the present alarm seems subsided; and indeed the exterior of

---

[3] These letters were first pub-lished by Lord Albemarle in his Memoirs of Lord Rockingham. vol. ii. p. 422.

London has been, as far as I have seen, very little affected by the state. There has been none of the confusion, and hardly any of the signs of anxiety which might be expected at such a moment. I still, however, feel very impatient to see you, as, although I think you must have been out of the reach of any great alarm, I cannot help being somewhat anxious to be more fully assured of it. I shall therefore leave London to-morrow (as I had before intended), and probably make the best of my way to Burton, in which case I shall arrive before this letter. If, however, I should before that time find less reason to be in so much haste, I may perhaps contrive to take Stowe in my way."

It would seem, however, that this intended visit to Stowe did not take place. Lord Temple was at this time in declining health, and he expired on the following 11th of September. He was succeeded as second Earl by his nephew George, eldest son of George Grenville, the late Prime Minister. The new Peer, born in 1753, had for some years been one of the members for the county of Buckingham, in which representation he was now succeeded by his next brother, Thomas Grenville, who was born in 1755, and who survived till 1846. Their third brother, William Wyndham Grenville, afterwards Lord Grenville, was born in 1759. All three were of course first cousins of Mr. Pitt; and each will be found to play a part, more or less important, in my future narrative.

Having passed the autumn weeks with Lady Chatham at Burton Pynsent, Mr. Pitt went back to Cambridge as usual in October, when his correspondence with his mother recommences:—

"Pembroke Hall, Oct. 15, 1779.

"I find everything going on admirably well relative to my object here, which I think it will be a satisfaction to you to know."

"Nerot's Hotel, Nov. 23, 1779.

"I cannot imagine that, according to any idea of law or right, any subsequent grant would affect anything but what might remain from the produce of the fund after yours should be discharged. Those therefore whose grants were later could have no right to be paid but out of the surplus after the payment to you, and their claims do not justify yours being in arrear. . . . . The pleas in your favour appear certainly so strong that it would be wrong to leave the matter as it stands at present, and I do not myself see how there can be any objections (in point of delicacy) to seeking redress by whatever is the proper method. Complaining of any abuses in the management of the fund cannot convey anything improper towards the *Great Person* from whom the grant originally came : and in any other light I do not conceive any reason for a moment's hesitation. Whatever you may resolve upon, I flatter myself that my brother or I being upon the spot there will be very little trouble in the detail."

"Lincoln's Inn, Dec. 18, 1779.

"My residence here is for the present very comfortable, and when everything is finished, of which at last there really seems to be a near prospect, will be as complete as a lawyer can aspire to. In that state I flatter myself I shall see it when I return hither after Christmas. I now think of going to Cambridge for a short time towards the end of next week, and shall indeed only wait for those means from you which are,

I am sorry to say, necessary to enable me. I trust I need not say how unwilling I am to make any demands at so inconvenient a time, but the approach of Christmas, and the expense of moving, oblige me to beg you to supply me with a draft of 60*l.*"

"Pembroke Hall, Jan. 3, 1780.

" MY DEAR MOTHER,

"I was very unwillingly prevented last post-day from thanking you for your last letter, and sending you a proper certificate of my health, which I think it will be a satisfaction to you to receive. The charge of looking slender and thin when the doctor saw me I do not entirely deny; but if it was in a greater degree than usual, it may fairly be attributed to the hurry of London, and an accidental cold at the time. Both those causes have equally ceased on my removal hither, and as my way of life has ever since been as fattening as any one could desire, I believe I now possess as much *embonpoint* as I have naturally any right to. I had followed the doctor's advice by drinking asses' milk before I received your letter; and so easy a prescription I have no objection to obeying, though I believe it unnecessary, for some time longer. The use of the horse I assure you I do not neglect, in the properest medium; and a sufficient number of idle avocations secure me quite enough from the danger of too much study. On the whole, I think I may give in short a very satisfactory account of myself, as I really feel perfectly well, and yet do nothing that even an invalid need be afraid of. Among the principal occupations of Cambridge at this season of Christmas are perpetual college feasts, a species of exercise in which, above all others, I shall not forget your rule of moderation. The character, too, of candidate supplies me always with some employment, which, without deserving the name of business, fills up a good deal of time. . . . My business here is in a prosperous train, but nothing materially new is to be expected at present. The new year in some measure seems to promise a happy one to Ministry, if not to the country. It can hardly promise and keep its word to both. . . .

"I am, my dear Mother, &c.,

"W. Pitt."

"Pembroke Hall, Jan. 12, 1780.

"I do not know whether to hope that your western climate has been as much milder than ours as usual; for the weather we have had, though very sharp for above a fortnight, has been uncommonly pleasant, and such as I think you would enjoy. Within two or three days the frost has been too hard for riding, which is the only thing I quarrel with in it; and even that I can forgive, while it makes walking so excellent. Your moor must be in the perfection of winter beauty; but I suppose with hardly any cattle upon it, except stalking horses.

"The Cambridgeshire fens are nearly enough related to it to put me often in mind of it, though I confess the family likeness, with such a difference of features, is not much to the advantage of this country.

"The counties in this part of the world are beginning to awaken, and most of them will, I hope, adopt the Yorkshire measures.[4] I do not yet hear anything to the honour of the West, which I am sorry for."

---

[4] The great petition agreed upon at York in December, 1779. It prayed for Economical Reform, and was signed by upwards of 8000 freeholders.

" Lincoln's Inn, Feb. 9, 1780.

" You will, I hope, have excused my trusting entirely
to my more constant correspondent Harriot for your
knowing that I was established in town.   I have really
been a good deal engaged, and in some measure necessarily, having begun to attend as a lawyer at Westminster Hall ; to which I confess has also been added
occasionally the less professional pursuit of Opera,
Pantheon, &c., &c., so that my time between business
and pleasure may be fully accounted for.   I am now
going to a scene where both are united, I mean the
House of Lords, who are to enter to-day on the consideration of Lord Shelburne's motion.   The pleasure
of it would be a good deal heightened if there were
any present prospect of its having any considerable
effect.   The ground is certainly very strong, and some
accessions to the minority are expected ; but I fear
there is little chance of their being for some time
numerous enough to turn it into a majority."

" Grafton Street,[5] Feb. 26, 1780.

" You will not, I believe, be sorry to hear that in the
House of Commons yesterday, on a motion for the
List of Pensions, which the Ministry strenuously
opposed, the minority was 186 against 188.   This, I
think, looks like the downfall of those in power ; and
I am willing to hope that the views of Opposition are
really such as would make that event a blessing for
the country.   The principles on which some persons
at bottom probably act (I need not explain whom I
mean) I have as little confidence in as any one, but
I think they are so deeply pledged for what is right that
no harm can be apprehended from them at present."

---

[5] Where at this time Lady Harriot Pitt resided in company with
Lady Williams.

"Lincoln's Inn, March 14, 1780.

"My Parliamentary engagements still continue, and have now afforded me a scene which I never saw before, a majority against a Minister.[6] I was in the gallery till near three this morning, when this great phenomenon took place. The debate was the most interesting imaginable, and not the less so from Sir Fletcher Norton's unexpected and violent declarations against Lord North. What the consequence will be cannot be guessed, but I have no ideas of Ministry being able to stand. There are rumours of Parliament being to be dissolved soon after Easter, which oblige me to work double tides in the business of canvassing. My prospect, though not more certain, is as favourable as ever. Harriot will, I know, have sent Burke's speech, which I think will entertain you both with real beauties and ridiculous affectations. I have heard two less studied harangues from him since in reply, that please me much more than this does now that it is upon paper."

"Grafton Street, April 4, 1780.

"Last night was the masquerade, the pompous promises of which the newspapers must have carried to Burton. Harriot went with Lady Williams to Mrs. Weddel's (who is, I believe, a sister of Lady Rockingham's) to see masks. She was very much pleased with it, principally, I fancy, because it was the first thing of the kind she has seen. I was there as well as at a much more numerous assemblage at a magnificent Mr. Broadhead's, to which *some few* ladies did not like to go, from little histories relative to the lady of the

---

[6] On the clause in Mr. Burke's Bill for abolishing the Board of Trade, when the numbers were : for the clause, 207 ; against it, 199.

house. These did not prevent its being the most crowded place I ever was in. The company I was not conversant enough in masks to judge of. I concluded my evening at the Pantheon, which I had never seen illuminated, and which is really a glorious scene. In other respects, as I had hardly the pleasure of plaguing or being plagued by any body, I was heartily tired of my domino before it was over."

" Harley Street, April 20, 1780.

" All my feelings with regard to the paper enclosed[7] I need not express. I am sure I should be far indeed from wishing to suggest a syllable of alteration. The language of the heart, of such a heart especially, can never require or admit of correction. May it remain as it deserves, a lasting monument of both the subject and the author. My pen does not easily go from this topic to that of common news, nor of that have I much to tell you. It is, however, an essential satisfaction to assure you that I find my sister Mahon mended greatly in looks and strength, and in all respects since I have been absent; more indeed than I could have flattered myself. If the weather should not be very unfavourable she will go with Harriot to-morrow to Hayes, and I

[7] Lady Chatham had consulted her son on the inscription which she had drawn up for the pedestal of a marble urn to the memory of her husband in the grounds of Burton Pynsent. The inscription will be found printed at length in the Chatham Correspondence, vol. iv. p. 531.

When, after Lady Chatham's death, the estate of Burton Pynsent was sold, the urn, with its inscription, was transferred to the gardens at Stowe. Upon the dispersion of the family relics at that place the urn passed into a stranger's hands. But it has subsequently been recovered by another relative, James Banks Stanhope, Esq., M.P., who has raised the interesting monument once again in his gardens at Revesby Park, in Lincolnshire.

hope return soon quite in established health. You will be glad too to hear that I have every reason to be satisfied with my visit to Cambridge, which gives me as promising an expectation as is possible in the circumstances. It seems not unlikely that there may be an election there even before the end of this Parliament.

"With regard to the business of my account[8] there is certainly no occasion to have it re-stated. I am only sorry it has already occasioned you so much trouble, and still more so to think that your affairs are still so full of such embarrassment. I hope it will not be necessary to think of selling the arrears."

"Lincoln's Inn, May 2, 1780.

"I was yesterday present at a great debate in the House of Commons, where, according to the old custom, which is, I fear, pretty nearly re-established, arguments and numbers were almost equally clear on opposite sides. The idea of a Dissolution seems not to prevail so much as it did, which is indeed very natural."

"Lincoln's Inn, June 1, 1780.

"The 'London Courant' will have given you, I believe, a pretty accurate account of what passed at Buckingham, which was not of a very pleasant kind. But it is a satisfaction that the person for whom we are the most interested had much the better in all respects. Lord Temple has been at Stowe since, so that we have none of us had an opportunity of meeting. These unfortunate divisions weaken if they do not extinguish all hope for the public."[9]

---

[8] The account of his fortune, &c., during his minority.

[9] At a Meeting of the County of Bucks (as reported in the 'London Courant,' May 31, 1780) Earl Temple proposed an Association

" Lincoln's Inn, June 8, 1780.

" The accounts which the papers will have given you of the religious mobs which have infested us for some days, will make you, I know, desirous to know in what state we now are. I have the satisfaction to tell you that from the appearance of to-night everything seems likely to subside, and we may sleep again as in a Christian country. Lincoln's Inn has been [surrounded] with flames on all sides, but itself perfectly free from danger.

" The only objects of resentment seem to have been public characters and the residences of Roman Catholics or felons. None of those you are particularly interested for have been exposed to any inconvenience or apprehension, or anything else than the disagreeable and disgraceful sight which such uncontrolled licentiousness exhibits."

" Lincoln's Inn, Thursday (June, 1780).

" You should certainly have found me a better correspondent, but that my time has really been infinitely taken up. Besides the military transactions of the times, I have had to assume within these few days the pacific character of a barrister-at-law, and now want nothing but my wig and gown to qualify me for the Western Circuit. Lincoln's Inn has continued uninsulted during the whole of this scene. It was, however, thought necessary that we should show our readiness to defend ourselves. Accordingly several very respectable lawyers have appeared with muskets on their shoulders, to the no small diversion of all spectators.

---

for Economical Reform. Lord Mahon moved an amendment to include the object of Parlia- | mentary Reform; and a sharp debate but no decision ensued.

Unluckily the appearance of danger ended just as we embodied, and our military ardour has been thrown away."

"Cambridge, July 7, 1780.

"I heard yesterday from Lord Mahon on the subject of my canvass, who mentions that he and my sister were to remove from town in a day or two. I trust the country air will bring back her strength, and add to the progress of her recovery, which for some time has scarcely kept pace with our expectations."

We learn from Bishop Tomline that Mr. Pitt was called to the Bar on the 12th of June, 1780. But a family bereavement, though little foreseen, was now close impending. Lady Mahon, a sister to whom Mr. Pitt was tenderly attached, died at Chevening on the 18th of July. She was only twenty-five years of age, but her health had never completely rallied from the birth of her last child. She left three daughters: the first her namesake, who, as Lady Hester Stanhope, will re-appear in the latter part of my narrative; secondly, Griselda, who in 1800 married John Tekell, Esq., and who died without issue in 1851; and, thirdly, Lucy, who in 1796 married Thomas Taylor, Esq., and who died in 1814, leaving three sons and four daughters. To this youngest niece, born in February, 1780, Mr. Pitt had been godfather.

In the course of the ensuing year Lord Mahon married again. The object of his choice was Louisa, only child of the Hon. Henry Grenville, who had filled in succession the posts of Governor of Barbadoes and

Ambassador at Constantinople. He was a younger brother of Lady Chatham; so that as the first Lady Mahon was sister, the second was first cousin of Mr. Pitt. Of this second marriage were born three sons: first, my father, the fourth Earl Stanhope; secondly, Charles Banks, a Major in the army, who was killed at the head of his regiment at the battle of Coruña; and, thirdly, James Hamilton, a Lieutenant-Colonel in the army, who married a daughter of the Earl of Mansfield, and who died in 1825.

In the August following, we find Mr. Pitt join for a short time the Western Circuit, and give a hasty report of his proceedings.

"Dorchester, Aug. 4, 1780.

"MY DEAR MOTHER,

"You will be glad to have early information of my having arrived prosperously at this place, and taken upon me the character of a lawyer. I have indeed done so, yet no otherwise than by eating and drinking with lawyers; and so far I find the Circuit perfectly agreeable. I write this in the morning, lest I should not have time after. There is not, to be sure, much probability of my being overwhelmed with business, but I may possibly have my time filled up with hearing others for the remainder of the day; and, therefore, to show how much I profit by our last conversation, I make sure of the present moment. I could also give you another instance, for, thanks to the sun and an eastern aspect, I was burnt out of my bed this morning before seven o'clock. My gown and wig do not make their appearance till two or three hours hence, as great part of the morning is taken up by the

Judges going to church, where it does not seem the etiquette for counsel to attend.

"You will not suppose that I have much news to tell you. The only thing worth mentioning is a curious enclosure which came to me by last night's post in a cover franked '*Tho. Pitt.*' Adieu.

> "Your ever dutiful and affectionate Son,
>
> "W. Pitt."

> "Exeter, Aug. 9, 1780.

" My dear Mother,

"I have but just time to write one line to tell you that I received your packet yesterday. Having been in Court till now, I fear I am too late for the regular post. . . . I have not forgot the Bonds of Award, and will return them as soon as I can find time, but so much is employed either in the hall or at table that I have not much to dispose of. Lord Mahon's letter was to inquire after you, and to tell me that a Dissolution was expected very soon. It must be rather uncertain, but I shall not be surprised if an express overtakes me with the news. If it should, I shall take Burton flying in my way to Cambridge.

> " Believe me, &c.,
>
> " W. Pitt.

"I shall leave this place on Saturday and proceed to Bodmin, unless summoned away by a Dissolution."

On the 1st of September accordingly the Parliament was dissolved. Pitt repaired in all haste to Cambridge, and an arduous contest began. But when it closed, he found himself at the bottom of the poll. He announced the result the same evening in a note, as follows :—

" Pembroke Hall, Sept. 16, 1780.

" MY DEAR MOTHER,

" Mansfield and Townshend have run away with the prize, but my struggle has not been dishonourable.

" I am just going to Cheveley[1] for a day or two, and shall soon return to you for as long as the law will permit, which will now be probably the sole object with me. I hope you are all well.

" Your ever dutiful and affectionate

" W. PITT."

Mr. Pitt appears to have paid his customary visit to Lady Chatham in the autumn; but on his return to town, his letters to her represent him as thoroughly immersed in the cares of his new profession.

" Lincoln's Inn, Nov. 23, 1780.

" I do not wonder that you seem to consider me rather as an idle correspondent, which, much against my will, I feel that I have been.

" If I had been able to give you any information worth knowing of what passed in Parliament, I certainly would; but really there has been nothing decisive, and all seems to be put off till after Christmas. You will, I am sure, be ready to excuse a little either of ignorance or laziness, when I assure you that ever since Term began I have been almost every day in Westminster Hall the whole time between breakfast and dinner, and that the rest of the day is sufficiently taken up by necessary business and incidental avocations which are unavoidable."

---

[1] The seat of the Duke of Rutland in Cambridgeshire.

At this very time, however, an opening to public life unexpectedly appeared. The brave and lamented Granby had been a friend and follower of Chatham. His eldest son, who was senior by five years to William Pitt, became one of the Members for the University of Cambridge, and in 1779 succeeded his grandfather as Duke of Rutland. Mindful of his hereditary friendships, he sought the acquaintance of William Pitt in the first years of Pitt at Cambridge. When Pitt came to live in London, the two young men quickly grew intimate, and the warm attachment between them was continued during the whole of the Duke's life.

It was natural, under such circumstances, that the Duke of Rutland should feel most sincere concern at the exclusion of Pitt from the House of Commons. He spoke upon the subject to Sir James Lowther, another ally of his house, and the owner of most extensive borough influence. Sir James quickly caught the idea, and proposed to avail himself of a double return for one of his boroughs to bring the friend of his friend into Parliament. The Duke mentioned the offer to Pitt; and Pitt, who was writing on the same day to his mother, added a few lines in haste to let her know. But it was not until after he had seen Sir James himself that he was able to express his entire satisfaction at the prospect now before him.

"Lincoln's Inn, Thursday night, Nov., 1780.
" MY DEAR MOTHER,

"I can now inform you that I have seen Sir James Lowther, who has repeated to me the offer he

had before made, and in the handsomest manner.
Judging from my father's principles, he concludes that
mine would be agreeable to his own, and on that
ground—to me of all others the most agreeable—to
bring me in. No kind of condition was mentioned,
but that if ever our lines of conduct should become
opposite, I should give him an opportunity of choosing
another person. On such liberal terms I could certainly not hesitate to accept the proposal, than which
nothing could be in any respect more agreeable.
Appleby is the place I am to represent, and the election will be made (probably in a week or ten days)
without my having any trouble, or even visiting my
constituents. I shall be in time to be spectator and
auditor *at least* of the important scene after the
holidays. I would not defer confirming to you this
intelligence, which I believe you will not be sorry to
hear.

　　　　　　" I am, my dear Mother, &c.,

　　　　　　　　　　　　" W. PITT."

　　　　　　　　　" Dec. 7, 1780.

　　" I have not yet received the notification of my
election. It will probably not take place till the end
of this week, as Sir James Lowther was to settle an
election at Haslemere before he went into the north,
and meant to be present at Appleby afterwards. The
Parliament adjourned yesterday, so I shall not take my
seat till after the holidays. . . . I propose before
long, in spite of politics, to make an excursion for a
short time to Lord Westmorland's[2] and shall probably look at my constituents *that should have been* at

---

[2] Apthorp, in Northamptonshire.

Cambridge, in my way. I have hopes of extending to
Burton in the course of the Christmas recess."

But the pleasure of Pitt at his approaching entrance
into Parliament was grievously dashed by another
domestic calamity. The sudden news came that his
youngest brother, James Charles, who was absent on
service, and already a Post-Captain, had died in the
West Indies. William set off immediately for Burton
Pynsent, and from thence wrote as follows to
Mr. Pretyman :—

"Dec. 1780.

. . . .

"You will, I know, be anxious to hear from me.
I have to regret the loss of a brother who had everything that was most amiable and promising, everything
that I could love and admire; and I feel the favourite
hope of my mind extinguished by this untimely blow.
Let me, however, assure you that I am too much tried
in affliction not to be able to support myself under it ;
and that my poor mother and sister, to whom I brought
the sad account yesterday, have not suffered in their
health from so severe a shock. I have prevailed on
them to think of changing the scene and moving towards
Hayes, which is a great comfort to me, as the solitude
and distance of this place must now be insupportable.
I imagine that we shall begin our journey in a few
days." [3]

---

[3] Life of Pitt, by Bishop Tomline, vol. i. p. 26.

CHAPTER II.

1781—1782.

Enters the House of Commons — State of parties — Attaches himself to Lord Shelburne — Goostree's Club — Pitt's first speech — Congratulated by Fox — Vindication of his father's opinions, and statement of his own, on the American war — On the Western Circuit, and in the Court of King's Bench — General character at the Bar — Readiness of debate — Speeches on Parliamentary Reform — Appointed Chancellor of the Exchequer — Letters to his mother.

ON the 23rd of January, 1781, when the Parliament met again, Mr. Pitt took his seat as member for Appleby. That date marks both the commencement and the close of his public life, for it was on the anniversary of the same day that he died.

At the time when Mr. Pitt first entered the House of Commons Lord North was still at the head of public affairs. Himself the most good-humoured and amiable of men, he might often as a Minister seem harsh, and still more often unfortunate. Yielding his own better judgment to the personal wishes of the King, he continued to maintain the fatal war against the revolted colonies, with a failing popularity and with a doubtful mind. His principal reliance at this time in debate was on Lord George Germaine, the Secretary of State, and on Henry Dundas, the Lord Advocate for Scotland.

The Opposition arrayed against him consisted, in fact, of two parties. They had been recently reconciled, and almost always voted together; yet still, as appeared shortly afterwards, the union between them was by no means thorough and complete. Of these two parties the largest by far in point of numbers was founded on the old Whig connexion of the Great Houses, or, as they loved to call themselves, the "Revolution Families." Men of this stamp could seldom— as Horace Walpole once complained of the Duke of Portland—extend their views beyond the high wall of Burlington House. To them birth and rank seemed the principal qualities for leadership. In former years they had chafed at the ascendency of the elder Pitt; and now they could never look on Burke in any other light than as a toiling and useful subordinate, to be rewarded on occasion with some second-rate place, and not worthy to sit in council with a Wentworth or a Cavendish.

With such views they had for many years acknowledged as their leader the Marquis of Rockingham, head of the house of Wentworth, a nobleman of vast estates, of highly honourable character, but of very slender ability either for business or debate. But their leader in the Commons and the true impelling and guiding spirit of their whole party was Charles James Fox. Born in 1749, a younger son of the first Lord Holland, he had entered Parliament at only nineteen as member for the close borough of Midhurst. His youth had been marked by a course of wild extravagance and by the assertion of strong anti-popular politics. On two occasions he had held a subordinate office under Lord North. But soon breaking loose from these tram-

mels and joining the ranks of Opposition, side by side
with Burke, he had made himself most formidable to his
recent chief. His admirable eloquence and his powers
of debate—never exceeded in any age or in any nation
—his generous and open temper, and the warm attachment, which ensued from it, of his political friends,
cast into the shade his irregular life and his ruined
fortunes, and extorted the wonder even of his enemies.
Under him at this time were two men whose genius
would have made them capable of leading, but who
were proud to serve under so great a chief. There was
Edmund Burke, the first philosophical statesman of his
country; there was Richard Brinsley Sheridan, the first
of her dramatists in recent times, who had already produced some masterpieces of wit upon the stage, and was
shortly to produce other masterpieces of oratory in the
House of Commons.

Besides this main body of the old Whig aristocracy,
there was also in Opposition a smaller band of the old
adherents of Lord Chatham. It comprised the Earl of
Shelburne and Lord Camden, who had filled the offices
of Secretary of State and Chancellor in Chatham's last
administration, and who to the close of his life had
enjoyed his highest confidence. Lord Shelburne was
indeed looked upon as the leader of his party since his
death. There were also among its chief men Mr.
Thomas Townshend, an active and useful politician,
who spoke often and not without effect; Mr. Dunning,
unrivalled in his own time for success at the Bar; and
Colonel Barré, a bold and unsparing, and therefore the
more applauded debater.

It was almost as a matter of course that Mr. Pitt on entering Parliament attached himself closely to this party. So had his eldest brother on coming of age. So had his friend the Duke of Rutland, on succeeding to the title. So had also his kinsman Lord Mahon, who had been returned at the General Election for the borough of High Wycombe, then a close corporation under the control of Lord Shelburne. So had also Mr. John Jeffreys Pratt, the only son of Lord Camden, and born in the same year as Mr. Pitt, who had come in for another close corporation, that of Bath.

But besides these, as I may term them, hereditary ties, Mr. Pitt began at this time to form some intimate friendships with other young men, chiefly, like himself, entering upon life, and more or less closely linked with him in politics. Such were Henry Bankes, of Corfe Castle in Dorsetshire, whom he had known well at Cambridge; Edward, the eldest son of Mr. Eliot, of Port Eliot, in Cornwall, who some years later became his brother-in-law; Richard Pepper Arden, afterwards Lord Alvanley; Robert Smith, at this time member for Nottingham, and head of a great banking-house in London. Unlike the rest, he was seven years the senior of Pitt, and yet he survived him thirty-two.

But, of all the intimacies formed at this time by Mr. Pitt, there was none that ripened into more cordial friendship than that with Mr. Wilberforce. The son of a banker at Hull, and the owner of a good estate in Yorkshire, William Wilberforce, though born in the same year as Pitt, was sent three years later to Cambridge. There the two young men were but slightly acquainted; but, at the General Election of 1780, Wilberforce was, after a sharp contest, returned for the town of Hull, and meeting Pitt both in the House of Commons and in social circles, they rapidly grew friends.

These young men and several others—about twenty-five in all—besides their resort at the larger clubs, as Brooks's and White's, formed at this time a more intimate society called Goostree's, from the name of the person at whose house they met in Pall Mall. Pitt was one of the chief frequenters of this little club, and during one winter—probably that from 1781 to 1782—is said to have supped there every night. How delightful was his conversation in his easier hours Mr. Wilberforce has warmly attested:

"He was the wittiest man I ever knew, and, what was quite peculiar to himself, had at all times his wit under entire control. Others appeared struck by the unwonted association of brilliant images; but every possible combination of ideas was present to his mind, and he could at once produce whatever he desired. I was one of those who met to spend an evening in memory of Shakespeare at the Boar's Head in Eastcheap. Many professed wits were present, but Pitt was the most amusing of the party, and the readiest and most apt in the required allusions." [1]

Another of the Boar's Head party, Mr. Jekyll, gives of it a similar account:

"We were all in high spirits, quoting and alluding

---

[1] Life of Wilberforce, by his Sons, vol. i. p. 18.

to Shakespeare the whole day, and it appeared that Mr. Pitt was as well and familiarly read in the poet's works as the best Shakespearians present." [2]

The clubs of London, Goostree's not excepted, all at this time afforded a dangerous temptation. Fox, Fitzpatrick, and their circle, had long since set the example of high play. It had become the fashion; and Wilberforce himself was nearly ensnared by it. On the very first day that he went to Boodle's he won twenty-five guineas of the Duke of Norfolk. His diary at this period records more than once the loss of a hundred pounds at the faro-table. He was reclaimed from this pursuit by a most generous impulse—not because he lost in private play to others, but because he saw and was pained at seeing others lose to him. Of the young member for Appleby he proceeds to speak as follows:

"We played a good deal at Goostree's, and I well remember the intense earnestness which Pitt displayed when joining in those games of chance. He perceived their increasing fascination, and soon after suddenly abandoned them for ever."

It was not long before Mr. Pitt took part in the debates. He made his first speech on the 26th of February, in support of Burke's Bill for Economical Reform. Under the circumstances, this first speech took him a little by surprise. Lord Nugent was speaking against the Bill, and Mr. Byng, member for Middlesex, asked Mr. Pitt to follow in reply. Mr. Pitt

---

[2] Note to Bishop Tomline's Life, vol. i. p. 43.

gave a doubtful answer, but in the course of Lord
Nugent's speech resolved that he would not. Mr. Byng,
however, had understood him to assent, and had said
so to some friends around him; so that the moment
Lord Nugent sat down, all these gentlemen, with one
voice, called out "Mr. Pitt! Mr. Pitt!" and by their
cry probably kept down every other member. Mr.
Pitt, finding himself thus called upon, and observing
that the House waited to hear him, thought himself
bound to rise. The sudden call did not for a moment
discompose him; he was from the beginning collected
and unembarrassed, and, far from reciting a set speech,
addressed himself at once to the business of reply.
Never, says Bishop Tomline, were higher expectations
formed of any person upon his first coming into Parliament, and never were expectations more completely
fulfilled. The silvery clearness of his voice, his lofty
yet unpresuming demeanour, set off to the best advantage his close and well arrayed though unpremeditated
arguments, while the ready selection of his words and
the perfect structure of his sentences were such as
even the most practised speakers often fail to show.
Not only did he please, it may be said that he astonished the House. Scarce one mind in which a reverent
thought of Chatham did not rise.

No sooner had Pitt concluded than Fox with generous warmth hurried up to wish him joy of his
success. As they were still together, an old member,
said to have been General Grant, passed by them and
said, " Aye, Mr. Fox, you are praising young Pitt for his
speech. You may well do so; for, excepting yourself,

there is no man in the House can make such another; and, old as I am, I expect and hope to hear you both battling it within these walls, as I have heard your fathers before you." Mr. Fox, disconcerted at the awkward turn of the compliment, was silent and looked foolish; but young Pitt, with great delicacy and readiness, answered, "I have no doubt, General, you would like to attain the age of Methuselah!"[3]

After Mr. Pitt several other members spoke, and the debate was continued until midnight, when, on a division, the measure of Burke was rejected by a majority of 233 against 190.

It deserves to be noted that warmly as the merits of Pitt's first speech were acknowledged by his hearers, those merits are scarcely to be traced in the meagre report of it which alone remains. So imperfect indeed was still, and for many years afterwards, the Parliamentary system of reporting, that it totally fails to give any just idea of the great orators of the time, except in a few salient passages, and unless, as was the case with Burke in his chief speeches, they prepared their own compositions for the press. For this reason, among others, I shall forbear from inserting in my narrative any but very few and very brief extracts of Mr. Pitt's published speeches, which my readers can, if they desire it, find elsewhere.

Next day the young orator wrote to Lady Chatham as follows:

---

[3] This anecdote was put on record by Fox's nephew, Lord Holland, and I give it in his own words. See the Memorials of Fox by Lord John Russell, vol. i. p. 262.

" Tuesday night, Feb. 27, 1781.

" MY DEAR MOTHER,

"If the length of the debate yesterday, and of a late supper after it, had not made me too lazy this morning, I intended to have been at Hayes to-day. To-morrow I must be early in the House of Commons, to attend the Lyme election, and am therefore doubtful whether I can ride to Hayes and back again in time, which makes me wish to write to you one line at least, in case I should not.

"I know you will have learnt that I heard my own voice yesterday, and the account you have had would be in all respects better than any I can give if it had not come from too partial a friend. All I can say is that I was able to execute in some measure what I intended, and that I have at least every reason to be happy beyond measure in the reception I met with. You will, I dare say, wish to know more particulars than I fear I shall be able to tell you, but in the mean time you will, I am sure, feel somewhat the same pleasure that I do in the encouragement, however unmerited, which has attended my first attempt.

"I hope when I come to find you better than I left you, and I trust that will not be later than Thursday at furthest. Pray give my love to Harriot, and best compliments to Mrs. Stapleton.[4]

" Your most dutiful and affectionate son,

" W. PITT."

"It is a curious fact," writes Lord Macaulay, "well remembered by some who were very recently living,

---

[4] Mrs. Stapleton was an aunt of the first Lord Combermere. She was the friend and frequent visitor, and at last for many years the constant companion, of Lady Chatham.

that soon after this debate Pitt's name was put up by
Fox at Brooks's."

The merits of Mr. Pitt's performance continued for
some days to be discussed in political circles. Lord
North said of it, with generous frankness, that it was
the best first speech he had ever heard. Still more
emphatic was the praise of Mr. Burke. When some
one in his presence spoke of Pitt as "a chip of the old
block," Burke exclaimed, "He is not a chip of the old
block: he is the old block itself!" Dr. Goodenough,
subsequently Bishop of Carlisle, exults in one of his
letters that the great Lord Chatham is now happily
restored to his country. "All the old members recog-
nised him instantly: to identify him there wanted only
a few wrinkles in the face." [5]

It appears that a little time previously, Pitt had made
the earliest trial of his debating powers in a party of
some young friends. Mr. Jekyll, who was at this time
like himself a barrister on the Western Circuit, thus
relates the fact:—" When he first made his brilliant
display in Parliament, those at the Bar who had seen
little of him expressed surprise; but a few who had
heard him once speak in a sort of mock debate at the
Crown and Anchor Tavern, when a club called the
Western Circuit Club was dissolved, agreed that he had
then displayed all the various species of eloquence for
which he was afterwards celebrated." [6]

---

[5] To the Rev. Edward Wilson,
Feb. 27, 1781. Life of Lord Sidmouth, by Dean Pellew. vol. i.
p. 27.

[6] See a valuable note (of which
I shall give the rest in another
place) contributed to Bishop Tomline's Life, and inserted in that

On the 31st of May Mr. Pitt made his second speech in the House of Commons. The subject was a Bill to continue an Act of the last Session for the appointment of Commissioners of Public Accounts. When Lord North, who had argued the question at considerable length, sat down, Fox and Pitt rose together. But Fox, with a feeling of kindness to the young member, immediately gave way,[7] and Pitt, proceeding in a strain of forcible eloquence, contended that the House of Commons, which the constitution had entrusted with the power of controlling the public expenditure, could not in the faithful discharge of their duty delegate any part of that trust to persons who were not of their own body.

In the division which ensued Colonel Barré and Mr. Pitt were appointed Tellers on the same side. It was far from affording any cause of triumph to the young orator, since Lord North carried his negative by 98 votes against 42.

A few days later we find Mr. Wilberforce refer to this second speech as follows in a letter to a friend at Hull : —" The papers will have informed you how Mr. William Pitt, second son of the late Lord Chatham, has distinguished himself. He comes out as his father did, a ready-made orator, and I doubt not but that I shall one day or other see him the first man in the country. His

---

work at vol. i. p. 42. The Bishop does not name the writer, but describes him as " very intimate with Mr. Pitt on the Western Circuit," and as " holding an honourable station in the Court of Chancery " in 1820 ; adding other circumstances also which plainly identify his correspondent with Mr. Jekyll.

[7] See Tomline's Life, vol. i. p. 33. Lord Macaulay, by a trifling oversight, has transferred this incident to Pitt's first speech (Biographies, p. 152).

famous speech, however, delivered the other night did
not convince me, and I stayed in with the old fat fellow
(Lord North)."

In the same month of May Wilberforce himself had
for the first time taken part in the debates. He seems
on this occasion to have attracted little notice. But ere
long he gained the success which his abilities and character deserved, and by degrees grew into high favour
with the House as an earnest and excellent speaker.

Mr. Pitt spoke for the third time this Session on the
12th of June, upon a motion of Mr. Fox tending to conclude a peace with the American colonies. It does not
appear that the young orator had any thoughts of
taking part in this debate, but he was unexpectedly
called up by several misrepresentations of his father's
sentiments. Here is his own account to Lady Chatham
the next day.

"June 13, 1781.

"The business of yesterday was a triumph to Opposition in everything but the article of numbers, which
was indeed some abatement of it—172 to 99. I found
it necessary to say somewhat which was very favourably
and flatteringly received, in answer to Mr. Rigby and
Mr. Adam, who chose to say that my father and every
other party in the kingdom who had objected only to
the internal taxation of America, and had asserted at
that time the other rights of this country, were acces-
sories to the American war. This you may imagine I
directly denied, and expressed as strongly as I could how
much he detested the principle of the war. I gave several
general reasons which occurred to me for the necessity, in
every point of view, for an inquiry into the state of the

war (which was what Mr. Fox moved for), but avoided saying anything direct on the subject of independence, which in that stage of the business I thought better avoided. I hope you will excuse the haste of this account, as I have a person waiting for me whilst I write."

But besides thus vindicating the opinions of Lord Chatham in regard to the American war, Mr. Pitt took occasion to state with the utmost force his own. " A Noble Lord who spoke early" (here he alluded to Lord Westcote) "has in the warmth of his zeal called this a holy war. For my part, though the Right Hon. gentleman who made the motion and some other gentlemen have been more than once in the course of the debate severely reprehended for calling it a wicked or accursed war, I am persuaded, and I will affirm, that it is a most accursed, wicked, barbarous, cruel, unnatural, unjust, and diabolical war. . . . The expense of it has been enormous, far beyond any former experience, and yet what has the British nation received in return? Nothing but a series of ineffective victories or severe defeats—victories only celebrated with temporary triumph over our brethren whom we would trample down, or defeats which fill the land with mourning for the loss of dear and valuable relations slain in the impious cause of enforcing unconditional submission. Where is the Englishman who on reading the narrative of those bloody and well fought contests can refrain lamenting the loss of so much British blood shed in such a cause, or from weeping on whatever side victory might be declared?"

In reply to Pitt rose Henry Dundas, Lord Advocate, the same who was destined through many coming years to be not only one of Pitt's Cabinet colleagues, but the most trusted and relied on of all. He defended, as he had always done and as he was bound to do, the whole course of the American war; but as regarded his young adversary in that debate, he could not refrain from complimenting "so happy an union of first-rate abilities, high integrity, bold and honest independence of conduct, and the most persuasive eloquence."

The debate on this occasion was summed up by Fox with his usual admirable ability, but his motion to go into Committee was rejected as we have seen by overwhelming numbers.

These three were the only speeches made by Mr. Pitt in that Session. It closed on the 18th of July. A little time afterwards, when a member of the Opposition happened to remark to Mr. Fox, "Mr. Pitt, I think, promises to be one of the first men in Parliament," Fox, without the smallest touch of jealousy, said at once, " He is so already."

In the summer of that year, as in the preceding, Mr. Pitt went the Western Circuit. It proved to be for the last time. His whole career at the Bar was indeed so short as to leave little opportunity for the display of his abilities. He was eager to apply himself to it, and resolved to neglect no business, however small. It used to be related by Mr. Justice Rooke how Pitt had dangled seven days with a junior brief and a single guinea fee waiting till a cause of no sort of importance should come on in the Court of Common Pleas. On another occasion, however, in the Court of King's Bench, there being a motion for a Habeas Corpus in the case of a man who was charged with murder, we are assured that Mr. Pitt made a speech which excited the admiration of the Bar, and drew down some words of praise from Lord Mansfield.

On the Circuit he had but little business, yet at Salisbury in the summer of 1781 he was employed by Mr. Samuel Petrie as junior counsel in some bribery causes that had resulted from the Cricklade Election Petition. There are reports of two speeches that he made in these causes, each report, however, extending only to a few lines; and in giving judgment on the point which the second of these speeches involved, Mr. Baron Perryn said that "Mr. Pitt's observations had great weight with him." [8]

It further appears that in the course of these trials Pitt received some high compliments from Mr. Dunning, the leader of the Bar. "I remember also," thus writes Mr. Jekyll, one of his brother barristers upon this Circuit, "that in an action of *Crim. Con.* at Exeter he manifested, as junior counsel, such talents in cross-examination, that it was the universal opinion of the Bar that he should have led the cause."

Of his general character at the Bar, we find Mr. Jekyll speak as follows: "Among lively men of his own time of life, Mr. Pitt was always the most lively and convivial in the many hours of leisure which occur to young unoccupied men on a Circuit, and joined all the little excursions to Southampton, Weymouth, and such parties of amusement as were habitually formed. He

---

[8] See the Report of the Cricklade Case (as published by Mr. Petrie), p. 301 and 321, ed. 1785.

was extremely popular. His name and reputation of high acquirements at the University commanded the attention of his seniors. His wit, his good humour, and joyous manners endeared him to the younger part of the Bar. . . . . At Mr. Pitt's instance an annual dinner took place for some years at Richmond Hill, the party consisting of Lord Erskine, Lord Redesdale, Sir William Grant, Mr. Bond, Mr. Leycester, Mr. Jekyll, and others. After he was Minister he continued to ask his old Circuit intimates to dine with him, and his manners were unaltered."

The Circuit of this summer having ended, Mr. Pitt passed some autumn weeks with his mother at Burton Pynsent, and during a part of this time they were joined by Mr. Pretyman. But in the first days of October we find him on a visit in Dorsetshire, and at the close of that month again in chambers.

" Kingston Hall,[9] Oct. 7, 1781.

" MY DEAR MOTHER,

" I have delayed writing to you longer than I intended, which I hope is of little consequence, as Harriot will have brought you all the news I could have sent—an account of that stupid fête at Fonthill,[1] which, take it all together, was, I think, as ill imagined, and as indifferently conducted, as anything of the sort need be. She will, I hope, also have acknowledged that although somewhat duller, she found it much less formidable than she imagined, which was one great point

---

[9] The seat of his friend Henry Bankes, Esq.
[1] The well-known seat of William Beckford, Esq.

in its favour. By meeting Lord Shelburne and Lord
Camden, we were pressed to make a second visit to
Bowood, which, from the addition of Colonel Barré and
Mr. Dunning. was a very pleasant party. Since that
time I have been waging war, with increasing success, on pheasants and partridges. I shall continue
hostilities, I believe, about a week longer, and then
prepare for the opening of another sort of campaign in
Westminster Hall. Parliament, I am very glad to hear,
is not to meet till the 27th of November, which will
allow me a good deal more leisure than I expected."

　　　　　　　"Lincoln's Inn, Oct. 24, 1781.

　　　" I rejoice that the prospect of seeing you at Hayes
draws nearer, and I flatter myself too with the hopes of
finding your course of amendment much increased and
confirmed. There is no fresh news in town. The last
account from America seems, if anything were wanting,
to complete our prospect there."

Parliament met again on the 27th November. Only
two days before had come the tidings of the surrender of
Lord Cornwallis at York Town. It was necessary for
that reason to new-cast the Royal Speech. The Ministers
were grievously depressed, while their opponents gathered
strength and energy in the same proportion. On the
Address, an amendment was moved by Fox, and both he
and Burke put forth all their powers of debate. So also
next day, on the Report of the Address, did Pitt. Such
was the applause in the House when he sat down that
it was some time before the Lord Advocate, who rose
immediately, could obtain a hearing.

The speech of Henry Dundas on this occasion was

not a little surprising. In a tone of great frankness, and paying the highest compliments to Pitt, he let fall some hints of discordant views or erroneous conduct in the Ministry to which he still belonged: but he would no further explain himself. So acute a politician must have clearly discerned the tottering state of Lord North, and may not have felt unwilling, even at this time, to connect himself with a young statesman of popular principles and rising fame.

Compliments to the young statesman were, however, by no means peculiar to Dundas. We are told in a youthful letter from Sir Samuel Romilly, that in one of these debates before Christmas, 1781, "Fox, in an exaggerated strain of panegyric, said he could no longer lament the loss of Lord Chatham, for he was again living in his son, with all his virtues and all his talents." [2]

About a fortnight after the Address, Pitt made his second speech of the Session, and his last before the holidays. Horace Walpole, who was still in his old age a most keen observer of everything that passed around him, has an entry as follows in his journal:— "December 14th, 1781. Another remarkable debate on Army Estimates, in which Pitt made a speech with amazing logical abilities, exceeding all he had hitherto shown, and making men doubt whether he would not prove superior even to Charles Fox."

In this speech Mr. Pitt gave a surprising proof of the readiness of debate which he had already acquired, or I may rather say which he had from the first displayed.

---

[2] Life of Romilly, by his Sons, vol. i. p. 192.

Lord George Germaine had taken occasion two days before to declare that, be the consequences what they might, he would never consent to sign the independence of the colonies. Lord North, on the contrary, had shown strong symptoms of yielding. Pitt was inveighing with much force against these discordant counsels at so perilous a juncture, when the two Ministers whom he arraigned drew close and began to whisper, while Mr. Welbore Ellis, a grey-haired placeman, of diminutive size, the butt of Junius, under the by-name of Grildrig, bent down his tiny head between them. Here Pitt paused in his argument, and glancing at the group exclaimed, " I will wait until the unanimity is a little better restored. I will wait until the Nestor of the Treasury has reconciled the difference between the Agamemnon and the Achilles of the American war."

A few days later, Parliament adjourned for several weeks of Christmas holiday. No sooner had it reassembled than the Opposition resumed their attacks with fresh spirit and success. Mr. Fox made the first onset on the 24th of January, 1782: it was directed against the Earl of Sandwich, as First Lord of the Admiralty. Pitt spoke several times to enforce these charges, which were renewed in various forms.

" I support the motion," he said, " from motives of a public nature, and from those motives only. I am too young to be supposed capable of entertaining any personal enmity against the Earl of Sandwich; and I trust that when I shall be less young it will appear that I have early determined, in the most solemn manner, never to allow any private and personal consideration

whatever to influence my public conduct at any one
moment of my life."

It should be observed that these remarkable words
have been put on record, though not so stated, from
the personal testimony of Mr. Pretyman, who appears
to have been present in the gallery that evening. They
are not to be found in the corresponding passage of the
' Parliamentary Debates.' [3]

Lady Chatham having before that period returned to
Hayes, there was probably scarce a week in which she
did not receive a visit from her son. His letters to her
during this spring are accordingly few and of little interest. Here, however, are some extracts:—

> "Lincoln's Inn, Wednesday (Jan. 1782).

"I am very unlucky in having been prevented by the
weather this morning from mounting my horse; and
the more so because fresh engagements arise every
hour which make it difficult for me to have the pleasure
of looking at you at Hayes. I thought it impossible
that anything should interfere with my intention to-
morrow; but (what is very *mal a propos*, considering
how seldom it has occurred) I have some law business
just now put into my hands, which must be done without delay."

> "March 9, 1782.

"I came to town yesterday in time for a very good
debate; and a division which, though not victorious, is
as encouraging as possible—216 against 226, on a ques-

---

[3] Compare Bishop Tomline's
Life, vol. i. p. 52, with the Parl.
Hist. vol. xxii. p. 939. The Bishop
has in like manner supplied some
expressions of Mr. Dunning in the
same debate.

tion leading directly to removal, is a force that can hardly fail. Another trial will be made in the course of the week, and probably on Thursday, on which day I shall be able to attend without much inconvenience. To-morrow morning I return to Salisbury, and unluckily the hour at which I must set out will not give me a chance of seeing you first. Knowing of some little business that I shall be engaged in there, it is of importance to me to be in time. I trust to have the pleasure of finding you here at my next glimpse of London."

"Goostree's, half-past one (March 16, 1782).

"After an excellent debate we have lost our question by a division of 236 against 227, which is indeed everything but a victory."

It is not necessary that I should go through in detail the long series of able and vigorous attacks upon the Government by which the Parliamentary annals of this spring are distinguished. In several of them Mr. Pitt took part with great applause. Sometimes the Ministers underwent defeat, and sometimes they only escaped it by most narrow majorities. Notwithstanding the King's wishes and entreaties, their resignation could be no longer deferred. It was announced on the 20th of March to the House of Commons by Lord North, speaking, as ever, with excellent taste and temper; and the King, though coldly and ungraciously, consented to accept the Marquis of Rockingham as his new Prime Minister.

In the distribution of offices which ensued it was sought to combine both the parties in Opposition. Mr.

Fox and Lord Shelburne became joint Secretaries of
State, Lord Camden President, the Duke of Grafton
Privy Seal, and Lord John Cavendish Chancellor of
the Exchequer.   He was recommended to that office
mainly by his name and rank; but still, as to his mental
qualities, does not quite deserve to be called, as Lord
Brougham calls him, "the most obscure of mankind."
Lord Thurlow, whose energy had gained him both the
personal favour of the King and the political guidance
of the House of Peers, was continued Lord Chancellor.
Henry Dundas, in like manner, was continued Lord
Advocate.   Burke was promoted to the lucrative office
of Paymaster, but not deemed worthy of a seat in the
Cabinet.   No more was Thomas Townshend, who accepted the post of Secretary-at-War.   Other rich offices
were bestowed on Barré and Dunning, the latter being
also shortly afterwards raised to the peerage as Lord
Ashburton.

The son of Chatham was not included in the new
arrangements.   Some ten days before Lord North had
announced his resignation, but while that resignation was
foreseen as close impending, Pitt had taken occasion, in
the House of Commons, to use words to the following
effect:—"For myself, I could not expect to form part
of a new administration; but were my doing so more
within my reach, I feel myself bound to declare that I
never would accept a subordinate situation."   Young as
he was, he had determined that he would not be held as
committed to measures in framing which he had no
share.   He had determined that he would serve his
Sovereign as a Cabinet Minister, or not at all.

Such a resolution is only to be justified by the consciousness and by the reputation of extraordinary powers. Even at the present time such a resolution might justly excite surprise, and be regarded as presumptuous from a young man not yet twenty-three; but in the time of Pitt it must have seemed more surprising and more presumptuous still. The Cabinet was then a much smaller body than at present. In 1770, on the first formation of his Government, Lord North made it of seven. In 1783, as we shall see hereafter, Pitt himself made it of seven also. Admission to such an assembly was of course a much higher distinction than it could be to Cabinets of fourteen and sixteen; and some men even of the most powerful intellects, as Burke and Sheridan, were never to the end of their lives invited to enter its doors.

It is said indeed that Pitt had no sooner sat down than he felt he might have gone too far, and consulted Admiral Keppel, who was next him, whether he should not rise again and explain. This was told by Sir Robert Adair to the Earl of Albemarle, as derived from Keppel himself.[4] All three authorities are entitled to high respect; yet it does not seem very likely that the determination announced by Pitt could have been formed at the spur of the moment, or could therefore have been liable to so sudden a revulsion. The statement of Bishop Tomline, on the contrary, implies that the determination of Pitt was deliberate, and not announced till some days after it was formed.

---

[4] See the Memoirs of Lord Rockingham, vol. ii. p. 423.

Certain it is that Mr. Pitt showed no irresolution when, upon the change of Government consequent on Lord North's resignation, he had before him the choice of several subordinate posts. These offers came to him through his friend Lord Shelburne, for with Lord Rockingham he had no more than a slight acquaintance. The Vice-Treasurership of Ireland was especially pressed upon him. It was an office of light work and high pay, the latter being computed at no less than 5000*l.* a-year. It was an office to which Pitt might the rather incline because his father had formerly held it; but the young barrister preferred his independence with chambers and not quite 300*l.* a-year.

Mr. Pitt did not evince the smallest displeasure or resentment at his own omission from the highest rank of offices. He publicly expressed, on several occasions, his good opinion of the Government; and he cheerfully gave it his general support, while still pursuing his own independent line.

The question to which, beyond any other at this time, Mr. Pitt applied himself, was to amend the representation of the people in the House of Commons. Parliamentary Reform had followed close in the wake of Economical Reform. The lavish expense and the ill success of the American war in its concluding stages led many persons to forget that the prosecution of that war, even at such expense, had been for some years a popular object with the country at large, as might be amply shown by the avowal, at the time, of the Opposition chiefs themselves. It was now on the contrary contended, from the experience of the last fifteen or twenty

months, that the members for the close boroughs had
been the main strength on which the war party relied.
A cry against these boroughs rapidly arose, and the
cause of Parliamentary Reform was espoused with great
ardour by many persons—by no one with greater than
by the Rev. Christopher Wyvill, a clergyman of an old
family in Yorkshire. His 'Correspondence' upon this
subject, which he subsequently published, extends over
six volumes and twenty years; and affords the best materials for the history, at that time, of a cause not until
long afterwards destined to prevail.

Under the influence of Mr. Wyvill and other zealous
party men, a general meeting of the friends of Parliamentary Reform was convened in London. It was held
at the house of the Duke of Richmond, who was then
Master of the Ordnance and a member of the Cabinet
in the new administration. Here it was determined that
the question should be immediately submitted to the
House of Commons. Mr. Pitt was fixed upon as the
fittest person to bring it forward, and the offer being
made to him he undertook the task.

On the 7th of May, after the House had been in due
form called over—a practice at that time customary to
secure a full attendance — Pitt brought forward this
great question in a speech of considerable length. To
combine in his support all classes of Reformers, he carefully refrained, both in his speech and motion, from any
specific statement of a plan: he moved only for a Select
Committee to examine into the state of the representation. With resolute boldness he inveighed against
" the corrupt influence of the Crown — an influence

which has been pointed at in every period as the fertile
source of all our miseries—an influence which has been
substituted in the room of wisdom, of activity, of exertion, and of success—an influence which has grown up
with our growth and strengthened with our strength, but
which unhappily has not diminished with our diminution,
nor decayed with our decay." Such is one of the very
few sentences that can well be cited from the abridged
and most tame report of his animated speech; but in
arguments, of which only the mere groundwork is preserved, he declared himself the enemy of the close
boroughs—the strongholds of that corruption of which
he had complained. He pointed out the great anomaly
(for an anomaly all must own it to be) that some decayed
villages, almost destitute of population, should send members to Parliament under the control of the Treasury, or
at the bidding of some great Lord or Commoner, the
owner of the soil; and he asked emphatically, " Is this
representation?" He further appealed to the memory
of a person of whom he said that every member of the
House could speak with more freedom than himself; and
he declared, as of his own knowledge, that this person
(I need scarcely say that he referred to his father)—a
person, he added, not apt to indulge in vague or chi-
merical speculations inconsistent with practice and ex-
pediency—had held the opinion that unless a more solid
and equal system of representation were established,
this nation, great and happy as it might have been,
would come to be confounded in the mass of those
whose liberties were lost in the corruption of the people.

When Pitt sat down, as he did amidst loud applause, a

veteran reformer, Mr. Alderman Sawbridge, rose and seconded the motion he had made.

The new Government was by no means united on this question. The Duke of Richmond, for example, had been among its first promoters. But the sentiments of Lord Rockingham, so far as we can trace them through the haze of faulty grammar and confused expressions in his letter to Mr. Pemberton Milnes,[5] were secretly adverse. Those of Burke were openly hostile. It was with some difficulty that Fox, who took the contrary part, prevailed on him to stay away from the debate. Fox himself spoke in favour of the motion; so also did Sheridan and Sir George Savile. On the other hand Pitt found himself opposed by his cousin Thomas Pitt of Boconnoc, who objected to the motion as too vague and undefined; by his coming friend, the Lord Advocate; by Rolle, the member for Devonshire; and by several besides. On dividing, the motion was lost by only twenty votes in a House of more than three hundred members, the numbers being 161 against 141. Lord Macaulay has observed that the Reformers never again had so good a division till the year 1831.

On the 17th of May a branch of the same subject was again brought forward by Alderman Sawbridge, who proposed a Bill "to shorten the duration of Parliaments." Both Fox and Pitt spoke in favour of the motion, but it was rejected by a large majority. Mr. Burke could not be withheld from taking part in this debate or from re-

---

[5] As published by Lord Albemarle in his Memoirs of Lord Rockingham, vol. ii. p. 395.

verting to the former question. Thus in a private letter to a friend in Ireland does Sheridan describe the scene : "On Friday last Burke acquitted himself with the most magnanimous indiscretion, attacked William Pitt in a scream of passion, and swore Parliament was and always had been precisely what it ought to be, and that all people who thought of reforming it wanted to overturn the Constitution."[6]

On the 19th of June Mr. Pitt spoke with much warmth and ability in support of a Bill which had been introduced by Lord Mahon for preventing bribery at elections. Mr. Fox, though with many expressions of courtesy to Pitt, took the opposite side, and "this," says Bishop Tomline, "was, I believe, the first question upon which they happened to differ before any separation took place between them. I must, however, remark that although they had hitherto acted together in Parliament, there had been no intimacy or confidential intercourse between them."[7]

In Committee on this Bill, Lord Mahon consented to give up several points in the hope to render the measure more palatable to the House. Thus he struck out the words that forbade candidates to hire horses or carriages for the conveyance of voters to the poll. But the clause still provided that the money for this purpose should not be paid to the elector on any account whatever, under the penalties of disfranchisement for ever of the elector, and of incapacity to the candidate of sitting in

---

[6] See the Memorials of Fox, edited by Lord John Russell, vol. i. p. 322.

[7] Life of Pitt, vol. i. p. 81.

that Parliament. Mr. Pitt supported this clause, which Mr. Fox and other gentlemen thought too severe, and on a division it was rejected by a majority of 26. " This incapacitating clause contained," said Lord Mahon, " the very pith and marrow of my Bill,"—which thus mutilated he declined any further to proceed with.

On the 25th of June both Fox and Pitt spoke in support of a motion which was levelled at Lord North and his colleagues. It was to direct the payment into the Exchequer of the balances remaining in the hands of Mr. Rigby, late Paymaster of the Forces, and of Mr. Ellis, late Treasurer of the Navy. The motion was opposed by Lord North, and rejected by a majority of 11, showing how powerful was still the party of the late administration in the House of Commons.

During the three months that had elapsed since the late administration fell, vehement differences had already arisen in the new. The Chancellor was on ill terms with most of his colleagues, and was suspected of caballing against them. Fox and Shelburne, as joint Secretaries of State, were jealous of each other, and the more so since the line between their departments had not been accurately drawn. The negotiations for peace were no easy task. The affairs of Ireland had grown to be most critical, and could not be adjusted without some conflict of opinion. So early as mid-April we find Fox in one of his private letters complain of " another very teasing and wrangling Cabinet." [8]

To quell these dissensions among his colleagues there

---

[8] Memorials, by Lord John Russell, vol. i. p. 315.

was needed a man of energy as Premier. Lord Rockingham on the contrary, with the best intentions, was
on every point timid, feeble, indecisive. It seems impossible that he could have much longer kept together
the jarring elements that were, at least nominally, committed to his charge; but in the course of June he fell
sick, and on the 1st of July he died.

The Cabinet at once fell asunder. His Majesty sent
for Lord Shelburne and offered him the vacant post of
First Lord of the Treasury. Lord Shelburne accepted
the offer. Most of the other Ministers acquiesced in it,
but Fox was fully determined not to bear the dominion
of his rival. He leagued himself with his chosen friend
Lord John Cavendish, the Chancellor of the Exchequer,
and they both came to the conclusion that the fittest man
for Prime Minister was Lord John's brother by marriage,
the Duke of Portland, at that time Lord Lieutenant of
Ireland. Portland was in all points the very counter-
part of Rockingham. Like him he was a man of high
birth, of princely fortune, of honourable character, of
nervous shyness, and of very moderate abilities. It was
plainly designed that Fox's own pre-eminent abilities
should govern the country under his Grace's name.

In fulfilment of their resolution Fox and Cavendish proceeded to press upon the King the nomination of the
Duke of Portland to the Treasury. But the King saw
no reason to revoke his appointment of Lord Shelburne,
and on His Majesty's refusal the two Ministers resigned.
They were followed by the Duke of Portland from Dublin Castle, as also by Burke, Sheridan, and some few
others from the lower ranks of office, and they continued

to be supported by a considerable body of adherents in the House of Commons.

But from the public they obtained little sympathy. The resignation of Fox was in general regarded as indefensible on any public grounds. Among his independent friends many of the most high-minded disapproved it. Such was especially the case with Sir George Savile. It seemed to carry out to their worst extreme the oligarchical principles at that time of the great Whig houses. Was it to be borne in a free country that no man but the heir of some one of these houses should ever be deemed fit for the highest place in public affairs? And there was another circumstance which, as Horace Walpole remarks in one of his letters of this date, added not a little to the ridicule of this pretension. "It is not merely," he says, "that a few great families claim the hereditary and exclusive right of giving us a head, but they will insist upon selecting a head without a tongue!"

Fortified as he hoped by popular opinion, but exposed to unfavourable chances in the House of Commons, the new Prime Minister proceeded to fill up the vacant offices. Earl Temple, the first cousin of Pitt, was appointed Lord Lieutenant of Ireland, with his brother William Grenville as Chief Secretary. The seals of Secretary of State, as relinquished by Fox and Shelburne, were entrusted to Thomas Townshend and Lord Grantham. The place of Chancellor of the Exchequer was offered to Pitt, and by him accepted. And thus did Pitt attain one of the highest offices of Government only a few weeks after he had completed the age of twenty-three.

In the new administration the leadership of the House of Commons was nominally vested in the senior member, Mr. Secretary Townshend; but it was Pitt on whom Lord Shelburne relied to confront the great orators ranged in the Opposition ranks; and in fact, as appeared in the sequel, it was Pitt who took the prominent part in every debate.

The Parliament was quickly prorogued after a day of Ministerial explanations in both Houses. In the Commons, Pitt, whose writ was not yet moved, whose appointment even was not yet announced, was able to take part in the debate, and there was now for the first time an altercation conducted with some keenness between him and Fox. "The late Right Hon. Secretary," said the young orator, "is to be looked upon as public property, and as such I have a right to question him as to his conduct in resigning an important post. . . . It was in my opinion a dislike to men, and not to measures; and there appears to be something personal in the business; for if the Right Hon. gentleman had such an aversion as he now professes to the political sentiments of Lord Shelburne, how came he only three months ago to accept him as a colleague?"

In the other House Lord Shelburne defended the stand which he had made against the dictation of Fox and Cavendish, by his adherence to the maxims of one whom he called his master in politics, the late Earl of Chatham. "That noble Earl," he said, "always declared that the country ought not to be governed by any oligarchical party or family connection, and that if it was to be so governed, the Constitution must of necessity expire.　And on these principles," added Shelburne, "I have always acted."

The familiar letters of Mr. Pitt to his mother will best portray his feelings and conduct at this time and for some time afterwards. I shall either insert them at length, or extract from them as usual all passages of interest, and with these extracts the present chapter shall conclude.

" Lincoln's Inn, June 27, 1782.

"My brother tells me he has mentioned to you that Lord Rockingham is ill, which is unfortunately in the way of anything more at present; but Lord S. told me yesterday that Lord R. had expressed himself as wishing to do something that might give you a security for the future. You are very good in thinking of communicating any share of what I am sure your own occasions may demand entire; mine are not so pressing but that they will wait very tolerably at present: and I shall expect that Westminster Hall will, in good time, supply all that is wanting.

"The Circuit begins on Tuesday sennight. I hope to call in my way westward, if not certainly in my return: and I shall undoubtedly be able to make some stay after it is over, though my plan for the remainder of the summer is not quite settled. I hope Mrs. Stapleton is by this time added to your society, and as well as usual. My brother, I believe, has not informed you of a match of which the world here is certain, but of which he assures me he knows nothing, between himself and the beauty in Albemarle Street.[9] There is no late public news;

---

[9] Mary Elizabeth, daughter of the Right Hon. Thomas Townshend. The match in question did not take place for upwards of a year.

but our fleet is, I believe, sailing, which will probably furnish some very important. Lord Rockingham's very precarious state occasions a great deal of suspense, and if it ends ill, may, I am afraid, produce a great deal of confusion. Whether that may not happen any way is indeed more than one can be sure of as things stand."

"Tuesday, July 2, 1782.

" MY DEAR MOTHER,

"I am much obliged to you for your letter, but very sorry to think that the unavoidable engagement which produced the interval in my letters left you in that state of suspense which distance too naturally produces. I hope you will have received at the due time the letter I wrote last Saturday. After what I then mentioned, it will not be a surprise to you to hear that the event of Lord Rockingham's death took place yesterday morning. What the consequences of it will be to the public cannot yet quite be foreseen. With regard to myself, I believe the arrangement may be of a sort in which I *may*, and probably *ought* to take a part. If I do, I think I need not say you pretty well know the principles on which I shall do it. In this short time nothing is settled, and I only saw what were the strong wishes of *some* who foresaw the event. But how different pretensions will be adjusted is a matter of great uncertainty. As soon as I am able to let you know particulars, I will do it by a safer conveyance, and give you notice. You will not wonder if I write in some haste. I am very glad to hear that Harriot is better.

"The business depending will probably be settled one way or other before I need decide about the Circuit.

"I am, my dear Mother, &c.,

" W. PITT.

" My poor servant John has had a violent attack of his old complaint, which has been of a very serious nature. He is getting better, and I hope in a good way, though still very ill. I think he seems very much to wish to see his wife, though he does not care directly to send for her. But I believe if you would have the goodness to send her up by the coach, and furnish what is wanting for her journey, it would be a great comfort to him, as he will, I fear, in no case be quite well a good while. I have got a servant that will do in his stead for the present."

"Friday, July 5, 1782.

" You will, I am sure, be impatient to hear something more from me. Things begin to be pretty near settled, and on the whole I hope well for the country, though not precisely as one would have wished. Fox has chosen to resign, on no ground that I can learn but Lord Shelburne being placed at the Treasury. Lord J. Cavendish also quits, which is not surprising, as he accepted at first merely on Lord Rockingham's account. Other inferior changes will take place in some departments; but the bulk stand firm. My lot will be either at the Treasury as Chancellor of the Exchequer, or in the Home department as Secretary of State. The arrangement cannot be finally settled till to-morrow or next day, but everything promises as well as possible in such circumstances. Mr. Townshend certainly makes part of this fresh arrangement, and probably in a more forward post, which is to me an infinite satisfaction. Lord Shelburne's conduct is everything that could be wished. Parliament adjourns in a day or two, and little or nothing can pass there till next Session. The principal thing I shall have to regret will be the probability of this delaying my having the happiness of seeing

you; though I trust it will not do that for the whole
summer.

"I have written in great haste, and at first with a view
to the post; but I believe it will become more the discretion which I must now have about me not to send it
by that conveyance. I forgot to say that Mr. J. Grenville either continues in his present situation or takes a
new one; perfectly disapproving of the step Fox has
taken. This I am sure you will be glad to hear."

"Grafton Street, July 16, 1782.

"Our new Board of Treasury has just begun to enter
on business; and though I do not know that it is of the
most entertaining sort, it does not seem likely to be
very fatiguing. In all other respects my situation
satisfies, and more than satisfies me, and I think
promises everything that is agreeable. . . . Lord North
will, I hope, in a very little while make room for me in
Downing Street, which is the best summer town house
possible."

"Grafton Street, July 30, 1782.

"I am not able to tell whether I can succeed as
I wish for your Welsh friend. Of all the secrets of my
office I have in this short time learnt the least about
patronage. I rather believe this branch belongs almost
entirely to the First Lord, though certainly recommendations will have their weight there. I think I need
not say that I will try as far as I can with propriety.
Harriot's request, or rather her neighbour's (for I certainly do not charge Harriot with being too pressing a
solicitor), is, I am afraid, of a sort which I cannot much
forward; but I will consider whether I can do anything,
and let her know. In the mean time she may be per-

feetly assured that I am not yet so tired of being asked as to take it very ill of her to have been the channel of it. I expect to be comfortably settled in the course of this week in a *part* of my vast, awkward house."

"Grafton Street, Aug. 10, 1782.

"I must certainly plead guilty to the charges you have to make against me as a correspondent, which, however, I hope you will have less cause for in future. At the same time, though I am very far from pretending never to have an hour of leisure, you may imagine that business may sometimes come at such a time as to prevent writing, or at least to prevent writing with great accuracy. I had understood before from Lord Shelburne the substance of what you mention out of his letter to you, which is certainly on the whole very favourable: and as I am sure he will not be disposed to lose any time in the business, I have no sort of doubt that you will soon perceive the good effect.[1]

"My secretary, whom you wish to know, is a person whose name you may probably never have heard, a Mr. Bellingham, an army friend of my brother. You will wonder at a secretary from the army; but as the office is a perfect sinecure, and has no duty but that of receiving about four hundred a year, no profession is unfit for it. I have not yet any private secretary, nor do I perceive, at least as yet, any occasion for it."

"Downing Street, Sept. 5, 1782.

"I have not had so much of a Hayes life as you seem to imagine, as I have been able to go there but for two nights this fortnight. I hope to be able to steal a few

---

[1] As regarded the payment of arrears in Lady Chatham's pension.

days before long for shooting, though I find the vacation by no means a recess from business. I wish I could see a prospect of its allowing me to look in upon you at Burton."

"Downing Street, Sept. 12, 1782.

"I am much obliged to you for your letter, which I received yesterday on my return from Cheveley, where I had been for two days. A short visit for such a distance; but as my brother was going there, I thought it worth the exertion, and it was very well repaid by a great deal of air and exercise in shooting, and the finest weather in the world. The finest part of all indeed is a fine east wind, which, as the fleet is just sailed for Gibraltar, is worth everything. I assure you I do not forget the lessons I have so long followed, of riding in spite of business; though I indeed want it less than ever, as I was never so perfectly well. All I have to do now is to be done quite at my own hours, being merely to prepare for the busy season; which is very necessary to be done, but which at the same time is not a close confinement. We are labouring at all sorts of official reform, for which there is a very ample field, and in which I believe we shall have some success."

"Sunday (Dec. 1782).

"The Gibraltar business, I reckon, stands fairer since our last debate; but I shall not be sorry if, finally, it does not come in question at the conclusion of the treaty, *of which there is some chance.*

"I shall be impatient to receive orders at the Treasury on a subject where I cannot well be the first to give them." [2]

---

[2] The settlement of Lady Chatham's arrears.

CHAPTER III.

1782 — 1783.

Acknowledgment of American independence — Proposed cession of Gibraltar — Preliminary treaties with France and Spain — Conference between Pitt and Fox — Coalition of Fox and North — Defeat of Lord Shelburne — Pitt's great speech in vindication of the Peace — Resignation of Lord Shelburne — Pitt refuses the offer of the Treasury — Resigns office of Chancellor of the Exchequer — Duke of Portland's Ministry — Pitt in private life — Again brings forward Parliamentary Reform, but is defeated — Prince of Wales — Marriage of Lord Chatham.

As the autumn advanced, and the period for the reassembling of Parliament drew near, the new Ministers became more and more impressed with the difficulties which they might expect in the House of Commons. It seemed most desirable that they should endeavour to gain strength from the ranks of Opposition. The Opposition at that time consisted, as we have seen, of two parties, as yet wholly unconnected and wide asunder—the party of Mr. Fox and the party of Lord North, and with either of these a junction might perhaps be made. On that point, however, the wishes of the First Lord of the Treasury and of his Chancellor of the Exchequer were by no means the same. Lord Shelburne, as was natural, resented the violence of Fox against himself, and inclined far rather to a coalition with Lord North. But Pitt positively declared that nothing should induce him to concur in this last scheme. He retained his strong aversion to the conduct of the American war and to its authors, but was willing and desirous to rejoin those who, like Fox, had been united with him in opposing that war and in hurling Lord North from power.

The wishes of Pitt in this direction were earnestly supported by several other members of the Cabinet, as by General Conway and by Admiral, now Viscount, Keppel. They had long been adherents of Fox; and, though continuing in office, chafed at their separation from him. But the repugnance of Lord Shelburne was as yet unconquerable. Amidst these jarring counsels the time went on to the meeting of Parliament: no resolution was taken, and no overtures in any quarter were made.

The meeting of Parliament had been fixed for the 26th of November. It was further prorogued to the 5th of the following month, in hopes that the peace might meanwhile be concluded. Provisional articles with America, to be hereafter inserted in a treaty of peace, were indeed signed at Paris on the 30th of November. By these the revolted colonies were in explicit words acknowledged; but the terms with France and Spain were found to require much longer time for their adjustment. On these there was also a material disagreement among the Ministers. Lord Shelburne was desirous of yielding Gibraltar to the Spaniards, receiving in return Porto Rico or some other West India island. Lord Keppel, the Duke of Grafton, and several more members of the Cabinet, were warmly opposed to this exchange. We learn from a cautious passage—the last in my preceding chapter—of Pitt's letters to his mother, that Pitt himself was among the Ministers who stood firm against Lord Shelburne's project, and who finally prevailed.[1]

It may be suspected that, on account of this twofold difference—as to the junction with Fox and as to the exchange of Gibraltar — the cordiality between the Chancellor of the Exchequer and his chief had become a little impaired.

It would seem that through the autumn Lord North among his friends had talked much—and as some of them thought, too much—of "absence, neutrality, moderation."[2] When the two Houses met on the 5th of December, he appeared in his place and spoke with great temper and forbearance. But nothing could exceed the vehemence of Burke and Fox. Burke especially, who, in the explanations of July last, had called Lord Shelburne "a Borgia and a Catiline," now inveighed against his "duplicity and delusion," and compared him to a serpent with two heads! Some discrepancy there certainly was to complain of in the explanations of the Ministers. In the House of Peers Lord Shelburne had said that the acknowledgment of American independence under the Provisional Articles was only contingent and conditional ; while in the Commons both Pitt and Conway declared that, in their

---

[1] An extract from the MS. Memoirs of the Duke of Grafton, giving a full account of the dissensions in the Cabinet relative to Gibraltar, has been already published by me in the Appendix, p. xxvi., to the seventh volume of my History of England.

[2] Letter of Gibbon to Holroyd, Oct. 14, 1782.

judgment, this acknowledgment must be regarded as positive and final.

The first part of this Session, which commenced on the 5th of December, was soon interrupted by the approach of the Christmas holidays, and the Parliament was adjourned for one month. There had been already some very keen debates. In all these Pitt had taken the lead on the part of Government, and had maintained the contest, on no unequal terms, with the great orators of the Opposition; and it deserves to be noted —so natural is the supremacy of genius in popular assemblies—that he had taken this chief part without giving any offence to his nominal leader, Mr. Secretary Townshend. That gentleman—once his father's friend, as now his own—continued to act with him on most cordial terms.

During these short holidays we find Pitt, in the following note, summon Lord Mahon to London, probably to concert with him a measure on Parliamentary Reform.

"Downing Street, Dec. 28, 1782.

"MY DEAR LORD,

"I am in great hopes you will be able to come directly to town. This is just the time in which we must fix on something; and, I think, in a day or two we could go through all the necessary discussion before any practical steps are taken.

"Yours most affectionately,

"W. PITT."

The preliminary treaties with France and Spain (for with Holland there as yet was only a truce concluded)

being at last brought to an adjustment, were signed at
Paris on the 20th of January, 1783. On the 27th they
were carried down to both Houses of Parliament—to
the Peers by Lord Grantham, to the Commons by his
brother Secretary, Townshend. Ample time was left
for their consideration, the Addresses to the King in
reply being fixed for the 17th of the ensuing month.

It has been admitted by nearly all the writers on
that point in the present century that the conditions of
these treaties were to the full as favourable as, with
such vast odds against us, we had any right to expect
or to demand. To the Americans we conceded only
the independence which, in fact, they had already
won. We gave back to the French Chandernagore and
Pondicherry, the settlement of Senegal, and the island
of St. Lucia. We gave back to the Spaniards Minorca
and both the Floridas. But we retained our Indian
empire, that mighty counterpoise to the colonies which
we lost on another continent. We retained the rock
of Gibraltar, against which the two great Bourbon
monarchies had tried their strength in vain. And, as
Lord Macaulay with much force observes, England
preserved even her dignity, for she ceded to the House
of Bourbon only part of what she had conquered from
that House in previous wars.

At the time, however, such considerations were by
no means duly weighed. No sooner were the terms
of the treaties divulged than considerable murmurs
arose. The necessity of such concessions was already
half forgotten, while the concessions themselves rose
full in view. Even those who had most loudly de-

nounced "a ruinous war" showed equal force of lungs
in crying out against "a ruinous peace."   Under such
circumstances the Cabinet found it far from easy to
frame the Addresses to be moved in both Houses,
and to express at least a qualified approval of the
treaties.   "We agreed," so writes the Duke of Grafton
in his manuscript Memoirs, "that no triumphant words
could be carried or ought to be proposed. Those which
pleased most were the most moderate, and such were
adopted."

At the time when the treaties were brought down to
Parliament the administration of Lord Shelburne was
nearly rent asunder by divisions. Already had Keppel
retired from the Admiralty, and Richmond ceased to
attend the meetings of the Cabinet. Other changes
soon ensued. Grafton and Conway expressed themselves as much dissatisfied, and Lord Carlisle threw up
his office of Lord Steward.

Thus estranged in great part from his colleagues,
and pressed by the want of a majority in Parliament
to approve the treaties, Lord Shelburne gave way at
last to the earnest representations of Pitt. He reluctantly agreed that Fox and his friends should be invited
to re-enter the service of the Crown. Certain it is
that, so late as February, 1783, such a junction might
have been effected without the smallest sacrifice of
public principle on either side. Pitt at once availed
himself of this authority. He called upon Fox by appointment at Fox's house, but the conference between
them was not a long one. No sooner had Fox heard the
object of the visit, than he asked whether it was intended

that Lord Shelburne should remain First Lord of the
Treasury. Pitt answered in the affirmative. "It is
impossible for me," Fox rejoined, "to belong to any administration of which Lord Shelburne is the head."
"Then we need discuss the matter no further," said Pitt;
"I did not come here to betray Lord Shelburne;" and so
saying he took his leave. Bishop Tomline adds to the
account which he has given of this interview, "This
was, I believe, the last time Mr. Pitt was in a private
room with Mr. Fox, and from this period may be dated
that political hostility which continued through the remainder of their lives."[a]

In another direction some active steps were taken of
his own accord by Henry Dundas, who, under the administration of Lord Shelburne, besides continuing Lord
Advocate of Scotland, filled the office of Treasurer of the
Navy. He had several conferences with William Adam,
a confidential friend of Lord North. "There is no longer
any prospect," he said, "none at least for the present,
that there will be any overture for a coalition to Lord
North from the present Ministry. Lord Shelburne and
I have pushed it, but we could not get the other Ministers
to agree to it. . . . If Lord Shelburne resigns, Fox and
Pitt may yet come together and dissolve Parliament,
and there will be an end of Lord North. I see no means

---

[a] Life of Pitt, vol. i. p. 89.
From the narrative of the Bishop
it might at first sight be inferred
that the interview between Fox
and Pitt took place towards the
close of the year 1782: but the
exact date was February 11, 1783,
as appears both from a letter of
William Grenville (Courts and
Cabinets of George III., vol. i. p.
148) and a statement of Henry
Dundas (Fox Memorials, vol. ii.
p. 33).

of preventing this but Lord North's support of the Address." And at parting he said again, "Nothing will answer but an absolute, unconditional support."

The object of Dundas in these hints was to alarm Lord North into compliance. But he had overshot the mark. Lord North was on the contrary roused into resentment, and altogether demurred to such a peremptory tone. In this altered mood of the late Prime Minister, and with the unabated hostility of Fox, it was plain, taking into account the public temper of the time, that were these two great party leaders to league themselves together, they might certainly command a majority against the Government on the conditions of the peace.

To this combination, however, there were, or there should have been, the strongest obstacles upon both sides. No two statesmen could be more estranged from each other in thought, word, or deed. Not only had Fox during many years opposed all the measures of Lord North's administration, but he had exhausted against him personally the whole vocabulary of invective; he had pronounced him "void of honour and honesty;" he had thundered for his condign punishment; he had declared, and this but eleven months before, that he would rest satisfied to be called "the most infamous of mankind" could he for a moment think of making terms with such a man.[4] North, on his part, though in gentler terms, had no less for many years arraigned and denounced the principles of Fox. Yet now, as the overthrow of Lord Shelburne rose before them as a

---

[4] See his speech in the House of Commons of March 5, 1782.

tempting prize, these two eminent men, in an evil hour
for their own fame, were gradually drawn together. The
secret agent and channel of communication at the outset was on Lord North's side his eldest son George North,
whose own leanings were to the Whigs. There was
also on that side William Eden, who some months since
had been Chief Secretary in Ireland, and was now perhaps a little impatient for another office. On Fox's part
may be mentioned especially his kinsman and close
friend Colonel Fitzpatrick, and another of his friends,
John Townshend.

The first interview between Fox and North took place
on the 14th of February, at the house of Mr. George
North. Both the statesmen showed a frank and manly
temper. They agreed to treat Reform of Parliament as
an open question between them. They agreed to lay
aside all former animosity, Fox declaring that he hoped
their administration would be founded on mutual good-
will and confidence, which was the only thing that could
make it permanent and useful. They also agreed to
oppose the Address upon the Peace, and Lord North
drew up the amendment to be moved by Lord John
Cavendish. This amendment went no further than to
reserve to the House the right at a later period of disapproving the terms; but there was also another clause
expressing the regard of Parliament for the American
loyalists which was less likely to be palatable to the
Whigs, and which therefore Lord North himself undertook to move in a separate form.

Meanwhile Lord Shelburne finding that he had nothing to hope from Fox, had determined to apply to

Lord North, even though aware that this step, if it succeeded, would cost him the secession of Pitt from office. It was settled that Rigby, as a personal friend of Lord North, should go to him and propose an interview with Shelburne. The veteran jobber, whetted by the appetite of office, waited accordingly on the late Prime Minister; but by that time Lord North had concluded his treaty with Fox, and he therefore replied to Rigby in few words, "I cannot meet Lord Shelburne now. It is too late."

According to notice the Address upon the Peace was moved in both Houses on the 17th of February. In the Lords it was carried by 69 votes against 55. In the Commons it was moved by Mr. Thomas Pitt, while at the special request of William, his friend Wilberforce stood forth as seconder. Lord John Cavendish then moved his amendment, not soaring in his speech above his usual mediocrity. But both North and Fox put forth all their powers. Already was the rumour rife of their confederacy, giving rise to no small amount of reprobation. Fox avowed it only so far as the vote of that evening was concerned, but defended it on broader grounds. "It is not in my nature," he said, "to bear malice or live in ill will; my friendships are perpetual, my enmities not so." In support of the Government Townshend was clear and full, Dundas acrimonious and able. Pitt, who did not rise till four o'clock, could produce no strong impression on an exhausted House. But he was himself exhausted, and his speech was not good. "There were perhaps few occasions," says Bishop Tomline, "upon which he spoke with less effect."

In one passage of this speech which was in reply to
Sheridan, Pitt dealt severely with what he called his
dramatic turns and his epigrammatic points. These he
advised Sheridan rather to reserve for the stage, where
they would always obtain, as they always deserved, the
plaudits of the audience. This taunt was unworthy both
of the man and of the occasion, and exposed Pitt to the
severest retort that he ever in his life received; for
Sheridan sprang on his feet again, as he declared " only
to explain," and with admirable wit and readiness said.
" If ever I again engage in those compositions to which
the Right Hon. gentleman has in such flattering terms
referred, I may be tempted to an act of presumption. I
may be encouraged by his praises to try an improvement on one of Ben Jonson's best characters in the play
of the Alchymist—the Angry Boy!"

At length a little before seven in the morning the
keen orations ended, the impatient numbers were arrayed, and the combined Oppositions were found to prevail by a majority of sixteen.

Before he retired to bed that morning Mr. Pitt found
time for a hasty note.

" Downing Street,
" Tuesday morning, quarter before Seven,
(Feb. 18, 1783.)

" My dear Mother,

    " You are, I hope, enough used to such things in
the political world as *changes*, not to be much surprised
at the result of our business in the House of Commons.
An amendment was moved on our Address, expunging
all commendation of the peace, and the two standards of
Lord North and Fox produced 224 against us, 208 for

us. This I think decisive. It comes rather sooner than I imagined, though certainly not quite unexpected. We shall at least leave the field with honour. I am just going to bed, and am perfectly well in spite of fatigue.

"Your ever dutiful

"W. PITT."

Notwithstanding this great defeat Lord Shelburne did not at once resign. He had some vague hopes of still maintaining his position, and determined at all events to expect a second blow. He had not long to wait. So early as the 21st Lord John Cavendish brought forward another string of Resolutions pledging the House to preserve inviolate the terms of the peace, but declaring that its concessions were too large. The debate which ensued has not often been surpassed in interest. By that time the new Coalition was openly avowed, and as one of its main authors, Colonel Fitzpatrick, confesses in a private letter, was universally cried out against. Two independent members, Thomas Powys, member for Northamptonshire, and Sir Cecil Wray, who had long been followers of Fox, rose in succession to denounce the "unnatural alliance." Many others who could not speak could at least mutter and growl. Fox had not much to say in defence of his own consistency, but that little he said to the best advantage, and he endeavoured to vindicate the Coalition on public grounds, while adverting to the loss of his friends in manly and becoming terms.

If, as may be thought, Pitt had lost some ground in the debate of the 17th, he much more than retrieved that ground in the debate of the 21st. That second speech in its energy and eloquence surpassed any other that he had yet delivered, and must be ranked among the very highest oratorical achievements of his life. Rising immediately after Fox he thus began :—

" Revering, Sir, as I do the great abilities of the Right Honourable gentleman who spoke last, I lament in common with the House when those abilities are mis-employed, as on the present question, to inflame the ima-gination and mislead the judgment.   I am told, Sir, ' he does not envy me the triumph of my situation this day,' a sort of language which becomes the candour of that Honourable gentleman as ill as his present principles. The triumphs of party, Sir, with which this self-appointed Minister seems so highly elate, shall never seduce me to any inconsistency which the busiest suspicion shall pre-sume to glance at.   I will never engage in political en-mities without a public cause.   I will never forego such enmities without the public approbation, nor will I be questioned and cast off in the face of this House by one virtuous and dissatisfied friend."

From this introduction Pitt proceeded to what still remains by far the most able and convincing among the many vindications of the peace. " But, Sir," he said, " I fear I have too long engaged your attention to no real purpose. For I will not hesitate to surmise, from the obvious complexion of this night's debate, that it has arisen rather in a desire to force the Earl of Shelburne from the Treasury, than in any real conviction that Ministers deserve censure for the concessions they have made. . . . Of the Earl of Shelburne I will say that his merits are as much above my panegyric as the arts to which he owes his defamation are below my notice. . . . I repeat then that it is not this treaty, it is the Earl of Shelburne alone whom the movers of this question are desirous to wound. This is the object which has raised this storm of faction—this is the aim of the unnatural Coalition to which I have alluded. If, however, the baneful alliance is not already formed, if this ill-omened marriage is not already solemnized, I know a just and lawful impediment, and in the name of the public safety I here forbid the Banns!"

Of Lord North in particular the son of Chatham spoke in terms to the full as bitter as Chatham had ever used. "In short, Sir, whatever appears dishonourable or inadequate in this peace is strictly chargeable to the Noble Lord in the blue riband, whose profusion of the public money, whose notorious temerity and obstinacy in prosecuting the war which originated in his pernicious and oppressive policy, and whose utter incapacity to fill the station he occupied, rendered a peace of any description indispensable to the preservation of the State." To the memory of Chatham Pitt appealed with reverent affection. "My earliest impressions were in favour of the noblest and most disinterested modes of serving the public; these impressions are still dear, and will, I hope, remain for ever dear to my heart; I will cherish them as a legacy infinitely more valuable than the richest inheritance." And the great orator (for so we may already term him) concluded with some lines of Horace expressing a thought not less lofty than his own.

　　" Laudo manentem ; si celeres quatit
　　　Pennas resigno quæ dedit—
　　　————　———— probamque
　　　Pauperiem sine dote quæro." [5]

The speech of Pitt on this occasion may be regarded as by far the greatest piece of oratory delivered either in ancient or in modern times by any man under twenty-five. Its exact length was of two hours and three-quarters ; and some persons who could find no other fault with it were inclined to blame it as too long. Marvellous as it appears when we consider the speaker's age, we must deem it more marvellous still on learning the circumstances of ill health under which he spoke.[6]

Rising after Pitt, Lord North, assailed as he had been, and provoked as he might be, did not lose his customary candour, but began by a tribute of just praise to the " amazing eloquence" of the last speaker. To Fox, as his new ally, he referred in frank and becoming terms : " In the early part of that gentleman's career, when I had the happiness to possess his friendship, I knew that he was manly, open, and sincere. As an enemy I have always found him formidable, and a person of most extraordinary talents, to whatever Minister he may be

---

[5] Horat. Carm. lib. iii. 29. Bishop Tomline relates, that being under the gallery while Mr. Pitt delivered this speech, a young man, afterwards a distinguished member of Opposition, turned round to him and asked eagerly, " Why did he omit ' Et meâ virtute me involvo?' " An omission, adds the Bishop, generally considered as marking the modesty and good sense of Mr. Pitt.

[6] " Pitt's famous speech...... Stomach disordered, and actually holding Solomon's Porch door open with one hand while vomiting during Fox's speech, to whom he was to reply."—Wilberforce's Diary, &c. (Life, vol. i. p. 26). " Solomon's Porch " was the portico behind the old House of Commons.

opposed. But in proportion as I had reason to dread him
while his principles were adverse to mine, now that they
are congenial we shall, with the greater certainty of
success, unite with one mind and one heart in the cause of
our common country. And let me hail it as an auspicious
circumstance in our country's favour, that those who were
divided by her hostilities are cemented by her peace."

Lord North then proceeded to give grounds for his
belief that the resources of America were reduced to
the lowest ebb:—" In Monday's debate I asked,—if
Congress are unable to raise a farthing to carry on a
war in the heart of their own country, is it to be supposed that their contributions would be either liberal
or cheerful for extending their hostilities to a foreign
one? I have had an opportunity since of satisfying
myself more fully of the fact, and I find my information
to be authentic in every respect. In most of the States
they have refused to pay the tax levied by Congress for
the service of the war. The Rhode Islanders in particular rose forcibly on the officers who came to collect it,
and drove them away. In Massachusetts the tax was dis-
counted in the province, and consequently never carried
to the public account." From these facts Lord North endeavoured to show that, had we insisted on better terms
of peace, the Americans must have yielded them. Yet
how often before had hopes of this kind been expressed,
and how constantly had they been disappointed!

At past three in the morning the House proceeded to
divide, when the Opposition found their former majority
of sixteen increased by one, the numbers being—for the
Government 190, and against it 207.

This second division decided the fate of Shelburne. On the 23rd he called a meeting of his Cabinet in the morning, and of his supporters in the evening; and to both these meetings announced his intended resignation. Next morning accordingly he went to the King and did resign. A few days afterwards, and as a posthumous act of his authority, his steady adherent Thomas Townshend, the Secretary of State, was raised to the peerage as Lord Sydney.

In laying down his office, Lord Shelburne did not, however, advise the King to bestow it upon any chief of the new Coalition. He rather pressed upon His Majesty an idea which Dundas and other friends had pressed upon himself—to make Mr. Pitt Prime Minister. The Chancellor concurred in the same counsel to his Sovereign; and George the Third, eager to escape the yoke already fitted to his neck—the yoke of the great Whig houses—grasped at the suggestion. He sent at once to Mr. Pitt, offering him the headship of the Treasury, with full authority to nominate his colleagues. Thus was the whole power of the State, without stint or reservation, laid at the feet of a younger son of a far from wealthy family—of a junior barrister who had received but very few briefs—of a stripling who had not quite attained the age of twenty-four. It is perhaps the most glorious tribute to early promise that any history records.

Pitt, however, was not dazzled. He asked, in the first place, for a day to consult and to decide. But the views and the conduct of the young statesman will best appear from the correspondence at this period of Henry Dundas, the Lord Advocate, with his brother at Edin-

burgh, and with Pitt himself. To that correspondence,
which in 1854 was kindly placed at my disposal by Mr.
Dundas of Arniston, I shall add, according to their dates,
Mr. Pitt's letters to his mother.

The Lord Advocate to his brother, President Dundas.

"February 24, 1783.

"Lord Shelburne last night, to a numerous meeting
of those who had come into office with him, announced
his intention of submitting to His Majesty, this day, the
necessity of new-arranging his Government. I am
going this day to Court, but I suppose it will be
Wednesday before we resign. I cannot yet say what
will be the result of all this confusion. Thank God, we
have got peace. I wish all this may not disturb the
definitive treaty, where several things still remain to be
settled. You cannot conceive how much Lord North
has fallen in character in the course of this fortnight,
from his forming a connection with Charles Fox. In
short, it is a contradiction to the whole tenor and principles of his life for thirty years back. In great confidence I send you a copy of a letter I this morning wrote
to Lord Shelburne.[7] You will see it is not for common
eye. I perhaps may write to you again this night or
to-morrow. I am not very sanguine that anything will
come of it, but I was resolved to lay it fairly before him.

"Yours,

"H. D."

---

[7] Urging that Lord Shelburne
should advise the King to send
for Mr. Pitt as the next Prime
Minister.

The Lord Advocate to his brother.

"MY DEAR LORD,   "February 25, 1783.

"I cannot be more particular than I was yesterday, except to say that my project in regard to Mr. Pitt
was yesterday laid before the King by Lord Shelburne
and the Chancellor, who is warm and sanguine in the
belief of the success, as are Lord Gower and that whole
set of interest. The King received it eagerly, and instantly made the offer to Mr. Pitt, with every assurance
of the utmost support. Mr. Pitt desired to think of it.
I was with him all last night, and Mr. Rigby and I have
been with him all this morning, going through the state
of the House of Commons. I have little doubt that he
will announce himself Minister to-morrow, and I have as
little doubt that the effects of it upon the House of
Commons will be instantly felt. Not a human being
has a suspicion of the plan, except those in the immediate confidence of it. It will create an universal con-
sternation in the allied camp the moment it is known.
Still, secrecy!

                                   "Yours,

                                        "H. D."

Mr. Pitt to Lady Chatham.

                          "Tuesday morning, half-past Nine.
"MY DEAR MOTHER,   Feb. 25, 1783.

"I wished more than I can express to see you
yesterday. I will, if possible, find a moment to-day to
tell you the state of things and learn your opinion. In
the meantime the substance is, that our friends, almost
universally, are eager for our going on, only without
Lord Shelburne, and are sanguine in the expectation of

success—Lord Shelburne himself most warmly so. The King, when I went in yesterday, pressed me in the strongest manner to take Lord Shelburne's place, and insisted on my not declining it till I had taken time to consider. You see the importance of the decision I must speedily make. I feel all the difficulties of the undertaking, and am by no means in love with the object. On the other hand, I think myself bound not to desert a system in which I am engaged, if probable means can be shown of carrying it on with credit. On this general state of it I should wish anxiously to know what is the inclination of your mind. I must endeavour to estimate more particularly the probable issue by talking with those who know most of the opinions of men in detail. The great article to decide by seems that of numbers.

" Your ever dutiful and affectionate,

" W. PITT."

Mr. Pitt to Lady Chatham.

" Wednesday night, Feb. 26, 1783.

" MY DEAR MOTHER,

" The Levee to-day has decided nothing. Many opinions are in favour of the step in question, and none apparently more than *the principal one;* but the difficulties are notwithstanding many. It must however, I think, end one way or other to-morrow.

" Your ever dutiful,

" W. PITT."

Mr. Pitt to the Lord Advocate.

"Thursday, Feb. 27, 1783,
Two o'clock.

" My dear Lord,

"I have just been at your house to tell you, which I must do with great pain, what has passed in my mind since I saw you on a subject which seemed then on the point of coming to another issue. I am anxious to apprise you of it the first moment possible. What you stated to me this morning seemed to remove all doubt of my finding a majority in Parliament, and on the first view of it, joined to my sincere desire not to decline the call of my friends, removed at the same time my objections to accepting the Treasury. I have since most deliberately reconsidered the ground, and, after weighing it as fully as is possible for me to do, my final decision is directly contrary to the impression then made on me. I see that the main and almost only ground of reliance would be this,—that Lord North and his friends would not continue in a combination to oppose. In point of prudence, after all that has passed, and considering all that is to come, such a reliance is too precarious to act on. But above all, in point of honour to my own feelings, I cannot form an administration trusting to the hope that it will be supported, or even will not be opposed, by Lord North, whatever the influence may be that determines his conduct. The first moment I saw the subject in this point of view, from which I am sure I cannot vary, *unalterably* determined me to decline. I write this while I am dressing for Court. I have to beg a thousand pardons for being the occasion of your having so much trouble in vain. This resolution will, I am afraid, both surprise and disappoint you; but you will not wonder at any reconsideration of so important a subject, or at my finally forming whatever decision is dictated by my principles and feelings. I am, with the deepest sense of the friendship you have shown me in all this business,   " Yours, &c.,

" W. PITT."

The Lord Advocate to his brother.

"Thursday, Feb. 27th, 1783,
" MY DEAR LORD,   Five o'clock, P.M.

"Things are in a more extraordinary state than I could have conceived. I send you copies of three notes I received from the Chancellor in the course of yesterday. I was with Mr. Pitt this morning from 8 o'clock till 11, and parted with him perfectly resolved to accept First Lord of the Treasury; Lord Gower President of the Council; in short, a Government consisting of a coalition with the Bedford interest and the present administration, joined by a great defalcation from the parties both of Lord North and Mr. Fox, and in a very short time Lord North himself supporting, for he and Fox have differed much. All this was settled at 11 o'clock, and I communicated the same to the Chancellor and Lord Gower, all of whom are in immense spirits. They will soon be damped, for the Chancellor, Lord Gower, Lord Aylesford, Lord Weymouth, Lord Mount Stuart, Mr. Rigby, and Mr. [Thomas] Pitt, dine with me, when, in place of our hailing the new Minister, I must communicate to them a letter I have received from Mr. Pitt within this hour, a copy of which I likewise send. How it will all end, God only knows. I don't think I shall give myself any more trouble in the matter.

"It is just upon dinner, and I must close.

" Yours faithfully,

" H. DUNDAS."

Mr. Pitt to Lady Chatham.

"MY DEAR MOTHER,   "Sunday, March 2, 1783.

"I have been coming to you all the morning, which I expected to have been entire leisure, but have been kept till now. I know nothing of the approaching arrangements, further than that Lord North has been with the King. I rejoice much at *Lord Sydenham's* honours. Lord Grantham will not be overlooked. Whether I refuse depends merely upon whether anything is offered. Taking I must consider as out of the question, as well as continuance in office under any arrangement which can be made; though I believe my *former* friends are not as much disinclined for it as I am. I am going this fine day to dine with Mr. Wilberforce, at Wimbledon, and shall be back early to-morrow morning, to settle some Treasury business, and a Bill which I must bring in to-morrow; after which I shall be a free man, and shall be able to see you again with a little more certainty.

"Ever, my dear Mother, &c,

"W. PITT."

It was not long ere authentic rumours spread abroad of the high offer to Pitt, which had thus been tendered and refused. How the public at the time talked or thought of it, may be surmised from a passage as follows, in the diary of the Duke of Grafton: "The good judgment of so young a man, who, not void of ambition on this

---

*This was the title at first de- | hend, but the title of Sydney was signed for Mr. Thomas Towns- | finally preferred.

trying occasion, could refuse this splendid offer, adds
much to the lustre of the character he had acquired, for
it was a temptation sufficient to have overset the resolution of most men."

Meanwhile, though holding office only till the choice
of his successor, Pitt found it requisite to bring in a
measure which admitted no delay. It was necessary at
the conclusion of peace to regulate in one way or other
our commercial intercourse with North America. The
views of Pitt upon this question were of the largest kind.
He thought that the feelings of animosity produced by
the war ought, as far as possible, to end with the war
itself. He desired to treat the United States on points
of commerce nearly as though they had been still de-
pendent colonies. But many other members of weight,
as Lord Sheffield and Mr. Eden, took a far more jealous
view; and the measure which Pitt actually proposed
was not a final, only a temporary Bill. Even thus it
was, said Pitt, "undoubtedly one of the most complicated in its nature, and at the same time one of the
most extensive in its consequences, that ever had been
submitted to Parliament." It was a good deal discussed
during the remainder of the Session. The Bill was
several times committed and re-committed with a variety
of amendments, and at last under the next administration was further altered by the Lords. It was no
doubt a money Bill. "But I am of opinion," said Fox,
" that the order of the House respecting money Bills is
often too strictly construed. . . . . . It would be very
absurd indeed to send a loan Bill to the Lords for their
concurrence, and at the same time deprive them of the

right of deliberation."[9]   At last there was passed a temporary Bill, merely vesting in the King, for a limited time, the power of regulation, and it afterwards came to be renewed from year to year.

Disappointed in Pitt, the King had next endeavoured to break the Coalition by appealing in the most earnest manner to Lord North to undertake the government singly. Lord North again and again refused, and the King found it necessary to admit into his service both the Coalition chiefs. But the rival pretensions of their followers caused a new and well-nigh insuperable difficulty. At one moment it seemed probable that Fox and North would relinquish the task which they had assumed, and declare themselves unable to form the government which they had announced. Fresh overtures to Pitt ensued.

The Lord Advocate to his brother.

"MY DEAR LORD,

> "Friday, (March) 21 (1783),
> Five o'clock.

"Last night the Duke of Portland waited upon the King, and informed him that he could not form an administration, he and Lord North having differed as to one particular. The King instantly sent for Mr. Pitt, and told him so. Mr. Pitt sent for me to come to him this morning at eight. I went and met the Duke of Rutland there. The result was that if they could not agree, and the country by that means (was) kept in anarchy, he would accept of the Government, and make an administration, which would indeed have been a

---

[9] Speech of Fox, May 8, 1783.

strong one, himself at the head of it. But he insisted
to have the secret kept, because he was determined to
have it distinctly ascertained before going again to the
King, that North and Fox, after making a profligate
conjunction, had quarrelled among themselves about
the division of the spoils. Mr. Pitt and the Duke of
Rutland have this instant called at my house to inform
me that the Coalition had again taken place, for that the
Duke of Portland and Mr. Fox had yielded the point in
dispute. The disputed point was whether Lord Stormont
should be President of the Council. So I suppose we
shall instantly have their arrangement published, and
they will kiss hands on Monday.

> " Yours, &c.,
>
> "H. DUNDAS."

The Lord Advocate to his brother.

> "March 24, 1783.

"I went to Langley on Saturday, and at two this
morning was called up by an express from Mr. Pitt. I
have seen him this morning, and although I shall not
be sanguine upon anything till it is actually fixed, I
flatter myself Mr. Pitt will kiss hands as First Lord of
the Treasury on Wednesday next."

The Lord Advocate to his brother.

> "March 25, 1783.

"I have just time to write to you, that since yesterday I have altered my mind; and it is now my opinion
that Mr. Pitt will not accept of the government. How
all this anarchy is to end God only knows.

> " Yours,
>
> "H. D."

The letters which passed, so late as the 24th, between the King and Mr. Pitt will be found with the rest of their correspondence at the close of the present volume. They evince how earnest was His Majesty in pressing, and how resolute the young statesman in continuing to decline, the highest political prize.

Thus for several weeks, at a most critical juncture of public affairs, was the country left without a government. Murmurs began to rise on every side. In the House of Commons there had already been a motion reflecting on these delays by Mr. Coke of Norfolk, and another to the same effect was announced by the Earl of Surrey. Thus pressed, the Coalition did at last consent to coalesce. On the 31st of March, the very day which had been fixed for Lord Surrey's motion, Pitt rose in his place and announced that he had that day with His Majesty's permission resigned the office of Chancellor of the Exchequer.

Lord Surrey, however, rose again and insisted on making his motion. After some debate he was induced to withdraw it, but declared that he should certainly bring it forward again in a few days unless a new administration was announced. He had no further delays to complain of, for on the 2nd of April the new Ministers kissed hands.

In the Cabinet thus formed, there was carried out the favourite idea of Fox, of a mere nominal headship of the Treasury; for the First Lord was declared to be His Grace of Portland. Under him were Fox and North as joint Secretaries of State, and with coequal authority, but far different shares of real power. The gentler spirit of Lord North was, on most occasions, content to yield, while under the wing of the Duke of Portland, Fox was in fact Prime Minister. Lord John Cavendish returned to the Exchequer, and Lord Keppel to the Admiralty. Lord Stormont was President, and Lord Carlisle Privy Seal. The Great Seal was put into commission, the King having striven in vain to keep Lord Thurlow in office. The new Cabinet, therefore, consisted of seven persons only.

An anxious wish had been felt to include Mr. Pitt in these Cabinet arrangements. His own intended successor, Lord John Cavendish, pressed him to resume the post of Chancellor of the Exchequer, intending in that case to take another office for himself. But Pitt would not listen to such overtures, nor consent to take any part in a combination of which he strongly disapproved.

In the appointments outside of the Cabinet, Burke returned to his old place of Paymaster, and Sheridan became Secretary of the Treasury. The Vice-Royalty of Ireland was bestowed on the Earl of Northington, son of the late Chancellor, and a friend of Fox, while a young man of the highest promise, William Windham, of Norfolk, went as Secretary. Lord Sandwich, with certainly a most tame submission to those who had once so bitterly arraigned him, consented to take the Rangership of St. James's and Hyde Parks; a post of no political importance, but to which at that time a large salary was joined.

The new government being formed, and having entered on its duties, Fox, without hesitation, took the lead in the House of Commons. Indeed, it was in contemplation to call Lord North, by writ, to the House of Peers. But the idea, if not relinquished, was at least postponed.

Thus did the Coalition triumph—if indeed the word triumph can be used whenever power is attained through the sacrifice of fame. Even at the outset this "unnatural alliance," for so it was commonly termed, was rebuked with great bitterness in the House of Commons. There the bitterness might be in some measure mitigated by the admirable suavity of Lord North, and by the warm attachment of so many friends to Fox. But in the country there was no such counteraction. "Unless a real good government is the consequence of this junction, nothing can justify it to the public;" such was the remark at the time of one of its main promoters.[1] And when Fox, on taking office, appealed to his old constituents at Westminster, he did indeed succeed in obtaining re-election, but the multitude received him with hootings and hissings, and his eloquent voice could not be heard.

Such was the public indignation. Nor yet did it quickly cool. On the contrary, it became more ardent when the Ministry formed by this alliance had been tried and been found to fail. A year later there were echoes from every part of England to the austere reproach against the Coalition, expressed by Mr. Wilberforce to the freeholders of Yorkshire. The Coalition, he said, was a progeny that partook of the vices of

---

[1] Letter of Colonel Fitzpatrick to his brother, Feb. 22, 1783, as printed in the Fox Memorials.

both its parents—the corruption of the one and the violence of the other.

Nor yet in present times have the ablest historical writers formed any very different opinion. Lord John Russell and Lord Macaulay might be suspected of some leaning to the views of Mr. Fox ; yet both, unable to vindicate this fatal Coalition, have given judgment against it with perfect candour and fairness. Lord Macaulay, above all, treats as a mere empty pretext the ground that was urged by Fox for this alliance—his objections to the terms of peace. There is not, says Lord Macaulay, the slightest reason to believe that Fox, if he had remained in office, would have hesitated one moment about concluding a treaty on such conditions.

In the month that preceded the formation of the Fox and North government, there had been several Parliamentary debates. Mr. Townshend had been called to the House of Lords, so that Mr. Pitt, during that period, was in name as well as fact the leader of the House of Commons. On the 31st of March, in the discussion which ensued after his announcement that he had finally resigned the office of Chancellor of the Exchequer, he took occasion to explain the principles of his future course. "I desire," he said, "to declare that I am unconnected with any party whatever. I shall keep myself reserved, and act with whichever side I think is acting right."

Accordingly in the remainder of the Session, which was protracted till the middle of July, Pitt did not attend in his place as a mere party man. It also frequently happened that the charms of advancing summer drew him from the House of Commons to the villa of his friend Wilberforce at Wimbledon. "Eliot, Arden, and I will be with you before curfew, and expect an early meal of peas and strawberries"—such is one of the notes at this period which Pitt wrote, and Wilberforce preserved. "One morning"—so Wilberforce relates—"we found the fruits of Pitt's earlier rising in the careful sowing of the garden-beds with the fragments of a dress-hat with which Ryder had over night come down from the opera."

How different I may observe the real Pitt of private life from him whom in the following year the authors of the 'Rolliad' portrayed! They make him even at the tea-table maintain his stately manner and his Parliamentary language.

> " Pass muffins in Committee of Supply,
> And buttered toast amend by adding dry."

Here are some further extracts from Wilberforce's diary at this time: "May 26th, House. I spoke. Dinner at Lord Advocate's; Mr. and Mrs. Johnstone, Thurlow, Pepper, Pitt. After the rest went we sat till six in the morning.—Sunday, July 6th, Wimbledon. Persuaded Pitt and Pepper to church.—July 11th, Fine hot day. Went on water with Pitt and Eliot fishing. Came back, dined, walked evening. Eliot went home; Pitt stayed."

Yet it must not be supposed that Pitt was neglecting his duty in the House of Commons. We find, for example, that he spoke in the debate upon the case of Powell and Bembridge—that painful case in which

Burke, so greatly to the discredit of his judgment, had reinstated in office two clerks publicly accused (and one of whom was afterwards convicted) of defalcations in their accounts. And on two other occasions Mr. Pitt took not only an active but a leading part.

On the 7th of May Pitt brought forward for the second time the question of Parliamentary Reform. Now there was a specific plan comprised in three Resolutions. By the first the House was pledged to take measures for the better prevention both of bribery and expense at elections. The second Resolution provided that whenever in any borough the majority of voters should be convicted of gross corruption, the borough itself should be disfranchised, and the minority not so convicted should be entitled to vote for the county. By the third Resolution the knights of the shire were to be increased in number. This, as is well known, was the scheme of reform which Lord Chatham had suggested to the extent of one hundred new county members; but the third Resolution of Pitt further proposed an increase of representatives to the metropolis.

In the debate which ensued the new confederates and joint Secretaries of State took opposite sides, Fox warmly supporting, and Lord North with equal vehemence denouncing the scheme. It was their first public disagreement since their late alliance.

On the other hand Pitt obtained some aid from the ranks of his opponents on the last occasion. First there was Dundas, now become or becoming the closest of his friends. "Last year," said Dundas, "I was against going into a Committee because there was no specific motion made; now I am for the motion because I think it a good one." Much to the same effect spoke Thomas Pitt, but in the course of his speech he also referred to himself as the proprietor, or as it was then termed the "patron," of the borough of Old Sarum. This he said he was willing to surrender into the hands of Parliament as a free sacrifice, as a victim to be offered up at the shrine of the British Constitution. Should the victim be accepted, he would suggest that the power of returning two members might be transferred to the Bank of England.

It must have been diverting as the debate of that night proceeded to contrast the liberal offer of Thomas Pitt with the anti-reforming zeal of the Right Hon. Richard Rigby. In his ardour for the close boroughs Mr. Rigby rose to declare that he would rather see another member added to Old Sarum, where there was but a single house, than another member to the City of London, which had members enough already.

On dividing, the Resolutions of Pitt, notwithstanding the accession to his ranks of Dundas and his kinsman Thomas, were rejected by a very large majority, the numbers being 293 and 149. The result shows how rightly Pitt had judged in the more general terms of his motion of last year.

On the 2nd of June Pitt produced some of the fruits of his labours at the Treasury. He brought in a Bill for the Reform of Abuses in the Public Offices. He hoped, as he said, to effect a saving of at least 40,000l. a-year, and on going into Committee on the 17th he gave some striking proofs of the abuses which prevailed. Thus, in the article of stationery, for which the annual charge was 18,000*l.*, he said, " I believe I shall somewhat astonish the Noble Lord in the blue riband (Lord North), when I tell the House and inform him, for I really believe the Noble Lord had no idea of any such circumstance, that the Noble Lord alone, as chief of the Treasury, cost the public the year before the last no less than 1,300*l.* for stationery. One article of the bill is 340*l.* for pack thread alone!"

Lord North, whose own upright and disinterested character is beyond all question, rose in his own defence. " I had given," he said, "the most positive direction that no stationery ware should be delivered for my use without the express order of my private secretary. If therefore any fraud has been committed, it must have been by a breach of this direction. I assure the House that I will make a most rigorous inquiry into this business, and if I find delinquency, I will leave nothing in my power undone to bring the delinquents to punishment. . . As to coals and candles, I found when I was placed at the head of the Treasury that my predecessors had been supplied with those articles at the expense of the public, and that it was according to an old and established custom. But I declined to avail myself of this custom, and I have supplied my house with coals and candles at my own expense." The vindication of Lord North personally was no doubt complete, but still from some other quarter the gross abuse, the wanton loss to the public, remained.

The conduct of the Coalition Ministers in regard to this Bill was certainly not creditable to them. They

did not venture to divide the House of Commons against
it in any of its stages, but when it reached the House
of Lords they put forth all their influence, and caused
the Bill to be rejected upon the second reading.

Here are some extracts of Pitt's own correspondence
with Lady Chatham at this time :—

" May 15, 1783.

" The little that has passed in the world since we
parted you know already as well, I believe, as I can tell
you ; for nothing has occurred in which I know anything
more than all the rest of the world. Politics have been
tolerably quiet, which for the present is, I think, much
the best. In the two circumstances of the loan, and the
restoration of Mr. Powell, our new Ministry have given
a pretty fair opening, if it were the time to seize it.
The latter business must still produce some further discussion, and probably a good deal to their discredit ; but
the Session is now so far advanced that probably nothing
very material will happen in the House of Commons.
What may happen out of it any day there is no knowing.
The same *fixed aversion*, I believe, still continues ; you
will easily guess where. My defeat on the Parliamentary Reform was much more complete than I expected. Still, if the question was to be lost, the discussion has not been without its use. Business of some
sort or other will probably keep Parliament sitting
through most of the next month at least. I have not
been able yet to arrange the whole of my summer plan
with any certainty, but undoubtedly Burton will never
be left out of it.

" The scene in Albemarle Street has been carried on
from day to day till it is full time it should end. I
rather hope it will be happily completed very soon.

though it has lasted so long already that it may still
last longer than seems likely.

"I hope you are gradually able to enjoy more of the
beauties round you, and of this delightful weather.
Delightful as it is, if it continues, even the moors will
begin to complain. The dust of this part of the world
is almost insufferable."

"May 24, 1783.

"I hardly need tell you how much the division about
Powell and Bembridge has exposed the weakness of
Ministry, and added to their disgrace. To rub through
the remains of the Session seems almost as much as
they can expect, all things considered."

"May 28, 1783.

"I am just going to the House of Commons on East
India business, which is not the most entertaining. The
Budget has, as you have seen, given us some more
debate. I was induced, from Fox's language, to mark
pretty strongly that I was not disposed always to stand
quite on the defensive; and the effect of attacking him,
not very civilly, was, that he took more pains afterwards to be civil to me than I ever knew when we were
friends."

During the last six weeks of the Session the members
of Parliament were as usual beginning to disperse, and
the Ministers seemed to be perfectly secure; yet at that
very time they were contending with a serious danger,
and their government was in their opinion near its
close.

The cause of this new entanglement was George
Prince of Wales, afterwards King George the Fourth.

In his education he had received from his Royal parents an excellent example of a moral life, but he had by no means adopted that example as his own. On the contrary, as Horace Walpole once remarked, he came forth from that Temple of Virtue, his father's palace, as though he had been brought up in a cider-cellar. Plunging headlong into a career of extravagance and dissipation, he eagerly attached himself to Fox as his familiar friend; and it may readily be supposed that this association was far from tending to conciliate the King either to the great Whig orator or to the giddy young Prince.

Born in August, 1762, the Prince was now within a few weeks of his majority. It became necessary to consider, without delay, the question of a separate establishment for His Royal Highness. Mr. Fox proposed to apply to Parliament for a grant of 100,000*l.* a-year. Lord North and Lord John Cavendish, although they thought the amount extravagant, acquiesced; but the King felt objection both to the largeness of the sum and to the independence of parental control which that vote would imply. In place of it he offered to allow 50,000*l.* a-year from his Civil List.

For some time neither side would yield. The King, as usual with him, was firm and unbending in his own opinion, and the Ministers considered themselves bound by their promise to the Prince of Wales. The notes of His Royal Highness to Fox, pending this negotiation, are still preserved: they begin with the friendly prefix of "Dear Charles." In the middle of June Fox and his colleagues looked upon their dismissal or resignation as close at hand, and they wrote accordingly to their friends at Dublin Castle.

It so chanced that at this very juncture Earl Temple arrived in London from his recent Lord Lieutenancy, and, as a matter of course on such occasions, had an audience of the Sovereign. His Majesty seized the opportunity to consult his late Viceroy. He expressed himself as much incensed at the pretensions put forth on behalf of his son, and as greatly inclined on that account to dismiss his Ministers. Lord Temple, however, though one of the keenest of party men, had sagacity enough to see that here neither the juncture nor yet the pretext would be favourable, and he strongly advised the King to await a better time.

On the other hand, His Royal Highness of Wales being assured that he should not be able to prevail in his pretension, was induced to release his friends from their engagement. With a calmer temper on each side, the business was soon adjusted. It was determined that the King should allow the Prince 50,000*l.* yearly from his Civil List, and that the House of Commons should be asked to grant the sum of 60,000*l.* as an outfit to His Royal Highness. A message on this subject to the Commons was brought down by Lord John Cavendish on the 23rd of June, and on a subsequent day the sum proposed was most cheerfully voted. The Prince was thus provided with what seemed to be an adequate establishment, and on the meeting of Parliament in the November following he took his seat in the House of Lords.

It does not appear that Mr. Pitt was in any manner

consulted in this affair, though no doubt he must have
been fully apprised of it in subsequent conversations with
Lord Temple. Unconnected with public affairs there
was an event at the same period which afforded him
great pleasure. His brother, Lord Chatham, had become attached to the Hon. Mary Elizabeth Townshend,
a daughter of his friend Lord Sydney. For upwards of
a year had the young Earl continued his attentions;
but with the procrastination that through life formed a
main feature of his character, it was not until June,
1783, that he brought them to a point. The offer being
made and accepted, was a source of much joy to Lady
Chatham, to whom we find Mr. Pitt write in terms of
affectionate congratulation :—

"Saturday, June 14, 1783.

"My dear Mother,

"I know too well your feelings on the happy
news you have received, and you, I trust, know too well
how much my feelings are your own, to make words of
congratulation necessary between us; and yet I have
had my pen in my hand several times, though I have
been as often interrupted, and I can now hardly imagine
how so many days have passed away without my employing it on this subject. You have, I am sure, easily
imagined, though not so near a spectator, how much joy
the long-expected declaration produced. Lord Sydney
is the happiest person in the world—at least two excepted—and is delighted with your answer to his letter.
I cannot learn with any certainty when the union is
likely to be completed; but as there are not many materials for the law's delay, I imagine it cannot be long.

"Lord Temple came to town yesterday, and made

his appearance at St. James's, where I met him. You will not be surprised that he was received in the most gracious manner possible. I have had since a great deal of conversation with him, and in all respects of the most satisfactory sort. Our economical and reforming Ministry will probably take another opportunity of showing their sincerity on Tuesday, on a Bill for remedying the abuses in several public offices. The establishment for the Prince of Wales is also to come on that day or the next. Rumour says strange things of it. The proposers probably expect to make their account by it, but they will lose in the nation more than they gain elsewhere.

"I am almost too late for dinner, even though at the Duke of Rutland's. Adieu.

"Your ever dutiful

"W. PITT."

The marriage thus agreed upon was solemnized on the 10th of July, and the happy pair went to pass the honeymoon at Hayes. There soon afterwards they received a visit from their brother William.

No children were born of this marriage. The second Countess of Chatham died in 1821, and the title was extinct at the decease of the second Earl in 1835.

Besides his excursion to Hayes, Pitt made also a visit at Stowe, which, from his description of it to his mother, he appears never to have seen before. He next proceeded to Brighton in company with Mr. Pretyman, and towards the middle of August joined Lady Chatham at Burton Pynsent.

"MY DEAR MOTHER,   "Savile Street,[2] July 22, 1783.

"I resume at last my pen, though with no other reason than ought to have made me do so every day for this month past. I can indeed hardly make out how that period has slid away, in which I have done little else but ride backwards and forwards between Wimbledon and London, and meditate plans for the summer, till I find the summer half over before I have begun to put any in execution.

"My excursion to Stowe was a very short one—the pleasantest, however, that could be. I found more beauties in the place than I expected; and the house, though not half finished in the inside, the most magnificent by far that I ever saw. Still, as far as the mere pleasure of seeing goes, I had rather be the visitor than the owner. Sedgemoor and Troy Hill are not to be exchanged for the Elysian Fields, with all the temples into the bargain. I had the discretion, you will believe though, to keep this opinion to myself. We were quite a family party—Mr. and Mrs. Fortescue, Miss Grenville, William, and myself. We had leisure, as you may imagine, for abundance of speculation and discourse, all of which was in the greatest degree satisfactory, and promises everything that you would wish in regard to those quarters. The Session is over, and everything seems very quiet, though whether the Ministry will gain much strength from their repose is very doubtful. Perhaps not. I rather think, if I can, to take leave of this neighbourhood in a day or two, and to take some dips at Brighthelmstone before our Somersetshire party, which I hope will take place not very late in next

---

[2] A house which had been taken by Lord Chatham before his marriage.

month, if nothing happens any day to derange my
summer schemes. I came this morning from Hayes,
where all is happiness, as you will believe, and where
indeed all ought to be so. I should be very much
tempted to stay there till they move, but that I want
to employ a few more studious hours in the interval
than I could easily find there. Brighthelmstone will
answer in that view, as well as in point of health,
though, as to that, it cannot make me better than I
am. . . . . .

> " Ever your dutiful and affectionate
>
> " W. PITT."

> " Brighthelmstone, Aug. 8, 1783.

" MY DEAR MOTHER,

" I imagine some of your visitors are by this time
with you, or at least on their way. I am so far separated from the main army that they may probably not
be able to give you any certain account of my motions,
though it is my intention very soon to rejoin it. I shall
leave this place probably on Wednesday, and by striking
across the country shall, I flatter myself, reach Burton
the next day. At all events, before the end of the
week, I shall certainly have the happiness of seeing
you, and, I trust, of finding you going on well. This
part of the world supplies no news, and I know of none
elsewhere. By all I learnt before I left London, I now
think things may possibly go through the rest of the
summer as they are, though much longer there is every
reason to believe they will not.

> " Ever, my dear Mother, &c.,
>
> " W. PITT."

CHAPTER IV.

1783.

Pitt's excursion to France — Abbé de Lageard — Return to England — Fox's India Bill — Great speech of Burke — Bill passes the Commons, but is thrown out by the Lords — Dismissal of Fox and North — The Royal Prerogative — Pitt appointed Prime Minister — Resignation of Lord Temple — The New Cabinet.

His legal pursuits being for this summer laid aside, Pitt had planned an excursion to France, in company with Wilberforce and Eliot. Early in September the three friends met and passed a few days at the seat of Henry Bankes in Dorsetshire. There one day in partridge-shooting Pitt had a narrow escape from Wilberforce's gun. "So at least," said Wilberforce, "my companions affirmed, with a roguish wish perhaps to make the most of my short-sightedness and inexperience in field-sports."

On the 10th of September Pitt attended the King's Levee at St. James's, and on the 12th embarked at Dover with his two travelling companions. But the events of his short tour will best be gathered from his own correspondence.

"My dear Mother,	"Sept. 10, 1783.

"I am just going to the Levee, and shall get into my chaise immediately after, and, I hope, shall reach Dover before night. I will write as soon as I am landed

on the other side of the water. London furnishes no
news but the long expected definitive treaty, and of
that no new particulars are known. I hope you are
perfectly free from the complaint Harriot mentioned in
her last letter. If the cross-post does me justice, she
will have heard from me in answer. Adieu. Ever, my
dear Mother, &c.,

" W. PITT."

" MY DEAR MOTHER,   " Calais, Sept. 12 (1783).

" Lest any howling at Burton should have given
you the idea of a storm, I am impatient to assure you
that we are arrived here after rather a rough but a very
prosperous passage. We shall set out to-morrow and
reach Rheims Sunday night or Monday morning. A
letter, directed to a Gentilhomme Anglois à la Poste
Restante, will, I find, be sure to reach me. I hope
I shall have the pleasure of hearing from you very
soon.

" Your dutiful and affectionate

" W. PITT."

" Rheims, Sept. 18, Thursday, 1783.

" MY DEAR MOTHER,

" We arrived here after a journey which had
little but the novelty of the country to recommend it.
The travelling was much better than I expected, and
the appearance of the people more comfortable, but the
face of the country through all the way from Calais the
dullest I ever saw. Here we are in very good quarters,
though as yet we have not found much society but our
own. The place is chiefly inhabited by mercantile
people and ecclesiastics, among whom, however, I suppose we shall by degrees find some charitable persons

who will let us practise our French upon them. At present, when I have told you that we are here and perfectly well, I have exhausted my whole budget of news. The post is also not well suited for a longer letter, as it goes out at nine in the morning, and I am writing before breakfast. This, however, is not so great an exertion as in England, for the hours are uncommonly early, to which we easily accustom ourselves, at night, and in some measure in the morning. I hope I shall have the happiness of a letter from Burton soon. You will probably have received one which I wrote from Calais. Kind love to Harriot, and compliments to Mrs. Stapleton.

" Your ever dutiful and affectionate

" W. PITT."

To Lady Harriot Pitt.

" MY DEAR SISTER,   " Rheims, Oct. 1, 1783.

. . . .

" This place has for some days been constantly improving upon us, though at this time of year it has not a numerous society. We are going to-day to dine at a country-house in the midst of vineyards, which, as this is the height of the vintage, will furnish a very pleasant scene. To-morrow we are to dine at a magnificent palace of the Archbishop's, who lives about five miles off, and is a sort of prince in this country. Most of those we see are ecclesiastics, and as a French Abbé is not proverbial for silence, we have an opportunity of hearing something of the language. . . . . .

" Your ever affectionate

" W. PITT."

To Lady Chatham.

"Rheims, Monday, Oct. 6, 1783.

"This will be the last time of my writing from this place, which we leave on Wednesday for Paris. The time has passed not unpleasantly or unprofitably, and I flatter myself has furnished a stock of French that will last for ten days or a fortnight at Paris. We shall arrive there on Thursday, and do not mean to be tempted by anything to prolong our stay much beyond the 20th of October. Parliament I hear meets on the 11th of November, and a fortnight or three weeks in England first is very desirable.

"The direction I sent became, from my manner of expressing it, more mysterious than I meant, as I had no intention to leave out my name. It is some proof of French politeness that they do not bear it any enmity, though they seem to know the difference between this war and the last. I believe you may venture to direct to me at full length at Paris, adding Hôtel du Parc Royal, Rue du Colombier, Faubourg St. Germain."

"Hôtel de Grande Bretagne, Paris,
Wednesday, Oct. 15 (1783).

"I am just setting out to Fontainebleau for two or three days, where I shall find the Court and all the magnificence of France, and with this expedition I shall finish my career here. Since I have been here I have had little to do but to see sights, as the King's journey to Fontainebleau has carried all the world from Paris except the English, who seem quite in possession of the town."

Some further details have been preserved of this, the only visit to the continent which Pitt ever made. Nearly all are derived from the letters and the Diary as published of Mr. Wilberforce. At Rheims Pitt had many conversations with Abbé de Lageard, a highly intelligent gentleman, then the Archbishop's delegate, and afterwards an emigrant in England. One day as the young orator was expressing in warm terms his admiration of the political system which prevailed at home, the Abbé asked him, since all human things were perishable, in what part the British Constitution might be first expected to decay? Pitt mused for a moment, and then answered:—"The part of our Constitution which will first perish is the prerogative of the King, and the authority of the House of Peers."

"I am much surprised," said the Abbé, "that a country so moral as England can submit to be governed by such a spendthrift and such a rake as Fox; it seems to show that you are less moral than you claim to be." "The remark is just," Pitt replied, "but you have not been under the wand of the magician."

On the French institutions they also sometimes conversed. Pitt made many careful inquiries, and summed up his impressions in the following words:—"Sir, you have no political liberty; but as to civil liberty you have more of it than you suppose." It is remarkable that this is the very conclusion which, in treating of that period seventy years afterwards, the last work of De Tocqueville has with so much force of argument maintained.

But, besides these well attested replies of Pitt in

France, there is another resting on no good authority;
a mere silly rumour which has often been repeated.
We are told that Monsieur and Madame Necker, through
the intervention of Horace Walpole, proposed to him
their daughter in marriage, with a fortune of 14,000*l.*
a-year, and that Pitt answered,—"I am already married to my country."[1]   Now in the first place Horace
Walpole was not then, and had not been for many years,
at Paris.   Secondly, it is most improbable that Monsieur
and Madame Necker, strongly imbued as they were
with the Swiss ideas of domestic happiness, should have
offered their child as the wife of a young foreigner after
only a few days' acquaintance.   And thirdly, the
theatrical reply ascribed to Pitt is wholly at variance
with his ever plain and manly, and sometimes sarcastic,
style.   I believe that he never had the opportunity of
refusing Mademoiselle Necker, but if he did I am sure
that it was not in any such melo-dramatic phrase.

At Fontainebleau we find Pitt take part in the chase.
Wilberforce dots down in his journal:—"October 17,
morning: Pitt stag-hunting, Eliot and I in chaise to see
King.   Clumsy, strange figure in immense boots.   Dined
at home; then play."   Both at Fontainebleau and at
Paris the son of Chatham was much noticed by persons
of distinction, from the Queen, Marie Antoinette, down-
wards.   "They all, men and women"—so writes Wilberforce to Bankes—"crowded round Pitt in shoals; and
he behaved with great spirit, though he was sometimes

---

[1] See the story as related in the Life of Wilberforce, but not on his
authority, vol. i. p. 39.

a little bored when they talked to him of Parliamentary Reform."

The three friends landed again at Dover on the 24th of October. Mr. Pitt, as we learn from Bishop Tomline, who despatches his tour in a single sentence, returned to England with the intention of resuming his profession of the law, if there should appear a fair probability of the administration being permanent. But the events of the coming Session speedily dispelled his legal dreams.

Pitt was full of Parliamentary topics, when a few days after his return he wrote as follows to Lord Mahon :—

"Berkeley Square, Nov. 3, 1783.

" My dear Lord,

"I was in hopes to have seen you and those with you at Chevening, all of whom I wished extremely to see before this time, but I have had so much to do ever since I have been in town that I have found it impossible. The meeting is now so near that time is every day more precious, and there is abundance of objects that require examination. I trust you will be in town in *a very few days*, for there are several things in which I am quite at a loss without you. If anything detains you, pray let me know, and I will endeavour to meet you at Hayes, but I rather trust to seeing you here. Adieu.

"Ever most affectionately yours,

"W. PITT."

Parliament met on the 11th of November. On that day Pitt spoke, admitting that there was no objection

to the Address proposed.   On the same day he addressed
to Lady Chatham a few hasty lines :—

> "Berkeley Square, Nov. 11, 1783.
>
> "My dear Mother,
>
> "I have been disappointed the two last posts in
> my intention of writing to you, which, just as the meet-
> ing of Parliament approached, you will, I am sure,
> readily excuse.   We have to-day heard the King's
> Speech, and voted the Address without any opposition.
> Both were so general that they prove nothing of what
> may be expected during the Session.   The East India
> business and the funds promise to make the two prin-
> cipal objects.   I am afraid it will not be easy for me
> by the post to be anything else than a *fashionable* cor-
> respondent, for I believe the *fashion* which prevails of
> opening almost every letter that is sent, makes it almost
> impossible to write anything worth reading.   .   .   .   .
> Adieu, my dear Mother."

In the course of the debate on the Address Mr. Secretary Fox announced that in a week from that time he
should bring forward the great Ministerial measure for
the government of India, which was foreshadowed in the
Royal Speech.   To that measure, almost in exclusion
of every other, the public attention was now directed.

The progress of our Eastern empire under Warren
Hastings, as its rise under Clive, displayed amidst all
its greatness and its glory some flagrant cases of oppression and misrule.   Echoes of these, though faint, had
gradually rolled across the wide expanse of sea.   Inquiry
and suspicion began to be rife in England.   Committees
of the House of Commons had sat and had reported.

By the witnesses examined the cases of oppression were in part revealed. By the voice of eloquent speakers—of Dundas especially and Burke—the oppressor still in office was denounced.

So recently as April, 1783, on the fall of the Shelburne administration, Dundas had brought in a Bill on this most important subject. His plan was to send out a new Governor-General, prepared to remedy abuses and armed with extensive powers, with authority to overrule, if he thought it needful, the wish and the opinion of his council. In such a case, as Dundas had observed, everything would depend on the weight and authority of the person so selected; and as the fittest person, Dundas had named Earl Cornwallis.

Under such circumstances the Coalition Government had scarce an alternative before it. The Ministers did no more than any other Ministers at that period must and would have done in undertaking to frame a measure that should reform the entire administration of our Indian provinces.

From the profound knowledge of Burke upon all branches of this subject it has been commonly supposed that, in framing the new measure, he had by far the largest share. This conjecture has been confirmed by the subsequent publication of his papers. "From Mr. Pigot, who finished the India Bill from my drafts"—such is the endorsement, in Burke's own handwriting, to a letter which he received in October, 1783.[2] There can be no doubt, however, that Burke, before he

---

[2] Correspondence of Burke, vol. iii. p. 22, as published in 1844.

sent in his measure to the Cabinet, consulted Fox on
every point of importance, and that Fox applied himself
to the whole subject with most anxious care.

The India Bill, prepared by these two eminent
statesmen and agreed to by their Cabinet colleagues,
was of a bold and sweeping character. It gave to a
Board of seven persons—all charters or vested rights
notwithstanding — the absolute power to appoint or
displace the holders of office in India, and to conduct
as they deemed best the entire administration of that
country. The names of these seven persons were left
in blank to be filled up in the Committee, and their
authority was to endure for four years from the passing
of the Act, whatever changes of administration might
meanwhile ensue. The members of the Board were
prohibited from the use of the ballot or any other mode
of secret voting, and they were required to lay their
accounts before both Houses at the beginning of every
Session.

It would be great injustice to the memory of both
Burke and Fox were we to doubt that in their deliberations the advantage of India and the cause of justice
and good policy were the foremost objects of their
thoughts. Burke showed on many occasions an eager,
nay a passionate anxiety for the welfare of the Indian
people, and Fox was never wanting in a generous
sympathy with every form of suffering and distress.
Nor is it to be denied that several arguments might
be pleaded in favour of the project they proposed.
Was it not most desirable to shield those distant provinces from the vicissitudes of party conflict at home,

and to obtain a clear field for the needed improvements and reforms?

But, while we may readily admit that the benefit of India itself was the main object with Fox when he devised or adopted his celebrated India Bill, some of his warmest admirers have been willing to acknowledge that he also allowed considerable weight to the future interests and influence of his own party friends in England.[3] He saw that the King had most unwillingly admitted them to office: he saw that His Majesty might at any moment turn them out. How useful, then, if they might construct for themselves some safe citadel of refuge independent of the Royal smiles! How useful if, concentrating in sure hands and during a fixed term of years the entire administration of India, they might confront the Treasury with a mass of patronage scarcely inferior to its own![4] Could the King hope to make head against such a combination? Would it not probably avert or certainly baffle any overt act of his disfavour?

While thus urged forward, first by public and in the second place by personal motives, Fox was by no means insensible to the perils that he ran. "It will be vigorous and hazardous." In these words do we find him describe his own measure in a confidential letter of the time.[5] But his nature was ever bold and fearless, and the prize glittered bright before him. On the

---

[3] See on this point, for example, Moore's Life of Sheridan, vol. i. p. 393.

[4] The patronage under the Bill cannot, I think, be taken at less than 300,000l. a-year. Wilkes makes it "above two millions." See the Parl. Hist. vol. xxiv. p. 24.

[5] To the Earl of Northington at Dublin, Nov. 7, 1783.

18th of November, according to the notice he had
given, he rose to explain to the House of Commons the
provisions of the Bill. He fixed the second reading
for the 27th of the same month, a time that was complained of as far too early; but Pitt, who rose immediately after him, could obtain no further delay.

The speeches of Fox, both in opening and defending
this momentous measure, have been acknowledged on
all hands as most lucid and able. "Such eloquence,"
said his great rival, "would lend a grace to deformity."
On one point only, that is, on the violation of the
Charters, Fox, as addressing an assembly jealous of
vested rights, may have faltered in his tone. For this
violation he could merely urge, in general terms, the
plea of necessity. But necessity—as Pitt exclaimed
with indignation, on the very first day of the Bill—
"necessity is the argument of tyrants, it is the creed of
slaves!"

During the interval between the introduction of the
Bill and its second reading we find Pitt write as follows
to his friend the Duke of Rutland:—

"Berkeley Square, Nov. 22, 1783.

"My dear Duke,

. . . .

"We are in the midst of a contest, and, I think,
approaching to a crisis. The Bill which Fox has
brought in relative to India will be, one way or other,
decisive for or against the Coalition. It is, I really
think, the boldest and most unconstitutional measure
ever attempted, transferring at one stroke, in spite of
all charters and compacts, the immense patronage and

influence of the East to Charles Fox, in or out of office.
I think it will with difficulty, if at all, find its way
through our House, and can never succeed in yours.
Ministry trust all on this one die, and will probably
fail. They have hurried on the Bill so fast, that we
are to have the second reading on Thursday next,
November 27th. I think we shall be strong on that
day, but much stronger in the subsequent stages. If
you have any member within fifty or a hundred miles
of you who cares for the Constitution or the country,
pray send him to the House of Commons as quick as
you can. .   .   .   .   .

" Ever most faithfully yours,

" W. PITT.

" For fear of mistakes, I must tell you that I am at
a house which my brother has taken here, and not at
Shelburne House.

" I do not see Lord Tyrconnel in town, nor Pochin,
nor Sir Henry Peyton. Can you apply to any of
them? They may still be in time for some of the
stages of the Bill."

Notwithstanding the strongest muster that the Opposition was able to make, the second reading of the
India Bill was carried by a majority of 229 to 120.
The struggle was resumed in its succeeding stages,
with no great gain as to numbers, but with some
splendid eloquence all through on either side. Pitt,
especially, put forth all his powers, and, stripling as
he might be termed, he shone forth no unworthy
antagonist to the riper genius of Fox. Henceforth
these two great orators, high above the common level,

might confront each other—it is a poet's thought—like two vast mountains, parted by the main.

> " We, we have seen the intellectual race
>   Of giants stand like Titans face to face :
>   Athos and Ida, with a dashing sea
>   Of eloquence between." [6]

These debates are further memorable for one of the great speeches of Burke—one of those great speeches which contemporaries might hear with indifference, but which the latest posterity will admire and revere. On this occasion he most happily applied to Fox some lines in Silius Italicus, prophetic through an ancestor in the Punic Wars of Cicero—"the only person to whose eloquence it does not wrong that of the mover of the Bill to be compared."

> " Indole proh quantâ juvenis, quantumque daturus
>   Ausoniæ populis venturum in sæcula civem ;
>   Ille super Gangem, super exauditus et Indos
>   Implebit terras voce, et furialia bella
>   Fulmine compescet linguæ." [7]

Of late years I have heard Lord Macaulay more than once refer to this passage, and observe how many persons he has known to misunderstand it—failing to catch the allusion to Cicero—and supposing from a hasty perusal or an imperfect recollection that the lines are " somewhere in Virgil," as, indeed, they are a manifest and successful imitation of the Virgilian manner.

In the same most beautiful passage Burke dwells on

---

[6] Lord Byron, in the ' Age of Bronze.' Some preceding lines give the application of the passage to Pitt and Fox.

[7] Sil. Italic., lib. viii. v. 407.

the merits of Fox with affectionate regard : "He is traduced and abused for his supposed motives. He will remember that obloquy is a necessary ingredient in the composition of all true glory ; he will remember that it was not only in the Roman customs, but it is in the nature and constitution of things, that calumny and abuse are essential parts of triumph. . . . . He is now on a great eminence, where the eyes of mankind are turned to him. He may live long, he may do much ; but here is the summit,—he never can exceed what he does this day. . . . . He has faults, but they are faults that, though they may in a small degree tarnish the lustre and sometimes impede the march of his abilities, have nothing in them to extinguish the fire of great virtues. In these faults there is no mixture of deceit, of hypocrisy, of pride, of ferocity, of complexional despotism, or want of feeling for the distresses of mankind. His are faults which might exist in a descendant of Henry the Fourth of France, as they did exist in that father of his country."

The descent of Mr. Fox from Henri Quatre, which Burke here indicates, may perplex some readers quite as much as the passage from Silius Italicus. They must remember that Mr. Fox's mother was a daughter of the Duke of Richmond; that the Dukes of Richmond are sprung by the *Bend Sinister* from Charles the Second; and that Charles the Second was, on the maternal side, a grandson of the fourth Henry.

In these debates two lawyers of rising fame—of opposite politics, but each destined to attain the height of his profession—made their maiden speeches. First, there was John Scott, in after years Lord Eldon. Having been returned in the previous June for a small borough through the Thynne family interest, he was called by his adversaries at this time "Lord Weymouth's law-yer." His first speech was but a slight one, though eliciting some compliments from Fox. His next effort appears to have been, as his biographer describes it, "vastly more ambitious than successful." [8] Quoting several verses from the Book of Revelation, he alleged the beast with seven heads and ten horns as an emblem of the awful innovation designed in the affairs of the East India Company; and he further garnished his oratory with a citation of the tragic fate of Desdemona. In reply he was severely lashed by Sheridan, and could receive but scant congratulation from his friends; but his mortification at the moment led, beyond all doubt, to his ultimate advantage. It induced him ever afterwards to renounce such soaring flights, and to place, as he well might, his reliance on his legal ability and learning and his great judicial powers.

Erskine also spoke for the first time in these debates. A seat had been found for him at Portsmouth, and he took his seat on the 11th of November. Not a week elapsed ere he rose to address the House. There was great eagerness to hear him, and the highest expecta-tion derived from his wonderful successes at the Bar. But deep in proportion was the disappointment that en-sued. Here, as derived from an eye-witness, is a graphic representation of the scene:—"Pitt, evidently intending

---

[8] Life of Lord Eldon by Twiss, vol. i. p. 153.

to reply, sat with pen and paper in his hand, prepared
to catch the arguments of this formidable adversary.
He wrote a word or two. Erskine proceeded, but with
every additional sentence Pitt's attention to the paper
relaxed, his look became more careless, and he obviously
began to think the orator less and less worthy of his
attention. At length, while every eye in the House was
fixed upon him, with a contemptuous smile he dashed
the pen through the papers and flung them on the floor.
Erskine never recovered from this expression of disdain ;
his voice faltered, he struggled through the remainder
of his speech, and sank into his seat dispirited and shorn
of his fame." A discussion is said to have arisen at the
time whether Pitt's pantomimic display of contempt was
premeditated, or arose from the feeling of the moment ;
but Lord Campbell, as the biographer of Erskine, inclines to the latter opinion.[9]

There is still in these debates another legal speech to
be commemorated. The Attorney-General, John Lee,
was seeking to repel the charge founded on the abroga-
tion of the Charters ; but he did so in terms which greatly
added to the popular excitement that prevailed. "For
what," cried Mr. Lee, "is a Charter? Only a skin of
parchment with a seal of wax dangling at one end of
it." He had added, "when compared with the happiness of thirty millions of subjects." But in such cases
modifications and qualifications are of little avail ; the

---

[9] Lives of the Chancellors, vol.
vi. p. 416. It should be noted,
however, that the meagre Parliamentary History of that day (though
here no doubt in error) represents
Erskine as speaking, not before
Pitt, but immediately after him
(vol. xxiii. p. 1245).

hostile echoes out of doors repeat only the obnoxious words.

In the Committee Fox filled up the blank space with the names of the Directors he proposed. First there was Earl Fitzwilliam, who was designed as Chairman of the Board. He was a man not as yet generally known, but highly respected in his private character, "whom," thus writes Horace Walpole, "the Cavendishes are nursing up as a young Octavius, to succeed his uncle Rockingham." [1] Next was George, eldest son of Lord North. All the rest were of the same complexion, staunch and tried friends of the new administration. There was not even in one case the pretence of an impartial choice; there was not the smallest doubt that the new Board thus composed would be wholly at the bidding of Fox, whether in or out of office.

On the 8th of December the India Bill finally passed the Commons, by a majority of 208 against 102. On the 9th it was carried up to the Peers by Fox, as in triumph, attended by a great concourse of members. The Duke of Portland fixed the second reading for the 15th, but the indignation of several Peers could not be so long restrained. Earl Temple started up at once, happy, he said, to seize the first opportunity of entering his solemn protest against so infamous a Bill. The words of Lord Thurlow, who followed, were much more weighty and almost as vehement. "As I abhor tyranny in all its shapes," said the late Chancellor, "I shall oppose most strenuously this strange attempt to destroy the true ba-

---

[1] Notes by Horace Walpole, March 17, 1783.

lance of our Constitution.   I wish to see the Crown great
and respectable, but if the present Bill should pass, it
will be no longer worthy of a man of honour to wear."
In using these words, Lord Thurlow looked full at
the Prince of Wales, who was present, and he thus proceeded : "The King will, in fact, take the diadem from
his own head, and place it on the head of Mr. Fox."

These two Peers did not confine themselves to speeches
in Parliament.   They had for some time been acting in
close concert together, and they had drawn up a joint
memorandum for the King.   This memorandum, after
remaining secret for many years, was published so recently as 1853, with other papers from Stowe.[2]   It is thus
endorsed in Lord Temple's own hand : " Delivered by
Lord Thurlow, on December 1, 1783."   We find it convey
the strongest warning against the India Bill in progress as
"a plan to take more than half the Royal power, and
by that means disable His Majesty for the rest of the
reign."   Such a warning could not fail to make the
strongest impression on the King, falling in as it did
with his own political feelings, and coming from two
statesmen, one of whom had been lately his Lord Chancellor, and the other his Lord Lieutenant of Ireland.

But could the danger be still averted?   This was a
question which the memorandum did not leave without
a reply.   It suggested that the India Bill could be
thrown out in the House of Lords ; but it added that
the result might be doubtful " if those whose duty to
His Majesty would excite them to appear, are not ac-

---

[2] See the Courts and Cabinets of George the Third, vol. i. p. 288.

quainted with his wishes, which would make it impossible to pretend a doubt of it."

In the further progress of this transaction, Thurlow appears with much prudence to have kept in the background, and allowed the less wary Temple to take the lead. It may be said, indeed, that Thurlow acted the part of Bertrand, and Temple the part of Raton, in the well-known French fable.

On the 11th of December the Earl asked for and obtained a private audience of the King. This is the interview described with so much spirit in that excellent satire, the Rolliad :

> " On that great day when Buckingham, by pairs,
> Ascended, Heaven-impelled, the King's back stairs,
> And panting, breathless, strained his lungs to show
> From Fox's Bill what mighty ills would flow ;
> Still, as with stammering tongue he told his tale,
> Unusual terrors Brunswick's heart assail,
> Wide starts his white wig from the Royal ear,
> And each particular hair stands stiff with fear ! "

In this audience it appears that Lord Temple urged the King to use his Royal influence against the Bill, and that the King consented. To remove all doubt upon this point, a card was written, apparently in the King's own hand, stating that " His Majesty allowed Earl Temple to say that whoever voted for the India Bill was not only not his friend, but would be considered by him as an enemy; and if these words were not strong enough, Earl Temple might use whatever words he might deem stronger and more to the purpose." There may be some doubt as to the exact words of this commission, but as to its purport and its meaning none.

Such a commission was at that time especially significant. At that time there sat in Parliament no inconsiderable number of persons who professed for His Majesty either a personal attachment or a political adherence, and who were known by the common designation of "King's friends." In the Commons the leader of this band on all occasions was Mr. Charles Jenkinson, in later years Lord Hawkesbury, and finally Earl of Liverpool. In the Lords they seem to have had no regular chief; but any Peer inclining to their sentiments would of course attach the greatest weight to the commission of Lord Temple.

But that commission could not from its very nature remain a secret; it had to be made known to many of the Peers. Those who yielded to it might be willing to keep silence, but those who were determined to stand firm divulged it as of course to their political friends. On the 15th, when the Bill was again before the House, and when Counsel at the Bar were heard against it, the many rumours already rife upon the subject were noticed vaguely by the Duke of Portland, and in more pointed terms by the Duke of Richmond. Earl Temple rose in reply. "That His Majesty," he said, "has recently honoured me with a conference is a matter of notoriety. It is not what I wish to deny, or have the power to conceal. It is the privilege of the Peers, as the hereditary counsellors of the Crown, either individually or collectively, to advise His Majesty. I did give my advice; what it was, I shall not now declare; it is lodged in

His Majesty's breast.   But though I will not declare what my advice to my Sovereign was, I will tell your Lordships negatively what it was not : it was not friendly to the principle and object of the Bill."

The effects of this advice, or rather of the commission which resulted from it, were, however, apparent that same evening.   A motion of adjournment being made, was carried against Ministers by a majority of eight.   "The Bishops waver, and the Thanes fly from us, and in my opinion the Bill will not pass," writes Colonel Fitzpatrick to his brother the same day.[3]

Still far greater was the effect of the Royal message upon the 17th of December, on the motion " that the Bill be committed."   Then after a long and keen debate the motion was negatived and the Bill thrown out by, including proxies, 95 votes against 76.   On this occasion all or nearly all the " King's friends " either took part against the Bill or stayed away.   The Prince of Wales had voted with his friends in office in the division of the 15th, but during the interval the King's aversion to the Bill was so clearly conveyed to him that he could no longer affect to doubt it, and on the 17th he was absent from the House.   Strange to say, one of the Cabinet Ministers, Lord Stormont, President of the Council, formed part of the final majority against the Bill. Stranger still, it would seem that his colleagues, considering his personal adherence to the King, bore him no ill will on that account.   Lord Holland in his notes writes of it as follows : " It is just to remark that

---

Lord Stormont, a stiff, formal man, of high Tory principles, always during his political connection with Mr. Fox conducted himself with great honour and fairness, and Mr. Fox has frequently told me that he behaved well."

In the midst of this crisis the Commons had adjourned for two days, in consequence of a death in the Speaker's family. But they met again upon the 17th. Then, and while the debate upon the India Bill in the other House was still depending, Mr. Baker, of Hertford, a personal friend of Burke, rose in his place and adverted in strong terms to the rumours of the conference between Lord Temple and the King, and he concluded by proposing a Resolution in the following terms: "That it is now necessary to declare that to report any opinion or pretended opinion of His Majesty upon any Bill or other proceeding depending in either House of Parliament, with a view to influence the votes of the Members, is a high crime and misdemeanor, derogatory to the honour of the Crown, a breach of the fundamental privileges of Parliament, and subversive of the Constitution of this country."

No sooner was the motion moved and seconded than Pitt rose. He denounced the Resolution as "one of the most unnecessary, the most frivolous and ill-timed that ever insulted the attention of the national Senate," since it neither contained any specific charge, nor yet was directed to any decisive issue. As against it he moved the Order of the Day, and he was seconded by Lord Mahon. But Lord North, speaking with especial weight as the King's Minister for so many years, warmly urged the propriety and necessity of the Resolution before the House ; and it was further supported by Fox in one of the most able and most animated of his many great speeches at this time. "The question is not," he said, "whether His Majesty shall avail himself of such advice as no one readily avows, but who is answerable for such advice. . . . . How, Sir, are Ministers situated on this ground ? Do they not come into power with a halter about their necks, by which the most contemptible wretch in the kingdom may despatch them at pleasure ? Yes : they hold their several offices, not at the option of the Sovereign, but of the very reptiles who burrow under the Throne : they act the part of puppets, and are answerable for all the folly and the ignorance, and the temerity or timidity, of some unknown juggler behind the screen !" And not content with such general terms of condemnation, Fox proceeded in no covert terms to point his invective against Pitt. "Boys without judgment, without experience of the sentiments suggested by the knowledge of the world, or the amiable decencies of a sound mind, may follow the headlong course of ambition thus precipitately, and vault into the seat while the reins of government are placed in other hands. But the Minister who can bear to act such a dishonourable part, and the country that suffers it, will be mutual plagues and curses to each other."

The masterly speech of Fox was followed by an overwhelming majority in favour of the motion—153 voting for it, and no more than 80 against it. Erskine—unabashed at his recent failure, and, rather than be silent, ready to encounter many other failures in Parliament—

then rose to move a second Resolution. This, which was carried by like numbers, declared that the House would pursue the redress of the abuses which had prevailed in the government of India, and would regard as a public enemy any person who should advise His Majesty to interrupt the discharge of this important duty.

Thus on the morning of Thursday, the 18th of December, the two Houses stood directly and keenly arrayed against each other. The Commons had pledged themselves to the principles of their India Bill, and denounced, in violent terms, the means employed against it, while the Peers, on their part, had flung out the Bill itself.

Supported by their vast majority in the Commons, Fox and his colleagues determined to stand their ground. They deemed it wisest to cast upon the King the entire responsibility of a change of Government. During the whole of the 18th, from hour to hour, the King was in expectation of receiving the resignation of his Ministers. Finding that none came, he took a step that could no longer be deferred. Very late that evening—it was indeed near midnight — Mr. Fox and Lord North, as Secretaries of State, received the King's orders, that they should deliver up their Seals of office, and send them by their Under Secretaries, since a personal interview on the occasion would be disagreeable to His Majesty. The Seals thus sent were given by the King next morning to Lord Temple, who immediately took the oaths as Secretary of State, and as such wrote letters of dismissal to the other Ministers.

That the course of the King in these transactions was

an extreme stretch of his prerogative is indisputable.
That it was, as Mr. Fox's friends have all along contended,
a manifest infringement of his Constitutional duty is not
to be so readily admitted. Perhaps we may think that,
when closely viewed, the Constitutional relation of the
Sovereign to his responsible advisers is by no means so
clear and well-defined as it might at first sight appear.
Perhaps we may come to the conclusion that it must
depend in many cases rather on good feeling and principle upon both sides than on any fixed and undeviating
rule. Let us for this inquiry assume the case of the
India Bill to be exactly such as its adversaries made it.
Here then was a Bill containing an insidious and disguised attack on the Royal Prerogative. On general
principles we can scarcely blame a King for being careful of his Prerogative, so long as we continue to applaud
each House of Parliament for being jealous of its privileges. Now, in the particular case which we suppose
before us, the Bill containing this attack had been by
the Minister so artfully and ably prepared, that in the
first instance neither the King nor yet the public at
large discerned the danger. But when the discussions
in Parliament arose, that danger was made manifest, and
painted in the strongest light by the Opposition speakers. With so much force of argument did they denounce
the Bill, that they brought a great portion of the public
round to their opinion. What then? Is the King to be
the only person in the kingdom forbidden to derive new
lights from the debates in Parliament? Is he to be
absolutely and in all cases bound to the assent which
the first draft of a measure, as glossed over by his

Ministers, may have received from him? Then if not, what course should he take? Is he bound to dismiss his Ministers at the very moment that these new lights have flashed upon his mind? Is he bound in that dismissal entirely to disregard the consideration whether that precise period may not be of all others the most inopportune for defeating their designs? Then if delay be allowed him, are his lips meanwhile to be altogether sealed? Is he bound to hide even from members of his family, from old servants or from trusted friends, the feelings or the wishes that are swelling in his breast? It will be owned, I think, by any candid inquirer that some of these questions might be found in practice most perplexing to decide. Without denying then that the course pursued in this emergency by George the Third was most unusual and most extreme, and one most undesirable to establish as a precedent, I greatly doubt whether it would be practicable to lay down with perfect clearness and precision the Constitutional rule which he is supposed to have infringed.

But whatever bolts of party indignation have been, or may be, hurled against the King or against Lord Temple, they at all events fall short of Pitt. He had taken no part in these transactions. So far as we can trace, he had not even been apprised of them beforehand. It was only after the final issue that the King, turning for aid to the only adequate antagonist of Fox, asked him to undertake his responsible support as his new Prime Minister. Nor did Pitt prove unequal to the crisis. Without one moment's faltering, he responded to the call. Thus when on the afternoon of the same day, the

19th of December, the House of Commons met—thronged with an expectant and buzzing crowd, and Fox and North taking their seats on the front Opposition benches, —there was seen to walk in a young Member, Mr. Richard Pepper Arden, holding an open paper in his hand; and soon afterwards rising in his place he moved a new Writ for the borough of Appleby, " in the room of the Right Honourable William Pitt, who, since his election, has accepted the office of First Lord of the Treasury and Chancellor of the Exchequer." So hazardous seemed the venture that, as we are assured, this motion was received with loud and general laughter on the Opposition side. The friends of Fox and North were not in the least depressed. They looked forward, and not unreasonably, to an early and triumphant resumption of their offices. They were even taunted by Lord Mulgrave, in the debate which ensued, as looking much too merry.

A discussion at once arose. Dundas, as representing the new Prime Minister, moved that the House should sit on the next day, a Saturday, to expedite the passing of the Land Tax Bill. But he did not venture to divide the House against Fox, who proposed the usual adjournment to Monday, his object being, as the event showed, rather to make manifest his power than to obstruct the progress of what he owned to be a necessary measure. In his speech Fox referred to the event of a Dissolution as certain and near impending. " No one." he cried, " would say that such a prerogative ought to be exercised merely to suit the convenience of an ambitious young man. And I here, in the face of the House, declare that if a Dissolution shall take place, and if very solid and substantial reasons are not assigned for it, I shall, if I have the honour of a seat in the next Parliament, move a very serious inquiry into the business, and bring the advisers of it to account."

To the same effect spoke also Lord North—" Though a new Writ has been moved for Appleby, I am not to be deceived by such a device. I believe that there is not a man in the House who is not sure that a Dissolution is at hand."

So exasperated indeed were the Opposition chiefs— so large the majority to back them in the House of Commons—and so doubtful as yet the prospects of a General Election—that Pitt found the greatest difficulty in forming his new Government. Many men who expressed to him their approval and good wishes had, or alleged they had, some special reason to hang back.

On the other hand, Pitt had one piece of good fortune which he had not expected. Earl Gower enjoyed at this time a large measure of public esteem. In the autumn of 1779 he had seceded from Lord North's Cabinet rather than continue the American war. In the spring of 1783 he had been solicited by the King to form an administration of his own. He was not on any terms of political connection or intercourse with Pitt. Yet at this juncture he sent through a friend a message to the new Premier. He stated that, desirous as he was of retirement for the remainder of his life, he could not be deemed a candidate for office, but that in the present distressed state of his King and country he was willing

to serve in any place where he could be useful. The
offer was eagerly accepted, and on that same day, the
20th of December, Earl Gower was declared Lord
President of the Council.

One disappointment to Pitt was, however, wholly unforeseen. He had reckoned upon his kinsman Lord
Temple to fill the office of Secretary of State, and to
lead the House of Lords; but Temple, who, on the
morning of Friday the 19th, had accepted the Seals,
suddenly, on the evening of Sunday the 21st, determined to resign them. Under all the circumstances
this was a "heavy blow and great discouragement" to
the not yet formed administration.

We obtain at this place, from Bishop Tomline, one of
those personal recollections which are so seldom to be
found in his pages. Adverting to the sudden resignation, he adds,—

"This was the only event of a public nature which I
ever knew disturb Mr. Pitt's rest while he continued
in good health. Lord Temple's resignation was determined upon at a late hour in the evening of the 21st,
and when I went into Mr. Pitt's bedroom the next
morning he told me that he had not had a moment's
sleep. He expressed great uneasiness at the state of
public affairs, at the same time declaring his fixed resolution not to abandon the situation he had undertaken,
but to make the best stand in his power, though very
doubtful of the result. Some of his confidential friends
coming to him soon after he was dressed, he entered,
with his usual composure and energy, into the discussion
of points which required immediate decision—all feeling

the present moment to be one of peculiar anxiety and difficulty." [4]

The resignation of Lord Temple was stated in the House of Commons that same day, the 22nd. His brother William, who announced the fact, attempted also to explain it. Having in the first place adverted to the Resolution which the House had passed on Mr. Baker's motion, Mr. Grenville added, " I am authorised by my Noble Relative to say that he is ready to meet any charge that shall be brought against him; and that he may not be supposed to make his situation as Minister stand in the way of, or serve as a protection or shelter from inquiry and from justice, he had that day resigned into His Majesty's hands the Seals of office with which His Majesty had so lately been pleased to honour him; so that my Noble Relative is now in his private capacity, unprotected by the influence of office. to answer for his conduct whenever he shall hear the charge that may be brought against it."

Fox rose next. He said, with something of disdain in his tone, that Lord Temple was no doubt the best judge of his own situation. He knew why he had accepted, he knew why he retired from office; but certainly no one had said that any Resolution would be levelled against the Noble Lord, and he (Mr. Fox) hoped that the members of the House would not be turned aside by that incident from the consideration of the important business which was that very evening to come before them.

[4] Life of Pitt, vol. i. p. 233.

The important business to which Fox referred was a motion by Erskine, which was made immediately afterwards in a Committee of the whole House, upon the state of the nation. It was an Address to the Crown against either a Prorogation or a Dissolution of Parliament. Mr. Bankes, as a personal friend of Pitt, rose and said that he had authority to declare that the new Prime Minister had no intention whatever to advise a Dissolution. Nevertheless Mr. Erskine, by the advice of his friends, persisted in his Address, which, after long debate but no division, was carried.

Later that same night, in a letter which Fox addressed to his confidential friend Lord Northington, we find him, notwithstanding his disclaimer in the House, refer to the secession of Lord Temple as to a great party advantage:—" I now think it necessary to despatch a servant to you to let you know that Lord Temple has this day resigned. What will follow is not yet known, but I think there can be very little doubt but our administration will again be established. The confusion of the enemy is beyond description, and the triumph of our friends proportionable." [5]

It is natural to inquire what was really the reason of this strange step on the part of Lord Temple. That reason, though often discussed, has never been clearly explained. I may therefore be forgiven if I enter at some length into this still controverted point.

In the first place it is to be observed that Lord Temple, on his resignation, at once retired to Stowe, and that

---

[5] Fox Memorials, vol. ii. p. 224.

for several years to come he took no farther part in politics; nor did he ever again fill any office in England. Secondly, it seems to be admitted on all sides that the explanation given by William Grenville in the House of Commons by no means suffices. The Resolution of Mr. Baker had passed the night before Lord Temple took office. If then that Resolution, or the personal attacks that might be expected to ensue from it, were to weigh with Lord Temple at all, they would have prevented his acceptance, and not produced his resignation, of the Seals.

Lord Macaulay, in his excellent sketch of Mr. Pitt, has made the following statement :—

" The general opinion (in December, 1783) was that there would be an immediate Dissolution ; but Pitt wisely determined to give the public feeling time to gather strength. On this point he differed from his kinsman Temple. The consequence was that Temple, who had been appointed one of the Secretaries of State, resigned his office forty-eight hours after he had accepted it."

Presuming on the cordial friendship which to my good fortune existed between Lord Macaulay and myself, I wrote to him upon this subject. While sending for his perusal an unpublished manuscript of Burke from another period, I expressed my doubts whether he had any good authority for the statement which I have here transcribed. With perfect frankness, Lord Macaulay replied as follows :—

" My dear Stanhope,   " Holly Lodge, Dec. 2, 1858.

      " I return Burke's paper. It is interesting, and very characteristic.

" I am afraid that I can find no better authority for
the account which I have given of Temple's resignation
than that of Wraxall, who tells the story very confidently
and circumstantially, but whose unsupported testimony
is of little value, even when he relates what he himself
saw and heard, and of no value when he relates what
passed in the secrecy of the Cabinet. After looking at
Tomline's narrative and at the ' Buckingham Papers,' I
am satisfied that I was wrong. Whenever Black re-
prints the article separately, as he proposes to do, the
error shall be corrected.

" Ever yours truly,

" MACAULAY."

Several weeks later Lord Macaulay pointed out to
me that the publication of the 'Cornwallis Papers,'
which had since occurred, might tend in some degree to
corroborate the statement of Wraxall. He referred to
a letter dated March 3, 1784, in which Lord Cornwallis
says, " I do not believe Lord Temple and Mr. Pitt ever
had any quarrel, and think that the former resigned
because they would not dissolve the Parliament. I
may, however, be mistaken in this."

It seems to me clear, from the concluding words, that
Lord Cornwallis spoke only from common report; and
when, in the first part, he assumes that there had been
no resentment on Lord Temple's part, he was, as will
presently be shown, quite mistaken.

There is no doubt, from what Wraxall and Lord Cornwallis write, that there was a prevalent rumour in 1784
of the resignation of Lord Temple having been caused
by his fixed desire for an immediate Dissolution ; but

the question remains how far that rumour was truly founded.

One document, hitherto unpublished, seems to me on this point decisive. There is a letter from the King to Mr. Pitt, dated April 12, 1789, and referring to Lord Temple, then Marquis of Buckingham and Lord Lieutenant of Ireland. In that letter the King speaks of "his base conduct in 1784." I know not to what these words can possibly refer, unless it be to the resignation just before the new year. Now at that very period, as we learn from other private letters of the King, His Majesty was warmly pressing a Dissolution on his Ministers, and he could not be angry with Lord Temple for holding the same opinion as himself.

Another document which bears upon this question was preserved among the Buckingham papers, and was published in 1853.[6] It is a letter of Lord Temple to Mr. Pitt only a few days after his resignation, and dated Stowe, December 29th, 1783. This letter will be found to breathe ire and resentment in every line. In it Lord Temple most bitterly complains that there has not been any mark of the King's approbation to him on account of his Lord Lieutenancy of Ireland. It appears that "various marks of favour" had been suggested by his brother William, and that Pitt had actually offered a peerage for his second son, which, however, Lord Temple thought insufficient, and declined.

This letter is further to be compared with several more written by Lord Temple in 1789, in reference to

---

[6] See the Courts and Cabinets of George the Third, vol. i. p. 291.

his second Lord Lieutenancy.   Here again we find him
pressing most warmly for some special mark of the
King's favour, and having in view a Dukedom.   For
this object he engaged the aid not only of his brother
William, but of Mr. Pitt.   The King, however, had
determined many years before to grant no more Duke-
doms except to Princes of the Blood.

On the whole then it seems to me the most probable
conclusion that in December, 1783, Lord Temple had
asked for a Dukedom, or some other personal object of
ambition.   Finding that the King refused him, and
that Mr. Pitt was not willing to make that personal
object a *sine quâ non* condition in so anxious a state of
public affairs, he flung down the Seals in anger and set
off to Stowe.

Undismayed by the adverse vote of the House of
Commons on Monday the 22nd, we find Pitt apply himself with energy all through the 23rd to complete his
appointments.   Here is his note to his friend the Duke
of Rutland :—

> " Berkeley Square, Tuesday, eleven o'clock,
> Dec. 23 (1783).

" MY DEAR DUKE,

"In this decisive moment, for my own sake
and that of the country, I trust I may have recourse to
your zeal and friendship.   My hands are so full that
I cannot be sure of calling on you.   Will you, if possible, come here at twelve?   I am to see the King at
one.

> " Ever most truly yours,
>
> " W. PITT."

The journal of Wilberforce that same day, the 23rd, has the following entry :—" Morning, Pitt's. Pitt nobly firm. Cabinet formed."

In forming his Cabinet Pitt experienced several disappointments. Already some days back his father's most intimate friend, Lord Camden, had declined to take part in the hazardous venture, and refused the Presidency of the Council. In like manner the Duke of Grafton, whom Pitt had summoned from Suffolk, refused the Privy Seal. From men also of less note and beyond the Cabinet pale there were answers in the negative. Thus for example Lord Mahon declined office, not apparently from any disinclination at that time to Mr. Pitt, but as I conjecture from his superior attachment to the pursuits of science.

Mr. Pitt proceeded to fill up the several offices—as Bishop Tomline tells us—in the best manner he could, though not exactly as he wished. Earl Gower was President of the Council. The Duke of Rutland took the Privy Seal. The Seals of Secretary of State were entrusted to two other Peers, Lord Sydney and the Marquis of Carmarthen, eldest son of the Duke of Leeds, who had been in his father's lifetime called up to the House of Lords. Lord Thurlow, almost as of course, resumed the Great Seal. Lord Howe was First Lord of the Admiralty. These with the Premier formed the new Cabinet, which was therefore of only seven persons, and of these seven one only, Pitt himself, was a member of the House of Commons.

The Duke of Richmond went back to his former office of Master-General of the Ordnance, but declined a seat in the Cabinet. But only a few weeks afterwards, as the fight grew hotter, he felt an ambition to serve in the front ranks, and he asked for and obtained the responsible post which he had at first refused.

In like manner Dundas, on whom Pitt relied as his principal assistant in debate, resumed the post which he had held in Lord Shelburne's administration as Treasurer of the Navy. Lloyd Kenyon became Attorney, and Pepper Arden Solicitor General. Of his other young friends, Pitt placed Eliot in the Board of Treasury, and Jefferies Pratt in the Board of Admiralty. William Grenville and Lord Mulgrave were (after some delay) joint-Paymasters of the Forces; George Rose and Thomas Steele joint-Secretaries of the Treasury.

In the evening of the same day, the 23rd, Pitt convened a meeting of his principal adherents in the House of Commons. Wilberforce, in his Recollections, gives of it a lively account :—" We had a great meeting that night of all Pitt's friends in Downing Street. As Pratt, Tom Steele, and I were going up to it in a hackney-coach from the House of Commons, 'Pitt must take care.' I said, 'whom he makes Secretary of the Treasury; it is rather a rogueish office.' 'Mind what you say.' answered Steele, 'for I am Secretary of the Treasury!' At Pitt's we had a long discussion, and I remember well the great penetration shown by Lord Mahon. 'What am I to do,' said Pitt, 'if they stop the Supplies?' 'They will not stop them,' said Mahon; 'it is the very thing which they will not venture to do.'"

Next day, the 24th, the King upon his Throne received the members of the House of Commons, who, with Fox at their head, brought up their Address of the 22nd. In his answer, as prepared by Pitt, the King assured them that, "after such an adjournment as the present circumstances might seem to require," he should not interrupt their meeting by any exercise of his prerogative, either of Prorogation or Dissolution. On this assurance Fox agreed that the House of Commons, after meeting again on the 26th for the issue of Writs, should adjourn for some Christmas holidays. But he insisted upon it that the adjournment should be only for the shortest period—not to extend beyond the 12th of January, and the House then to go again into Committee on the state of the nation. It was useless to divide the House against a chief who commanded a sure majority.

Fox and his friends continued sanguine of the issue. Thus he wrote to Lord Northington at Dublin:—"I neither quit your house nor dismiss one servant till I see the event of the 12th." And in the same strain spoke his friend Mrs. Crewe. "Well," she said to Wilberforce, "Mr. Pitt may do what he likes during the holidays; but depend upon it, it will be only a mince-pie administration."

So overwhelmed with business was Pitt at this period, that among Lady Chatham's papers I find only one letter from him between the 11th of November and the 16th of March. Here is what that letter says of politics:—

"Berkeley Square, Dec. 30, 1783.

"You will easily believe it is not from inclination I have been silent so long. Things are in general more promising than they have been, but in the uncertainty of effect the persuasion of not being wrong is, as you say, the best circumstance and enough; though there is satisfaction in the hopes at least of something more."

CHAPTER V.

1784.

Difficulties of Pitt's position — His India Bill — His public spirit — Fox's popularity declines — Proceedings of the "Independents" — Party conflicts in the Commons — Address to the King — Pitt attacked in his coach — Revulsion of national feeling — Schemes of Fox — The Great Seal stolen — Dissolution of Parliament.

WHEN, at the age of twenty-four, Mr. Pitt was called upon to fill the highest place in the councils of his Sovereign, he found himself surrounded by most formidable difficulties—the greatest perhaps that any Prime Minister of England ever had to grapple with. Arrayed against him was a compact majority of the House of Commons, led on by chiefs of consummate oratorical ability—by Burke and Sheridan, by Fox and Lord North. The finances, at the close of an unprosperous war, were in the utmost disorder. The commercial system with the now independent colonies was as yet undetermined, and required prompt and final regulation. Our foreign relations, which at last had left us almost without a single ally, called for vigilant foresight and conciliatory care. But as claiming precedence above all others was the East India question. It was necessary for the new Cabinet, without the loss of a single hour, to frame a new measure in place of that which the House of Lords had rejected. It was necessary also that the measure should be submitted both to the Court of Directors and the Court of Proprietors, and their approval, if possible, obtained before that of the House of Commons was asked.

By incessant labour Mr. Pitt and his colleagues attained this object. Their Draft Bill was not only prepared, but was approved by both sections of the East India body, previous to the meeting of the House of Commons on January the 12th.

The expected day came at last. Fox rose at the unusual hour of half-past two, and moved the order of the day. He was soon interrupted by the newly-elected members, Pitt among them, who came up to the table to take the oaths. When that ceremony had concluded, Pitt and Fox rose together—the Minister holding in his hand, as he stated, a Message from the King which he desired to deliver; but the Opposition chief insisted on his own previous right to speak, and the Speaker, being appealed to, decided that Mr. Fox was in possession of the House.

A debate of many hours ensued. Mr. Fox, in his principal speech, took up very dangerous ground. His great object seemed to be to secure himself against a Dissolution. With this view he ventured to assert that the Crown did not possess the right, as Burke afterwards termed it, of a " penal Dissolution "—the privilege, namely, of dissolving Parliament in the midst of a Session, and in consequence of the votes it had given. There had been no instance of the kind since the Revolution; and there was a pamphlet by Lord Somers, in which it might be thought, from some doubtful expressions, that the right was controverted. "But we are told," continued Fox, "that nothing has yet happened to make the Dissolution of the Parliament necessary. No! What does that signify? Let us go into the Committee, and make it impossible!"

Mr. Pitt, on his part, strongly pressed that the Members should not pledge themselves by any vote against him until they had an opportunity of seeing the new Bill for the government of India, which he had prepared and was ready to bring in. Being, in the course of the debate, repeatedly attacked on the point of secret influence, he was permitted to speak a second time. This he did in a tone of lofty denial and disdain. "I came up no back stairs," he said. "When I was sent for by my Sovereign to know whether I would accept of office, I necessarily went to the Royal Closet. I know of no secret influence, and I hope that my own integrity would be my guardian against that danger. This is the only answer I shall ever deign to make to such a charge; but of one thing the House may rest assured, that I will never have the meanness to act under the concealed influence of others, nor the hypocrisy to pretend, when the measures of my administration are blamed, that they were measures not of my advising. If any former Ministers" (and here he looked at Lord North) "take these charges to themselves, to them be the sting."

At half-past two in the morning the House divided on the question of going into Committee, which was carried by a majority of 39. In Committee Fox proceeded to move three Resolutions:—First, that any per-

son issuing money for the public service, without the
sanction of an Appropriation Act, would be guilty of a
high crime and misdemeanor; secondly, that an account should be rendered of all sums of money issued
since the 19th of December for services voted, but not
yet appropriated by Act of Parliament; and thirdly, to
postpone the second reading of the Mutiny Bill to the
23rd of February.

These three Resolutions being carried without dividing
the Committee, two more were moved by Lord Surrey,
and gave rise to another violent debate:—First, as to
the necessity of an administration which should have
the confidence of that House and of the public; and,
secondly, to state that the late changes in His Majesty's Councils were preceded by universal reports
of an unconstitutional abuse of His Majesty's sacred
name.

As the readiest means to get rid of these Resolutions,
Dundas moved that the Chairman should leave the
Chair; but he was defeated by the increased majority of
54, and the two further Resolutions were adopted.

It was not till the close of these stormy proceedings
that Pitt was allowed to deliver the Message from the
King. This was merely to announce, in the usual form,
that on account of the river Weser being frozen up, it
had been found necessary to disembark in England two
divisions of Hessian troops on their return from the
American contest; but that His Majesty had given
directions that as soon as the Weser should be open
they should be sent to Germany. An Address of thanks
to the King for his gracious communication was agreed

to, and at half-past seven in the morning the House adjourned.

The result was certainly, to all appearance, most inauspicious to the Government. On the very first day when Pitt appeared in the House of Commons as Prime Minister, five hostile motions were carried against him; and he was left in two minorities, the one of 39 and the other of 54. Mr. Pitt, however, was not dispirited. He gave notice, before the members separated, that he should next day move for leave to bring in his India Bill; and the King, on learning the event of the first divisions, came up from Windsor, and in an audience that same evening assured the Minister of a firmness not inferior to his own.

Next day, the 14th, according to his notice, Pitt proceeded to lay his India Bill before the House of Commons. So far, he said, from violating chartered rights, he had sought to frame his measure in amicable concert with the Company, while at the same time he trusted that it would be most effectual for the reformation of abuses. He proposed to establish a new department of State, without, however, any new salaries— a "Board of Control" which should divide with the Directors the entire administration of India, but leave the patronage untouched. "It is my idea," said Pitt, "that this should be a Board of political control, and not, as the former was, a Board of political influence." All the details of this plan were unfolded by Pitt at great length in a speech of consummate ability; but no sooner had he sat down than Fox, without allowing a moment of further consideration to his rival's scheme, started up, and, with equal ability, denounced every part of it, although on that occasion he did not divide the House.

The attacks upon the Government were now in various forms, but with incessant activity, renewed. Again and again was Pitt put on his defence. Finding that he did not resign in consequence of the proceedings on the 12th, Fox, so early as the 16th, insisted that the House should go again into Committee. There Lord Charles Spencer moved a Resolution that the continuance of the Ministers in office was contrary to Constitutional principles. After a sharp debate, the Resolution was affirmed by the diminished majority of 21.

This diminished majority may in great part be ascribed to the conciliatory temper which at this time began to appear among the independent members. In the debate upon Lord Charles's motion, there were, for the first time, public expressions of the wish that Pitt and Fox might be induced to act together as colleagues in the same Cabinet. Such a junction seemed to the more tranquil spirits to afford the only hope of safety, or at least of quiet. Foremost among those who called for it were Thomas Grosvenor, Member for Chester, and Charles Marsham, Member for Kent, both well known and esteemed. But the ablest of this respectable little band, and more especially its spokesman, was Thomas Powys, Member for Northamptonshire, an upright and active country gentleman, and not undistinguished in debate.

Mr. Powys might, with the more propriety, attempt in his speeches at least the character of mediator, since he did not at this time belong in fact to either party. He had been a follower of Fox, but had loudly condemned his coalition with Lord North. He did not like, he said, the ground on which the new Ministers came into office, but was much impressed with the tokens that he saw of the ability and public spirit of Pitt.

The next great trial of parties was on the 23rd, when Pitt's East India Bill stood for its second reading. Then Fox exerted all his influence, and on the motion for commitment the Bill was thrown out, but by a majority of no more than eight.

It will be seen from the very small majority that the House of Commons came to this last vote with some reluctance. It was felt as bringing matters to a crisis with the Ministry; it was felt to render probable an immediate Dissolution. No sooner then was the India Bill rejected, than the chiefs of the Opposition, one after another, rose, and vehemently questioned Pitt as to his intentions. The fiercest threats and the bitterest invectives were freely used. To these questions so intemperately urged the Minister gave no reply. There were loud cries from the Opposition benches for Mr. Pitt to rise, but Mr. Pitt sat still.

At length, in the midst of the tumult, started up General Conway, the former colleague of Pitt in the Shelburne administration. He was a man who in the course of a long public life had shown little vigour or decision, but who was much respected for his honourable character and his moderate counsels. Now, as often happens to weak men, he had caught the contagion of the violence around him. He inveighed in furious terms against what he called "the sulky silence" of the Minister. "The Right Hon. gentleman," he said, "is bound to explain for the sake of his own honour; but all the conduct of these Ministers," he added, "is dark and intricate. They exist only by corruption, and they are now about to dissolve Parliament after sending their agents round the country to bribe men."

But here Pitt, though with lofty calmness, interrupted Conway. He rose, he said, to order. He had a right to call upon the Right Hon. General to specify the instances where the agents of Ministers had gone about the country practising bribery. It was a statement which he believed the Right Hon. General could not bring to proof, and which, as he could not prove, he ought not to assert. For his own honour, he claimed to be the sole and sufficient judge of it; and he concluded by a most felicitous quotation (which in reply to such an onset could have been in no degree premeditated) of some words in which Scipio as a young man rebukes the veteran Fabius for his intemperate invectives: "Si nullâ aliâ re modestiâ certe et temperando linguae adolescens senem vicero."[1]

Finding that no answer could be wrung from the Minister on the point of the expected Dissolution, Fox insisted, although the hour was two in the morning and the day was Saturday, that the House should adjourn only till twelve o'clock, at which time he hoped members would attend to vindicate the honour and assert the privileges of the Commons.

---

[1] (Liv. lib. xxviii. c. 14.) The Parliamentary History at this place mentions only "a classical text," but the precise reference has been happily preserved by Bishop Tomline (Life of Pitt, vol. i. p. 299).

At the appointed hour, the House having met in large numbers, Mr. Powys rose. His emotion was such that he shed tears while he was speaking. He declared that the scene of confusion which he beheld last night had so haunted his mind that he had never since been able to divert his thoughts one moment from it. He entreated the Minister to reply, at least thus far, whether on Monday next the House might expect to meet again to proceed to business. Mr. Pitt remained silent, but Mr. Powys with the greatest earnestness renewed his question. Then at last Pitt rose. " I have laid down to myself," he said, " a rule from which I do not think I ought in duty to depart. I decline to pledge myself to the House that in any possible situation of affairs I would not advise His Majesty to dissolve Parliament. However, as the Hon. gentleman has brought the matter to a very small point, I will so far gratify him as to answer that I have no intention to prevent the meeting of the House on Monday next." Fox said nothing, and the House immediately adjourned.

While these things were passing in Parliament, Pitt had an opportunity to give a most signal proof of his public spirit in office. To this instance Mr. Powys had referred, with expressions of the highest praise, in his speech on Lord Charles's motion. It so chanced that on the 11th of January, the very day before Parliament met, Sir Edward Walpole, a younger son of the great Sir Robert, had died. By his death there fell in the Clerk-ship of the Pells, a sinecure place for life, worth 3000*l.* a-year. It was in the gift of the Prime Minister, and tenable with a seat in the House of Commons. Every

one expected that Pitt would take the office for himself.
Such a course would have been in complete conformity
with the feelings and the practice of his age. Such a
course was strongly advised by his private friends. Such
a course was commended to him by a stronger temptation than any of his predecessors in the premiership, his
father alone excepted, can have felt. Unlike the rest,
he had a most slender patrimony. If he failed in his
struggle with the Opposition, he could only return to his
practice at the Bar, and that he would so fail was the
common belief. It is plain from the private letters of
the time, that many even of those who wished him victory, by no means expected it; at the very best it was
a perilous and doubtful issue. But by taking for himself the brilliant prize which was already in his hands,
he might make himself independent, so far as fortune
went, of all party vicissitudes. He might, with 3000*l.*
a-year secured to him, apply himself wholly to the aims
of public life.

But as Wilberforce had lately said, Pitt was " nobly
firm." Instead of taking the office for himself, he determined to save its income to the public. He undertook to efface a scandalous job which Lord Rockingham
had perpetrated. That well-meaning, but most feeble
nobleman, during his last administration, had sanctioned as a Government measure the Bill for Economical
Reform drawn up by Burke. According to that Bill the
Crown was precluded from granting a pension to any
higher amount than 300*l.* a-year. But while that Bill
was still before Parliament, and while therefore its
clauses were only morally binding on its authors, Lord

Rockingham had granted a pension more than tenfold beyond the limits which he was seeking to enact—a pension, namely, of 3200*l.* a-year to Colonel Barré. By this grant he was certainly not seeking profits or emoluments for himself. He was not even seeking them for any of his personal friends. His object was to gratify and conciliate the section of Lord Shelburne, with which he was at that time bound up in administration. He had no ill design, but it is lamentable that he failed to see the glaring contrast between the legislation which he proposed, and the course which he pursued.

To obliterate the pension which had been—to say the least—so improvidently granted, Pitt made arrangements that Barré should now resign it, receiving in return the Clerkship of the Pells for life. This appointment made at once a strong impression on the country. It fixed as on a rock for the whole of his life the character of Pitt for personal disinterestedness. "It is a great thing," says Lord Macaulay, "for a man who has only three hundred a-year to be able to show that he considers three thousand a-year as mere dirt beneath his feet when compared with the public interest and the public esteem."

Two or three weeks after the event we find Lord Thurlow, in a debate of the House of Lords, refer to this patriotic act in terms of manly frankness :—" I must acknowledge," he said, " that I was shabby enough to advise Mr. Pitt to take this office, as it had so fairly fallen into his hands ; and I believe I should have been shabby enough to have done so myself, since other

great and exalted characters had so recently set me the
example." Bishop Tomline states that he saw Colonel
Barré soon after this offer was made him, and that
nothing could exceed the warm terms in which he spoke
of it in a public view :—" Sir," said Barré, " it is the act
of a man who feels that he stands upon a high eminence
in the eyes of that country which he is destined to
govern."

There were other favourable indications in the country.
Fox in his ardour had certainly overshot his mark. He
had made it with his Sovereign a struggle as of life and
death. He had made it, as Dr. Johnson afterwards
said, a contest whether the nation should be ruled by the
sceptre of George the Third, or by the tongue of Fox.[2]
On the 16th of December he had joined in a Resolution
against the King's conduct, when not yet dismissed from
the King's service. On the 12th of January he had
seemed to question two of the most important and most
undoubted of the King's prerogatives—the right to
appoint the Ministers, and the right to dissolve the
Parliament. He would not grant the ordinary courtesy
to postpone his attacks in the House of Commons until
after the re-election and re-appearance of the new
Minister. He refused the least respite, the smallest
interval for consideration of the measures which that
Minister might desire to bring forward. So much
violence of conduct, so much acrimony of invective, are
not easily to be defended. At the present day a writer
of high authority, who loves the memory of Fox, but

---

[2] Conversation with Boswell at Oxford, June 10, 1784.

who has still higher regard for the cause of truth and
law, gives it as his opinion that "the conduct of
Mr. Fox and the majority of the House of Commons
was wanting in dignity and in adherence to the spirit of
the Constitution." [3]

Such also grew to be in great measure the public
opinion at the time. The violent conduct of Fox served
as a counterpoise to the violent conduct of the King.
Men began to forget the Royal interference with the
votes of the House of Lords, as they beheld night after
night the most unbridled faction triumphant in the
House of Commons.

Pitt, with great sagacity, discerned those signs of the
times. He saw that the popularity of Fox had waned,
but not departed. He saw that the public opinion was
changing, but not yet changed. He saw that although
an immediate Dissolution might gain him some votes,
a deferred Dissolution might gain him many more.
Therefore, when on the rejection of his India Bill upon
the 23rd of January, he was pressed by several friends
to appeal at once to the people, and pressed by no one
more warmly than by the King. Pitt did not yield
to the Royal solicitations any more than to the Parliamentary attacks; and he practised that hardest of all
lessons to an eager mind in a hard-run contest—to
wait.

The battle in the House of Commons therefore recom-
menced. In debates, which often extended beyond the

---

[3] These are the words of Lord John Russell.   Fox Memorials,
vol. ii. p. 229.

morning dawn, Pitt was again assailed by the utmost force of eloquence, and the utmost acrimony of invective. The public beheld with astonishment the young man of twenty-four—the boy, as his adversaries love to call him —wage this unequal conflict almost single-handed. The common idea seems to have been that the more numerous and experienced party of the late administration must ere long prevail. As Gibbon once exclaimed in a most picturesque phrase,—" Depend upon it Billy's painted galley must soon sink under Charles's black collier." [1]

Up to this time the Lords had remained spectators of the contest. But an opportunity now arose for them to strike a blow. On the 4th of February the Earl of Effingham brought forward a motion— grounded on some late Resolutions—which charged the House of Commons with attempting of their own authority to suspend the execution of the law. The motion was affirmed by 100 votes against 53, and an Address to the King being framed from it, and presented, received from His Majesty a most gracious reply.

The King's prerogative was also brought into action. His Majesty had refused to create any Peers at the request of the Duke of Portland, but was most willing to do so at the request of Mr. Pitt. So early as the 30th of December Thomas Pitt had been raised to the Upper House as Lord Camelford; and before the close of January there was a batch of three. Mr. Eliot, one of the Members for Cornwall, and the father of Pitt's

---

[1] See the Reminiscences of Charles Butler, vol. i. p. 161.

friend, became Lord Eliot. An English Barony was granted to Mr. Henry Thynne as Lord Carteret, and another to the Duke of Northumberland, to descend to his second son. These creations were in a most unusual manner bitterly inveighed against by Mr. Fox in the House of Commons. Indeed it might be difficult to say which branch of the Royal Prerogatives Mr. Fox at that period would have been content to spare.

At this period also Pitt found an opportunity, most welcome to his feelings, to provide for both the tutors of his youth. Mr. Wilson became a Canon of Windsor, and Mr. Pretyman a Canon of Westminster. The last appointment had the further advantage, as it was considered, that it did not call Mr. Pretyman from town. He remained in Downing Street with the Prime Minister, and filled for some time longer the place of his private secretary. Mr. Pretyman, in the same year that he received this preferment, married Elizabeth, daughter of Thomas Maltby, Esq. She became ere long an intimate friend of Lady Harriot Pitt.

Pitt found also that he could no longer defer his arrangements with respect to Ireland. He induced his friend the Duke of Rutland to undertake the office of Lord Lieutenant, and adjoined to him an excellent man of business, Mr. Thomas Orde. The Duke set out for his mission in the middle of February, and immediately afterwards we find Pitt write to him as follows:

" My dear Duke,   " Berkeley Square, Feb. 17, 1784.

"Nothing passed of material consequence yesterday. The House came to Resolutions relative to the proceedings of the Lords which will not have much

effect one way or other. The House, however, sat so
late that we adjourned till to-morrow. We shall then
probably come to the question of postponing the supplies,
though I think the enemy rather flinches. What the
consequence will be is as doubtful as when you left us.
At all events, I trust nothing can arise to interrupt
your progress; for come what may, your taking possession is, I think, of the utmost consequence. I hope to
be able to send you further accounts before you reach
Holyhead. My brother has given me the memorandums
you left, which must be managed as well as they can.
The *independents* are still indefatigable for Coalition,
but as ineffectual as ever.

" Believe me always, my dear Duke, &c.,

" W. PITT."

The proceedings of these *independents* will now require
some detail. So early as the 26th of January they had
held a meeting at the St. Alban's Tavern. They had
met to the number of fifty-three, and placed in the chair
Mr. Thomas Grosvenor. They had felt that the two
great rival champions, flushed with their nightly conflicts
in the House of Commons, could scarcely be expected
to confer in the day time, and to negotiate a treaty of
peace with any prospect of success. Under such circumstances it seemed to them that the Duke of Portland, so
lately the First Lord of the Treasury, would be the
most proper representative of Fox's side. An Address
was agreed to and subscribed by all the Members present, entreating the Duke and Mr. Pitt to communicate
with each other, and endeavour to remove every impediment to a cordial concert of measures. A Special Committee also was appointed to present the Address and
to assist in the negotiation.

To this overture Pitt responded with the utmost frankness. He declared that whatever might be the difficulties in the way of the union itself, there was no difficulty on his part in the way of an immediate intercourse with the Duke of Portland on the matter that had been suggested to them. But the Duke having consulted Fox, said that he must decline even to meet the Prime Minister, until he had first, in compliance with the vote of the House of Commons, resigned his office. To this preliminary condition Pitt, as was natural, demurred. Thus the gentlemen of the St. Alban's had the mortification to find that so far from effecting a junction, they could not even effect an interview.

By no means yet discouraged, these gentlemen induced Mr. Grosvenor, as their Chairman, to move a Resolution in the House of Commons, on the 2nd of February, declaring that the state of the country called for an extended and united Ministry. Both Pitt and Fox held nearly the same language on this subject. Both declared that they felt no personal objections, but would not consent to combine except on public principles. On this general ground the motion of Mr. Grosvenor passed without a single negative.

But no sooner was this motion disposed of than Mr. Coke of Norfolk, acting in concert with Fox, rose to move another Resolution—that the continuance of the present Ministers in office was an obstacle in the way of forming another administration, which should have the confidence of the House of Commons.

It was still insisted by Fox and Portland—for the dignity, as they said, of the House of Commons—that

Pitt should absolutely resign his office before they would hold a single conference with him respecting the new arrangements. " With what regard to personal honour or public principle can this be expected ? " cried Pitt, with lofty indignation, in the course of this debate. " What, Sir, that I, defending—as I believe myself to do—the fortress of the Constitution, and that fortress alone, should consent to march out of it with a halter about my neck, change my armour, and meanly beg to be re-admitted as a volunteer in the army of the enemy ! . . . . The sacrifice of the sentiments of men of honour is no light matter ; and when it is considered how much was to be given up to open a negotiation—what insulting attacks had been made, and what clamours had been excited—I think that some regard ought to be paid to my being willing to meet the wishes of these respectable gentlemen, who call for an union of parties." But not-withstanding this earnest appeal, the motion of Mr. Coke was carried in a full House by a majority of 19.

The truth is, that except the gentlemen at the St. Alban's Tavern, none of the parties to this negotiation had much wish for its success. The King had given his consent to it with great reluctance. Pitt was determined to bate nothing of his honour. Fox was sanguine of being borne back to office on the shoulders of the House of Commons. At his instigation the Duke of Portland made every possible difficulty. First he must see the King's writing ; next he must see the King himself. The former point was conceded, and the second all but promised. Then the Duke began to cavil at Pitt's phrase of a junction " on fair and equal terms." Instead

of the word "equal" His Grace desired to use the word
"equitable," the object being manifestly that Fox might
obtain a large preponderance, and leave only a few
crumbs of office to Pitt's friends. On this subject Pitt
finally wrote as follows to Mr. Powys:

"Feb. 29, 1784.

"Mr. Pitt has all along felt that explanation on all
the particulars, both of measures and arrangements,
with a view to the formation of a new administration,
would be best obtained by personal and confidential intercourse. On this idea Mr. Pitt has not attempted to
define in what manner the principle of *equality* should
be applied to all the particulars of arrangements, nor
discuss by what precise mode it may be best carried
into effect; but he is so convinced that it is impossible
to form any union except on that principle, that it
would be in vain to proceed, if there is any objection to
its being stated in the outset that the object for which
His Majesty calls on the Duke of Portland and Mr. Pitt
to confer is the formation of a new administration on a
wide basis, and on a fair and *equal* footing."

But the Duke of Portland would not give way; and
at this point, to the great concern of the St. Alban's
gentlemen, the whole negotiation ended.

On a review of all these semi-diplomatic proceedings,
it might at first sight be supposed that the main obstacle
to them turned on two points: first, the position of Lord
North; and secondly, the plan of Fox for the government of India; but with neither was this the case. It
is no more than justice to the Minister of the American
war if I point out how frank, how fair, how thoroughly

in the spirit of a gentleman, was his conduct at this crisis. Pitt had openly declared that he never would consent to act with Lord North as a colleague. This declaration, though made entirely on public grounds, might well justify some strong resentment on the other side; but, far from this, Lord North was eager to see Fox and Pitt united. "And God forbid," he said in Parliament, "that I should be the person to stand in the way of so great and necessary a measure." He plainly intimated that in such a case he should, with the greatest readiness, relinquish all pretensions of his own.

With respect to the East India Bill, Fox, seeing the unpopularity of his former measure, had been forward and eager to declare in Parliament that he was willing to give up some of its chief provisions. In private he was still more explicit. He told Mr. Marsham, on the part of the St. Alban's gentlemen—and Marsham afterwards repeated it in the House of Commons—that "provided Mr. Pitt would agree that the government of India should be in this country, and should be permanent at least for a certain number of years, he would leave it to that Right Honourable gentleman to settle the point of patronage as he pleased. With this information" (thus continued Marsham) "I waited on the Minister, who told me that the point of patronage being thus given up, an opening was so far made to a negotiation." [5]

It is not to be imagined that this negotiation, while it still went on, had suspended the party conflicts in the

---

[5] Parl. Hist., vol. xxiv. p. 633.

House of Commons. There, on the contrary, the battle continued; and it was indeed, as it has been called, "a battle of giants." Scarce any debate which did not elicit a most masterly speech of Fox, and another not less able of Pitt upon the other side—each enforcing the same topics with an ever fresh variety of illustration and of language. Thus how happily, on one occasion, does Fox advert to a celebrated passage from Lord Chatham in defence of his own coalition with Lord North!—"I recollect," he said, "to have seen a beautiful speech of a near relation of the Right Honourable gentleman over against me, in which, to discredit a coalition formerly made between the Duke of Newcastle and my father, it was compared to the junction of the Rhone and the Saone. Whatever the effect and truth and dread of that comparison might have been at that time and upon that occasion, I am not at all afraid of it now. I would not have admitted that great and illustrious person, were he now living, to have compared the late Coalition to the Rhone and the Saone as they join at Lyons, where the one may be said to be too calm and tranquil and gentle, the other to have too much violence and rapidity; but I would have advised him to take a view of those rivers a hundred miles lower down, where, having mingled and united their waters, instead of the contrast they exhibited at their junction, they had become a broad, great, and most powerful stream, flowing with the useful velocity that does not injure, but adorns and benefits the country through which it passes. This is a just type of the late Coalition; and I will venture to assert, after mature experience, that whatever the enemies of it may have hoped, it is as impossible now to disunite or separate its parts as it would be to separate the waters of those united streams."

On the other hand, with how much admirable force and spirit did Pitt vindicate his own position and the King's!—"Where" (with these words did he close one of his most celebrated speeches), "where is now the boasted equipoise of the British Constitution? Where is now that balance among the three branches of the Legislature which our ancestors have meted out to each with so much care? Where is the independence—nay, where is even the safety of any one prerogative of the Crown, or even of the Crown itself, if its prerogative of naming Ministers is to be usurped by this House, or if—which is precisely the same thing—its nomination of them is to be negatived by us without stating any one ground of distrust in the men, and without suffering ourselves to have any experience of their measures? Dreadful therefore as the conflict is, my conscience, my duty, my fixed regard for the Constitution of our ancestors, maintain me still in this arduous post. It is not any proud contempt or defiance of the Constitutional Resolutions of this House—it is no personal point of honour, much less is it any lust of power—that makes me still cling to office. The situation of the times requires of me, and, I will add, the country calls aloud to me, that I should defend this castle, and I am determined therefore that I will defend it!"

On the 18th of February Fox ventured an experiment upon the feelings of the House. He proposed that the

Report of the Committee of Supply, which stood for that evening, should be postponed for only three days. He disclaimed all intention of obstructing the public business, and pleaded only for a short delay that the House might have leisure to consider the anomalous position of the Government. Pitt treated the motion as a direct refusal of supply, and on a division it was carried by a majority of only 9.

On the 20th Mr. Powys moved and resolved that the House relied on the King's readiness to form an united and efficient administration. But several more of the independent members appear on this occasion to have rallied round Mr. Powys. His Resolution was carried by a majority of 20, and an Address to the King, which Fox immediately founded upon it, by 21. To give the more solemnity to this Address, it was ordered to be presented by the whole House. Then, after a most stormy sitting, and at past five in the morning, the House adjourned.

On the 25th accordingly, the Speaker, attended by a numerous train of members, was summoned to the Royal presence, and heard the King deliver the reply which his Minister had carefully prepared. The tone was frank and explicit, and at the same time conciliatory. His Majesty stated the very recent endeavours which he had made to effect an union of parties on a fair and equal footing, and lamented that these endeavours should have failed. He declared himself unable to perceive how such an object could in any degree be advanced by the dismissal of those at present in his service, more especially as no specific charge was urged against them. " And under these circumstances," said the King in conclusion, " I trust my faithful Commons will not wish that the essential offices of Executive Government should be vacated until I see a prospect that such a plan of union as I have called for, and they have pointed out, may be carried into effect."

Much chafed at this new rebuff, Fox determined that on the 1st of March he would himself move another Address of the same tenor, but in stronger terms.

During this interval, however, Pitt was exposed to an onset of a different nature. Earlier in the month the Corporation of London had passed a vote of thanks to him for his public conduct, as also the freedom of the City to be presented in a gold box of the value of one hundred guineas. A Committee appointed to carry these Resolutions into effect went on Saturday the 28th in procession—preceded by the City Marshal, and accompanied by the Sheriffs and Town Clerk—to the house in Berkeley Square, where Pitt then resided with his brother Lord Chatham. After the presentation of the Vote of Thanks and gold box the whole party went on together to the hall of the Grocers' Company in the Poultry, where the Prime Minister was engaged to dine. Great crowds had been assembled in Berkeley Square from an early hour in the morning, and an immense concourse of people joined the procession after it left Lord Chatham's house, marching through the City amidst the loudest acclamations, and shouts of welcome. At Grocers' Hall Pitt was also loudly cheered as he took the usual oath administered to freemen, and was addressed in a speech of most laudatory purport by the Chamberlain—no other than John Wilkes. In returning at night there was the same throng, there were the same acclamations. Such tokens of the rising popular favour to Pitt must have been of course gall and wormwood to those who desired to be called exclusively the " Friends of the People." Thus, at night, when the crowd of artisans was dragging up St. James's Street the coach in which sat Pitt himself, Lord Chatham, and Lord Mahon, and when they had come opposite Brooks's Club, at that period the stronghold of his political opponents, the coach was suddenly attacked by men armed with bludgeons and broken chair-poles, among whom— so at least it was at the time asserted and believed—were seen several members of the Club. Some of the rioters made their way to the carriage, forced open the door, and aimed blows at the Prime Minister, which were, with some difficulty, warded off by his brother's arm. At length Mr. Pitt and his companions, after a severe struggle, made their way into White's Club. Hearing of this attack, " I called there," writes Wilberforce, " and to bed about three." The servants were much bruised, and the carriage was nearly demolished.

At a later period we find the authors of the " Political Eclogues" refer to this transaction, which, for their own credit, surely they had better have avoided. But being ashamed to name Mr. Pitt in connexion with it, they transfer their raillery to Lord Mahon :—

> " Ah ! why Mahon's disastrous fate record ?
> Alas, how fear can change the fiercest Lord !
> See the sad sequel of the Grocers' treat ;
> Behold him dashing up St. James's Street,
> Pelted and scared by Brooks's hellish sprites,
> And vainly fluttering round the door of White's."

On the day but one ensuing, the 1st of March, Fox fulfilled his intention of moving a new Address to the Crown for the dismissal of Ministers. He was supported by Lord Surrey and General Conway; opposed by Pitt, Wilberforce, and Sir William Dolben. In the division which ensued the Address was carried by a majority of 12. But the only result from it was an answer from the King on the 4th, declining compliance on the grounds which he had already stated. What more was now the Opposition to do?

Fox during the greater part of February appears to have thought the game in his own hands. The time had passed when Pitt could dissolve the Parliament, and convene another previous to the 25th of March, on which day the Mutiny Act would expire. And by his command of the majority within the House, Fox expected that he could at any time deal as he pleased, either with the new Mutiny Bill or the Supplies, and thus force his rival to an unconditional surrender. But in this view he had not reckoned on the revulsion of national feeling.

Within a month from the re-assembling of the House symptoms of this change appeared. The Corporation, and also the merchants and traders of London, took the lead; they presented Addresses to the King, in which they expressed their approval of the conduct of the House of Lords in rejecting Mr. Fox's India Bill, and thanked His Majesty for dismissing his late Ministers. Several other towns and districts immediately bestirred themselves to follow this example, and sent in Address upon Address of the same kind. The earliest of these were scoffed at and derided by Fox as mere make-believes:—"To such shifts and impositions," he cried, "are the Ministers and those who support them driven to prop up their tottering fabric!" But, although Fox might thus delude himself as to the first few of the Addresses, the time came when he could no longer close his eyes to their growing number.

The effect on others was at all events clear. Several watchers of the times in the House of Commons, who had hitherto been most staunch in Opposition, began to waver and hang back. Already, after the vote which they had given with Fox, postponing the Supplies for only two months, several Members—no doubt pressed by their constituents still more than by their consciences—had risen in their place to protest most earnestly—one Member even as he said upon his honour—that they had never meant, never wished, never dreamt to refuse their Sovereign a Supply. And Fox saw with bitter mortification that he could no longer propose any vote of the same kind with the smallest prospect of success.

Still, however, one resource remained. Fox hoped that, though he could not stop the Supplies, he might shorten the Mutiny Bill. On two occasions in debate he sounded the House as to the propriety of passing a Mutiny Bill for only a month or six weeks, so that their privileges might not be curtailed, nor their period of Session broken through. In this suggestion he was zealously supported by the ancient champion of preroga-tive, Lord North. But here again the force of public feeling told against him. The members for cities and counties could scarcely venture to give such votes in the teeth of the loyal Addresses that were daily pouring in. Under such circumstances the idea of a short Mutiny Bill was so coldly received that it could not be pressed. Fox had no alternative but to relinquish the present struggle, and lie in wait for any future slips of his opponent. And thus the contests between these mighty statesmen were in truth decided by the voice of the nation, even before it was appealed to in due form by a Dissolution.

But before Fox threw down his arms he determined to aim another blow. It was his object both to put on record the maxims which he had recently maintained, and to try the numbers that might still adhere to him. He gave notice that on the 8th he would move for the adoption of the House a long state-paper. This he called a Representation to the King, though in fact it was rather intended as a manifesto to the people. It had been drawn up by Burke with great care and skill.

The rumour ran already that this was to be the last great movement on Fox's side. By eleven o'clock in the morning the gallery for strangers was thronged. The gentlemen who could obtain admittance sat with the utmost patience from that hour till the meeting of the House at four. Then a severe disappointment was in store for them. Then Sir James Lowther by a freak of capricious displeasure insisted on the unwise privilege which is still allowed even to any single member, and ordered the gallery to be cleared. The loss has extended even to future times, since it has deprived them of all except the most summary reports

of this memorable and crowning debate. At length at
midnight, and in breathless suspense, the House divided.
The motion was found to be carried, but by a majority
of only one, the numbers being 190 and 191. Such a
result was felt to be at once decisive. We may picture
to ourselves the blank looks of the Opposition, and the
rising cheers of the Ministerial ranks.

Next day, the 9th of March, came on the long-expected Committee on the Mutiny Bill. When the
Secretary at War moved in the customary form that
the blank as to the time should be filled up for the usual
period of one year, it was found that in spite of all the
previous threats no opposition was attempted. Only
two independent Members, Sir Matthew White Ridley
and Mr. Powys, rose to lament what they termed the
degradation of the House. "Not a century ago," cried
Mr. Powys, "a vote of the Commons could bestow a
Crown; now it cannot even procure the dismissal of a
Minister!" Sir Matthew White Ridley on his part
declared—no doubt as a remedy to the evils complained of—that he had resolved to cease his own
attendance in a House which had been sacrificed by its
constituents.

On the same day we find Pitt write as follows to the
Duke of Rutland:

"Berkeley Square, Tuesday night,
"My dear Duke,   March 10, 1784.

"I am happy more than I can tell you in all the
good accounts you have sent us from Ireland. I ought
long before this to have made you some return, but I

could never have done it so well as this evening. We yesterday were beat only by *one*, on the concluding measure of Opposition, a long representation to the King, intended as a manifesto to the public, where its effect is not much to be dreaded. To-day the Mutiny Bill has gone through the Committee without any opposition (after all the threats) to the duration for a twelvemonth. The enemy seem indeed to be on their backs, though certainly the game left in our hands is still difficult enough. They give out that they do not mean to oppose supplies, or give any interruption to business; but their object is certainly to lie in wait, or at least catch us in some scrape, that they may make our ground worse with the public before any appeal is made there. The sooner that can be done I think the better, and I hope the difficulties in the way are vanishing.

"You see I am so full of English politics that I hardly say a word on Irish, though I am sure you have a right to expect a considerable mixture of them. Another messenger will follow this in a day or two, and I will then acquit my promise of sending the paper Orde left with me, with the necessary remarks. . . . . I write now in great haste, and tired to death, even with victory, for I think our present state is entitled to that name. Adieu, my dear Duke.

"Believe me ever yours,

"W. PITT."

Thus had Pitt remained the conqueror in the hard fight which he had fought with such unflinching courage and such consummate skill—worn out indeed as he describes himself, and as it were sinking to the ground with the labours of the conflict, but grasping firmly the palms of triumph in his hand.

A few days later he wrote to Lady Chatham also:

> "Downing Street, Tuesday night,
> March 16 (1784).
>
> "MY DEAR MOTHER,
>
> "Though it is in literal truth but a single moment I have, I cannot help employing it to thank you a thousand and a thousand times for the pleasure of your letter. I certainly feel our present situation a triumph, at least compared with what it was. The joy of it is indeed doubled by the reflection of its extending and contributing to your satisfaction. Among other benefits I begin to expect every day a little more leisure, and to have some time for reading and writing pleasanter papers than those of business.
>
> "Ever, my dear Mother, &c.,
>
> "W. PITT."

Obviously in this state of public feeling, it had become the game of Fox to offer no obstruction to public measures, and afford no plea for the Dissolution of Parliament. Thus Pitt was enabled to carry without hindrance the necessary votes of Supply, but did not propose an Appropriation Bill, on which his enemy might have made a stand with some advantage. During this time he was constantly plied with questions and invectives as to the expected Dissolution. But he remained steadily silent. At length, on the 23rd, all the necessary preparations were completed, and we find Pitt announce the fact as follows to the Duke of Rutland:

"Downing Street, Tuesday night,
March 23, 1784.

"MY DEAR DUKE,

"The interesting circumstances of the present moment, though they are a double reason for my writing to you, hardly leave me the time to do it. *Per tot discrimina rerum*, we are at length arrived within sight of a Dissolution. The Bill to continue the powers of regulating the intercourse with America to the 20th of June will pass the House of Lords to-day. That and the Mutiny Bill will receive the Royal Assent to-morrow, and the King will then make a short speech and dissolve the Parliament. Our calculations for the new elections are very favourable, and the spirit of the people seems still progressive in our favour. The new Parliament may meet about the 15th or 16th of May, and I hope we may so employ the interval as to have all the necessary business rapidly brought on, and make the Session a short one. . . . .

"We shall now soon have a little more leisure, and be better able to attend to real business in a regular way, instead of the occurrences of the day.

"Believe me, &c.,

"W. PITT."

Everything therefore was brought in readiness for the Dissolution of Parliament. But at this very juncture there occurred a most strange event. Early in the morning of the 24th some thieves broke into the back part of the house of the Lord Chancellor, in Great Ormond Street, which at that time bordered on the open fields. They went up stairs into the room adjoining the study, where they found the Great Seal of England, with a small sum of money and two silver-hilted swords. All these they carried off without alarming any of the servants, and though a reward was afterwards offered for their discovery, they were never traced.

When the Chancellor rose and was apprised of this singular robbery, he hastened to the house of Mr. Pitt, and both Ministers without delay waited upon the King. The Great Seal being essential for a Dissolution, its disappearance at the very time when it was most needed might well cause great suspicion, as well as some perplexity. But Pitt took the promptest measures; he summoned a council to meet at St. James's Palace the same morning, and there an order was issued that a new Great Seal, with the date of 1784, should be prepared with the least possible delay. It was promised that, by employing able workmen all through the night, this necessary work should be completed by noon the next day.

That same morning Pitt found time for a letter to his friend in Yorkshire.

"DEAR WILBERFORCE,

"Parliament will be prorogued to-day and dissolved to-morrow. The latter operation has been in some danger of delay by a curious manœuvre, that of stealing the Great Seal last night from the Chancellor's, but we shall have a new one ready in time.

"I send you a copy of the Speech which will be made in two hours from the Throne. You may speak of it in the *past* tense, instead of the *future*.

"A letter accompanies this from Lord Mahon to Wyvill, which you will be so good as to give him.

K 3

I am told Sir Robert Hildyard is the right candidate for the county. You must take care to keep all our friends together, and to *tear the enemy to pieces.*

"I set out this evening for Cambridge, where I expect, notwithstanding your boding, to find everything favourable. I am sure, however, to find a retreat at Bath.

"Ever faithfully yours,

"W. Pitt."

The requisite measures having thus been taken, the King, according to his original intention, went down to the House of Lords the same afternoon, and in a short Speech closed this eventful scene. "On a full consideration," thus began His Majesty, "of the present situation of affairs, and of the extraordinary circumstances which have produced it, I am induced to put an end to this Session of Parliament. I feel it a duty which I owe to the Constitution and to the country in such a situation, to recur as speedily as possible to the sense of my people by calling a new Parliament. . . And I trust that the various important objects which will require consideration may be afterwards proceeded upon with less interruption and with happier effect." Next day, the new Great Seal being ready according to promise, the Parliament was dissolved by Royal Proclamation.

This disappearance of the Great Seal has ever since remained a mystery. It may be observed that in his letter to Wilberforce Pitt speaks of it as "a curious manœuvre." Certainly it seems difficult to suppose that a theft so critically timed was altogether unconnected with political design. On the other hand, no man of

common candour will entertain the least suspicion that
Fox or North, or any one of the Whig chiefs, was in any
measure cognisant of this mean and criminal device.
Such a slander against them would only recoil on the
man who made it. But their party, like every other in
England, both before and since, had no doubt within,
or rather behind its ranks, some low runners ready to
perform, without the knowledge of their leaders, any
dirty trick which they might think of service, and
the dirtier the better to their taste. Such runners
would have been constantly hearing that a Dissolution
at that juncture might be the ruin of their party views :
that even a few days' delay might be of service, as giving the people time to cool. Can it be deemed incredible that under such circumstances even common
thieves and burglars should be taken into pay by men
in real fact perhaps baser than thieves and burglars are ?
It may be objected that on this supposition a greatly
overstrained importance was attached to the possession
of the Great Seal. But we may well imagine that an
humble and heated partisan should be under the same
delusion as was, in 1688, the King of England himself,
when, hoping to embarrass his successor, he dropped his
Great Seal into the Thames.

CHAPTER VI.

1784.

Pitt elected for the University of Cambridge, and Wilberforce for the County of York — Fox's Westminster Contest — Numerous defeats of Fox's friends — New Peerages — Meeting of Parliament — Predominance of Pitt — Disorder of the Finances — Frauds on the Revenue — Pitt's Budget — his India Bill — Westminster Scrutiny — Restoration of Forfeited Estates in Scotland — Letters to Lady Chatham — Promotions in the Peerage — Lord Camden President of the Council.

Now rose the war-cry of the hustings throughout England. Almost everywhere Fox's banner was unfurled, and almost everywhere struck down. The first election in point of time was as usual for the City. There Pitt was put in nomination without his knowledge or consent, and the show of hands was declared to be in his favour, but when apprised of the fact he declined the poll. He was pressed to stand for several other cities and towns, more especially for the city of Bath, which his father had represented ; and the King was vexed at his refusal of this offer. But the choice of Pitt was already made. He had determined, as we have seen, to offer himself again for the University of Cambridge.

As another candidate on the same side, Pitt was aided by the eldest son of the Duke of Grafton, his father's friend. They were opposed by the two late Members, Mr. John Townshend and Mr. Mansfield, both of whom had held office in the Coalition Ministry. After a keen contest Mr. Pitt and Lord Euston were returned—Pitt at the head of the poll. It was a great triumph, and no merely fleeting one, for Pitt continued to represent the University during the remainder of his life.

It has been said that Paley, who was then at Cambridge, suggested one evening as a fitting text for an University sermon: "There is a lad here which hath five barley loaves and two small fishes; but what are they among so many?" But the author, whoever he was, of this pleasantry, altogether mistook the public temper of the time. In most cases the electors voted without views of personal interest; in some cases they voted even against views of personal interest.

Such was the fact, for example, in the strongholds of the Whig estates. Thus in Norfolk the late Member had been Mr. Coke, lord of the vast domains of Holkham—a gentleman who, according to his own opinion, as stated in his Address to the county, had played "a distinguished part" in opposing the American War. But notwithstanding his alleged claims of distinction, and his much more certain claims of property, Mr. Coke found it necessary to decline the contest.

But of all the contests of this period the most important in that point of view was for the county of York. That great county, not yet at election times severed into Ridings, had been under the sway of the Whig Houses. Bolton Abbey, Castle Howard, and Wentworth Park had claimed the right to dictate at the hustings. It was not till 1780 that the spirit of the county rose. "Hitherto"—so in that year spoke Sir George Savile—"I have been elected in Lord Rockingham's dining-room. Now

I am returned by my constituents." And in 1784 the spirit of the county rose higher still. In 1784 the independent freeholders of Yorkshire boldly confronted the great Houses, and insisted on returning, in conjunction with the heir of Duncombe Park, a banker's son, of few years and of scarcely tried abilities, though destined to a high place in his country's annals—Mr. Wilberforce. With the help of the country-gentlemen they raised the vast sum of 18,662l. for the expense of the election; and so great was their show of numbers and of resolution, that the candidates upon the other side did not venture to stand a contest. Wilberforce was also returned at the head of the poll by his former constituents at Hull. " I can never congratulate you enough on such glorious success," wrote the Prime Minister to his young friend.

In this manner throughout England the Opposition party was scattered far and wide. To use a gambling metaphor, which Fox would not have disdained, many threw down their cards. Many others played, but lost the rubber. A witty nickname was commonly applied to them. In allusion to the History, written by John Fox, of the sufferers under the Romish persecution, they were called " Fox's Martyrs." And of such martyrs there proved to be no less than one hundred and sixty.

Nor were these losses to the Coalition party confined to the rank and file. Several of their spokesmen or their leaders also fell. At Hertford, Mr. Baker succumbed to Baron Dimsdale; at Portsmouth, Mr. Erskine to a brother of Lord Cornwallis; at Bury, General Conway to a son of the Duke of Grafton. Lord Galway, an Irish peer of no great pretensions, prevailed in the city of

York over Fox's most trusted friend and colleague Lord John Cavendish. Some escapes there were of course, though for the most part narrow ones. In Bedfordshire, Mr. St. John carried his election by a single vote; at Norwich, Mr. Windham had on his side nearly thirteen hundred voters, but a majority of only fifty-four. Burke was safe at Malton, Sheridan was safe at Stafford, and Lord North was safe at Banbury.

Amidst all these reverses, however, Fox's high courage never quailed. On the 3rd of April we find him write as follows to a friend: "Plenty of bad news from all quarters, but I think I feel that misfortunes when they come thick have the effect rather of rousing my spirits than sinking them."[1]

The case of Fox himself in these elections should be the last recorded, since it extended very far beyond the date of the rest. He had appealed again to his old constituents at Westminster. So had also his late colleague, Sir Cecil Wray. That gentleman had been formerly not only his colleague, but his follower; but had become estranged from him by his ill-starred Coalition, and was now inclined to support the Government of Pitt.

As their principal candidate at Westminster the Government set up a Peer of Ireland, and naval chief of high repute, Lord Hood. It soon appeared that Lord Hood would be at the head of the poll, and that the real contest would be between Fox and Wray. The voters came forward slowly, and the poll continued open

---

[1] Memorials by Lord John Russell, vol. ii. p. 267.

from day to day and from week to week—that is from
the 1st of April to the 17th of May. During this time
every nerve was strained on either side. Several ladies
of rank and fashion stood forth as Fox's friends—at their
head, Georgiana, the eldest daughter of Earl Spencer,
and the wife, since 1774, of the fifth Duke of Devonshire. Of great beauty and unconquerable spirit, she
tried all her powers of persuasion on the shopkeepers
of Westminster. Other ladies who could not rival her
beauty might at least follow her example. Scarce a
street or alley which they did not canvass in behalf of
him whom they persisted in calling "the Man of the
People," at the very moment when the popular voice
was everywhere declaring against him.

Fox had one supporter of even higher rank and importance. The Prince of Wales, after attending the
King at a review, rode through the streets of Westminster wearing Fox's colours, and partook of a banquet
which was given to his friend at Devonshire House.
Henceforth, as of course, the influence of Carlton House
was set up against the influence of St. James's. It came
to be not only Fox against Pitt, but Prince against
King.

At the hustings in Covent Garden, hour after hour,
the orators strove to out-argue and the mobs to out-
bawl each other. All day long the open space in front
resounded with alternate clamours, while the walls were
white with placards, and the newspapers teeming with
lampoons. Taverns and public-houses were thrown open
at vast expense. Troops of infuriated partisans, decked
with party ribbons and flushed with gin and wine, were

wont to have fierce conflicts in the streets, often with severe injuries inflicted, and in one instance even with loss of life.

Up to the twenty-third day of the polling Fox was in a minority, notwithstanding the immense exertions that had been made in his behalf. The Ministerial party were sanguine in the hope of wresting from him the greatest and most enlightened, as it was then considered, of all the represented boroughs of England.

"Westminster goes on well in spite of the Duchess of Devonshire and the other *Women of the People ;* but when the poll will close is uncertain,"—so writes Pitt to Wilberforce on the 8th of April. Here is another letter which he wrote a few days afterwards to his cousin James Grenville, the same who, in 1797, became Lord Glastonbury.

"Downing Street, Friday,
April 23, 1784.

" My dear Sir,

      " Admiral Hood tells me he left Lord Nugent at Bath, disposed to come to town if a vote at Westminster should be material. I think from the state of the poll it may be very much so. The numbers on the close to-day are—

    H. 6326.   Wr. 5699.   F. 5615.

And Sir Cecil has gained four on Fox to-day. There is no doubt, I believe, of final success on a scrutiny, if we are driven to it ; but it is a great object to us to carry the return for both in the first instance, and on every account as great an object to Fox to prevent it. It is uncertain how long the poll will continue, but pretty clear it cannot be over till after Monday. If you will

have the goodness to state these circumstances to Lord
Nugent, and encourage his good designs, we shall be very
much obliged to you; and still more, should neither
health nor particular engagements detain you, if besides
prevailing upon him you could give your own personal
assistance. At all events I hope you will forgive my
troubling you, and allow for the importunity of a hard-
ened electioneerer.

"We have had accounts from Bath which alarm us
for Mr. H. Grenville, but I hope you will have found
him mended. I have not yet heard the event of Bucks,
but William was sure, and by the first day's poll Aubrey's
prospect seems very good. Mainwaring and Wilkes are
considerably a-head in Middlesex, and Lord Grimston
has come in, instead of Halsey, for Herts.

"Adieu, my dear Sir, and believe me ever faithfully
and affectionately yours,

"W. PITT."

The early minority of Fox was, however, at last retrieved. On the twenty-third day of the polling he
passed Sir Cecil, and he continued to maintain his
advantage till the fortieth, when by law the contest
closed. Then on the 17th of May the numbers stood:
for Lord Hood, 6694; for Mr. Fox, 6233; and for Sir
Cecil Wray, 5598. There was strong reason, however,
to suspect many fraudulent practices in the previous
days, since it seemed clear that the total number of
votes recorded was considerably beyond the number of
persons entitled to the franchise. For this reason Sir
Cecil Wray at once demanded a scrutiny, and the High
Bailiff—illegally, as Fox contended—granted the request. But further still, the High Bailiff, Mr. Corbett,

who was no friend to Fox, refused to make any legal
return until this scrutiny should be decided. Thus
Westminster was left for the present destitute of Representatives, and Fox would have been without a seat in
the new Parliament but for the friendship of Sir Thomas
Dundas, through which he had been already returned
the member for the close boroughs of Kirkwall.

In considering the causes which, taken together,
produced this almost unparalleled accession to the
Ministerial ranks, we must allow something to the
disgust of the Coalition, and something to the alarm of
the India Bill. We must allow something both for the
reverent remembrance of Chatham, and for the rising
fame of Pitt. But above all, we must bear in mind that,
owing to these motives, Pitt won a combined aid from
quarters hitherto in public life most wide asunder. He
had with him many Dissenters, and many Churchmen;
many friends of the King's prerogative, and many as-
sertors of the people's rights. He had from the one side
such men as Jenkinson and Thurlow; from the other
such men as Sawbridge and John Wilkes. For the
Coalition, as Lord Macaulay well observes, had at once
alienated the most zealous Tories from North, and the
most zealous Whigs from Fox.

Looking back to these eventful four months—from
December 1783, to April 1784—it will be found perhaps
that by far the nearest parallel to them which our
history affords is the first administration of Sir Robert
Peel—that other period of four months from December
1834, to April 1835. Some points of essential difference
between them have indeed been pointed out by Sir

Robert Peel himself.[2] But on the other hand there
are many points of similitude which he did not and he
could not state. In both there was the same oratorical
pre-eminence—in both the same absence of colleagues
efficient for debate—in both, therefore, the same glory
to have fought such a battle single-handed. Of both
Pitt and Peel it may be said with truth, as I conceive,
that besides the ability which their enemies have never
denied, courage, temper, and discretion were evinced
by them in the highest degree amidst all the circumstances that could most severely task and try these
eminent qualities. Not one hasty or inconsiderate expression, not a single false step, can perhaps within these
periods be charged upon either. Both were opposed by
eloquent and powerful antagonists exasperated by recent
dismissal from office, through the unjust exercise, as
they deemed it, of the Royal prerogative. In both
cases the violence of the press exceeded all customary
bounds. In both there was the same appeal by a Dissolution to the judgment of the people, though in the
one case the appeal preceded and in the other followed
the conflict in the House of Commons. Yet how opposite the result, since—though without at all implying
on that account any inferiority of genius in the latter
statesman—Pitt succeeded and Peel was overthrown.

At the close of the Elections the King showed his
entire approval of his Minister by the grant—perhaps a
little lavish—of seven new peerages. The others were to
Baronies; but one, Sir James Lowther, whose influence

---

[2] See the second volume of his Memoirs, pp. 44-48, ed. 1857.

at Appleby had not been forgotten, was raised at once to higher rank as Earl of Lonsdale. Three other Earldoms were now conferred, and three more in the ensuing summer, on Peers who were Barons already.

The King also consented, at the request of Pitt, that in place of Sir Lloyd Kenyon, who became Master of the Rolls, Mr. Archibald Macdonald should be made Solicitor General. But it is remarkable that His Majesty, even at that early period, expressed his own preference for Mr. Scott.

On the 18th of May the new Parliament met, and on the 19th was opened by the King in person. After several days consumed in swearing in Members, the debates began upon the 24th. The proceedings in the House of Commons are related as follows by Mr. Pitt himself in a letter the same night to the Duke of Rutland:

"Downing Street, May 24, 1784.

" MY DEAR DUKE,

"I cannot let the messenger go without congratulating you on the prospect confirmed to us by the opening of the Session. Our first battle was previous to the Address on the subject of the return for Westminster. The enemy chose to put themselves on bad ground by moving that two Members ought to have been returned without first hearing the High Bailiff to explain the reasons of his conduct. We beat them on this by 283 to 136. The High Bailiff is to attend today, and it will depend upon the circumstances stated whether he will be ordered to proceed in the scrutiny, or immediately to make a double return, which will bring the question before a Committee. In either case I have no doubt of Fox being thrown out, though in

either there may be great delay, inconvenience, and
expense, and the choice of the alternative is delicate.
We afterwards proceeded to the Address, in which
nothing was objected to but the thanking the King
expressly for the Dissolution.   Opposition argued everything weakly, and had the appearance of a vanquished
party, which appeared still more in the division, when
the numbers were 282 to 114.   We can have little
doubt that the progress of the Session will furnish
throughout a happy contrast to the last.   We have
indeed nothing to contend against but the heat of the
weather, and the delicacy of some of the subjects which
must be brought forward.   Adieu.

"Ever affectionately yours,

"W. PITT."

The predominance of Mr. Pitt, as shown in these
first divisions, was maintained, it may be said, not only
through this Session, but through this Parliament and
through the next.   Henceforth an historical writer may
glide far more rapidly over the debates than when the
fate of a Government or of a party hung suspended and
trembling in the balance.

There were two subjects which at this time demanded
immediate attention from the Legislature: first, the
public finances; and secondly, the affairs of the East
India Company.

As to the first, they were in deplorable disorder.
Lord North by no means wanted knowledge or skill in
his department, but he was wholly deficient in resolution
to look his difficulties fairly in the face.   His administration of the finances was merely a series of make-
shifts and expedients.   As the readiest means of meeting

any sudden call, he had allowed the unfunded debt to
grow to an enormous magnitude, so that the outstanding
bills issued during the war were at a discount of fifteen
or twenty per cent. Consols themselves were at 56 or
57, scarcely higher than during the most adverse periods
of the recent contest. So vast was the prevalence of
smuggling—so numerous were the frauds on the revenue
—that the income of the country during the last year
had fallen far below even its reduced expenditure, and
it was foreseen as almost inevitable (and yet how severe
a trial to the popularity of any Minister!) that the
return of peace must be celebrated by the imposition of
new taxes.

Of these many and gigantic evils, the frauds on the
revenue might be deemed to call the loudest for a
remedy. Tea was then the staple of smuggling. All
other branches of illicit traffic seemed slight and insig-
nificant by the side of this. According to Pitt's calcu-
lation, about thirteen millions pounds weight of tea were
consumed every year in England, while only five
millions and a half were sold by the East India Company, so that the illicit trade in this article was more
than double the legal trade. It had been reduced to a
regular system. Forty thousand persons by sea and by
land were said to be engaged in it ; and the large capital
requisite for their operations came, as was believed, from
gentlemen of rank and character in London. Ships—
some of 300 tons burden—lay out at sea and dealt out
their cargoes of tea to small colliers and barges, by
which they were landed at different places along the
coast. where bands of armed men were stationed to

receive and protect them. " Not merely the revenue "
—this is the statement of Captain Macbride—" is affected by smuggling, though that would be mischief
enough, but the agriculture and manufactures of the
island are in danger of being ruined. The farmers
near the coast have already changed their occupation,
and instead of employing their horses to till the soil,
they use them for the more advantageous purpose of
carrying smuggled goods to a distance from the shore.
The manufacturers will catch the contagion, and the
loom and the anvil will be deserted. In former wars
the smugglers had not conducted themselves as enemies
to their country, but in the late war they enticed away
sailors from the King's ships, concealed such as deserted,
gave intelligence to the enemy, and did everything in
their power hostile to the interest of Great Britain." [3]

Such was the spirit that had grown up under Lord
North, and which Pitt had determined to quell. First,
he brought in a general measure against smuggling,
with some new or more stringent regulations. Thus
the right of seizing vessels allowed to the revenue
officers under certain circumstances of suspicion was
extended from the distance of two to four leagues from
the shore. But these were only palliatives, and Pitt
was bent upon striking at the very root of the evil. " It
has appeared to the Committee of this House," he said,
" that the best possible plan for the purpose is to lower
the duty on tea to such a degree as to take away from

---

[3] On this whole subject compare
with Tomline's Life of Pitt, Mac-
pherson's History of Commerce,
vol. iv. p. 49, and Sinclair's History
of the Revenue, vol. ii. p. 392.

the smuggler all temptation to his illicit trade; and this idea has my hearty approval." In the discussion which ensued Pitt said of Lord Mahon that his Noble Friend had an especial right to speak on this subject, since it was he who "originally suggested the reduction of duties as beneficial to the revenue."

In pursuance of the plan which his speech had indicated, the Minister proposed that the duties on tea, which brought in upwards of 700,000*l.* yearly, should be reduced so far that they might probably yield no more than 169,000*l.* To set against these diminished duties there was the certain decline of smuggling, so that the fair trader would no longer be exposed to any unequal competition. There would be, however, in the first instance, a considerable loss to the revenue, which Pitt proposed to supply by means of a new impost—"the Commutation Tax," as it was afterwards called—namely, an additional duty upon all houses above the poorest kind, estimated according to the number of their windows.

This scheme found great favour both with Parliament and with the public, and was carried through by an overpowering majority. It was obviously much in favour of the poorest classes, since they were relieved from the old tax upon tea without being made subject to the new tax upon windows. Fox, however, raised an objection to the new plan as being compulsory—that is, as obliging every householder above the lower rank to pay an equivalent for drinking tea, whether he drank it or not. But this argument, though specious in theory, was deemed to carry no great weight, since in point of

fact at that time there was scarce a family in the kingdom, rich or poor, in which tea of some kind was not
every day consumed.   So vast had been the change
since the days of Locke, who but a century before speaks
of tea by its French designation of " Thé," and enume-
rates it among the " foreign drinks " to be found in the
London coffee-houses.[4]

Exactly the same principle was applied by Pitt to
the similar case of spirits.   Here again fraudulent devices had spread so wide that, for instance, the distillery
from molasses in the city of London, which had yielded
to the revenue 32,000*l.* in 1778, produced no more than
1098*l.* in 1783.   The Minister therefore brought in and
carried a measure regulating the duties upon British,
and greatly reducing those upon foreign spirits.   But
expecting as the result a considerable increase of consumption in spirits legally imported, he did not think
it necessary as in the case of tea to propose any new
impost as a substitute.

These might be called the preliminary measures.
But on the 30th of June Pitt unfolded his entire plan
of finance—the first of those luminous and masterly
Budgets which were heard in the House of Commons
year by year so long as he continued Minister, and
which had not been equalled by any of his predecessors.   Hard and irksome was the task, he said,
to propose not only new taxes but also a new loan in
the second year of peace.   But the necessities of the

---

[4] See his Memoranda of 1679, | his Life by Lord King (vol. i. p.
and his Journal of April, 1685, in | 251 and 297).

State made that task his duty, and for these necessities others, and not he, had to answer. The floating or unfunded debt he estimated at fourteen millions. Pitt was very desirous to fund the whole of this sum in the present Session, but he was assured by the monied men that so large a quantity of Stock coming at once into the market must greatly depress the other public securities, and prevent them from supplying the new loan on favourable terms. "After an arduous effort for the whole," said Pitt, "I was obliged to compound the business, and therefore I propose to fund only six millions and a half of the unfunded fourteen millions."

"It was always my idea"—thus in his great speech the Minister continues—"that a fund at a high rate of interest is better to the country than those at low rates; that a four per cent. is preferable to a three per cent., and a five per cent. better than a four. The reason is that in all operations of finance we should always have in view a plan of redemption. Gradually to redeem and to extinguish our debt ought ever to be the wise pursuit of Government. Every scheme and operation of finance should be directed to that end, and managed with that view."

Such a maxim might at that time be regarded as a considerable innovation on established views. Not less novel was the course which Pitt announced himself to have pursued with respect to the loan of six millions he required. Former Ministers had made such loans a source of patronage—the means of gain to their friends and followers. Pitt loftily resolved to consult the public interest only. He gave notice through the Governor and Deputy Governor of the Bank that he was ready to contract for the loan with those who would offer the lowest terms, and that the lottery tickets should be distributed among the persons who lent the money, in proportion to the sums lent. The sealed tenders which were sent in accordingly were opened in the presence of the Governor and Deputy Governor. Pitt at once accepted the terms that were the lowest; and as he assured the House of Commons, on his honour, not one shilling was retained for distribution in his hands. The example thus set has served as a precedent and model in all loans of later times.

It is worthy of note, in passing, how different was the spirit which Lord Rockingham and Lord John Cavendish upon the one part, or Pitt upon the other, applied to questions of finance. The danger of undue influence by allowing to Members of Parliament any share in the contracts for loans and lotteries was acknowledged on all sides. Rockingham and Cavendish dealt with this evil by pruning its branches—by a Bill to prohibit every contractor from sitting in the House of Commons. Pitt dealt with this evil by striking at its roots—by providing that every contract should be free from any possible admixture of party favour.

Reverting to the first Budget of the new Minister, we find him in his speech enumerate the Army Estimates for the year as upwards of four millions, the Navy as upwards of three millions, the Ordnance as upwards of 600,000l. The Miscellaneous Services would amount to nearly 300,000l., including a large arrear, which Pitt had the painful duty of announcing, in the Civil List.

The interest of the National Debt in all its manifold
denominations might be taken at nine millions. On
the other hand, the revenue would fall short of the required charges by no less than 900,000*l.*, and Pitt proposed to supply the deficiency at once and boldly by
the imposition of new duties. "Irksome as is my task
this day," he said, "the necessities of the country call
upon me not to shrink from it; and I confide in the
good sense and the patriotism of the people of England."
He added, as the maxim which he designed to follow as
Minister of the Finances, "to disguise nothing from the
public."

The taxes proposed by Pitt to yield what he termed—
and what, according to the estimates of that time, he
might well term—this "enormous sum," were upon
hats, ribbons, and gauzes, coals not employed in certain
branches of our manufactures, horses not employed in
husbandry, an additional duty upon linens and calicoes,
an additional duty of one halfpenny in the pound upon
candles, upon licences to dealers in exciseable commodi-
ties, certificates for killing game, paper, hackney-coaches,
and bricks and tiles. According to Pitt's estimate the
yearly consumption of bricks was about three hundred
millions, and of these one hundred and five were used in
and near London alone. All these intended imposts he
explained and defended at length, in the course of his
speech, with so much perspicuity and knowledge of
details as might justly delight his friends, and in the
same measure disconcert his adversaries.

In pursuance of the views which his speech explained,
Pitt on the same evening moved no less than 133

Resolutions of Finance. He added several others on
subsequent days, on all which numerous Bills were
founded. His new taxes passed for the most part with
little difficulty, excepting that on coals, which was
assailed by so many and so strong objections that the
Minister consented to withdraw it, substituting several
other small imposts or new regulations in its place.

To the tax on bricks and tiles there was also some
demur. Lord Mahon assailed it in a speech of considerable violence, and he went on to denounce the arguments of Mr. George Rose in its support as "the most
weak, ridiculous, and absurd that could be advanced."
It was the manifest duty of Pitt to defend his own
Secretary of the Treasury. He retorted in a strain of
irony on Lord Mahon; and this appears to have been
the first estrangement between these so lately most
cordial friends.

Several of the new financial regulations which Pitt
was proposing applied to the privilege of franking by
Peers and Members of Parliament. Up to that time
nothing beyond the signature of the person privileged
had been required, nor was there any limit as to place
or number. Several banking firms especially were
possessed of whole box-fulls of blank covers signed by
some friend or partner, and kept ready for use in their
affairs. Letters were constantly addressed to some
Member, at places where he never resided, so that by a
secret arrangement other persons might receive them
post-free. It was computed, though probably with some
exaggeration, that the loss to the revenue by such means
might amount every year to no less than 170,000*l.* By

new rules it came to be provided that no Member of
either House should be entitled to frank more than ten
letters daily, each of these to bear in his own handwriting, besides his signature, the day of the month and
year, the name of the post-town, and the entire address;
nor were any letters to be received by him post-free
except at his actual abode. These regulations, which
continued in force until the final abolition of Parliamentary franks in 1839, were carefully framed, and productive of considerable savings. Yet no amount of
public forethought is ever quite a match for private
skill, and many cases of most ingenious evasion are
recorded. Thus on one occasion the franks of a Scottish
Member, Sir John Hope, having been counterfeited, the
person accused on that account protested that he had
done no more than write at the edge of his own letters,
"Free I hope." A Peer with whom I was acquainted
is said to have franked the news of his own decease
—that is, having died suddenly one morning, and
left some covers to friends ready written on his own
escritoire, his family availed themselves of these to
enclose the melancholy tidings.

The arrear of the Civil List, first made known by
the Prime Minister in his speech upon the Budget,
was afterwards more formally communicated by a
message from the King. It amounted to 60,000l.,
which was voted with no opposition, and with little
remark.

It is worthy of note that the Appropriation Act of
this year was framed to include the supplies voted in
the preceding as well as in the present Session. It

passed quietly through, without a word of remonstrance, or even of remark. No Bill of Indemnity to Ministers was either solicited by themselves or called for by their opponents. Thus worthless was the Resolution which the last House of Commons had carried on this subject! So completely had all the threats antecedent to the Dissolution fallen to the ground!

Next in importance to the settlement of the finances, stood the question of the government of India. On the 6th of July Pitt brought in and explained his new measure for that object. It differed but little from the scheme which he had laid before the last Parliament at the beginning of the year, and by establishing a " Board of Control " laid the foundation of that system of double government for India which, with some modifications, continued till the Act of 1858. Every possible objection was urged against it by Fox and Burke, by Sheridan, and by Philip Francis, who had now for the first time obtained a seat in the House of Commons. But they had little success. In the only division which they ventured to try upon the general principle, no more than 60 Members were found to oppose the Bill, while 271 voted in its favour. And it passed still more smoothly through the House of Lords.

Another question, prolific of debates, was the Westminster Scrutiny. It called forth one of the most admirable and least imperfectly reported of the many admirable speeches of Fox. The High Bailiff defended himself at the bar. Witnesses were examined and counsel heard. Among these, Erskine, now no longer in Parliament, summed up the case on Fox's side. At

last the House by a large majority affirmed the legal
character of the Scrutiny, and directed that it should
proceed with all possible despatch—a most unhappy
decision for the interests of all the parties concerned.
" I have had a variety of calculations made upon this
Scrutiny," said Fox in his great speech of the 8th of
June, "and the lowest of all the estimates is 18,000l."
It is said that Pitt was misled upon this question by
the authority of Sir Lloyd Kenyon, the new Master of
the Rolls.[5]

The last measure of this Session had the rare good
fortune of being supported from all sides. On the 2nd
of August Dundas brought in a Bill to restore to the
rightful heirs the estates in Scotland which had been
forfeited in consequence of the last rebellion. The return, said Dundas, to a more conciliatory system was
commenced by the late Lord Chatham, who with admirable judgment and most complete success had raised
regiments of Highlanders to fight the battles of our
common country, declaring that he sought only for merit,
and had found it in the mountains of the North. " It is
an auspicious omen," thus Dundas proceeded, "that the
first blow to this proscription was given by the Earl of
Chatham, and may well justify a hope that its remains
will be annihilated under the administration of his son,
who will thus complete the good work that his great
father began. But let me not be understood to mean
that my Right Hon. friend has the sole merit of the

---

[5] Nichols's Recollections during the Reign of George the Third,
vol. ii. p. 151.

present measure. In justice to the Noble Lord in the blue riband (Lord North), I must say that, having conversed with him several times on the subject while he was at the head of affairs, I always found him disposed to act in that business upon the most liberal, generous, and manly principles. I found precisely the same favourable disposition in the Ministers who immediately preceded the present; and I know that had they remained longer in office, they would have brought forward the same proposal as I have now to make." Accordingly Fox rose to express his continued and hearty approval of the scheme, and it passed the House of Commons without even a whisper of objection. Nor was it resisted in the Lords. There, however, it provoked from the Chancellor a peevish burst of spleen, the cause of which may perhaps be detected at the outset of his speech, when he "lamented, as a private man, that he had not heard anything of the project of bringing the measure before Parliament till it had actually been brought in." He declared that he did not mean to vote against the Bill, and contented himself with drawing in array against it a great number of doubts and scruples.

In the course of this Session Alderman Sawbridge brought forward a motion for Reform in Parliament. Pitt, Wilberforce, and others endeavoured to dissuade him on account of the pressure of other business. "In my opinion," said Pitt, "it is greatly out of season at this juncture. But I have the measure much at heart, and I pledge myself in the strongest language to bring it forward the very first opportunity next Session." Nevertheless the Alderman persisted, and a long debate ensued. The motion was rejected by 199 votes against 125, Pitt himself being one of the minority.

On the 20th of August this short but busy Session, the second of the year, was closed with a brief speech by the King in person.

On the 3rd of September following, the new India Board was published. It was intended that the substantial power should remain wholly in the hands of Dundas; but the arrangement was not effected without some difficulties on the part of the other Commissioners, as will appear from a letter which one of them addressed at this time to Mr. Pitt, complaining above all of the undue number of Scotch appointments.

Lord Sydney to Mr. Pitt.

"Albemarle Street, Sept. 24, 1784.

"DEAR SIR,

"I went into the Closet to-day to carry in the business of the various departments which now fall upon my very inefficient shoulders. To begin with the War Office, upon the business of which I thought it necessary to say something, in consequence of a letter which I received from Sir John Wrottesley. . . .

". . . Moore cannot, I find, come in upon any vacancy in the first regiment of Guards, as he has behaved in a strange manner to the commanding officer of that regiment upon the subject of a Court Martial held upon his brother, who was a surgeon's mate. This I had from the King. I do not think His Majesty much edified with the keen appetite and quick digestion of the Phipps family.

"So much for military matters. As to the subject

upon which you know how much I hate to talk, and
upon which I wish I could never think, His Majesty
asked me what the Directors meant ?—the question of
all others to which I was most incompetent to answer.
I could have referred him to others who are masters of
the subject, but I find that you sent him only the Resolution of the Directors. He asked why they thought that
no one above the rank of Major-General could command
in chief, and how they came to ask the question whether
it is inconsistent or not for a Lieutenant-General to be
under the command of a Major-General.

"I have this moment received your note. I cannot
say how much it hurts me. My opinions as much as
my feelings are against the step that is taken, and what
I am most concerned about is that you will be imagined
to have been a party to this business. I am sure you
are not. You will find a combination of the most in-
satiable ambition and the most sordid avarice and vil-
lany at the bottom of this base work. As to the men
with whom I have hitherto treated, very imprudently,
with great openness, while I have a bolt to my door
they shall never come into my room. I must be allowed to show myself not to be their accomplice.

"I enclose you a list of the field-officers in India, to
show you the drift of that intended operation upon the
King's troops in India with which so many persons have
acquainted me. I believe there are as many English
or Irish names as there are among them. I will leave
the subject, as I feel it difficult to suppress my sense of
my own situation.

"Let me off from any connection with this Indian
business. I am ready to abandon it to the ambition of
those who like the department. But I must have the
rest of my department, while I hold it, unencroached
upon by others. I hope you will not suppose yourself

included in this last sentence, as I shall always look upon the patronage of my office as yours.

"Assure yourself that, hurt and disgraced as I feel myself, I am, with great and unalterable truth and regard, &c.,

"SYDNEY."

During the remainder of this year Pitt continued to apply himself most earnestly to the finances. He lived for the most part within easy reach of London, in a house which he had hired upon Putney Heath. Sometimes he indulged himself with one or two days at Brighton, or, as it was then called, Brighthelmstone. But he found it necessary to relinquish the longer journey to Burton Pynsent which he had designed.

The letters of Pitt to Lady Chatham from the time that he became Prime Minister appear less numerous and also of smaller interest. He appears to have felt it his duty in his new station to refrain from writing to her upon State affairs, except in rare cases and in general terms. His correspondence, therefore, turns chiefly on family matters. But he was most anxious and unremitting in attention whenever any point arose in which her comfort was concerned, as the following extracts from his letters will clearly show :—

"April 20, 1784.

"Everything continues to prosper here. I only wish you were a nearer spectator, and that I could have an opportunity of telling you all you would like to hear."

" Downing Street, May 6, 1784.

" With regard to the 4½ Fund itself, I still retain
my opinion that it will in no very distant time become
again adequate to all it is to pay; but in the mean
time I feel more than I can express the continuance of
the inconvenience to which you are subjected by the
delay. The best measure that I see in the present circumstances is that which, independent of any views of
our own, must, I believe, take place; and if it does, it
will, I think, be an effectual relief. That is an application to Parliament, stating the arrears of the fund and
the cause of the deficiency, and desiring that the charge
now upon it may be carried to the general fund of the
revenue of the Customs. I believe if this is properly
done, there will be no difficulty in it; and such a plan
is in forwardness on the part of the agents of the West
India governors. In the interval, there is one thing I
must most anxiously beg of you—not to entertain an
idea of contracting any further in the present moment
your own establishment, which is indeed too narrow to
admit of more economy. What Harriot said to me on
this subject makes me press this request. I have the
fullest persuasion that the thing will finally be put on a
satisfactory footing, and I hope it may soon. But while
we wait for this, which is a debt from the public, we
have some of us what may in part serve in lien of it.
I assure you I shall be a rich man enough myself (while
we continue in a state which seems to have every prospect of permanence) to give me a right to beg you to
be at ease with regard to any exceeding that may be
incurred while the suspense continues. I hope you will
be good enough to believe that whatever concerns your
satisfaction, more immediately concerns my own than
any articles that consume the salary of the Treasury.

What I beg you to believe also, is that my means, though they will not reach at the extent of my wishes on this point, will without a moment's difficulty go some way to it. I am sure you will forgive the haste in which I write, and believe that I have not time to express half what I feel on the subject. But before I end, I must repeat how anxiously I beg you, if you will let me urge it for my own comfort, not to let the delay of this business give you any additional uneasiness, and above all not to think of putting yourself to any fresh inconvenience or restraint. I will pledge myself for your finding ultimately no reason for it."

" Downing Street, May 29, 1784.

" MY DEAR MOTHER,

" I have had but one thing to complain of in the prosperous course of this busy time—that I have really been obliged day by day to relinquish my intention of writing to you, though every moment of delay was mortifying to me, more than I can express, knowing the suspense which it occasioned to you. I had also some inquiries to make before I could ascertain the present means of furnishing the accommodation, which I so much wish I could render perfectly complete. I trust in a little while our home Treasury will be punctual enough in its payments to leave no difficulty in making up, in some measure, the irregularity of other funds. The income of the Lord of the Treasury and Chancellor of the Exchequer together will really furnish more than my expenses can require; and I hope I need not say the surplus will give me more satisfaction than all the rest, if it can contribute to diminish embarrassment where least of all any ought, I am sure, to subsist. In the mean time, as even our payments are in some arrear, I cannot in the instant answer for all I could wish. But let me beg you to have the goodness to name what sum is necessary to the exigencies of the present moment, and I am sure of being able to supply it. I shall without any other steps have 600*l.* paid into Mr. Coutts's hands the day after to-morrow, and will immediately direct whatever part of it you will allow to be placed to your account. If anything more is necessary, pray let me know the extent of it. I have no doubt of finding means, if they are wanting, at present; though, for the reasons I have related, the facility may be greater a little while hence. I should add that I still continue to think some effectual arrangement may take place as to the $4\frac{1}{2}$ Fund, or a productive substitute for it. Forgive the haste in which I am obliged to write, and have the goodness to let me hear from you as soon as you conveniently can. The mode I have mentioned will enable you to draw on Mr. Coutts without trouble, and I think is the easiest, unless any other occurs to you.

" Believe me, my dear Mother, &c.,

" W. PITT."

" Putney Heath, August 28, 1784.

" The end of the Session has hardly yet given me anything like leisure, as the continual hurry of some months leaves of course no small arrear of business now to be despatched. I hope, however, in about ten days, or possibly a week, to be able to get as far as Brighthelmstone. My brother has, I believe, written to tell Harriot that a house is secured. I shall be happy to see her either in Downing Street or there the first moment she pleases. I am already in a great measure a country gentleman, because, though full of business, it is of a nature which

I can do as well at Putney, from whence I now write, as in town. I look forward with impatience to being enough released to be with you at Burton, and work the more cheerfully in hopes of it."

" Putney Heath, October 7, 1784.

" I have not been without some useful and agreeable mixture of idleness in my Brighthelmstone excursions, though in them I have had pretty constant experience that I could not afford more than a day's distance from town. I have been for a good while engaged to a large party which was to take place, for two or three days about this time, at a famous place of Mr. Drummond's in the New Forest. But as the party was to be made up principally of the Treasury and the new India Board, it is not very certain that the business of one or the other will not prevent it. The principal cause of my being detained at present is the expectation of materials from Ireland, and persons to consult with from that country, on the subject of all the unsettled commercial points, which will furnish a good deal of employment for next Session. The scene there is the most important and delicate we now have to attend to, but even there I think things wear a more favourable aspect."

" December 24, 1784.

" I have deferred from time to time saying anything respecting the grant, hoping to have the opportunity of talking it over fully. I hope, however, that I may safely beg you to be at ease upon it; for though I cannot at this moment say precisely what mode must be taken, I am convinced the business may be soon satisfactorily settled. I shall feel too much interested on what so nearly concerns that which has the first claim to my attention, not to take care that it shall be early adjusted. The only thing you must allow me to beg and insist on, is that you will in the interval feel no difficulty in calling for whatever you find necessary from Mr. Coutts. I hope you know that while it is accidentally in my power to diminish a moment's embarrassment or uneasiness to you, the doing so is the object the most important to my happiness. Inconvenience, if it existed, ought to be out of the question with me ; but I can assure you very sincerely that it cannot be produced in the slightest degree by your consulting your own ease and my pleasure in the interval that now remains."

During the autumn there were two considerable promotions in the Peerage. No Marquisate was at that time remaining in England. The title of Lord Winchester was merged in the Dukedom of Bolton, and the title of Lord Rockingham had become extinct at his death. Pitt now resolved to raise to the vacant rank two noblemen, one of whom had high claims on himself, and the other high claims on the King. On the same day in November the Earl of Shelburne became Marquis of Lansdowne, and Earl Temple Marquis of Buckingham. Of the former, we find the Duke of Rutland write confidentially to Pitt as follows in the previous June :—" I have reason to believe that though he (Lord Shelburne) has entirely relinquished all views of business and office, yet some mark of distinction such as a step in the Peerage would be peculiarly gratifying to him." [6]

Similar hints may perhaps have come from Lord

---

[6] The Duke of Rutland to Mr. Pitt, June 16. 1784.

Temple's friends. It is even probable, as I have shown
elsewhere, that he aspired to the highest rank.   His
eager wish in December, 1783, seems to have been
baffled only by the resolute refusal of the King. The
letter of Pitt to Lord Temple—which is not in my possession, but which I have seen—offering him a Marquisate in November, 1784, goes on to say that his
claim to a Dukedom should be considered in the event
of His Majesty ever granting any more patents of that
title.   I have been informed that the letter to Lord
Shelburne of the same date conveys the same assurance.

On the 1st of December Pitt was most highly gratified by an important accession to his ranks. Lord
Camden, though from the weight of years unwilling to
engage once more in active life, would no longer refuse
to join the son of Chatham.   He consented to take the
office of President of the Council, which Earl Gower gave
up for his sake, receiving in return the Privy Seal, left
vacant by the Duke of Rutland.   It was also designed,
and indeed made a condition by Lord Camden, that his
intimate friend the Duke of Grafton should become a
member of the Cabinet.   From various causes His Grace
postponed his decision for a considerable time.   At last
the affair of Ockzakow arising, he finally declined.

During the administration of Lord North it had been
usual to convene Parliament in the month of November.
But under Pitt the custom was changed.   Unless in
special cases, the Houses did not meet till after the
New Year.   Thus in 1784, at the time of which I speak,
the opening of the new Session was appointed for the
25th of January, 1785.

CHAPTER VII.

1784 — 1785.

Gibbon's character of Pitt — Pitt's application to business — Parallel between Pitt and Fox — The King's Speech on the opening of Parliament — Westminster Scrutiny — Success of Pitt's Financial Schemes — Reform of Parliament — Commercial intercourse with Ireland — The Eleven Resolutions — Pitt's Speech — Opposed by Fox and North — Petition from Lancashire against the measure — Opposition in the Irish House of Commons — Bill relinquished by the Government — Mortification of Pitt.

WHILE thus throughout the country parties were fiercely contending, we may desire to consult the more dispassionate opinion of an Englishman of superior intellect residing at a distance from England. It is, therefore, with especial pleasure that I insert the following letter. I owe the communication of it, and of several others, to the kindness of my friend the present and third Earl of St. Germans.

Mr. Gibbon to Lord Eliot.

"Lausanne, Oct. 27, 1784.

. . . .

"Since my leaving England, in the short period of last winter, what strange events have fallen out in your political world! It is probable, from your present connections, that we see them with very different eyes; and, on this occasion, I very much distrust my own judgment. I am too far distant to have a perfect knowledge of the revolution, and am too recently absent to

judge of it without partiality. Yet let me soberly ask
you on Whig principles, whether it be not a dangerous
discovery that the King can keep his favourite Minister
against a majority of the House of Commons? Here,
indeed (for even here we are politicians), the people
were violent against Fox, but I think it was chiefly
those who have imbibed in the French service a high
reverence for the person and authority of Kings. They
are likewise biassed by the splendour of young Pitt, and
it is a fair and honourable prejudice. A youth of five-
and-twenty, who raises himself to the government of an
empire by the power of genius and the reputation of
virtue, is a circumstance unparalleled in history, and,
in a general view, is not less glorious to the country
than to himself."

At the time when Gibbon wrote thus, Pitt had not
merely secured his high position by his triumph at the
General Election. He had done much more. He had
brought into order the finances of the country, and
found the public favour stand firm against that most
trying of all tests, the imposition of new taxes. He had
decided and settled for seventy years to come that most
anxious and perplexing of all questions—the principle
of our government in India. At this period, the
autumn of 1784, "he was," says Lord Macaulay, "the
greatest subject that England had seen during many
generations. His father had never been so powerful,
nor Walpole, nor Marlborough."

It is no less true, and this should above all be noted,
that the high supremacy which even at this distance of
time may dazzle us, never seems to have dazzled the
" boy-statesman," as his opponents loved to call him, of

twenty-five. Young as he was, and victorious as he had
become, he was never tempted to presume upon his
genius, or relax in his application. He continued, as I
have just now shown him, through all the Recess of
1784, seldom allowing himself any holiday, and earnestly intent on business for the coming Session.

But before I pass on to the events of that Session, and
of many Sessions more in which Pitt and Fox continued
to confront each other, I will attempt to draw a parallel
in some detail between these two most eminent men,
towering, as each did, high above the rest in the opposite ranks. As to Pitt, there could be no idea of competition with any of his colleagues ; and as to Fox,
though there stood beside him such men—hardly else to
be paralleled—as Burke, as Sheridan, as North, yet, as
Bishop Tomline says, " in conversation with me, I
always noticed that Mr. Pitt considered Mr. Fox as far
superior to any other of his opponents as a debater in,
the House of Commons."

Charles James Fox being born in January, 1749, was
older than Pitt by upwards of ten years. Each was the
younger and the favourite son of a retired Minister.
Each grew up amidst the sanguine expectations of his
father's friends. But in their training they were wide
as the poles asunder. Pitt, as we have seen, was
brought up by Lord Chatham in habits of active study,
and his mind was cultivated with unremitting care.
Fox, on the other hand, had the great misfortune of
a too indulgent father. It is clear from the letters published that the first Lord Holland connived at—it might
almost be said that he abetted and encouraged—the

early excesses of his son. The gaming-tables at Spa and elsewhere became familiar to young Fox even in his teens. His losses, his debts, his drinking bouts, and his amours were the theme of fashionable scandal. Such had been the life of Fox, far more through the fault of others than his own, when at the age of nineteen the burgage tenures of Midhurst first sent him to the House of Commons.

Pitt and Fox, as they grew up, differed greatly in aspect and in frame. The tall, lank figure, and the lofty bearing of the former might often be contrasted with Fox's increasing corpulence, and gay, good-humoured mien. With these, or the exaggerations of these, the caricatures of that day have made us all familiar. Caricatures, so far at least as any wide diffusion of the prints is concerned, may be said to have begun in the last days of Sir Robert Walpole. But it was not until the coalition of Fox and North — a most tempting subject for satire—that they, and above all such as came from the pencil of Gillray, attained any high degree of merit. With their merit so likewise grew their political importance. It is said that Mr. Fox was wont to ascribe in part the unpopularity stirred against him on his East India Bill to the impression produced by Sayer's caricatures, especially " Carlo Khan's Triumphal Entry into Leadenhall Street ;" and " A Transfer of East India Stock." " They have done me more mischief," he said, " than the debates in Parliament." [1]

---

[1] Anecdote-Book of Lord Eldon, | i. p. 162. See also Mr. Thomas
as cited in Twiss's Biography, vol. | Wright's ingenious disquisition

In able hands the pen may be almost as graphic as
the pencil. Thus, for instance, does Horace Walpole
describe the eloquent framer of the India Bill about the
very time when that Bill was framed: "Fox lodged in
St. James's Street, and as soon as he rose, which was
very late, had a levee of his followers, and of the
members of the gaming-club at Brooks's — all his
disciples. His bristly black person and shagged breast
quite open, and rarely purified by any ablutions, was
wrapped in a foul linen night-gown, and his bushy hair
dishevelled. In these Cynic weeds, and with Epicurean
good humour, did he dictate his politics, and in this
school did the Heir of the Crown attend his lessons and
imbibe them." The value of this portrait is enhanced
from the judgment formed upon it by one of Fox's
relatives and most warm admirers—his nephew, Lord
Holland. He speaks of it as, of course, a strong carica-
ture; "yet," he adds, "from my boyish recollection of a
morning in St. James's Street, I must needs acknowledge that it has some truth to recommend it."[2]

Take as a side-piece the portrait of Pitt as he appeared in 1783 to a Member of Parliament who was gar-
rulous and inexact, and extremely sore as disappointed
in his hopes of office, but still keen-eyed and observant.
Sir Nathaniel Wraxall, to whom I am referring, speaks
as follows: "In the formation of his person he was tall
and slender, but without elegance or grace. In his
manners, if not repulsive, he was cold, stiff, and without

---

upon caricatures, 'England under
the House of Hanover,' vol. ii. p.
81, ed. 1848.

[2] See the Memorials of Fox by
Lord John Russell, vol. ii. p. 45.

suavity or amenity.   He seemed never to invite
approach, or to encourage acquaintance, though when
addressed he could be polite, communicative, and occasionally gracious.   Smiles were not natural to him even
when seated on the Treasury Bench. . . . .   From the
instant that Pitt entered the door-way of the House of
Commons, he advanced up the floor with a quick and firm
step, his head erect and thrown back, looking neither to
the right nor to the left, nor favouring with a nod or a
glance any of the individuals seated on either side,
among whom many who possessed 5000*l.* a-year would
have been gratified even by so slight a mark of attention.   It was not thus that Lord North or Fox treated
Parliament." [3]

In vigour of frame, as in outward aspect, the two
statesmen differed greatly.   The health of Pitt, as I
have shown, was very delicate in his early youth, and it
again became so ere he had passed the prime of man-
hood.   Fox, on the contrary, had been gifted by nature
with a buoyant spirit and a most robust constitution.
For a long time even his own irregularities could not
impair it, and he used to say that a spoonful of rhubarb
was sufficient remedy for all the bodily ills that he had
ever known.   As a proof of his youthful vigour, it is
recorded by tradition at Killarney that at twenty-two
years of age he twice swam round a lake upon a moun-
tain summit of large extent, and of icy coldness, called
"the Devil's Punch-Bowl."   Mr. Herbert, of Mucross,
was his host on that occasion, and it is added that some

---

[3] Memoirs of his Own Time, vol. iv. p. 633.

months afterwards meeting that gentleman in London he asked him, "Pray, tell me—is that shower I left at Killarney over yet?"

So far as regards mental culture on other subjects than on politics, Pitt and Fox were exactly opposite in their position. Pitt had received a most excellent education, but from early office had afterwards little leisure for reading. Fox in his youth had read only by snatches, and it is greatly to his credit that he had read at all. When, however, his Coalition Ministry fell, and when a long period of exile from Downing Street loomed before him, he applied himself often with excellent effect and most unaffected relish to literary studies.

The best classic authors in Greek and Latin were to Fox a never-failing source of recreation. In these he might be equalled or indeed surpassed by Pitt, but as to modern literature there could be no kind of comparison between them. Pitt never carried any further his colloquial studies of Rheims and Fontainebleau. But Fox, besides some knowledge of Spanish, had made himself perfect master of both the French and Italian languages. It was partly for this reason that he took especial pleasure in foreign affairs.

It is said—and even the personal tastes of a great man may be to us a matter of interest—that Ovid was the poet Fox loved the best among the Latin poets, and Euripides among the Greek tragedians. For poetry in every language he had indeed a great predilection, and for poetry in English he had talent as well as taste. His own attempts in it were only of a cursory kind. Yet, slight as the praise may seem to certain ponderous

writers of unread dissertations, he is said to be the author
of perhaps the very best, and the truest, enigma in the
English language:

> " My first does affliction denote,
>   Which my second is destined to feel,
>   My whole is the best antidote
>   That sorrow to soften and heal."

Here is another, scarcely less excellent, which is also
ascribed to him:

> " Formed long ago, though made to-day,
>   I'm most employed when others sleep;
>   What few would wish to give away,
>   And none would ever wish to keep."

In his retirement, one of the projects that he fondly
cherished was to prepare a new and improved edition of
the works of his favourite Dryden. " Oh !"—he exclaims,
in the familiar correspondence of his later years—" oh,
how I wish that I could make up my mind to think it
right to devote all the remaining part of my life to such
subjects, and such only ! Indeed, I rather think I shall."

In prose compositions Fox was far less happy. His
private letters indeed deserve the praise of a clear,
frank, and perfectly unaffected style. But his pen
lacked pinions for a higher flight. During the last years
of his life he began with great care and pains to write
the History of England at the period of the Revolution,
and the work, so far as it had proceeded, was published
by Lord Holland after Fox's decease. Universal disappointment—such was the impression that this fragment
made. No trace of the great orator can be discovered
in the narrative; scarce any in the comments and

reflections. It was found that besides the natural defects of his written style, Fox had entangled himself with some most needless and fantastic rules of his own devising—as, for instance, to use no word which his favourite Dryden had not used before.

Pitt, besides his boyish tragedy, made no attempt in authorship. But parts of his correspondence, written on great emergencies, and to eminent men, seem to me of admirable power. I know of no models more perfect for State Papers than his letter to the King of January 31, 1801, or his letter to Lord Melville of March 29, 1804.

It is a harder as well as a more important task to compare the two great rivals in their main point of rivalry—in public speaking. Each may at once be placed in the very highest class. Fox would have been without doubt or controversy the first orator of his age had it not been for Pitt. Pitt would have been without doubt or controversy the first orator of his age had it not been for Fox. It may fairly be left in question which of these two pre-eminent speakers should bear away the palm. But they were *magis pares quam similes*—far rather equal than alike. Mr. Windham, himself a great master of debate, and a keen observer of others' oratory, used to say that Pitt always seemed to him as if he could make a King's speech off hand. There was the same self-conscious dignity—the same apt choice of language—the same stately and guarded phrase. Yet this, although his more common and habitual style, did not preclude some passages of pathetic eloquence, and many of pointed reply. He loved on some occasions to illustrate his meaning with citations from the Latin poets—sometimes giving a new grace to well-known passages of Horace and Virgil, and sometimes drawing a clear stream from an almost hidden spring—as when, in reference to the execution of Louis the Sixteenth, he cited the lines of a poet so little read as Statius, lines which he noticed as applied by De Thou to the massacre of St. Bartholomew. Never, even on the most sudden call on him to rise—did he seem to hesitate for a word, or to take any but the most apt to the occasion. His sentences, however long, and even when catching up a parenthesis as they proceeded, were always brought to a right and regular close—a much rarer merit in a public speaker than might be supposed by those who judge of Parliamentary debates only by the morning papers. I could give a strong instance of the contrary. I could name a veteran Member, whom I used, when I sat in the House of Commons, constantly to hear on all financial subjects. Of him I noticed, that while the sentences which he spoke might be reckoned by the hundred, those which he ever finished could only be reckoned by the score.

It is worthy of note, however, that carefully as Pitt had been trained by his illustrious father, their style of oratory and their direction of knowledge were not only different, but almost, it may be said, opposite. Chatham excelled in fiery bursts of eloquence—Pitt in a luminous array of arguments. On no point was Pitt so strong as on finance—on none was Chatham so weak.

Fox, as I have heard good judges say, had the same defects, which, in an exaggerated form, and combined with many of his merits, appeared in his nephew Lord

Holland. He neither had, nor aimed at, any graces of manner or of elocution. He would often pause for a word, and still oftener for breath and utterance, panting as it were, and heaving with the mighty thoughts that he felt arise. But these defects, considerable as they would have been in any mere holiday speaker, were overborne by his masculine mind, and wholly forgotten by his audience as they witnessed the cogency of his keen replies—the irresistible home-thrust of his arguments. No man that has addressed any public assembly in ancient or in modern times was ever more truly and emphatically a great debater. Careless of himself, flinging aside all preconceived ideas or studied flights, he struck with admirable energy full at the foe before him. The blows which he dealt upon his adversaries were such as few among them could withstand, perhaps only one among them could parry: they seemed all the heavier, as wholly unprepared, and arising from the speeches that had gone before. Nor did he ever attempt to glide over, or pass by, an argument that told against him; he would meet it boldly face to face, and grapple with it undeterred. In like manner any quotations that he made from Latin or English authors did not seem brought in upon previous reflection for the adornment of the subject at its surface, but rather appeared to grow up spontaneously from its inmost depths. With all his wonderful powers of debate, and perhaps as a consequence of them, there was something truly noble and impressive in the entire absence of all artifice or affectation. His occasional bursts of true inborn sturdy genuine feeling, and the frequent indica-

tions of his kindly and generous temper, would sometimes, even in the fiercest party conflicts, come home to
the hearts of his opponents. If, as is alleged, he was
wont to repeat the same thoughts again and again in
different words, this might be a defect in the oration,
but it was none in the orator. For, thinking not of
himself, nor of the rules of rhetoric, but only of success
in the struggle, he had found these the most effectual
means to imbue a popular audience almost imper-
ceptibly with his own opinions. And he knew that to
the multitude one argument stated in five different
forms is, in general, held equal to five new arguments.

The familiar correspondence of Fox, as edited with
ability and candour by Lord John Russell, has not
tended on the whole to exalt his fame. Such, at least,
is the opinion which I have heard expressed with sincere regret by some persons greatly prepossessed in his
favour—some members of the families most devoted to
his party cause. It seems to be felt, that although a
perusal of his letters leaves in its full lustre his reputation as an orator, it has greatly dimmed his reputation
as a statesman. There are, in his correspondence, some
hasty things that are by no means favourable to his
public spirit, as where he speaks of the "delight" which
he derived from the news of our disasters at Sara-
toga, and at York-town.[4] There are some hasty
things that are as far from favourable to his foresight
and sagacity. Take for instance a prophecy as follows, in 1801: "According to my notion the House
of Commons has in a great measure ceased, and will

---

[4] To Lord Holland, October 12, 1792.

shortly entirely cease, to be a place of much importance." [5] Perhaps also, after the perusal of these letters, we may feel more strongly than before it that many parts of Fox's public conduct—as his separation from Lord Shelburne, or his junction with Lord North —are hard to be defended.

But on this point there is one reflection that we should always bear in mind. The more we dwell on Fox's errors, the higher we are bound to rank those eminent qualities by which, in the opinion of so many of his contemporaries, his errors were outweighed. In spite of all his errors—and what is much more trying, in spite of the party reverses and discomfiture which proceeded from them—we find his friends, comprising some of the most gifted men of that age, adhere to him, except in one memorable crisis—the period of 1794— with fond admiration and unhesitating confidence.

Of this attachment on the part of his friends, I have seen a striking instance on the walls of All Saints' Church at Hertford. In that church lies buried Lord John Townshend, who died in February, 1833. The inscription on his monument terms him " the friend and companion of Mr. Fox ; a distinction which was the pride of his life, and the only one he was desirous might be recorded after his death."

As the cause of this enduring attachment on the part of Fox's friends, we may acknowledge in a great degree his wondrous powers of mind, but chiefly and above all his winning warmth of heart. How delightful must Fox have been as a companion ! How frank, how rich, how varied

---

[5] To Mr. Charles Grey, Fox Memorials, vol. iii. p. 341.

his flow of conversation! How high the privilege to
visit him in the country retreat that he loved so well—
of sitting by his side beneath the cedars that he planted
at St. Ann's! With what schoolboy fun would the
retired statesman at such times rally his own short
fits of utter idleness! Thus when Mr. Rogers once
said that it was delightful to lie on the grass with a
book in one's hand all day, we are told that Fox answered
" Yes—but why with a book?"[6] How genial his aspect,
as I have heard it described by another associate of his
later years—walking slow, and with gouty feet, along
his garden-alleys, but with cheerful countenance and
joyous tones—expanding his ample breast to draw in the
fresh breeze, and exclaiming from time to time, "Oh.
how fine a thing is life!"—"Oh, how glorious a thing is
summer weather!"

Several testimonies which I have already cited speak
of Pitt in his earlier years as a most delightful companion, abounding in wit and mirth, and with a flow
of lively spirits. As the cares of office grew upon him,
he went of course much less into general society. He
would often, for whole hours, ride or sit with only Steele,
or Rose, or Dundas for his companion. Nor was this
merely from the ease and rest of thus unbending his
mind. Men who know the general habits of great
Ministers are well aware how many details may be
expedited and difficulties smoothed away by quiet chat
with a thoroughly trusted friend in lesser office. Pitt,
however, often gave and often accepted small dinner
parties, and took great pleasure in them. The testimony

---

[6] Rogers's Recollections, p. 44.   This was at St. Ann's in 1803.

of his familiar friend, Lord Wellesley, which goes down
to 1797, is most strong upon these points. " In all places
and at all times," says Lord Wellesley, " his constant
delight was society. There he shone with a degree of
calm and steady lustre which often astonished me more
than his most splendid efforts in Parliament. His manners were perfectly plain ; his wit was quick and ready.
He was endowed, beyond any man of his time whom I
knew, with a gay heart and a social spirit." [7]

The habits of Pitt in Downing Street were very simple.
He breakfasted every morning at nine, sometimes in-
viting to that meal any gentleman with whom he had
to talk on business,[8] and it was seldom when the House
of Commons met that he could find leisure for a ride.

When retired from office, and living in great part at
Walmer Castle, Pitt, like Fox, reverted with much
relish, although in a desultory manner, to his books.
The Classics, Greek and Latin, seemed to be, as my
father told me, Pitt's favourite reading at that period.
Yet he was by no means indifferent to the literature of
his own day. On this point let me cite a statesman
who has passed away from us, to the grief of many
friends, at the very time when the page which records
his testimony has reached me from the press. Let me
cite the Earl of Aberdeen, who once, as he told me,
heard Pitt declare that he thought Burns's song " Scots,
wha hae wi' Wallace bled" the noblest lyric in the
language. Another time he also mentioned Paley to
Lord Aberdeen in terms of high admiration, as one

---

[7] Letter of November 22, 1836, as published in the Quarterly Review, No. 114.

[8] See the Wyvill Papers, vol. iv.
p. 23.

of our very best writers. Perhaps the great fault of his private life is that he never sought the society of the authors or the artists whom all the time he was admiring. Perhaps the great fault of his public life is that he never took any step—no, not even the smallest —to succour and befriend them.

With every drawback, however, and I have now named the most considerable, it certainly appears to me that Pitt was foremost among all the statesmen that England has ever seen. I will not pursue the invidious task of seeming to disparage other great men in contrast to one who was greater still; and the merits of Pitt himself will best appear as my narrative proceeds. But I shall think it the fault of that narrative if at its conclusion my readers should not be disposed to own that Pitt surpassed the Ministers who came before him, and has not been equalled by any of those who have since borne sway.

From this digression—I must own a very long one— I return to the Session of Parliament in 1785. It was opened on the 25th of January, by the King in person. His Majesty's Speech expressed congratulations on the improvement of the revenue, resulting from the measures of last Session. It invited the Houses to consider the further regulation of the public offices, and the final adjustment of the commercial intercourse with Ireland.

In another sentence the King's Speech took notice of "differences on the Continent." These were owing to the Emperor Joseph the Second. Since the year 1780

the death of Maria Theresa had left him sole chief of
the Austrian Monarchy. Eager to emulate his still
surviving neighbour, the great Frederick of Prussia, he
plunged headlong into a career of active innovation.
But it proved a contrast rather than a parallel. Frederick had made many changes, but none without full
inquiry and careful thought. In general, therefore, the
popular voice had been upon his side. On the contrary, it
seemed to be the practice of Joseph the Second to act first,
and inquire afterwards. So rash and heedless was his
course, so little regard did he pay to long-rooted feelings,
or to established rights, that at last the very nations which
he desired to serve, from Transylvania to Flanders, rose
almost in rebellion against his measures of reform.

As regards Flanders and Brabant, the first object of
the Emperor had been by his own authority to release
them from the obligations of the Barrier Treaty of 1715.
He demolished all the fortifications except at Luxem-
burg, Ostend, and the citadels of Antwerp and Namur;
and required the Dutch garrisons to withdraw from the
Barrier towns. The full effect of these unwise measures
was not apparent till ten years afterwards, when the
French revolutionary army, having defeated the Austrian
on the plain of Fleurus, overspread with perfect ease
the open country, and annexed it to their own.

But further still, in no generous spirit, Joseph the
Second desired to avail himself of the internal discords
of the Dutch to wring from them whatever he desired.
He claimed especially the possession of Maestricht and
the free navigation of the Scheldt. In the spring of
1784 he surprised a fort which belonged to Holland, at

the mouth of the river. In the autumn of that year
he sent out two brigs with orders to resist the usual de-
tention and examination in the Scheldt, and he announced
that he should consider as a declaration of hostilities
any insult offered to either of these ships. Nevertheless
the Dutch officers quietly took possession of both. The
Emperor, who was then in Hungary, immediately re-
called his envoy from the Hague, and a war was
supposed to be close at hand. But the measures of
Joseph were as feebly prosecuted as they had been
rashly commenced. He found the aid of France, upon
which he had reckoned, altogether fail him; and thus
after some negotiation and demur he was reduced in the
autumn of 1785 to sign a treaty far from honourable to
his arms, receding from most of the pretensions that he
had put forward, and accepting in return a sum of money
which the States of Holland consented to disburse, as
the price of peace.[9]

In this Session the first business brought before the
House of Commons was the Westminster Scrutiny. Nothing could have answered worse. All the resources of
chicanery—resources well-nigh inexhaustible in our ancient law of Parliament—had been called forth on either
side. Counsel were employed whenever a bad vote was to
be struck off; and their speeches had been of the longest,
especially whenever their arguments were slight or few.
Thus in the eight months which had elapsed no effectual
advance had been made; and it was computed that the
process would require two years more. Under such

_____

[9] See on these transactions especially the Malmesbury Papers, vol. ii.
p. 75-170.

circumstances the Scrutiny had grown hateful to both parties—quite as hateful to Sir Cecil Wray as it was to Mr. Fox. Still, however, a sense of consistency and a regard to the course he had formerly pursued induced Pitt to maintain it in the House of Commons. But he found the general feeling of hardship and injustice in this case prevail against him. A motion by Mr. Ellis, requiring the High Bailiff to make an immediate Return, was negatived by the decreasing majority of thirty-nine. On a second motion to the like effect by Colonel Fitzpatrick, the majority fell to only nine. Alderman Sawbridge then brought on a third motion in nearly the same words, which Pitt endeavoured to stave off by a proposal of adjournment; but he found himself in a minority of 124 against 162, and the original motion was carried without further hindrance. Next day, accordingly, the High Bailiff sent in the names of Lord Hood and Mr. Fox as highest on the poll; and thus was the great Whig statesman reinstated as Member for Westminster.

With this result the Westminster Scrutiny was certainly not a little damaging to the Prime Minister. In the first place there was the pain to see many of his friends vote against him—the mortification to find himself defeated in a House of Commons so zealous on his side. There was next the charge which, however unfounded, the Opposition did not fail to urge—of a vindictive rancour to his rival. But even the most impartial men might justly arraign him for a want of foresight and good judgment in his first preference of so faulty a tribunal.

On the other hand, Pitt was able to point with pride

to the prosperous result of his financial schemes. He could show smuggling, for the time, almost annihilated. and the revenue in all its branches rising from its ruins ; and he could promise for next year the creation of a Sinking Fund, to redeem the National Debt. But towards this end, and for the settlement of the remainder of the floating bills, the legacy of the last war, he required some new taxes, to produce at least 400,000*l.* a year. Accordingly, in his Budget, on the 9th of May, Pitt proposed an additional tax on male, and a new one on female, servants; and duties on retail shops, on post-horses, on gloves, on pawnbrokers' licences, and on salt carried coastwise.

On the Opposition side, the speakers—Fox especially, with Eden and Sheridan—attempted to denounce the Minister as both inaccurate in his statements and over sanguine in his hopes. Their general charges, flung out almost at random, made little impression on the public, but they were more successful in dealing with the details of the taxes proposed. The assessment on shops was open to some strong objections, which were strongly urged. The duty on maid-servants, besides several valid arguments against it, drew forth an infinite number of jests, not perhaps very diverting, and certainly not very decorous. Nevertheless the proposals of the Minister passed, though not without considerable modification ; and after the experience of a few years the two most obnoxious taxes were repealed.

Besides these and other financial measures—as Bills for the regulation of the Navy Office, and for the better Auditing the public Accounts—Pitt brought before the

House of Commons, in this Session, two subjects of paramount importance: first, the Reform of Parliament; and secondly, the commercial intercourse with Ireland.

On the question of Reform, Pitt had all through the winter been intent. He conferred at some length with the Rev. Christopher Wyvill, and other leaders of the cause. To them he renewed his promise of a measure of his own in the coming Session, adding, that to carry it, he would "exert his whole power and credit, as a man and as a minister." Mr. Wyvill, without any authority asked or given, made known these expressions of Pitt in a circular letter to the Chairmen of the several Committees, dated December 27th, 1784; a step far from prudent, since it was not till some weeks afterwards that Pitt received the King's assent to the introduction of the measure, and His Majesty's promise to use no influence against it. "I wish"—thus writes Pitt to the Duke of Rutland—"Mr. Wyvill had been a little more sparing of my name." But he adds, "Parliamentary Reform, I am still sure, after considering all you have stated, must sooner or later be carried in both countries. If it is well done, the sooner the better."

Conscious of the difficulties of his task, more especially within the walls of Parliament, Pitt spared no exertion to gain it votes. He prevailed upon Dundas once more to give it his support. He wrote to Wilberforce, who was passing the winter with his family at Nice, entreating him to return for this special object. Wilberforce came accordingly, and as an intimate friend was a guest of Pitt in Downing Street, as he was also on many subsequent occasions. Next day but one after his arrival, his Diary has an entry as follows: "Pitt's maid burnt my letters"—a dangerous mistake, as his biographers observe, to the young Representative of Yorkshire. The motion of Pitt for Parliamentary Reform was fixed for the 18th of April. Then, amidst a great throng of strangers, and to an attentive and expectant House, the Minister unfolded his scheme. In part it was prospective, and in part of present application. He proposed to disfranchise thirty-six decayed boroughs, each returning two Members, and by means of the seventy-two seats thus obtained to assign additional Representatives to the largest counties, and to the cities of London and Westminster. "But in the counties," added Pitt, "there is no good reason why copyholders should not be admitted to the franchise as well as freeholders; and such an accession to the body of electors would give a fresh energy to Representation." And in the boroughs he disclaimed all idea of compulsion. A fund of a million sterling was to be established to compensate in various degrees the several borough proprietors, and each borough should be invited to apply by petition from two-thirds of its electors.[1] Thus even in the case of burgage tenures, or of the very smallest hamlet, the franchise would not be forcibly resumed, but freely surrendered. Thus the extinction of the thirty-six small boroughs would be in a short time quietly effected. But as to the future, if any boroughs beyond these thirty-six either were, or grew to

---

[1] The amount of the fund and the number of the electors are not stated in Pitt's speech, but appear in Mr. Wyvill's 'Summary Explanation.' See a note to the Parl. Hist., vol. xxv. p. 445.

be, decayed and below a certain definite number of houses, such boroughs should have it in their power to surrender their franchise on an adequate consideration, and their right of sending Members to Parliament should be transferred from time to time to populous and flourishing towns.

Such was the general outline of Pitt's scheme, which he earnestly entreated the Members who heard him to consider, without suffering their minds to be disquieted with visionary terrors. "Nothing," he cried, "is so hostile to improvement as the fear of being carried further than the principle on which a person sets out." In the debate which ensued he had the pleasure to hear both Dundas and Wilberforce speak in favour of his Bill. Fox also, though finding an infinite number of faults with it in detail, expressed his support of the measure in its present stage. But, on the other hand, Lord North, in perfect consistency with his previous course, delivered an able and powerful speech not only against this scheme, but against all schemes of Parliamentary Reform; and on the division, at nearly four in the morning, the Minister had the mortification to find himself defeated by 248 votes, there being on his side only 174. Wilberforce, in his 'Diary,' says: "Terribly disappointed and beat. Extremely fatigued. Spoke extremely ill, but was commended. Called at Pitt's; met poor Wyvill."

Pitt considered the result as final for that Parliament at least. He saw that not even Ministerial power and earnest zeal, and that nothing but the pressure of the strongest popular feeling, such as did not then exist, could induce many Members to vote against their own tenure of Parliament, or in fact against themselves.

In Ireland it had been hoped that lasting peace and concord would have followed the full concession of legislative equality under the Rockingham administration; but, on the contrary, fresh grounds of agitation had almost immediately arisen, founded in part on the question of Parliamentary Reform, and in part on the claims of the National Volunteers. In 1783 we find Burke write as follows to his friend the Earl of Charlemont:—" I see with concern that there are some remains of ferment in Ireland, though I think we have poured in to assuage it nearly all the oil in our stores." [2]

It had also been supposed, considering how signal and how recent were the services of Grattan, that he would for many years to come guide the feelings of his countrymen. Yet another man of great ability, Henry Flood, started up at once in open competition with him. In a few months Flood appears to have even shot above him in popular favour. Flood gained the ear of the Volunteers' Convention when they met in Dublin, and was deputed to bring forward the question of Parliamentary Reform in the Irish House of Commons, though Grattan was also one of its supporters.

In October, 1783, the contending orators gave battle to each other in the Irish House of Commons. It was a memorable conflict, which General Burgoyne in his letters describes as far exceeding in violence anything that he had ever beheld in England. Then it was that Grattan in his speech described Flood as " hovering

---

[2] Memoirs of Lord Charlemont, by Hardy, vol. ii. p. 100.

about this dome like an ill-omened bird of night, with
sepulchral note, cadaverous aspect, and a broken beak,
watching to stoop and pounce upon its prey!" It is
worthy of note that this last phrase of Grattan, "a
broken beak," contained a peculiar sting as applied to
a manifest defect in the face of his rival.

The Convention of the Volunteers at Dublin had likewise two contending leaders: first the Earl of Charlemont, and secondly the Earl of Bristol, who was also
Bishop of Derry. This Prelate was son of the famous
Lord Hervey in the days of George the Second, and a
singular character, recalling the feudal Bishops of the
Middle Ages. He proposed to the Volunteers that in
the new Reform Bill which they were seeking to frame,
the franchise should be granted to Roman Catholics.
To this proposal Lord Charlemont gave his decided
opposition, and by far the greater number of the delegates sided with Lord Charlemont. Accordingly Flood,
as their spokesman, brought forward in the Irish House
of Commons a measure of Reform for the benefit of
Protestants only. He was defeated by a majority of
more than three to one.

Such then was the state of Irish parties when in
February, 1784, the new Lord Lieutenant, his Grace of
Rutland, arrived at "the Castle." At nearly the same
time Flood came back from England, whither he had
gone to present at the King's Levee the Address voted
by the Volunteers at the close of their Convention. But
he had also another object. He had been returned to
the English House of Commons also, through the influence of the Duke of Chandos; and he wished to try

his powers—as he did with very indifferent success—in
the debates upon Fox's India Bill. Many years later,
after his untimely death in 1791, his rival in politics
made, in a noble spirit, some excuses for his failure.
"He misjudged," said Grattan, "when he transplanted
himself to the English Parliament; he forgot that he
was a tree of the forest, too old and too great to be
transplanted at fifty." Of this truth, which Grattan
states in so solemn a strain, Grattan himself, at a still
later period, was to be a far more conspicuous example.

Flood, on his return to Dublin in the spring of 1784,
renewed with unabated spirit his motion on Irish Parliamentary Reform. Again it was negatived by overwhelming numbers.

The rejection of Flood's second motion gave rise, or
at least gave pretext, to a serious tumult, when some
noisy rioters broke into the House of Commons, and
two of them were apprehended by the Serjeant-at-Arms.
Yet ere long—especially considering the fixed resolve of
continued exclusion to the Catholics—the question of
Reform ceased to be uppermost in the public mind.
There was a more pressing grievance in the growth, at
this period, of great distress among the manufacturers
and traders of the kingdom. Each of the numerous
non-importation agreements, which had been taken up
as a weapon against England towards the close of the
last war, had now recoiled with violence upon its
authors. So far they had only themselves to blame,
but they also suffered severely from the high duties
which, mainly at the instance of the manufacturers of
England, had been imposed from early times on the

commerce between the two countries, and which in 1779 were relaxed only in the smallest possible degree.

In April, 1784, the question of trade was brought before the Irish House of Commons by Mr. Gardiner, with perspicuity and candour ; and several long debates ensued. Still, however, the distress increased. Through the summer many artisans who had been thrown out of employment came thronging into the great towns with violence, or threats of violence. One of their favourite devices, as derived from the early example of the insurgent colonies, was to tar and feather those whom they regarded as their enemies ; and they were disposed to regard as their enemies all who dealt in imported goods. In the country districts, notwithstanding the earnest remonstrances of the Catholic as well as the Protestant clergy, the Whiteboys began to reappear. Other persons of higher station were willing to take part in any movement which they might hope to lead. In that point of view Parliamentary Reform, or commercial distress, or any other question, were exactly of equal moment. Such men subscribed an Address to all the Sheriffs of Ireland, calling upon them to summon meetings for the appointment of delegates to a new assembly which should be held in Dublin, and which, by another imitation of America, should bear the name of Congress. On this occasion Napper Tandy, the son of a Dublin ironmonger in large business—a name subsequently noted in the ranks of Irish faction—came forth for the first time. The Earl of Bristol was also active. With his Lordship at that time, as with his ally Sir Edward Newenham, hostility to the English connection appears to have been the leading principle. The former published a pamphlet so closely bordering upon treason that the Lord Lieutenant for some time seriously considered whether the Earl-Bishop should not be arrested and brought to trial. The question was referred to Mr. Pitt and his colleagues in England, and was by them decided in the negative.

On the 15th of August we find the Lord Lieutenant, in writing to Pitt, describe the state of things as follows:—"This city (of Dublin) is in a great measure under the dominion and tyranny of the mob. Persons are daily marked out for the operation of tarring and feathering; the magistrates neglect their duty; and none of the rioters—till to-day, when one man was seized in the fact—have been taken, while the corps of Volunteers in the neighbourhood seem as it were to countenance these outrages. In short, the state of Dublin calls loudly for an immediate and vigorous interposition of Government."

In many other letters, public and private, did the Duke of Rutland consult his friend on the open violence which he saw, and on the secret conspiracy which he suspected. Nor did the Prime Minister leave him to deal singly with his difficulties. Neither then nor afterwards was any important step taken in Ireland without Pitt's advice and direction. Above all he now applied himself with earnest assiduity to the question most beset with obstacles in England—the question of the shackles and restrictions upon the trade of Ireland. That question was embarrassed by the resolute attachment to the existing system which prevailed at Manchester and our other manufacturing towns. There, at

that period, the feeling in favour of high protective
duties was quite as strong as in our own day we have
seen it in favour of Free Trade.

Pitt well knew, and could not undervalue, the current
of opinion in these vast centres, as they were rapidly
becoming, of our manufacturing importance; but for
his own part he was, as we have seen, a student and a
disciple of the great work of Adam Smith. We find
him, at the beginning of his deliberations on this subject (the 7th of October, 1784), write as follows, in strict
confidence, to the Duke of Rutland:—" I own to you
that the line to which my mind at present inclines is
to give Ireland an almost unlimited communication of
commercial advantages, if we can receive in return
some security that her strength and riches will be our
benefit, and that she will contribute from time to time
in their increasing proportions to the common exigencies
of the empire."

To determine the details that might be requisite. or
to weigh the objections that might arise, Pitt summoned
from Ireland two advisers of great knowledge and experience—Mr. John Foster, the Chancellor of the Exchequer; and Mr. John Beresford, the Chief Commis-
sioner of the Revenue in that kingdom. With these
gentlemen, and with Mr. Orde, the Irish Secretary, he
held frequent conferences all through the autumn and
mid-winter. There was no doubt that the Irish would
gladly accept the commercial advantages, but the difficulty was how to render palatable to them any contribution in return. " I really believe," writes Pitt, " that
these objections may be removed; and I do not see the

possibility of agreeing to complete the system of equal
commerce (which is what must be now done) without
some return being secured to this country. . . . . I am
ready at the same time to admit that the equivalent
due from Ireland is not to be expected immediately.
Give us only a certainty that if your extended commerce
increases your revenue, the surplus, after defraying the
same proportion of Irish expenses as at present, shall go
to relieve us. This, I think, no Irishman can rationally
object to; and Englishmen will be satisfied, though at
present the equivalent will certainly be below the just
proportion." [2]

In January, 1785, the scheme framed by Pitt in concert with his colleagues, and embodied in Eleven Resolutions, was transmitted to Dublin Castle; but the Duke
of Rutland and Mr. Orde, apprehensive of difficulties in
their own Parliament, took it upon themselves to make
one considerable alteration. They tacked a condition to
the words stipulating for a Return from Ireland, so as to
leave that Return, at least according to one construc-
tion, disputable and doubtful. This alteration was not
known to the public; but when imparted to the Cabinet
in England it caused much embarrassment to the Ministers, and drew forth two angry letters from the King. [3]

The Eleven Resolutions, as submitted to the Irish Parliament, in their general outline are as follows:—First.

---

[2] To the Duke of Rutland, Dec.
4, 1784. On the full development
of his plan see his able letter of
Jan. 6, 1785, published at full
length in the Quarterly Review,
No. cxl., p. 300. As privately
printed in 1842 it takes up eighteen
octavo pages, and is the longest
that I have seen of Mr. Pitt's.

[3] The King to Mr. Pitt. February 18 and 22, 1785.

to allow the importation of the produce or manufacture of other countries through Great Britain into Ireland, or through Ireland into Great Britain, without any increase of duty on that account. Secondly, in all cases where the duties on any article of the produce or manufacture of either country were different on importation into the other, to reduce them in the kingdom where they were the highest down to the lower scale. And thirdly, that whenever the gross hereditary revenue of Ireland should rise above 656,000*l.* in any year of peace (the actual gross income at that time being 652,000*l.*), the surplus should be appropriated towards the support of the naval force of the empire; and since this hereditary revenue was in the main derived from duties of Customs and Excise, any augmentation in them year by year would, as Pitt contended, exactly measure the growth of the prosperity of Ireland, derived from striking off the shackles on her trade.

Such is the outline of the measure which, in the name of the Government, Mr. Orde laid before the Irish Legislature at the beginning of February, 1785. Through the House of Commons the Eleven Resolutions passed with no serious opposition, and through the House of Lords with none at all. When thus transmitted back to England, Pitt resolved, notwithstanding the reluctance of some around him, to proceed. He was still bent upon his final object; and therefore, though not wholly adopting the Eleven Resolutions, he laid them before the English House of Commons on the 22nd of the same month. He moved only a general Resolution expressing the wish of the House for the final adjustment of the question, but he took the opportunity of explaining in detail the views which he had formed.

The speech of Pitt on this occasion may, even in its imperfect report, serve as a model of luminous statement in finance. Nor is it less conspicuous for its large and statesmanlike views of Irish policy. There were, he said, but two possible systems for countries placed in relation to each other like Britain and Ireland. The one of having the smaller completely subservient and subordinate to the greater—to make the one, as it were, an instrument of advantage, and to cause all her efforts to operate in favour and conduce merely to the interest of the other: this system we had tried in respect to Ireland. The other was a participation and community of benefits, and a system of equality and fairness which, without tending to aggrandize the one or depress the other, should seek the aggregate interest of the empire. Such a situation of commercial equality, in which there was to be a community of benefits, demanded also a community of burthens; and it was this situation in which he was anxious to place the two countries.

"Adopt then," cried Pitt in his peroration, "adopt that system of trade with Ireland that will have tended to enrich one part of the empire without impoverishing the other, while it gives strength to both; that like mercy, the favourite attribute of Heaven,—

> "'It is twice blessed,
> It blesseth him that gives and him that takes.'

Surely, after the heavy loss which our country has sustained from the recent severance of her dominions, there ought to be no object more impressed on the feelings of the House than to endeavour to preserve from further dismemberment and diminution—to unite and to connect—what yet remains of our reduced and shattered empire. . . . . I ask pardon for the length at which I have spoken. Of all the objects of my political life, this is in my opinion the most important that I ever have engaged in; nor do I imagine I shall ever meet another that shall rouse every emotion of my heart in so strong a degree as does the present."

To the views of Pitt a formidable opposition was at once announced. Fox, with his usual energy and eloquence, threw himself forward as the uncompromising adversary of Free Trade. Lord North espoused the same cause with less of vehemence, and also perhaps less eloquently, but certainly with far more of financial knowledge. And the further consideration of the subject was for some days adjourned.

The day but one after this debate we find Pitt write again to the Duke of Rutland : " Be assured of our firm persuasion that you made no concession but what at the moment of the decision you thought necessary and conducive to the general object. You must at the same time allow for the absolute impossibility of our maintaining this system while so essential a part is left in any respect disputable. . . I think it perfectly possible, upon its being understood that everything depends upon it, that the Irish Parliament will give the necessary explanation without difficulty. All we ask of Ireland is to clear from doubt and uncertainty a principle which they must consider themselves as having assented to."

But meanwhile in many parts of England a loud

and angry cry arose. At Manchester and other great
towns the manufacturers for the most part vehemently
declared that they should be ruined and undone. In
all haste they sent up to London the most stirring ad-
vocates and the most pathetic petitions. One of these,
presented by Mr. Thomas Stanley, was signed by no
less than eighty thousand manufacturers of Lancashire.
"It lies at my feet," said Mr. Stanley, "for it is too
heavy to be held in my hands. After stating some other
grievances, the framers of this great petition go on to
say that the admission of Irish fustians and cottons into
England was all that was wanting completely to anni-
hilate the cotton trade of this country."—We may smile
perhaps to find them on this occasion employ exactly the
same arguments which they or their successors afterwards denounced with so much indignation when applied
to the Corn Laws, and coming from the lips of the
landed gentlemen. Loaded as they were with heavy
taxes, how could they possibly compete with the Irish
in their own markets? What great advantages had
Ireland in the low price of labour! From that single
consideration how easy for her to undersell us!—No
arguments but only time and the test of experience
could solve such doubts beyond dispute.

Then again an alarm was raised that the measure
would be destructive of our Navigation Laws, the main
source (for so all parties then regarded them) of our
maritime strength. Yet, as Pitt showed, his proposal
was fully in the spirit of those laws. Already, by their
own express permission, goods the produce of any part
of Europe might be imported into Britain through Ire-

land. All that was now contemplated was to extend
the same licence to the settlements in America and
Africa, for by the monopoly of the East India Company
Asia would be still excluded.

As to the Colonies, however, it is to be borne in mind
that according to the common and almost undisputed
opinion of that time, Ireland had properly no part or
share in them. Thus do we find Mr. Pitt write in confidence to the Duke of Rutland: "Here, I think, it is
universally allowed that however just the claim of Ireland is, not to have her own trade fettered and restricted,
she can have no claim, beyond what we please to give
her, in the trade of our Colonies. They belong (unless
by favour or by compact we make it otherwise) exclusively to this country. The suffering Ireland to send
anything to these Colonies, to bring anything directly
from thence, is itself a favour, and is a deviation too, for
the sake of favour to Ireland, from the general and
almost uniform policy of all nations with regard to the
trade of their Colonies." Exactly similar to this was,
I may observe, the old claim of the Crown of Castille as
against the Crown of Aragon to the American Colonies.
Hence the epitaph on the son of Columbus, which may
still be seen in the cathedral of Seville:

> A Castilla y a Leon
> Mundo Nuebo dio Colon.

Amidst all these entanglements the measure of Pitt
made slow progress in the House of Commons. Two
months were consumed in hearing counsel and examining
witnesses, mingled with snatches of debate. Some of the
principal manufacturers and merchants gave evidence ex-
pressive of their disapprobation and alarm. Many objec-

tions of minute detail were plausibly, and several justly, urged. On the whole Pitt found it necessary to admit modifications in order to maintain his majority—above all, since no hopes of a specific promise came to him from the Irish Parliament. He brought forward his amended proposals on the 12th of May. Thus in his Diary writes Wilberforce : "May 12, House all night till eight o'clock in the morning. I differ from constituents. So affected that I could not get on. Pitt spoke wonderfully."

The ultimate proposals of Pitt as he now explained them were found to be attended with numerous exceptions and additions. Thus from eleven the Resolutions had grown in number to twenty. They had come to deal with patents, the copyright in books, and the right of fishing upon the coasts of the British dominions. Further, they provided that all the Navigation Laws which were then, or which might hereafter be, in force in Great Britain should be enacted by the Legislature of Ireland ; that Ireland should import no goods from the West Indies except the produce of our own Colonies ; and that so long as the Charter of the East India Company existed, Ireland should be debarred from all trade beyond the Cape of Good Hope to the Streights of Magellan.

By such means, and such means only, could the majority of Pitt be maintained. "Do not imagine"— thus he writes in strict confidence to the Duke of Rutland—"because we have had two triumphant divisions, that we have everything before us. We have an indefatigable enemy, sharpened by disappointment, watching and improving every opportunity. It has required infinite patience, management, and exertion to meet the clamour without doors, and to prevent it infecting our supporters in the House. Our majority, though a large one, is composed of men who think, or at least act so much for themselves, that we are hardly sure from day to day what impression they may receive. We have worked them up to carry us through this undertaking in its present shape, but we have had awkwardness enough already in many parts of the discussion." This important communication is dated May 21, 1785. We may be well pleased that the Duke omitted to comply with the postscript: "Be so good as to destroy this letter when you have read and considered it."

Notwithstanding the jealous spirit which compelled these changes, there remained enough of the first proposal to render it, as all parties have since owned, a boon of great value to the sister country. But in the very same proportion as it grew palatable to the English, it lost ground in the Irish House of Commons. Indeed during the last debates on this side of the Channel, and after the trials of party strength, Fox had entirely shifted his ground against the scheme. He had ceased to hope for its defeat in London, and he had begun to hope for its defeat in Dublin. With this view the measure was no longer in his eyes one of undue favour to Ireland; it was a signal breach of her newly granted legislative independence. "I will not," thus the great orator concluded, "I will not barter English commerce for Irish slavery; that is not the price I would pay, nor is this the thing I would purchase." [4]

Expressions of this kind found a ready echo across the Channel. When towards midsummer the Bill, as

_____

[4] Parl. Hist. vol. xxv. p. 778.

finally passed in England, came to Dublin, it was received with general disfavour. The Duke of Rutland and Mr. Orde found that they had most difficult cards to play. They had hoped for the aid of the leading patriot, the popular chief of 1782, who had supported the original Eleven Resolutions. But the changes made in them had wrought a corresponding change in him. "I have seen Mr. Grattan," writes the Lord Lieutenant on the 4th of July, "but found him impracticable." And again, on the 13th of August, when the measure was already before the Irish House of Commons: "The speech of Mr. Grattan (last night) was, I understand, a display of the most beautiful eloquence perhaps ever heard, but it was seditious and inflammatory to a degree hardly credible." Under such circumstances the result was soon apparent. Even on the mere preliminary motion that leave be given to bring in a Bill there was a fierce debate, continued till past nine in the morning, and "the Castle" could prevail by a majority of no more than nineteen. A victory of this kind was a sure presage of defeat in its further stages. The Bill was in consequence relinquished by the Government, to the great joy of the people. For so great was then the jealousy of their new legislative powers as entirely for the moment to absorb all other thoughts of national advantage. In Dublin there was even a general illumination to celebrate the withdrawal of the Bill.[5]

Thus did Ireland lose a most favourable opening for

---

[5] On the reception in Ireland of the Irish Propositions see the Correspondence of the Right Hon. John Beresford, vol. i. p. 265– 295, ed. 1854; and also Plowden's History of Ireland, vol. ii. p. 205, ed. 1809.

commercial freedom. Yet on other points her prospects
had brightened. The restoration of peace with foreign
States, and the restoration also of order in the finances,
had begun to draw prosperity in their train. The attempts in the winter of 1784 and again in the spring of
1785 to hold a Congress of delegates in Dublin had
been encountered with firmness by the Government,
and had signally failed. In like manner the hostile
factions had found themselves unable, as they wished, to
prolong the power of the Volunteers in time of peace,
and to turn them into a standing weapon against the
State. The Volunteers still continued to exist; they
had still the Earl of Charlemont for General-in-chief,
and by him were yearly reviewed; but their numbers
rapidly dwindled, and they became the mere shadow of
a shade. Meanwhile the Duke of Rutland, as Lord
Lieutenant, was gaining great personal popularity.
Young, of noble aspect, and of princely fortune, he was
generous, frank, and amiable, as became the son of the
gallant Granby. Fond of pleasure, he held a court of
much magnificence; and the succession of various enter-
tainments that he gave, splendid as they were in themselves, derived a further lustre from his Duchess, a
daughter of the house of Beaufort, and one of the most
beautiful women of her day. But besides and beyond
his outward accomplishments, the confidential letters of
the Duke to Pitt, all of which have been preserved, and
some printed, show him to have possessed both ability
and application in business. Perhaps had not his life
so prematurely ended, his name might have deserved
to stand as high in politics as does his father's in war.

To Pitt the failure of the Irish commercial measures was a deep disappointment, a bitter mortification. To them, to the framing or to the defence of their details, he had applied himself for almost a twelvemonth, and here was the result—the object of public good not attained, the jealousy of both nations stirred anew, and to himself for a time the decline of public favour, alike, though on exactly opposite grounds, in England and in Ireland. The journal of Wilberforce in the midst of the contest on this subject has this significant entry: "Pitt does not make friends."[6] On the other hand, Fox, as the champion of high protective duties, enjoyed in many quarters the gleam of returning popularity. Being at Knowsley in the course of that autumn on a visit to Lord Derby, the two friends went together to Manchester, and were warmly welcomed by the great metropolis of manufactures. Here is Fox's own account of it: "Our reception at Manchester was the finest thing imaginable, and handsome in all respects. All the principal people came out to meet us, and attended us into the town with blue and buff cockades, and a procession as fine, and not unlike that upon my chairing in Westminster. We dined with one hundred and fifty people. . . . . The concourse of people to see us was immense, and I never saw more apparent unanimity than seemed to be in our favour."[7]

---

[6] Diary, dated March 10, 1785.
[7] Letter dated September 10, 1785. See the Fox Memorials, vol. ii. p. 270.

CHAPTER VIII.

1785 — 1786.

Four-and-a-half Fund — Marriage of Pitt's sister, Lady Harriot — Pitt purchases a Country Seat — Embarrassment of Lady Chatham's, and of Pitt's private affairs — The Rolliad — Captain Morris's Songs — Peter Pindar — Pitt's Irish Propositions — Contemplated Treaty of Commerce with France — Proposed Fortifications of Portsmouth and Plymouth — Pitt's Sinking Fund — Impeachment and Trial of Warren Hastings — New Peers.

DURING the Session of 1785 Pitt was able to make, as he trusted, a satisfactory arrangement with respect to the Four-and-a-half Fund. The frequent arrears and defalcations of payment in the Pensions that were charged upon it were certainly not more inconvenient to the holders than they were discreditable to the Government. We find Pitt write as follows on the subject :

"Putney Heath, June 14, 1785.

" MY DEAR MOTHER,

"From a thousand circumstances I have been even longer than I thought possible in executing my intention of writing. Latterly I have delayed it till I could have the satisfaction of giving you positive accounts on the interesting and long depending subject of the grant. I have infinite pleasure in being at length able to tell you that it is settled in a way which is perfectly unexceptionable, and will, I think, answer every purpose.   A sum of 56,000*l.* was voted yesterday to make good the arrears of the 4½ per cent. up to the 5th of April last, and it was agreed to transfer the Duke of Gloucester's annuity of 9000*l.* to the aggregate fund. Relieved from this, there can be no doubt that the produce of the fund will be adequate to the remaining charges.   We may therefore fully depend on the discharge of the arrears very speedily, probably in the course of a few weeks, and on a punctual payment in future.   Not a word of opposition was offered to the proposal.   I cannot say how much I feel in a period being put to the embarrassment and inconvenience of a situation which ought to experience everything that is the contrary.

"Our Session is cruelly protracted, to the disappointment of my hope of seeing you, which I had promised myself I should do before this time.   How much longer it will last us is still uncertain, but I rather think we shall be at full liberty in less than a month.   Our principal difficulties are surmounted, and the chief trial now is that of patience.

.   .   .   .

> "Believe me ever, &c.,
>
> > "W. PITT."

The health of Lady Chatham had become in some degree impaired.   She suffered at intervals from a painful disorder, and since 1783 did not repeat her visit to Hayes.   Indeed so far as I can trace during a period of twenty years, she never again quitted Burton Pynsent even for a single night.   Under such circumstances, her daughter, Lady Harriot, sometimes paid visits of several weeks either to Lord Chatham or to Mr. Pitt.   There she was often in company with Mr. Edward Eliot, the early friend of her brother, and since the beginning of 1784 one of the Lords of the Treasury. An attachment sprang up between them, to the great satisfaction of their respective families. The offer of Mr. Eliot was accepted by Lady Harriot; and their marriage ensued September 21st, 1785. A few days later Pitt wrote to his mother in these words:

"Brighthelmstone, September 28, 1785.

"I look forward to the happiness of being with you on Tuesday in next week, and am to meet the bride and bridegroom in my way at Salisbury. You will have heard from my sister since the union was completed, which I trust furnishes a just prospect of increasing happiness to both."

And here is the commencement of another letter after his return from Burton:

"Downing Street, October 20, 1785.

"Your letter found me exceedingly safe at Brighthelmstone, notwithstanding all the perils of thunder and lightning, which overtook me at Mr. Bankes's at the end of a long day's shooting, and were attended with no more consequences than a complete wetting. My conscience has reproached me a good deal for not having sent this certificate of myself sooner."

In the course of this autumn Pitt became possessor of a country seat. This was Holwood, or as he always spelled it, Hollwood. It lies in Kent, one or two miles beyond his birth-place of Hayes. The purchase of the property as it now exists was not made at once, but extended over several years, the first payment being November, 1785, and the last August, 1794; and the total sum paid by Mr. Pitt in all these years was nominally 8,950*l.* In fact, however, it was only 4,950*l.*, since in 1786 he raised 4,000*l.* as a mortgage on the land. Holwood was a small house, but in a beautiful country. The view from it extends over a varied and undulating plain, from the heights of Sydenham on the one side to the heights of Knockholt Beeches on the other. In the grounds are considerable remains of a Roman camp, in part overgrown by some fine trees. Holwood now belongs to a highly accomplished and amiable man, retired from office, who cherishes with care any memorial that may remain of Mr. Pitt. It is from him, Lord Cranworth, that I have received the particulars, as abstracted from his own title-deeds, of Mr. Pitt's purchases and mortgages. But a former proprietor has pulled down the house which the great Minister dwelt in, and has reared a suburban villa in its place.

In the winter Pitt was concerned to find that the arrangement which he had made of the Four-and-a-half Fund did not, as he hoped, avert all future embarrassment from Lady Chatham. Thus he writes:

"Downing Street, December 1, 1785.

" MY DEAR MOTHER,

"I have learnt with more concern than I can express the feelings of your mind on the subject of your last letter. My great consolation is that the circumstances you state will not, I trust, upon reflection, give ground to the serious anxiety which I am sorry to find it has occasioned to you at the moment. Though there may exist a present balance against you in Mr. Coutts's books, beyond what you had imagined, there are, I am sure, but too many reasons to prevent your having anything to reproach yourself with on that account; and the inconvenience will be, I flatter myself, of very short duration; or rather that the business may be so arranged as to prevent its producing any. As to the two thousand pounds you mention, I have only to entreat you not to suffer a moment's uneasiness on that account. I can arrange that with Mr. Coutts without difficulty, and without its coming across any convenience or pleasure of my own; though none I could have would be so great as to be able to spare you a moment of trouble or anxiety. If Mr. Coutts wishes any further security for the 700*l.* which you mention as due to him, it will also be very easy to settle that to his satisfaction. I do not precisely know whether there are any arrears or debts of any sort, independent of the balance to Mr. Coutts, which will prevent your income being free in future. But as the two quarters of the grant which are due will be probably paid very soon, and the fund is so fully equal to the charges upon it, I persuade myself that you will find in future ample means to carry on your establishment, at least on its present footing. I wish very much I could relieve you from any of the anxiety and fatigue of looking into all the points relative to the state of your affairs. If it will contribute at all to it, I am sure, from the forwardness in which public business fortunately is, I can command a few days between this and Christmas to come down to you for that purpose; and which, independent of that, I am exceedingly desirous of doing. In the mean time it will be a great satisfaction to me if you could let me know nearly the amount of any demands outstanding upon you. Indeed it is the only point I want for complete satisfaction; because, as to the sums due to Mr. Coutts, I assure you that they ought not to give you any sort of disquietude. I thought once of sending this letter by a messenger, but I considered that you would perhaps answer it less at your leisure and convenience than by the common post; and though I shall wish much to hear from you, I hope you will not take up your pen at any time that may be troublesome to you.

" I am, my dear Mother, &c.,

" W. PITT."

At this period Mr. Pitt, wholly intent on public business, had much neglected his private affairs. Already had they fallen into some degree of embarrassment. In 1786 he requested his friend Mr. Robert Smith to examine them. Mr. Smith found that there was very great waste, and probably worse than waste, among the servants.[1] The evil might be checked for the moment; but through the ensuing years no effectual supervision was applied.

I now pass to matters of more public interest. But a few words on poetry before I come to prose.

It was not only by speeches or by essays, on the hustings or in the Houses, that the contest between Pitt and Fox was waged. Some of the political satires of that period attained a high degree of merit, and produced

---

[1] See a note by the editors to Wilberforce's Life, vol. iii. p. 245.

a powerful effect. But as to their effect there was a striking contrast between the early and latter part of Pitt's administration—a contrast that may be measured as between the *Rolliad* on the one side and the *Antijacobin* on the other. In the first period the superiority was beyond all doubt with the Opposition, in the second quite as clearly with the Minister.

The Rolliad—or to give the title more exactly, the 'Criticisms on the Rolliad'—came forth in parts during the last six months of 1784 and the first of 1785. It was first published in the 'Morning Herald,' a paper founded three years before. Other short pieces which soon afterwards appeared—the 'Political Eclogues,' and the 'Probationary Odes'—were combined with it to form a small volume, which has gone through a great number of editions, and which may still be read with pleasure. The principal writers were George Ellis and Tickell, Dr. Laurence, General Fitzpatrick, and Lord John Townshend.[2] At the outset Sheridan was suspected to be one of them, but in April, 1785, he took occasion in the House of Commons to deny the charge.

These gentlemen—the wits of Brooks's—being much disappointed at the results of the political conflict of 1784, gave some vent to their spleen in verse. For their subject they selected an imaginary epic of which

---

[2] On the authors of the Rolliad see some valuable contributions made in 1850 to the *Notes and Queries* by Lord Braybrooke, Mr. Markland, and Sir Walter C. Trevelyan (vol. ii. pp. 114, 242, and 373).

they gave fictitious extracts, and for their hero they took the Member for Devonshire, John Rolle. This gentleman, who became Lord Rolle in 1796, and who survived till 1842, was justly all through his life respected by his neighbours for hospitality and honour, for his consistent politics and his ample charities. But in 1784 he had provoked the Opposition by some taunts on the Westminster Scrutiny. He had besides been noticed as one of those impatient sitters who fretted at Burke's long speeches, and endeavoured to cough him down. The wits, in revenge, conferred upon him an epic immortality.

But in truth Mr. Rolle was little more to them than the peg on which they hung the shafts designed for higher game. They soon dismiss him with a few brief pleasantries upon his name or pedigree.

> " Illustrious Rolle! oh, may thy honoured name
> Roll down distinguished on the rolls of fame!
> . . . .
> Hot rolls and butter break the Briton's fast,
> Thy speeches yield a more sublime repast!"

With Mr. Pitt himself there was some difficulty in finding a good ground of attack upon his conduct. But then there was his age:

> " A sight to make surrounding nations stare,
> A kingdom trusted to a schoolboy's care."

As regards his friends, the authors of the Rolliad by no means confined themselves to political attacks. They eagerly sought out any peculiarities of habit, or even of face. Thus, in allusion to his frugal table, they address the Duke of Richmond :

> " Whether thou goest while summer heats prevail
> To enjoy the freshness of thy kitchen's gale,
> Where, unpolluted by luxurious heat,
> Its large expanse affords a cool retreat."

Or they refer, as follows, to the long chin of Lord Sydney :

> " Oh ! had by nature but propitious been
> His strength of genius to his length of chin,
> His mighty mind in some prodigious plan
> At once with ease had reached to Hindostan ! "

Or again as to the Marquis Graham, one of the Lords of the Treasury, who, in an unwary moment, had said in the House of Commons, " If the Hon. gentleman calls my Hon. friend Goose, I suppose he will call me Gosling," the Rolliad first in due precedence touches on the Duke. Then as to his son :

> " His son, the heir-apparent of Montrose,
> Feels for his beak, and starts to find a nose ! "

However trifling the theme of the Rolliad and the Political Eclogues, it is always commended to us by a consummate mastery of the English heroic couplet. So graceful in that metre are their inversions, and so sonorous their cadences, and so uniformly are these merits sustained, that it suggests the idea of a single writer much more than of a confederated band of friends. And when, in addition to their metrical skill, their pleasantries were fresh and new, it can scarcely be doubted that they had political effect, and tended to assist the cause which they espoused.

Besides the authors of the Rolliad, Captain Morris attained at this time some reputation as a writer of songs. He was a boon companion of the wits at Brooks's; and he thought that abuse of their opponents gave new zest to his praises of love and wine. But in one or two places he has indulged in a savage strain such as no man of common feeling could approve. In 1784, for example, he wrote a ballad entitled "Billy Pitt and the Farmer." It tells, with some humour, a story how Pitt and Dundas missed their way one dark night near Wimbledon, and were fired at by mistake from a farm-house at Wandsworth. And here are some of the stanzas with which the gallant Captain concludes his tale.

"Then Billy began for to make an oration,
    As oft he had done to bamboozle the nation;
    But Hodge cried 'Begone! or I'll crack thy young crown
        for't;
    Thou belong'st to a rare gang of rogues, I'll be bound
        for't.'

"Then Harry stepped up; but Hodge, shrewdly supposing
    His part was to steal while the other was posing,
    Let fly at poor Billy, and shot through his lac'd coat;
    Oh, what pity it was it did not hit his waistcoat!"[3]

At nearly the same time another political poet of much higher celebrity arose. This was John Wolcott, a

---

[3] This ballad is comprised in the Asylum for Fugitive Pieces, vol. ii. p. 246, ed. 1786.

native of Devonshire. He had taken Holy Orders, but
had not the smallest inclination to clerical duty, and he
subsisted mainly by his pen. Writing under the assumed
name of Peter Pindar, he soon attracted notice by the
humour of his grotesque descriptions, and still more perhaps by the audacity of his personal attacks. He loved
especially to portray any respectable character in a
ridiculous situation. Thus he represents the King, whom
he spared less than any, as visiting a cottage near
Windsor, and as struck with amazement at the sight of
an apple-dumpling, not being able to discover any seam
by which the apple was introduced! Thus he represents
Sir Joseph Banks as boiling fifteen hundred fleas in a
saucepan to ascertain if, when boiled, they might not
turn scarlet like lobsters! And as to Mr. Pitt, the
Reverend gentleman is never weary of taunting him
with his too faithful observance of the seventh com-
mandment.

The loss of the Irish Propositions was, as I have said, a
most bitter disappointment to Pitt; but, as he writes to
the Duke of Rutland, "we have the satisfaction of having
proposed a system which I believe will not be discredited
even by its failure, and we must wait times and seasons
for carrying it into effect. . . . All I have to say in the
mean time is very short: let us meet what has happened,
or whatever may happen, with the coolness and determination of persons who may be defeated, but cannot be
disgraced, and who know that those who obstruct them
are greater sufferers than themselves. . . . . I believe
the time will yet come when we shall see all our views
realized in both countries, and for the advantage of

both. . . . . . I write this as the first result of my feelings, and I write it to yourself alone."

It was still the hope of Pitt to renew his plan with some modifications during the next year; but finding his friends in Ireland afford him little hope of a more successful issue, he relinquished the idea, and applied himself to carry out the same principles in another sphere. He was most anxious to lighten the shackles which at that period weighed down our trade with France, and during the autumn he planned a mission to Paris for that object. A little to his own surprise, perhaps, he found a ready agent in the foremost ranks of Opposition. William Eden came at this time to be detached from his party ties with Fox and North, mainly by the intervention of his personal friend John Beresford. So far as I am able to discover, he did not alter his politics on any public ground, nor, indeed, allege any such in his own defence. In his first letter to Pitt he expressed a wish to become Speaker of the House of Commons, if any opening should arise; but Pitt gave no encouragement to this idea, and early in 1786 sent over Mr. Eden as special envoy to Paris, under the Duke of Dorset as Ambassador, to negotiate a treaty of Commerce with France. In that post his great ability and address were of signal service: but, as might be expected, his secession stung to the quick his former friends. There ensued some stanzas on 'the Loss of Eden' by the authors of the 'Rolliad,' and some taunts of no common asperity in the House of Commons.

Parliament met again on the 24th of January, and

almost the first business of importance which engaged
its time was a plan of the Duke of Richmond, as Master-
General of the Ordnance, to fortify the Dockyards of
Portsmouth and Plymouth. This plan had been already
mooted in the House of Commons in the preceding year,
but was then postponed. It was now brought forward by
Mr. Pitt in the name of the Government. During the
last war the unprotected state of our great naval arsenals
had been painfully apparent. Nevertheless the scheme
to fortify them was much opposed. In the first
place, the Duke himself was not popular. Then there
was the expense, estimated at 760,000*l.* Then again
there was the constitutional jealousy of any new strongholds in England. Surely—so Sheridan in a most able
speech contended—these unassailable fortresses might,
in the hands of an ambitious and ill-advised King, be
made the instruments for subverting the liberties of the
people. Yet, as Pitt had already asked, in allusion to
the system of Lord North, "Is it less desirable for us to
be defended by the walls of Portsmouth and Plymouth,
garrisoned by our own Militia, than to purchase the protection of Hessian hirelings?" So far, however, did the
eloquence of Sheridan, of Fox, and of Barré—for Barré
also opposed the scheme—prevail in the House of Commons, that on the division the numbers were exactly
equal: 169 on each side. The Speaker, Mr. Cornwall,
gave his casting vote with the Noes, so that the entire project, to Pitt's great mortification, fell to the
ground; nor was it ever afterwards renewed. "After
all," so wrote Eden to John Beresford, "it proves what
I have said to you, that it is a very loose Parliament,

and that Government has not a decisive hold of it upon any material question." [4]

If, however, these failures both on Irish trade and on English fortifications be taken as evincing some decline in Pitt's popularity and influence, they were more than redeemed by the general applause which greeted his measure for the redemption of the National Debt. Last Session he had promised it for this ; and all through the Recess, says Bishop Tomline, he received an almost incredible number of schemes and projects. Many of these came from amateur financiers in the country—the " provincial Chancellors of the Exchequer," as on one occasion they were termed by Sir Robert Peel—and such schemes might be quickly tossed aside ; but others were of a different order, and required thought and care. Nor did Pitt neglect the published lucubrations of Dr. Richard Price. That remarkable man was then in the zenith of his fame. Though a Dissenting Minister of the Socinian school, and though well skilled in philosophical controversies, he had by no means confined his attention to them. He was an ardent champion of popular claims, and a profound adept in financial calculations. During the last war the American Congress had by Resolution expressed their desire to consider him a citizen of the United States, and to receive his assistance in regulating their finances—an offer which his advancing years induced him to decline.[5] So early as 1773 he had pub-

---

[4] Beresford Correspondence, vol. i. p. 302.

[5] This was in 1778. See a note to Franklin's Works, vol. viii. p. 354, ed. 1844. Franklin, who knew him well in England, speaks of him as the "good Dr. Price." Ibid. vol. x. p. 365.

lished an elaborate 'Appeal on the National Debt,' in which he strongly urged the importance of an inalienable Sinking Fund; and in 1786 he was able to assert that "the plan which Mr. Pitt has adopted is that which I have been writing about and recommending for many years."[6]

In this assertion, however, we must understand Dr. Price to mean the principle or leading idea rather than the means of execution; for Dr. Price himself, as also several of Pitt's later correspondents, had framed divers ingenious devices for converting low Stocks into high, as easier for future redemption, and as holding out, in theory at least, an ultimate advantage to the public. But on full consideration Pitt had become convinced that of all the modes of redemption, the simplest and the plainest—merely to take the Funds from time to time at the market price of the day—would be also the surest and the best.

Having laid a great variety of accounts before the House, and paved the way by the Report of a Select Committee, Pitt brought forward his proposal on the 29th of March. On this occasion Bishop Tomline has indulged us with some personal reminiscences which appear of great interest, and are among the very few that his 'Life' contains:—

"Mr. Pitt passed the morning of this day in providing the calculations which he had to state, and in examining the Resolutions which he had to move; and at last he said

---

[6] Letter to Earl Stanhope, as read in the House of Lords, May 22. 1786.

that he would go and take a short walk by himself, that
he might arrange in his mind what he had to say in the
House. He returned in a quarter of an hour, and told
me he believed he was prepared. After dressing himself he ordered dinner to be sent up ; and learning at
that moment that his sister (who was then living in the
house with him) and a lady with her were going to dine
at the same early hour, he desired that their dinner
might be sent up with his, and that they might dine
together. He passed nearly an hour with these ladies,
and several friends who called in their way to the House,
talking with his usual liveliness and gaiety, as if having
nothing upon his mind. He then went immediately to
the House of Commons, and made this ' elaborate and
far-extended speech,' as Mr. Fox called it, without one
omission or error."

The speech of Pitt on the 29th of March, though
most imperfectly reported, was indeed conspicuous, even
among his own, for its masterly expositions of finance.
With some pride might he point to the re-establish-
ment of the public credit and to the thriving state of
the revenue under his administration. Already did the
surplus of income and revenue nearly approach one
million sterling ; and this sum—namely, one clear million annually—whatever the future state of the Exchequer might be, Pitt proposed to place beyond the
control of Government in the hands of Commissioners
for the yearly redemption of the public debt. To this
" Sinking Fund " was also to be added the yearly amount
of the interest of the sums to be redeemed, so that it
was in fact a million at compound interest.

The establishment of a Sinking Fund was by no means new. It may be traced up, as I have shown in another work, to the year 1716; but until now the Fund which was created in peace might always, at the will of the Government, be resumed in war. Such was the course which the preceding Ministers had always pursued; such was the course which Fox acknowledged that he still preferred. Pitt, on the contrary—and this was the peculiar and distinguishing point in his system—proposed to make his Sinking Fund the creation of an Act of Parliament, and inalienable except by another Act of Parliament. His proposal being regarded as the surest bulwark of our national credit, was accepted with eagerness—nay, almost enthusiasm—both by the House of Commons and the public. In vain did Fox, in several eloquent speeches, contend that our system should be to discharge in time of peace the debts contracted in time of war; and in the event of a new war to cease from paying off debts, and direct our entire resources against the foe. So strong was the current in Pitt's favour that Fox did not venture to call for a division.

In the Lords the main attack upon Pitt's measure came from his own brother-in-law, Charles Lord Mahon, who in March of this year had succeeded his father as Earl Stanhope. During the contests of 1783 and 1784 he had been, as we have seen, among the most strenuous supporters of his kinsman; but there was in him, conjoined with great powers of mind, a certain waywardness of temper which made him, it may almost be said, dislike the winning side as such. He loved better to act in a small minority; and in after years, as the disposition grew upon him, he loved best to act alone, coming in the House of Lords to be often surnamed, as in truth he sometimes was, the " Minority of One."

In May, 1786, Lord Stanhope having framed a plan of his own for the redemption of the National Debt, both published a pamphlet and delivered a speech against Pitt's. His main objection, however, was exactly the reverse of that which Fox had urged. He was not satisfied to secure the Sinking Fund by an Act of Parliament. He wished to carry its inalienability further still by certain changes of Stock and arrangements with the public creditor, so that any future diversion of the Sinking Fund would be equivalent to an act of national bankruptcy. Many compliments on his speech and pamphlet were paid him by Lord Loughborough, Lord Stormont, and other Opposition Peers, who already began to look upon him as their own ; but they appear to have dissuaded a division, and none in fact took place.

Thus almost by general consent did Pitt's measure become law. During many years did it retain both the support of Government and the favour of the people. During many years did we continue to hold sacred a million sterling for the Sinking Fund, even when compelled, by the exigencies of war, to borrow that million sterling, and scores of millions sterling besides. But by degrees there came to be a doubt upon the public mind. The policy of a Sinking Fund, whenever propped up by loans, began to be greatly questioned ; and the death-blow, it may be said, to the system of Pitt upon that subject was struck at last by a hand that had been most forward and active in assisting him to rear it. That hand was no other than Lord Grenville's. In 1786 he had been the Chairman of that Committee, as moved by Pitt, which immediately preceded the introduction of the Bill upon the Sinking Fund; and no man had been more zealous to promote or to vindicate the measure of his chief; but after the lapse of more than forty years it was found that experience and reflection had wrought an entire change in his views. A pamphlet published by him in 1828, and forming an era on this question, avows with noble frankness his sense of former error, and denounces with great force the inutility of a borrowed Sinking Fund.

It was under cover of the first great popularity of this measure that Pitt was able to propose and carry a vote of 210,000*l.* to discharge a new debt, which, in spite of the King's personal economy, had accrued upon the Civil List of 850,000*l.* a-year.

In this Session, as in those which followed, Pitt refrained from renewing his motion on Parliamentary Reform; but he gave his cordial aid to a Bill which had been framed and brought in by Lord Mahon for the improvement of County Elections. The object was in great part the same which has been since with general assent adopted —to provide an annual registration of the freeholders, and to admit several other polling-places besides the county town. Lord Mahon being called to the Upper House, Wilberforce undertook in his place the further conduct of the Bill. By his exertions, and the support of the Prime Minister, the Bill passed, though not without some difficulty, through the House of Commons; but in the Lords it was thrown out, mainly—so Mr. Wyvill states—by a "coalition of the King's Friends and the Whig aristocracy." [7]

In this Session Pitt also achieved a considerable change in the Revenue Laws. "I am just going," thus he writes to the Duke of Rutland, April 29, 1786, " to introduce a plan for excising wine, which, although it had nearly overthrown Sir Robert Walpole, will, I believe, meet with very little difficulty." So accordingly it proved.

But perhaps the Session of 1786 is chiefly memorable for the first Parliamentary steps that were taken towards the Impeachment and the Trial of Warren Hastings.

The career of Hastings in the East and the divers grounds of charge that might be urged against him have been related at length by several writers, and by myself among the rest.[8] He left India at last in perfect peace, retiring from his post not as dismissed, nor even as rebuked, but of his own free will. In June, 1785, he once more set foot on English ground, there rejoining Mrs. Hastings—the fair Marian Imhoff of Germany— who had preceded him by about a year. His reception at home was highly favourable. The Directors of the East India Company greeted him with a public Address ; the King and Queen were most gracious at the Levee. Her Majesty even condescended to accept from Mrs.

---

[7] Wyvill's Papers, vol. iv. p. 542 ; and the Life of Wilberforce, vol. i. p. 114.

[8] I venture on this subject to refer the reader to the 68th and 69th chapters of my History of England. The private letters of Hastings, both at that period and after his return, will be found in the three volumes of the Biography by the Rev. G. R. Gleig.

Hastings the present of an ivory bed—a gift by no means forgotten in the satires of that day.

In the House of Commons Hastings had two most bitter enemies in Edmund Burke and Philip Francis; the one impelled by high public spirit, the other, we may assert, mainly by personal rancour. Only a few days after Hastings's arrival in London, Burke rose in his place and gave notice that if no other Member would undertake the business, he would himself on a future day make a motion respecting the conduct of a gentleman just returned from India. But the Opposition was at that time, as we have seen, wholly broken and enfeebled, and among the Ministers Hastings had many friends. He might regard as such—so greatly had circumstances changed—even his old antagonist Dundas, who had moved the Vote of Censure upon him in 1782. Hastings himself in his private correspondence observes as of Dundas in July, 1785, that "the Board of Control has been more than polite to me." Lord Thurlow went much further still. He espoused the interests of Hastings with a warmth which, considering his own post of Chancellor, may be justly condemned as indecorous. And some of his expressions on the subject deviated from truth even further than from decorum. "The fact is," he cried, "that this is Hastings's administration, and that he put an end to the late Ministers as completely as if he had taken a pistol and shot them through the head, one after another!" Even in the previous year he had eagerly pressed Pitt for a peerage. Pitt, however, had preserved something more of a judicial mind. He owned the great merits and services of the late

Governor-General, but alleged the Vote of Censure still standing upon record in the Journals of the House of Commons. "Until," he said, "the sting of those Resolutions is done away by a Vote of Thanks, I do not see how I can with propriety advise His Majesty to confer an honour upon Mr. Hastings."[9]

In this state of affairs, so far as Hastings was concerned, the members of the Opposition were little inclined to cheer on or to follow Burke. The inquiry which he had announced must of necessity be long and laborious, while the prospect of party advantage from it was extremely small. Had no fresh provocation arisen, the old quarrel would scarcely have been further pursued. Had Hastings remained quiet, there seems every reason to surmise that Burke would have, though reluctantly, remained quiet too.

But it was the misfortune of the late Governor-General to rely at this time on a most incompetent adviser. There was under his patronage a Major of the Bengal army, John Scott by name, whom the rupees of his patron had seated for the small borough of West Looe. In the House of Commons this gentleman avowed himself the agent and representative of Hastings. Zeal and industry were qualities possessed by Major Scott in the highest perfection; of judgment and discretion he was wholly destitute. He proved to be a most tedious speaker and a most injudicious friend. As to the last point, his private letters to Hastings are still on record, evincing his passionate and distorted views of public

[9] Memoirs of Hastings by the Rev. G. R. Gleig, vol. iii. p. 171 and 174.

men and public measures. Thus in August, 1784, we
find him vilifying his great opponent as "that reptile
Mr. Burke," and with still more signal folly boasting
that over the reptile he, Major Scott, had "triumphed
most completely!"

Acting on such notions as these, Major Scott rose in
his place on the very first day of the Session of 1786.
Reminding the House of the notice which Burke had
given, he called upon Burke to bring forward his
charges, and to fix the earliest possible day for their discussion. This unwise defiance received a prompt reply.
It bound Burke to pursue his design, and it induced his
friends to rally round him. Henceforward the zeal of
Fox in this cause became fully equal to his own.

The first steps of the great twin leaders were motions
for papers, which, being in part refused, gave rise to
some keen debates. In these Pitt took occasion to declare his line—a line far different from Thurlow's. It
was such as every Minister would profess at present, but
such as hardly any Minister except himself appears at
that time to have kept in view. "For my part," he
said, "I am neither a determined friend nor foe to Mr.
Hastings, but I am resolved to support the principles of
justice and equity. Mr. Hastings, notwithstanding all
the assertions to the contrary, may be as innocent as
the child unborn; but he is now under the eye and suspicion of Parliament, and his innocence or guilt must be
proved by incontestable evidence."

Early in April Burke, with the active aid of Francis,
brought forward eleven specific Charges, which soon
afterwards he increased, by successive accessions, to

twenty-two.   But by far the chief ones in importance
were those on the Rohilla war, on Cheyte Sing, the
Rajah of Benares, and on the two Begums or Princesses
of Oude.   On the other part Hastings sent in a petition
praying to be heard in reply, and his petition being
granted, he appeared at the Bar bending under the
weight of a State paper which he had prepared, of immense length, according to the approved India Company fashion.   He read on as long as his own strength
and much longer than his hearers' patience endured.
Then the Clerks at the Table supplied his place, and
mumbled through the interminable document for some
hours more, while the Members stole away one by one,
comparing perhaps in their own minds the speeches of
Scott with the essays of Hastings, and doubting whether,
after all, the agent was one whit more tedious than his
principal.

The reading of this document at the Bar as at the
Table took up not merely one day, but part of the next.
Yet Hastings, looking no doubt to the great Bengal
models, thought it much too short.   "Stinted as I was,"
he says, "and indeed most dreadfully, as to time"—so
he writes to one of his friends May 20, 1786.   Lord
Macaulay has well shown in one of his excellent
essays how total and complete was the misapprehension of Hastings on all points of the temper of the
House of Commons.[1]

After the late Governor-General had concluded, Sir
Robert Barker and other witnesses were examined at

---

[1] Lord Macaulay's Essays, vol. iii. p. 427-437.

the Bar from time to time, and on the 1st of June Burke
brought forward his first, the Rohilla Charge. He had
with good judgment selected this as his vantage ground.
The cruel attack on the Rohillas had been at one time
condemned by the Court of Directors. It had been the
ground of the Vote of Censure passed by the Houses.
It had been in an especial manner the mark for the
indignation and the invective of Dundas, who was now,
beyond any other Member of Parliament, responsible
for the conduct of Indian affairs. When, therefore, it
was rumoured that Dundas intended to uphold Hastings
on the very point as to which he had formerly arraigned
him, the Opposition heard the news with exulting glee,
and Fox turned it to the best account in one of his
masterly speeches. Dundas, however, was at all times
bold and " cunning of fence." And on this occasion he
had specious arguments to urge. He declared that he
still thought, as in 1781, that the attack on the Rohillas
was a war of injustice. But he pointed out that he and
the other members of the old Committee, the framers
of the Vote of Censure—and to some of those in person
he might still appeal—had in view not any penal prosecution of Hastings, but only his recall. That recall was
the object which they had striven for and failed in.
Subsequently to that period an Act of Parliament had
been passed re-appointing Warren Hastings by name Governor-General of Bengal. The Statute therefore might
be considered as a Parliamentary pardon, unless some
fresh circumstances of aggravation had since occurred.
Had there been any such ? On the contrary there had
been services of the most essential character during

the latter periods of the war—services so great, Dundas continued, that we might almost be tempted to term Hastings the saviour of India. On these grounds, Dundas said, he must oppose the motion. Pitt, though he said nothing, had taken the same view. The Ministerial phalanx followed its chief, and upon a division Burke found himself defeated by 119 against 67.

Such a majority upon such a question might seem to the friends of Hastings the sure presage of approaching triumph. They expected that Fox and Burke would try perhaps one or two Charges more, would find the numbers to back them grown smaller still, and would then in anger fling down their brief and walk away. Had such proved to be the issue, Hastings would no doubt have ascribed it—so blind is human vanity!— to the transcendent merits of his essay at the Bar. Already in his private letters about this period does he declare that "it instantly turned all minds to my own way." Already does he speak of his demand to be heard in person as conceived "in a happy hour and by a blessed inspiration." But a complete reverse of fortune was now close at hand.

The great Benares Charge had been entrusted to Fox's care. He brought it forward on the 13th of June with his usual surpassing ability, resting his argument solely on this principle, that Cheyte Sing was an independent prince, no way liable to be called on for succour by the Bengal Government. "I must acknowledge," said he near his conclusion, "that there was something like a colour for the vote to which we came respecting the Rohilla war. The extreme distance of the time at

which it happened, the little information the House had
of it till lately, the alleged important services of Mr.
Hastings since that period (although I maintain that
they were neither meritorious nor in truth services)—all
these, with other causes and justifications, might then
be urged. But there are none such on the present
occasion. The facts are all of them undeniable; they
are atrocious, and they are important; so much so that
upon the vote of this night, in my judgment, the fate of
Bengal depends."

Fox was seconded by Francis, with far less ability indeed, but even superior bitterness. Then, after a short
speech from Mr. Nicholls, tending to the complete innocence of Hastings, the Prime Minister rose. In the
first place he utterly denied the independent position
ascribed to Cheyte Sing by Fox. The Rajah of Benares was, as he contended, a vassal of the Bengal
empire, bound in extraordinary perils to give extraordinary aid. For his contumacy in withholding such aid
a fine might justly be inflicted. But then the question
arose, what fine? Now to levy a fine of 500,000*l.* for
the mere delay of paying a contribution of 50,000*l.*,
which contribution had after all been paid, was to destroy all connection between the degrees of guilt and
punishment—it was a proceeding shamefully exorbitant,
and repugnant to reason and justice. On this ground,
and this ground only, Pitt declared that after a long
and laborious study of the question, he felt it his duty
on the whole to vote for the Benares charge.

Until Pitt rose, and indeed for a long time afterwards,
the House had been firmly persuaded that he intended to

side with Hastings. Great, therefore, and general was
the surprise at his conclusion. Several gentlemen in
office, as Mr. Grenville and Lord Mulgrave, were already
committed by their words or had already formed their
opinions; and they declared themselves bound in conscience to vote against the motion. But the majority
of the House was obedient to the voice of its leader.
The Yeas for Fox's Resolution were 119, and the Noes
but 79. Dundas had taken no part in the debate, but
he voted with Pitt.

In a letter written more than thirty years afterwards,
and only a few weeks before his death, we find Hastings
revert to the proceedings of that memorable day. He
declares that from information which he received at the
time, Dundas had called on Pitt at an early hour of that
morning, awoke him from his sleep, and engaged him
in a discussion of three hours, the result of which was a
total inversion of the Ministerial policy that night.[2] It
is difficult to lay any great stress on the statements of
that letter, since in the next sentence the writer goes
on to say, "I must stop, for my mind forsakes me."
Nevertheless it seems highly probable that the final
decision upon the Benares charge may have been deferred till close upon Fox's motion, and may have been
preceded by an anxious conference between the First
Lord of the Treasury and the President of the Board of
Control.

So general, however, had been the surprise at Pitt's
conclusion, that all kinds of rumours and surmises were

---

[2] To Mr. Elijah Impey, April 19, 1818.

noised abroad in order to account for it. Most of these were low and base, as coming from the mere runners and lackeys of faction. Hastings might excite the jealousy of Dundas; Hastings might excite the jealousy of Pitt; he might become a formidable rival in the Cabinet; he might draw to himself the entire management of the Board of Control. Yet, though Dundas had many faults, mean jealousy was never one of them; still less can it be imputed to the lofty mind of Pitt. And, moreover, in this case the imputation almost answers itself; for how, in a Parliamentary Government, can any man—unless, perhaps, at a former period, some great Peer like Rockingham—aspire to fill any high office at home, or be the cause of jealousy lest he should fill it, without some degree of fluency at least in public speaking? Now of such fluency, Hastings, by his own confession, had none at all. Many years afterwards we find him write as follows to a younger friend:— "Your father knows that I am in a singular degree deficient in the powers of utterance."[3]

But why in this case seek for any hidden or mysterious causes? Does not the true motive of Pitt lie clear upon the surface? Is it not to be found in the merits of the question itself? His full consideration of it had been long—perhaps too long—postponed; but when at length he went through the documents before him, they led him to exactly that conclusion which even now, on calm retrospect, we may be inclined to form. Hastings was right in regarding Cheyte Sing as a vassal.

----

[3] To Mr. Charles Doyley, April 15, 1813.

and in punishing his contumacy by the imposition of a fine; but Hastings was wrong—grievously wrong, and beyond all doubt misled by personal rancour and revenge—in the exorbitant amount of the fine imposed.

This conclusion as to the motive of the Ministers is confirmed by the unaffected language of Dundas to Lord Cornwallis, who only six weeks before—early in May, 1786—had sailed from England to fill the post of Governor-General of India. To him, in March, 1787, Dundas wrote as follows :—" The only unpleasant circumstance (in our public situation) is the impeachment of Mr. Hastings. . . . . But the truth is, when we examined the various articles of Charges against him, with his defences, they were so strong, and the defences so perfectly unsupported, it was impossible not to concur; and some of the Charges will unquestionably go to the House of Lords." [4]

In June, 1786, however, the Session was drawing to an end; and although Major Scott pleaded in the most vehement manner against all delay, the Charges against Hastings were of necessity postponed to the ensuing year.

On the 11th of July this busy Session was closed by the King in one of the shortest Speeches ever delivered from the Throne. Immediately afterwards we find Pitt returned to his favourite Holwood, but applying himself at once to fresh arrangements of business. Thence he writes :—

---

[4] See the Cornwallis Correspondence, vol. i. p. 281.

"Holwood, July 13, 1786.

"MY DEAR MOTHER,

"The pleasure I have received from your letter, which reached me at nearly the eve of our Prorogation, added, I assure you, not a little to the satisfaction of that welcome period. . . . . I cannot indeed boast to be yet perfectly at leisure, but I have at least comparatively holiday, and shall, as I hope, be really in possession of them in a few weeks. . . . . But I must be in town the very beginning of August, when our first payment of the Public Debt is to take place.

"I am just now in the beginning of some very necessary arrangements to put the business of Government into a form that will admit of more regularity and despatch than has prevailed in some branches of it. The first step is in the appointment of a new Committee of Trade, which becomes every day more and more important, at which Mr. Jenkinson is to preside, with the honour of a Peerage. This, I think, will sound a little strange at a distance, and with a reference to former ideas; but he has really fairly earned it and attained it at my hands."

The reconstruction of the Board of Trade, which the Economical Bill of Burke had swept away, was almost a necessity in a commercial country, and in view of the commercial changes which Pitt designed. We have seen that Mr. Jenkinson, now raised to the Peerage as Lord Hawkesbury, was the President of the new Board, while for its Vice-President Pitt named William Grenville.

The Peerage of Lord Hawkesbury was followed by several more. Thus, Sir Guy Carleton became Lord

Dorchester, and Sir Harbord Harbord Lord Suffield;
and English Baronies were granted to the Irish Earls
of Shannon and Tyrone. Earlier in the year Pitt also
obtained from the King two promotions in the Peerage
on strong grounds of merit: the advancement of Lord
Camden to be an Earl and Viscount Bayham; and the
advancement of Earl Gower to be Marquis of Stafford.
Yet the Minister was anxious at this time to stand firm
against most new claims. On the 19th of July he writes
as follows to the Duke of Rutland: " I have no difficulty
in stating fairly to you that a variety of circumstances
has unavoidably led me to recommend a larger addition
to the British Peerage than I like or than I think
quite creditable; and I am on that account very desirous not to increase it now farther than is absolutely
necessary."

CHAPTER IX.

1786 — 1787.

State of the Ministry — William Grenville — Lord Mornington —
Henry Dundas — Lord Carmarthen — Death of Frederick the
Great — Margaret Nicholson's attempt on the life of George the
Third — Death of Pitt's sister, Lady Harriot — Treaty of Com-
merce with France — State of Ireland — Dr. Pretyman becomes
Bishop of Lincoln and Dean of St. Paul's — Parliamentary Debates
on French Treaty — Mr. Charles Grey — Proceedings against
Hastings resumed — Unanimous testimony to Sheridan's eloquence
— Pitt's measures of Financial Reform — The Prince of Wales
and Mrs. Fitzherbert — Attempted Repeal of the Test Act —
Settlement in Botany Bay.

In the Session which was just concluded, Pitt had
been able to strengthen himself in the House of Commons. He was still the only Cabinet Minister in that
assembly; but there were two young men of high
promise, one of whom he had just promoted, and the
other just placed in office. These were the new Vice-
President of the Board of Trade, William Grenville,
afterwards Lord Grenville, and the new Lord of the
Treasury, Richard Wesley, Earl of Mornington in the
Irish Peerage, afterwards Marquis Wellesley. It was
some time, however, ere Pitt obtained from them much
assistance in debate. The oratorical eminence of both
was a plant of later growth.

Writing to the Duke of Rutland in October, 1785,
Pitt had thrown out the idea of Grenville for Irish
Secretary in the place of Orde. He added: "I do not
know that he would take it, and rather suppose that he

would not. I think, too, that his near connection with
Lord Buckingham is itself, perhaps, a sufficient objection ; though in temper and disposition he is much the
reverse of his brother, and in good sense and habits of
business very fit for such a situation." Grenville had
also taken part in several important debates, always
with authority, and sometimes with success. But he
did not, according to the common phrase, " make way "
in the House of Commons. To his style of speaking
the House of Lords was certainly the appropriate
sphere, and to this it appears that so early as 1786
Grenville in his secret hopes aspired.[1]

Lord Mornington at the Treasury did not for a long
time do justice to himself. Some years elapsed before
he spoke at much length or with much effect. Even
after he had made manifest his great oratorical powers,
it required much persuasion of others and much prepa-
ration of his own before he would engage to take part
in a debate. Pitt once said of him that he was the
animal of the longest gestation he had ever seen. His
speeches, when at last they came, were excellent and
justly admired, above all for their classic taste, their
graceful elocution, and their vivid style.

The main reliance of Pitt in all debates was still,
therefore, that able and zealous friend who had stood by
him ever since his outset in official life. Henry Dundas,
sprung from a family most eminent in Scottish juris-
prudence, was the son of one President of the Court of
Session, the brother of a second, and the uncle of a

---

[1] See the Courts and Cabinets of George the Third, vol. i. p. 315,
ed. 1853.

Lord Chief Baron. Born in 1742, and sent to Parliament in 1774 by his native county of Edinburgh, his outset in public life among "the Southron" might be compared to Wedderburn's, twelve years before. But there was all the difference between a very cold heart and a very warm one. Wedderburn, with no predilections except for his own rise, took the utmost pains, and with success, to divest himself of the Scottish dialect and accent. Dundas, on the contrary, in a far more manly spirit, as he clung to all other kindred ties, retained the speech and the tones of his fatherland. Intent only on the matter, to which he applied his masculine good sense, he never seemed to care for or to hesitate in the choice of words. Thus the graces of elocution and delivery were perhaps despised, or certainly at least neglected, by him. Throwing himself boldly into the van of the Parliamentary conflict, he would grapple at once with the strength of the arguments before him, and strike home at their vulnerable points. His adversaries might now and then indulge a smile at some provincial phrase or uncouth gesticulation, but they had often to quail before the close pressure of his logic and the keen edge of his invectives. They quickly found that it was difficult to answer, and impossible to daunt him. In business, as in public speaking, his turn of mind was eminently practical, clear, and to the point. Frank and cordial in his temper, fond of jests and good fellowship in private life, convivial to the full extent admitted by the far from abstemious habits of his age, he was much beloved in the circle of his friends, nor always disliked even by his political opponents.   Besides that his temper was to every one generous and kindly, his heart warmed to a fellow-countryman as such.   I have heard a Scottish Peer of the opposite party, but a discerning and long-experienced man—the second Earl of Minto—say that, as he believed, there was scarce a gentleman's family in Scotland, of whatever politics, which had not at some time and in some one of its members received some Indian appointment or other act of, in many cases quite disinterested, kindness from Henry Dundas.

In the House of Lords, the venerable Camden was enfeebled by the weight of advancing years. Lord Thurlow was most powerful and ready, but in an equal degree wayward and impracticable. Lord Carmarthen, at this time Secretary of State for Foreign Affairs, brought to the Government more of polish than weight. After Wilberforce had one day in 1785 dined with Pitt, we find him in his Diary contrast "pompous Thurlow and elegant Carmarthen." And at the same period the new American Minister, John Adams, writes: "The Marquis of Carmarthen is a modest, amiable man; treats all men with civility, and is much esteemed by the Foreign Ministers, as well as the nation, but is not an enterprising Minister." [2]

Such was the general state of the Ministry at the close of the Session of 1785, and for a long time afterwards.

In August of this year died Frederick the Second, or

---

[2] To Secretary Jay, November 4, 1785: Adams's Works, vol. viii. p. 336.

the Great, King of Prussia. With all his faults, and
they were many, he towered high above all the princes
of his time in genius and renown; and in his reign of
forty-five years he had doubled the extent, and much
more than doubled the wealth and resources, of his
kingdom. His nephew and successor, under the name
of Frederick William the Second, was cast in a different
mould. Pleasure, not ambition, was the ruling object
of his life. As Sir James Harris in the same year
aptly writes: "The late King had Solomon's wisdom;
this King seems disposed to have only his concu-
bines."

In the same month the life of George the Third was
exposed to some danger. As His Majesty was one day
stepping from his coach at St. James's Palace, he saw
a woman of respectable appearance hold forth a paper
to him, and as he extended his arm to receive it, she
made a thrust at him with a knife which she held in
her other hand. Starting back, the King escaped the
blow, while the woman was at once seized and secured.
But the King's first thought, greatly to his honour, was
to protect her from any hasty violence. "I am not
hurt," he said: "take care of the poor woman; do not
hurt her." She was in due course examined before the
Privy Council, when it appeared that her name was
Margaret Nicholson, a single woman, who gained her
living by needle-work. No less apparent were the
insane delusions to which she had been lately liable;
one above all, that she was entitled as of right to the
Crown of England. On a medical certificate to that
effect she was removed to Bethlehem Hospital, where,

without any recovery of her reason, she survived almost forty years.

A grievous family affliction was at this time sustained by Mr. Pitt. Mr. and Lady Harriot Eliot had settled in town during August on account of her expected confinement; and on the 20th of September Pitt could announce to his mother the prosperous event:

"I have infinite joy in being able to tell you that my sister has just made us a present of a girl, and that both she and our new guest are as well as possible."

But, unhappily, these prosperous symptoms did not long continue. Causes of alarm arose: she grew weaker and weaker; and on the 25th no hope of her life was left. Then Pitt wrote as follows to Mrs. Stapleton, his mother's companion and friend:

> "Downing Street.
> Sunday, September 25, 1786,
> 11 o'clock.

"Dear Madam,

"In a most afflicting moment it is some consolation to me to have recourse to your kind and affectionate attention to my mother, which she has so often experienced. The disorder under which my poor sister has suffered since Friday morning appears, I am grieved to say, to have taken so deep a root, that all the efforts of medicine have served only in some degree to abate it, but without removing the cause. This circumstance and the loss of strength render her case now so alarming, that although hope is not entirely extinguished. I cannot help very much fearing the worst; and unless some very favourable change takes place, there is too much reason to believe the event may be soon decided.

In this distressful situation I scarce know what is best for my mother—whether to rely for the present on the faint chance there is of amendment, or to break the circumstances to her now, to diminish if possible the shock which we apprehend. I have on this account addressed myself to you, that, knowing what is the real state of the case, you may judge on the spot whether to communicate any part of it immediately or to wait till the moment of absolute necessity. I need make no apology for committing to you, my dear Madam, this melancholy task. You will make, I am sure, every allowance for the feelings under which I write.

<blockquote>
" Sincerely and affectionately yours,

" W. Pitt.
</blockquote>

"Since writing this the symptoms are become decided; and though the sad event has not actually taken place, it is inevitable. My brother is probably at Burton, but I will send to Weymouth. I trust all to your goodness and attention."

Lady Harriot died the same day, the 25th of September. Bishop Tomline—then still Dr. Pretyman—tells us in his Biography : "It was my melancholy office to attend this very superior and truly excellent woman in her last moments; and afterwards to soothe, as far as I was able, the sufferings of her afflicted husband and brother — sufferings which I shall not attempt to describe. It was long before Mr. Pitt could see any one but myself, or transact any business except through me. From this moment Mr. Eliot took up his residence in Mr. Pitt's house, and they continued to live like brothers. But Mr. Eliot never recovered his former cheerfulness and spirits, nor could he bring himself again to mix in general society. He passed great part of his time in my family, both in town and country, and seemed to have a peculiar satisfaction in conversing unreservedly upon the subject of his loss with Mrs. Pretyman, who had been the intimate friend of his lamented wife and deeply shared in his affliction."

The letters of Pitt to his mother at this period are, as might be expected, full of affectionate sympathy. On the 4th of October, the morning after the funeral, he set out to join her at Burton Pynsent, and early in November renewed his visit to that place.

In the interval between these visits he writes to his mother from Downing Street, October 27: "Tuesday or Wednesday next is fixed for christening the poor child; and as the weather is favourable, Eliot hopes in a very few days afterwards to begin his journey westward and bring her to you." At the request both of Mr. Eliot and Mr. Pitt, Mrs. Pretyman became her godmother, with the Dowager Lady Chatham. She received her mother's name of Harriot, and was brought up by her father so long as he survived, and subsequently by her grandmother at Burton Pynsent. In 1806 she married Colonel, afterwards Lieutenant-General Sir William Pringle, by whom she had one son and four daughters; and she died in 1842.

Ever since the beginning of the year Pitt had been anxiously intent on the conclusion of the treaty which was negotiating at Paris. Mr. Eden had written to

him by almost every post, and consulted him on almost
every step. There had been great difficulties and great
delays, and Mr. Eden had found the energy of the
Prime Minister combining with his own to overcome
them. At length, the articles being adjusted, the
Treaty of Commerce was signed by Mr. Eden and M.
de Rayneval on the 26th of September—the very day
after Lady Harriot's death. Under such mournful
auspices did the long wished-for tidings arrive. Another
proof of the sad truth which the French moralist long
since expressed, that in this world joyful events scarce
ever come to us at the time when they would give us
most joy.

The great object of Pitt in negotiating this treaty
was to put an end, as far as possible, to prohibitions and
prohibitory duties. He did not seek to reduce or en-
danger the revenue by abolishing the custom duties
altogether. On the contrary, he expected to benefit
the revenue from that source by imposing only moderate
duties, which would really be levied on all articles imported, and which would deal almost a death-blow on
the contraband trade. For in spite of Pitt's previous
measures, the contraband trade in several of its branches
continued to prevail. Take the instances of brandy and
of cambrics. Only six hundred thousand gallons of
French brandy were legally imported in a year, while
no less than four millions of gallons were believed to be
every year smuggled into England.[3] And since there

---

[3] Speech of Pitt, February 12, 1787, as reported in Tomline's Life, vol. ii. p. 227. In the Par- liamentary Debates the four mil- lions are misprinted as four hun- dred thousand.

was a total prohibition of French cambrics, every yard
of them sold in England must have come in by illicit
means. "I am obliged to confess," said Pitt, in the
House of Commons, "that increase of revenue by means
of reduction of duties once was thought a paradox; but
experience has now convinced us that it is more than
practicable."

The Treaty of Commerce with France, as signed by
Mr. Eden, was to continue in force twelve years. It
stipulated that the subjects of the two contracting
parties might import, in their own vessels, into the
European dominions of each other every kind of mer-
chandise not especially prohibited. They and their
families might reside, either as lodgers or as house-
holders, free from any restraint in matters of religion,
and from any impost under the name of head-money or
argent du chef; free also to travel through the country, or depart from it, without licences or passports.
The wines of France were to be admitted into England
at no higher duties than those of Portugal, and the
duties on French vinegar, brandy, and oil of olives were
also much reduced.

The amount of duty, in both nations, on hardware,
cutlery, and a great variety of other articles, was in
like manner determined by this treaty; mostly at very
moderate rates, not exceeding twelve or fifteen per cent.
And in case of either nation being engaged in war, the
right of interference of the other party by equipping
privateers, or by other means, was expressly provided
against and renounced.

We find Pitt during his second visit to his mother

resume his correspondence on business, and write an important letter to the Duke of Rutland.

> "Burton Pynsent, Nov. 7, 1786.

" MY DEAR DUKE,

. . . .

" I have thought very much since I received your letter respecting the general state of Ireland, on the subjects suggested in that and your official letters to Lord Sydney. The question which arises is a nice and difficult one. On the one hand, the discontent seems general and rooted, and both that circumstance, and most of the accounts I hear, seem to indicate that there is some real grievance at bottom, which must be removed before any durable tranquillity can be secured. On the other hand, it is certainly a delicate thing to meddle with the Church Establishment in the present situation of Ireland; and anything like concession to the dangerous spirit which has shown itself is not without objection. But on the whole, being persuaded that Government ought not to be afraid of incurring the imputation of weakness by yielding in reasonable points, and can never make its stand effectually till it gets upon right ground, I think the great object ought to be, to ascertain fairly the true causes of complaint, to hold out a sincere disposition to give just redress, and a firm determination to do no more, taking care in the interval to hold up vigorously the execution of the law *as it stands* (till altered by Parliament), and to punish severely (if the means can be found) any tumultuous attempt to violate it. I certainly think the institution of tithe, especially if rigorously enforced, is everywhere a great obstacle to the improvement and prosperity of any country. Many circumstances in practice have made it less so here; but even here it is felt; and there are a variety of causes to make it sit much heavier on Ireland. I believe, too, that it is as much for the real interest of the Church as for the land to adopt, if practicable, some other mode of provision. If from any cause the Church falls into general odium, Government will be more likely to risk its own interests than to serve those of the Church by any efforts in its favour. If, therefore, those who are at the head of the clergy will look at it soberly and dispassionately, they will see how incumbent it is upon them, in every point of view, to propose some temperate accommodation; and even the appearance of concession which might be awkward in Government, could not be unbecoming if it originated with them. The thing to be arrived at, therefore, seems, as far as I can judge of it, to find out a way of removing the grievances arising out of a tithe, or, perhaps, to substitute some new provision in lieu of it; to have such a plan cautiously digested (which may require much time), and, above all, to make the Church itself the quarter to bring forward whatever is proposed. How far this is practicable must depend upon many circumstances, of which you can form a nearer and better judgment, particularly on the temper of the leading men among the clergy. I apprehend you may have a good deal of difficulty with the Archbishop of Cashel;[4] the Primate[5] is, I imagine, a man to listen to temperate advice: but it is surely desirable that you should have as speedily as possible a full communication with both of them; and if you feel the subject in the same light that I do, that, while you state to them

---

[4] Dr. Charles Agar, afterwards translated to the Archbishopric of Dublin. In 1795 he was created Lord Somerton, and in 1806 Earl of Normanton.

[5] Dr. Richard Robinson, Archbishop of Armagh. He had been in 1777 created Lord Rokeby.

the full determination of Government to give them all just and honourable support, you should impress them seriously with the apprehension of their risking everything if they do not in time abandon ground that is ultimately untenable. To suggest the precise plan of commutation which might be adopted is more than I am equal to, and is premature ; but, in general, I have never seen any good reason why a fair valuation should not be made of the present amount of every living, and a rent in corn to that amount be raised by a pound rate on the several tenements in the parish, nearly according to the proportion in which they now contribute to tithe. When I say a rent in corn, I do not actually mean paid in corn, but a rent in money regulated by the average value, from time to time, of whatever number of bushels is at present equal to the fair value of the living. This would effectually prevent the Church from suffering by the fluctuations in the value of money, and it is a mode which was adopted in all college leases, in consequence, I believe, of an Act of Parliament in the time of Queen Elizabeth. I need not say that I throw out these ideas in personal confidence to yourself; and I shall wish much to know what you think of them, and whether you can make anything of your prelates, before any measure is officially suggested. It seems material that there should be the utmost secrecy till our line is decided upon, and it must be decided upon completely before Parliament meets.

" Yours faithfully and sincerely,
" W. PITT."

It cannot fail, I think, to strike the reader how many ideas of Mr. Pitt, which in his own day were dissuaded or opposed by others as dangerous, have since come to be adopted almost by universal assent as indispensable.

On his second return from Burton Pynsent, Pitt applied himself with ardour to his works at Holwood, as the following extracts will evince :—

               " Downing Street, Nov. 13, 1786.

" MY DEAR MOTHER,

. . . .

   " Having been all the morning in the Court of Exchequer, I have not yet seen my brother ; but Eliot and I are both going to dine there ; which I am very glad to do on many accounts, and I reckon it as a step gained for Eliot. I flatter myself he has even made some progress in these two days, and I dare say will, in a little while, more and more. To-morrow I hope to get to Holwood, where I am impatient to look at my works. I must carry there, however, only my passion for planting, and leave that of cutting entirely to Burton."

               " Holwood, Nov. 18, 1786.

   " My works are going on very prosperously, and furnish a great deal of very pleasant employment, which just at present I have more leisure for than usual. I expect, however, Mr. Eden to arrive in a day or two, with abundance of details relative to the Treaty, which will break in a little upon planting. All, however, is going on as easily as possible, and I flatter myself with the hopes of seeing everything in good train for the Session by Christmas, which I am eager to accomplish for more reasons than one. Mrs. Stapleton's friend Lord Mansfield is supposed to be certainly resigning at length, and will probably not long survive his business."

Where Mr. Pitt says in one of these letters that he must not carry his "passion for cutting" to Holwood, he did not answer for the future. Three seasons later I find an entry as follows in the Diary of Mr. Wilberforce, who was visiting his friend at Holwood: "April 7th, 1790. Walked about after breakfast with Pitt and Grenville. We sallied forth armed with bill-hooks, cutting new walks from one large tree to another, through the thickets of the Holwood copses."

Besides the points that were settled in the Treaty of Commerce, there were some others reserved for a subsequent Convention; and to this new negotiation Mr. Eden applied himself with indefatigable industry, assisted as before by the zealous exertions of Pitt. At length on the 15th of January, 1787, the Convention was signed at Versailles, between Mr. Eden and the Comte de Vergennes, the French Minister for Foreign Affairs.

In January there was also concluded an Ecclesiastical appointment which Pitt had eagerly wished. The Bishop of Durham having died, it was intended to translate to that rich See Dr. Thomas Thurlow, who was already Bishop of Lincoln and Dean of St. Paul's. Pitt was most desirous that Dr. Pretyman should succeed Dr. Thurlow in both these offices. The draft of his letter to the King upon this subject is one of the very few preserved among his papers. It is dated the day before the meeting of Parliament. We find him press strongly for the King's consent, and assure His Majesty that there is "nothing which Mr. Pitt has more anxiously and personally at heart." His Majesty, though with strongly expressed reluctance, complied with this double request, and thus did Dr. Pretyman, according to the bad custom of those times, become both Bishop and Dean.

Parliament met again on the 23rd of January. The King's Speech announced the conclusion of the Treaty of Commerce, "and I trust you will find," His Majesty added, " that the provisions contained in it are calculated for the encouragement of industry, and the extension of lawful commerce in both countries." The provisions contained in it were still unknown to the public. Yet no sooner had the Address been moved and seconded than Fox sprang to his feet to denounce in vehement terms the idea of any concert or alliance with the French. In his own account of this evening he says, "There was no more debate and no division, so that I was time enough to go to dinner at Derby's, where everybody seemed to think I had done right." [6]

This was only a skirmish. But soon after the Treaty had been laid upon the table a battle in due form began. It may be of interest on this occasion to contrast the language as to France used by the two great party leaders.

Mr. Pitt said, " Considering the Treaty in its political view, I shall not hesitate to contend against the too frequently expressed opinion that France is and must be the unalterable enemy of England. My mind revolts from this position as monstrous and impossible. To suppose that any nation can be unalterably the enemy of another is weak and childish."

---

[6] Fox Memorials, vol. ii. p. 276.

On the other hand Mr. Fox said, "Undoubtedly I will not go the length of asserting that France is and must remain the unalterable enemy of England, and that she might not secretly feel a wish to act amicably with respect to this kingdom. It is possible, but it is scarcely probable. That she, however, feels in that manner at present I not only doubt, but disbelieve. France is the natural political enemy of Great Britain. . . . . I say again I contend that France is the natural foe of Great Britain, and that she wishes, by entering into a commercial treaty with us, to tie our hands and prevent us from engaging in any alliance with other Powers."

With passages such as these, and there are many more such upon record, it will be seen how just and well deserved is the rebuke which Lord Macaulay gives to some of the foreign accounts of Mr. Pitt. "Those French writers who have represented him as a Hannibal, sworn in childhood by his father to bear eternal hatred to France, and as having been the real author of the Coalition, know nothing of his character or history." On the contrary, as Lord Macaulay goes on to state, "Pitt was told in the House of Commons that he was a degenerate son, and that his partiality for the hereditary foes of our island was enough to make his great father's bones stir under the pavement of the Abbey."

Of the taunts which Lord Macaulay has thus commemorated, some of the most bitter came at this time from Philip Francis. It might seem as if the author of Junius stood half revealed before us by the similar scope of his reflections, and the innate vigour of his style: "Nations which border on each other never can agree; for this single reason, because they are neighbours. All history and experience assure us of the fact. As long as the Scotch and English stood in the relation of neighbours to each other, how was it possible they should agree? That cause of opposition ceased at their union, and instead of mortal enemies I trust in God they are immortal friends. . . . But now it seems we are arrived at a new enlightened era of affection for our neighbours, and of liberality to our enemies, of which our uninstructed ancestors had no conception. The pomp of modern eloquence is employed to blast even the triumphs of Lord Chatham's administration. The polemic laurels of the father must yield to the pacific myrtles which shadow the forehead of the son. Sir, the glory of Lord Chatham is founded on the resistance he made to the united power of the House of Bourbon. The present Minister has taken the opposite road to fame; and France, the object of every hostile principle in the policy of Lord Chatham, is the *gens amicissima* of his son."

Besides these veteran characters, if I may so term them, a new actor at this time appeared upon the scene. This was Mr. Charles Grey, known subsequently as Lord Howick, and then as the second Earl Grey. Born in 1764, he had come in for Northumberland in June, 1786, upon an accidental vacancy. From his outset he warmly attached himself to the politics of Fox, and he delivered his first speech in opposition to the Treaty with France. Then were heard the first accents of that most lofty and thrilling and as it were most thorough-bred eloquence, which was not extinguished, and scarcely even dimmed, after an interval of fifty years.

As to the outset of Mr. Grey in the House of Commons, there is the following account in a letter from General Grant to Earl Cornwallis: "Sir Charles Grey's son, who comes in for Northumberland, in his first speech made a violent attack upon the Minister, who, in reply, said many civil things, complimented him upon his abilities, and took no notice of the abuse. Mr. Fox said nothing could be handsomer or better judged than Mr. Pitt's conduct on the occasion. But Grey has returned to the charge, and upon making a motion to inquire into the state of the Post Office, he made use of stronger language than ever was heard in the House of Commons, and was not approved by either party. The Minister was firm, and without losing temper treated his violence and threats with contempt. He was attacked at the same time by Fox and Sheridan, and i short with all the abilities of Opposition."

In this last debate there was present a keen observer of many years' experience—the Right Hon. Richard Rigby. He now very seldom attended the House of Commons, but he expressed as follows to General Grant his impressions of that day: "You know that I am not partial to Pitt, and yet I must own that he is infinitely superior to anything I ever saw in that House; and I declare that Fox and Sheridan and all of them put together are nothing to him. He, without support or assistance, answers them all with ease to himself, and they are just chaff before the wind to him."[7]

[7] Cornwallis Correspondence, vol. i. p. 291.

It was hoped by the Opposition that there might arise in the commercial classes an impulse against the French Treaty as against the Irish Propositions. But this did not prove to be the case. Our merchants and manufacturers were upon the whole well pleased, or at least acquiescing and quiet. There came from any body of them to the House of Commons only one considerable petition, and that petition prayed only for postponement. Notwithstanding every effort, and in spite of all the eloquence of Fox and Sheridan, of Francis and Grey, an Address in approval of the Treaty was carried by overwhelming numbers—236 against 116.

In this Session the proceedings against Warren Hastings were resumed with unabated zeal. Witnesses were from time to time examined at the Bar; and on the 7th of February Sheridan brought forward the charge numbered as the fourth, and relating to the Begums of Oude. His speech on that occasion, taking up in the delivery five hours and forty minutes, and combining within it every kind of oratorical excellence, stands forth perhaps without a parallel in history from its effects upon its hearers. When he sat down, neither the Members in the House, nor the Peers below the Bar, nor even the strangers in the Gallery, could restrain their rapturous delight: they testified it contrary to all rule and precedent by the loud clapping of hands. An adjournment was moved by Sir William Dolben, who declared that in the state of mind in which that speech had left him, he was unable to form a determinate opinion; and Pitt, in supporting this adjournment, which was carried, observed that they were still under the wand of the enchanter.

Never certainly was there such unanimous testimony to surpassing merit. Burke declared this speech to be "the most astonishing effort of eloquence, argument, and wit united of which there is any record or tradition." Fox said: "All that he had ever heard, all that he had ever read, when compared with it, dwindled into nothing, and vanished like vapour before the sun." And Pitt, though censuring some parts of it, as marked with unmeasured asperity to the person accused, did not hesitate to own that " it surpassed all the eloquence of ancient and modern times, and possessed everything that genius or art could furnish to agitate and control the human mind." Nor was this a mere transient impression of the hearers. More than fifteen years afterwards, Fox, being asked by his nephew, the late Lord Holland, which was the best speech ever made in the House of Commons, answered without hesitation, "Sheridan's, on the Begum charge." [8]

With such high certificates of merit who is there but would eagerly seek out the records or reports of this great oration, and who but would grieve on ascertaining that none, or next to none, are to be found? Only the day after, and in the midst of the general enthusiasm, Sheridan was offered a thousand pounds if he would himself correct it for the press. This, however, he left undone, perhaps it might be from indolence, or perhaps

---

[8] On the circumstances of this wonderful effort of eloquence compare Moore's Life of Sheridan, vol. i. p. 450, and Macaulay's Essays, vol. iii. p. 443.

from a tender regard to his own fame. For certainly
no human composition could fail to leave open some
loop-holes for attack, or could safely stand the test of
comparison with the panegyrics which it had produced.
Thus, beyond a most jejune and meagre outline in the
Parliamentary History, nothing now remains of this
great oration. It has gone to the same limbo as the
speeches of Halifax and Bolingbroke, of Sir William
Wyndham and Charles Townshend.

The adjourned debate upon Sheridan's motion was
resumed on the following day. Francis spoke with
much rancour against Hastings, and Major Scott at
great length in his defence. Then Pitt rose. Going
over the whole of the argument, and listened to in
breathless suspense, since his opinion was as yet
unknown, he declared that the conduct of Hastings
to the Begums seemed to him utterly unjustifiable, and
that the charge on that subject ought to be affirmed.
It was affirmed accordingly, in the division, by a
majority of more than two to one.

Other Charges were on other days brought forward
by other Members. But the decisions of the House in
the case of Benares, and in the case of the Begums,
were of themselves sufficient to determine the question
of State Trial. When, therefore, it came to be moved
by Burke "that there is ground for impeaching the
said Warren Hastings, Esq., of high crimes and misde-
meanors," the Resolution was carried without the
appearance of one dissenting vote. And on the 10th
of May, Burke, with a great majority of members in his
train, appeared at the bar of the House of Lords, and

solemnly impeached Warren Hastings according to the
ancient form. Shortly afterwards Hastings was taken
into the custody of the Serjeant at Arms. Then he
was transferred to the Black Rod. Finally he was admitted to bail, and the further prosecution of his trial
was deferred till the ensuing year.

In this Session several important measures of financial reform were framed and carried by Pitt. There
was the farming of the duty on post-horses, to guard
against the minute but numerous frauds which had
hitherto prevailed. There was the regulation of lotteries to suppress a gambling practice pernicious to the
morals of the people, and called the insurance of
tickets. But above all there was the consolidation of
duties in the Customs, Excise, and Stamps. These
duties having been imposed or augmented at different
periods, and assigned to separate services, became at
last in the highest degree complicated, and as such vex-
atious and oppressive, and scarce any payment could be
determined without a series of calculations combined
from several departments. But perhaps the best idea
of these complications, and of the skill and patience
required to unravel them, may be gathered from the
fact that the remedial Resolutions moved by Pitt in the
House of Commons—as abolishing the old duties and
substituting new ones on a simpler plan—amounted in
number to no less than 2537. Burke, on this occasion,
did himself high honour. Instead of indulging any
party-spirit, or seeking to find any fault with Pitt's
proposal, "it rather," he said, "behoves us to rise up
manfully, and, doing justice to the Right Hon. gentle-

man's merit, to return him thanks on behalf of ourselves
and of the country."

Important as were these financial measures, the
public looked with much keener interest to the discussions on the conduct of the Prince of Wales. Since
1783 His Royal Highness had set up a separate establishment, and unreservedly thrown himself into the arms
of Opposition. With Fox especially, and Sheridan,
he lived in familiar friendship. But whatever useful
lessons he may have learned in that school, economy
and thrift were certainly not among the number.
It was not long ere he found himself deeply involved
in debt. He had spent above 50,000l. in building
at Carlton House; and most kinds of frolic and dissipation had their share. Altogether, in 1786, his
liabilities amounted to upwards of 150,000l. These,
however, were, it might be said, the faults of youth
and inexperience. A graver subject of apprehension
had meanwhile arisen. The Prince had become deeply
enamoured of Mrs. Fitzherbert, a widow lady who
held the Roman Catholic faith. She was of gentle
birth, and of great beauty; and both in her widowhood
and in her two former marriages had borne an irre-
proachable character. To avoid the Prince's importunities she had gone abroad in 1784, but on her return
at the close of the ensuing year those importunities
were renewed. Any legal alliance between them was
impossible from the terms of the Royal Marriage Act;
but, to quiet her scruples, the Prince offered to go
through the religious ceremony. A rumour to that
effect was quickly noised abroad; and Fox, in the true

spirit of an honourable friend, wrote at once to His
Royal Highness remonstrating in the strongest manner
against this "very desperate step." The intention was
denied, but it was persevered in. On the 21st of
December, 1785, the ceremony was performed in private
by a Clergyman of the Church of England and in the
form prescribed by the Book of Common Prayer; and
the certificate, bearing the same date, was attested by
two witnesses. Thus, it might be said, did the Heir
Apparent attempt to take to wife a private gentle-
woman in the teeth of the Royal Marriage Act, and a
Roman Catholic in the teeth of the Act of Settlement.
A breach of the law in the one alternative, or a for-
feiture of the Crown in the other.

Fox, in his excellent letter to the Prince, had fore-
told that if the marriage took place at all, it could not
be kept perfectly secret. Whispers of it soon began,
and, though contradicted, grew. Men in general knew
not what to believe as to the fact alleged; and the
public uncertainty found a vent in the public press.
Several pamphlets came forth upon this question; and
one by Horne Tooke attracted especial notice from its
boldness: for it maintained that the ceremony was perfectly legal, notwithstanding the provisions of the Royal
Marriage Act, and he therefore spoke of Mrs. Fitzherbert without reserve as of Her Royal Highness the
Princess of Wales.

So early as the spring of 1785, the Prince, through
Lord Southampton, applied to the King for aid. He
was met by a request for some explanation how in so
short a time so enormous a debt had been incurred.

This natural inquiry was construed by the Prince as a direct refusal. In 1785 he stated his positive intention to go immediately abroad. In 1786 he no less positively announced that he would break up his entire establishment : he advertised for sale not only his stud and his hunters, but even his carriage and his riding-horses, declaring that he would henceforth walk on foot, and devote two-thirds of his income to the payment of his debts. He desired, no doubt, by this step to excite the public sympathy in his favour ; but it does not appear that this object was in any degree attained.

In the spring of 1787 the Prince's friends, with his consent, if not at his instigation, determined to apply to Parliament for the payment of his debts, and for some addition to his income. Alderman Newnham gave notice of a motion with that view. Even the notice gave rise to some preliminary skirmishes, in the course of which Pitt declared that if, unhappily, this proposal were persisted in, he should feel it his duty to give it an absolute negative. And Mr. Rolle, the now celebrated member for Devonshire, rose to say that for his part, if such a motion were made, he would move the previous question upon it, because the question itself " went immediately to affect our Constitution both in Church and State." These words were well understood as applying to the rumours of a secret marriage with a Roman Catholic lady.

Fox himself, as it chanced, was not present when Mr. Rolle was speaking ; but in another of the preliminary debates took the opportunity of reverting to these words. In the most direct and peremptory terms that language could convey, he treated the report in question as an utter calumny. "I know," said Mr. Rolle, in rejoinder, "that there are certain laws and Acts of Parliament which forbid it, but still there are ways in which it might have taken place." "I deny it altogether," cried Fox; "I deny it in point of fact as well as in law. The fact not only never could have happened legally, but never did happen in any way whatsoever; and was from the beginning a base and malicious falsehood." "Do you speak from authority?" asked Rolle. "I do," answered Fox, "from direct authority."

It is painful to carry this question further. It ought at least to give no pleasure to any one who has lived as a subject of King George the Fourth. On the other hand, the memory of an eminent statesman demands the fullest justice; and I am bound to state, without doubt or hesitation, as my view of the case, that Mr. Fox had no intention whatever of deceiving, but was himself deceived.

At the time, however, and on the report of what had passed in the House of Commons, Mrs. Fitzherbert, believing herself wronged, was most vehemently incensed against Fox. To the end of his life, indeed, she would never be reconciled to him. The Prince, on his part, was half distracted between his concern for the lady and his apprehensions from the public. He sent for Mr. Charles Grey, who found him, as he states, in an agony of agitation.[9] His Royal Highness now confessed that the ceremony of marriage had taken place, and he most earnestly pressed Grey to say something in Parliament

---

[9] See Lord Grey's own notes to the Fox Memorials, vol. ii. p. 288.

for the satisfaction of Mrs. Fitzherbert ; but this Grey
steadily declined, and at length the Prince ended the
conversation abruptly by exclaiming, " Well, if nobody
else will, Sheridan must ! "

A few days later Sheridan accordingly, though with
manifest embarrassment, addressed himself to this point
in the House of Commons.   He did not attempt, however, to controvert in the slightest degree the accuracy
of Fox's statement, and merely referred to Mrs. Fitzherbert in some general expressions of respect and
sympathy.

Meanwhile the best friends of the Monarchy, in and
out of Parliament, had begun to feel that any public
discussion on the Prince of Wales's affairs, even though
confined to money matters, would be most unseemly.
In compliance with the general wish, Pitt had two interviews with the Prince at Carlton House.   " He was to
see the King to-night," thus reports His Royal Highness to Fox, " and would endeavour to get everything
settled if he could." [1]   This was no easy task.   George the
Third was now more than ever incensed against his son,
since the appeal which seemed to have been made from
himself to the House of Commons.   At last, however, a
Royal Message was obtained and brought down, commending to the faithful Commons the payment of the
Prince's debts, which amounted to 161,000l., besides a
grant of 20,000l. for the new works at Carlton House.
" His Majesty could not, however "—in these words the
Message proceeds—" expect or desire the assistance of

---

[1] Letter dated May 10, 1787.

the House but on a well-grounded expectation that the Prince will avoid contracting any new debts in future. With a view to this object, His Majesty has directed a sum of 10,000*l.* a-year to be paid out of his Civil List, in addition to the allowance which His Majesty has hitherto given him; and His Majesty has the satisfaction to inform the House that the Prince of Wales has given His Majesty the fullest assurances of his firm determination to confine his future expenses within his income." How far these assurances were fulfilled may be seen in the sequel; but for the present the money was cheerfully voted, and the quarrel was hushed.

Half a century had now elapsed since the Protestant Dissenters had applied to Parliament for the repeal of the Test Act. In the Session of 1787 their effort was renewed. For the most part they had warmly espoused the cause of Pitt at the last General Election, and they thought themselves entitled to some share of his favour in return. Their first step was to circulate among the Members of the House of Commons a paper entitled 'The Case of the Protestant Dissenters with reference to the Corporation and Test Acts,' in which they more especially laboured to distinguish their case from that of the Roman Catholics. With equal prudence they selected as their spokesman Mr. Beaufoy, a member of the Church of England, and a zealous supporter of the Government.

Pitt appears to have felt a disposition to support their claims, if he could do so with the assent of the Church of England. Without that assent, as expressed by its Heads, it was scarcely possible or scarcely proper for any Prime Minister to move onward. A meeting of the Bishops was held at the Bounty Office, on a summons from the Archbishop of Canterbury, and at the request, as the Bishops were informed, of Mr. Pitt. The question laid before their Lordships was as follows:— "Ought the Test and Corporation Acts to be maintained?" Of fourteen Prelates present, only two— Watson of Llandaff, and Shipley of St. Asaph—voted in the negative; and the decision of the meeting was at once transmitted to the Minister.[2]

When, on the 28th of March, Mr. Beaufoy did bring on his motion, Lord North spoke in opposition to it, and Fox in its favour. Pitt rose and said that he did not think he could with propriety give a silent vote. He observed that some classes of the Nonconformists had injured themselves in the public opinion greatly, and not unreasonably, by the violence and the prejudices which they had shown. "Were we," he said, "to yield on this occasion, the fears of the members of the Church of England would be roused, and their apprehensions are not to be treated lightly. It must, as I contend, be conceded to me that an Established Church is necessary. Now there are some Dissenters who declare that the Church of England is a relic of Popery; others that all Church Establishments are improper. This may not be the opinion of the present body of Dissenters, but no means can be devised of admitting the moderate part of the Dissenters and excluding the violent; the bulwark must be kept up against all."

---

[2] Anecdotes of the Life of Bishop Watson, written by himself, vol. i. p. 261, ed. 1818.

The division which ensued gave no great hopes to the claimants. Only 98 members went with Mr. Beaufoy, while 176 declared against him.

In this Session of 1787 was passed the measure which laid the foundation of new Colonies, scarcely less important than those which we had recently lost. The want of some fixed place for penal exile had been severely felt ever since the American War, and the accumulation of prisoners at home was counteracting the benevolent efforts of Howard for the improvement of the British gaols. The discoveries of Captain Cook were now remembered and turned to practical account. An Act of Parliament empowered His Majesty, by Commission under the Great Seal, to establish a Government for the reception of convict prisoners in New South Wales. An Order in Council completed the necessary forms. Captain Arthur Phillip of the Royal Navy was appointed Governor, commanding a body of marines, and conveying six hundred male and two hundred and fifty female convicts. The expedition set sail in May, 1787; and early in the following year laid the foundation of the new settlement at Port Jackson in Botany Bay.

Notwithstanding the many important measures or debates of this Session, the business was conducted with so much despatch that Parliament could be prorogued on the 30th of May.

CHAPTER X.

1787 — 1788.

State of parties in Holland — Differences respecting the French trade in India — Prussian troops enter Holland — Death of the Duke of Rutland — France and England disarm — Trial of Hastings — India Declaratory Bill — Budget — Claims of American Loyalists — First Steps in Parliament for the Abolition of the Slave Trade — Exertions of Wilberforce and Clarkson — Pitt's Resolution — Sir W. Dolben's Bill — Horrors of the Middle Passage — Controversies on Slavery.

FOR some months past the conflict of parties in the Dutch Republic had been the subject of much uneasiness and much deliberation to the Ministers in England. The Prince of Orange found his authority as Stadtholder not merely eluded, but struck at and defied. He had retired to Nimeguen, leaving Van Berkel and the other chiefs of the Democratic party in full possession of power at the Hague; and they on their part continued, as during the late war, closely connected with France, and obedient to every dictate that came from the Court of Versailles.

Such was the general picture of Holland at this time, but scarce any month elapsed without some fresh aggression or contumely on the Prince of Orange. In his own character there was nothing of spirit or energy; but both these qualities were possessed in a high degree by the Princess. She addressed in private earnest entreaties for aid to her brother, who had recently succeeded as King of Prussia, and also to the King of Eng-

land. Sir James Harris, our Minister at the Hague,
espoused her cause with zeal. We find him in his
despatches constantly urge that if the Democratic party
were allowed full play, Holland would sink ere long into
a mere dependency and almost a province of France.
These representations prevailed at once with Lord Carmarthen, the Secretary of State, who became not less
eager in the cause than Sir James himself; but by Pitt
they were more doubtfully received. Pitt indeed on
this occasion, as on several others previous to the great
crisis of 1793, proved himself to be in truth and emphatically a Peace Minister.

At the beginning of May, 1787, Sir James Harris
wrote again to Lord Carmarthen, pressing with more
than common urgency "a plan of vigorous measures."
But since objections would of course arise, and explanations be required, he further suggested that he might
himself go over for a few days to England. He received
the desired permission, and was invited to attend two
Cabinets that were held upon the subject. Of the first of
these Cabinets his notes are still preserved. The Chancellor, he says, took the lead, and "in the most forcible
terms that could be employed, declared against all half-
measures." So did also, besides Lord Carmarthen, the
Duke of Richmond and Lord Stafford. "I own," said
Mr. Pitt, "the immense importance of Holland being
preserved as an independent State. It is certainly an
object of the greatest magnitude. I have no hesitation
as to what ought to be done, if we do anything at all;
but if we do anything, we must make up our minds in
the first instance to go to war as a possible, though not

a probable, event. Now the mere possibility is enough to make it necessary for England to reflect before she stirs. It is to be maturely weighed whether anything could repay the disturbing that state of growing affluence and prosperity in which she now is, and whether this is not increasing so fast as to make her equal to meet any force France could collect some years hence."[1]

At the last Cabinet, however, it was determined that a sum of 20,000*l*., as derived from the Secret Service Fund, should be entrusted to Harris, and applied to assist our friends in Holland. Thus was Sir James enabled to return to his post armed with the same weapon as Jove (it is his own comparison) when invading the tower of Danae. In pursuit of the like policy, the Court of Versailles had sent to its Minister at the Hague a lavish letter of credit. " And I can assure your Lordship"—thus had Sir James written on the 1st of May— "I keep greatly within the mark when I declare that in this period of time (a fortnight) France has expended at least a million of livres."

Holland was not the only field on which the Courts of London and Versailles seemed at this time likely to contend. A serious difference had arisen between them as to the extent and meaning of the thirteenth article of the Treaty of Peace, stipulating for the French trade in India; and the French on this occasion received the full support of the ruling party at the Hague. Both

---

[1] Malmesbury Papers, vol. ii. p. 303, &c. For the French view of Dutch affairs see among others De Ségur's 'Histoire du Règne de Frédéric Guillaume II. Roi de Prusse,' vol. i. p. 100-136, with the Memoir of M. Cailland appended.

Powers had greatly increased their naval force in the
Indian seas; and this increase alone (to say nothing of
some new works at Pondicherry, and some fresh in-
trigues with Tippoo) gave us reason for apprehending a
combined attack on our newly-conquered territories.
Not that any result could at that time be foreseen with
certainty from the feeble and fluctuating Govern-
ments of France. The Comte de Vergennes, who had
concluded the Treaty of Commerce with us, had become
unpopular with many of his countrymen on that account.
The manufacturers of France were full of angry re-
proaches and of boding fears, and already in ima-
gination saw their produce undersold and their looms
deserted. Still, however, Vergennes had retained his
credit at Court: but he died in February, 1787, and his
death was followed at no long interval by the retirement of M. de Calonne, Minister of the Finances—a
victim to that Assembly of Notables which he had himself convened. Then it was that the way was opened
for the accession to power of a most vain and empty
statesman, a mere minion of Court favour, Lomenie
de Brienne, Archbishop of Toulouse. It was possible
that he might incline to peace on account of the ruined
state of the finances. It was equally possible that he
might incline to war, as seeking to divert the people
from their own distresses. But in any case it was most
desirable for us to reinforce our garrisons in the East,
to be ready with a powerful fleet, and, even on Indian
grounds alone, to break the intimate concert of councils
between the despotic Court of Versailles and the democratic rulers at the Hague.

A crisis in the affairs of Holland seemed to all parties near at hand, but the form in which it came at last was wholly unforeseen.　Towards the close of June the Princess of Orange determined to go in person to the Hague.　She carried with her letters from the Prince to the States-General and to the States of Holland, by which she was empowered to act or negotiate as circumstances might require; but at the frontier of the province her carriage was stopped by a detachment of Free Corps, and Her Royal Highness was detained in custody while the question was referred to the States. Finally, even after an answer had come from the Hague, she was prevented from proceeding on her journey, and obliged to return whence she came.

Such an insult to the wife of the Chief Magistrate of the Republic, and to the sister of a reigning Monarch, could only be atoned for by prompt apologies and adequate punishment of the offenders.　The King of Prussia demanded this reparation in peremptory terms, and to enforce his demands he collected at Wesel an army of 20,000 men under the Duke of Brunswick.　Even the Court of Versailles, on being consulted, owned that the act had been unjustifiable, and that the reparation was due; but the patriots (for so the Stadtholder's opponents called themselves) were rather inclined to defend the conduct of the soldiers, and blindly refused any, even the smallest, concession.　They saw that they were not upheld by France on this particular occasion.　Still they hoped that they might reckon on her general sympathy and succour, and they knew that at this very time she was forming for their sake a camp of 15,000 men at

the frontier town of Givet. Therefore, when threatened
by the Prussian army, they in specific terms applied to
France for protection.

In September the Court of France notified in form to
the Court of London that it had determined to afford to
the States-General the assistance they had requested.
By Pitt's direction an immediate reply was returned to
the purport that we on our side should take an active
part in favour of the Stadtholder. Already, with cha-
racteristic energy, had the British Minister decided his
measures. Despatches had been sent, both by sea and
over land, to the Governor-General of Bengal and to
the Governor of Madras, directing them to be prepared,
in case of war, to attack the French settlements in
India, and to take possession of the Dutch on the Stadtholder's behalf and in his name. At home, orders had
been given to augment both our navy and army. A
guarantee was sent to Berlin to promise our support in
the event of French hostility. Nor was this merely a
vague promise: we undertook to back the Duke of
Brunswick's advance by a fleet of forty ships of the line.
A treaty was concluded for the term of four years with
the Landgrave of Hesse, by which that little potentate,
ever ready as before to sell his subjects, agreed, in
return for a yearly subsidy of 36,000*l.*—"a retaining
fee," as Pitt called it in the House of Commons—to
send forth for our service a body of 12,000 troops whenever it might be required.

Yet the hopes of peace were still maintained. To
assist in the negotiations on this subject, Mr. Grenville
was despatched for some days to confer with the Ministers at Paris.

Hostilities were already in progress. On the 13th of September the Prussian troops entered the Dutch territory in three columns. Then it was that the utter weakness of the Democratic party came to be apparent. Almost everywhere the Prussians were received not as foemen, but rather as liberators and allies. Almost everywhere the Orange flag was hoisted, the Orange ribbons were worn. So easy and so rapid was the Duke of Brunswick's progress, that in the course of eight days the whole of the United Provinces, except Amsterdam, had yielded to him, and even Amsterdam surrendered after only a fortnight's siege. The Prince of Orange made his triumphal entry into the Hague amidst the loudest acclamations and every sign of public joy, and he found himself reinstated in all his former rights and powers as Stadtholder. "Your Lordship," so writes Harris to Carmarthen, "on reading this letter, will, I am sure, consider its contents as incredible; and I confess I can scarce bring myself to believe what has passed. . . . . If St. Priest (the French Minister) comes soon, he must enter the Hague decorated with Orange-coloured ribbons, or else he will not be suffered to enter it at all."

Pitt had for this summer planned an excursion to the north. His friend Wilberforce, who had now given up his villa at Wimbledon, had on the other hand taken one among the Lakes, and looked forward to make the Prime Minister acquainted with his favourite scenes. The 'Public Advertiser' of June 20, 1787, contains the following paragraph:—"Mr. Pitt, in his way into Scotland, will take Alnwick, Castle Howard, and other prin-

cipal places, but he will not make any stay, except with
Mr. Wilberforce." Unhappily, however, the affairs of
Holland marred this agreeable scheme. Pitt went no
farther north than Cambridgeshire. But his progress, and
the progress also of public events, will be best illustrated
by his correspondence with his mother at this time.

"Downing Street, September 13, 1787.

"I returned yesterday from Cheveley, which I reached
on the preceding Monday, and had the pleasure of finding my brother and Lady Chatham established very
much to their satisfaction. My visit was not a long one,
but afforded me a good deal of riding in the way there
and back, and as good a day's sport of shooting as could
be had without ever killing. I was in some hopes of
returning again the end of the week; but as I find
things are clearly coming to a point in Holland, and a
very few days may now decide a good deal as to the
future, I shall hardly stir further than Holwood for
some days."

"Downing Street, September 19, 1787.

"I am just going to Wimbledon to dine with M. de
Calonne at his villa there, and hear all the politics of
France, which form no bad variety in the interval of
our own."

"Downing Street, September 22, 1787.
" MY DEAR MOTHER,

"The business abroad is at length come to a
point, and with every appearance of success. France
has indeed notified to us that she will give assistance to

the province of Holland, and we are therefore under the
necessity of preparing with vigour, and are accordingly
pressing to arm the fleet. But there seems still every
reason to think France will quickly give way, as she
has no army prepared, and in the mean time the Duke
of Brunswick's success is in a manner decisive. News
came last night that most of the towns in Holland had
surrendered without any resistance. A complete revolution had taken place at the Hague, and the States of
Holland had resolved to restore the Stadtholder to all
his rights, and invited him back to the Hague. The
only question is whether the Free Corps will make any
stand at the Hague. If the issue there is as favourable
as may be expected, every effort the French can make
will come too late ; and they will hardly engage in an
unpromising contest for a mere point of honour. You
will not wonder if I have not time to write more at present. Pray give my love to Eliot, and affectionate compliments to Mrs. Stapleton.

" Ever, my dear Mother, &c.,

" W. PITT.

"It happens that there is just now a vacancy in the
place of Housekeeper to the Levee Rooms at Whitehall, which may be executed by deputy, and has, indeed, hardly anything to do. I am sorry to say it is
worth no more than 40l. a year ; but as there are so few
places of this kind which do not require some attendance, if you think Mrs. Sparry [2] would like this, as a
mark of old friendship, I shall be much obliged to you
if you will have the goodness to propose it to her."

---

[2] Lady Chatham's housekeeper; a much-valued servant of many
years' standing.

"Downing Street, September 29, 1787.

"This last fortnight has not allowed me to make much use of it anywhere, nor to venture so far as Holwood; but I trust it has been better employed. We are, I flatter myself, going on very satisfactorily in our preparations, only, what is much pleasanter, there is at present every reason to think we shall not be obliged to use them, and shall carry our point quietly. It may still, however, be a fortnight or three weeks before we can judge decisively, as we must allow time for consulting at Berlin; and in that interval one cannot be quite sure that some change of circumstances may not produce new intentions. At present all looks pacific, though each side must continue to arm till a final explanation takes place. You will not wonder if I have not time for much but this sort of news at present. . . . I rejoice that Mrs. Sparry likes my proposal."

"Downing Street, October 13, 1787.

"MY DEAR MOTHER,

"I write one line to say things are going on well. Amsterdam, though it has not actually opened its gates, has submitted to everything, and the settlement in Holland seems likely to be peaceably completed. France will probably in the end acquiesce, but we continue to be watchful in the mean time. Admiral Hood, who has been called to town again on account of some of the objects which may possibly arise, gives me the satisfaction of receiving a very good account of you. I hope the weather is still favourable to your drives. Adieu.

"Ever, my dear Mother, &c., &c.,

"W. PITT."

"Downing Street, October 29, 1787.

" MY DEAR MOTHER,

"The newspapers have probably conveyed to you the accounts which have arrived within these few days of the health of the poor Duke of Rutland. You will, I am sure, on many grounds, have entered into the anxiety which I must feel on this subject. It is therefore with additional regret I write to tell you that I received last night the affecting news of his death. His illness was a fever which had been hanging upon him for some time, and which within a few days took an unfavourable turn, and proved of the putrid sort. I am informed by his agent that by his will (which is in Ireland) he has appointed me as one of his executors and guardians of his children, a mark of kindness and confidence which must add to what I feel for him. I am sorry to dwell on so melancholy a subject, but still I thought it better you should learn it from my pen than through any other channel.

"You will, I am sure, excuse my not having found time to return Mr. Coutts's letter sooner. I should have been very glad on every account to have been able to obtain his request. But on speaking to Lord Sydney about it, it seemed from the line which the King has laid down to be a point which could not well be attempted.

"The account of the dear little girl made me, you will easily believe, very happy; I have not heard from Eliot himself very lately, but by an indirect channel I have just had very good accounts of him. I expect every hour news from Paris which I think likely to put an end to the present suspense to our perfect satisfaction, but there is no certainty on such a subject till it is actually completed. Affectionate compliments to Mrs. Stapleton, and kind remembrances to Mrs. Sparry.

" Ever, my dear Mother, &c.,

" W. PITT."

The expectations held out in this last letter of good news from Paris were most speedily fulfilled. Two days before its date the French Ministers announced in form to the British ambassador that they had relinquished any hostile design against the new Government of Holland; and on the same day, the 27th of October, a Joint Declaration was signed at Paris, by which France and England agreed that the armaments and warlike preparations should be discontinued on each side. Thus was happily averted the war which we had bravely dared; and thus amidst general satisfaction was renewed our ancient and close alliance with the United Provinces.

The judgment on the whole of this transaction of Count Woronzow, the Russian ambassador in London, seems well worthy of record. He wrote to his brother to the following effect: " The part played by England in these affairs has been brilliant and courageous, and the conduct of Mr. Pitt on this occasion is very like that which his late father pursued. Such conduct was very little known and very little practised in England during the interval between his father's retirement and his own accession to power. I had so strong an attachment and so thorough a respect for the late Lord Chatham, that I take a warm interest in the conduct and character of his son. How would the father have rejoiced in them had he lived on till now!"[3]

At the same time and at the opposite extremity of Europe another contest was raging. The Sultan and the Czar were again at strife, and the Emperor Joseph the Second was preparing to join the Russian side. But the war having been commenced with great rashness and some appearance of ill faith on the part of Turkey, there was the less sympathy for the disasters which her arms ere long sustained.

The satisfaction of Pitt at the maintenance of peace to England was grievously damped by the unhappy news from Dublin. Besides the loss of his early friend, there was the check to the prosperous course of Irish business. There was the difficulty, and a very great one, in the choice of a successor. To the surprise of many persons the choice of Pitt fell upon the Marquis of Buckingham.

With the prospect of a war impending, it was judged right to convene the Parliament before Christmas. Parliament met accordingly on the 27th of November, after the alarm had passed. During the last Session the views of Fox had been so strongly expressed as Anti-Gallican—he had in speaking of the Treaty of Commerce so thundered against all French objects and French alliances—that he was already and by anticipation pledged to the approval of our recent policy with respect to Holland. That approval he did express in

---

[3] Letter of Count Woronzow, published in the original French, but without a date, in Tomline's Life of Pitt, vol. ii. p. 316.

strong terms, though not without several qualifications and reserves; and his approval ceased when the Minister proposed a permanent increase of our land forces to the amount of 3,000 men for the better security of our West Indian islands. "No person," said Pitt, "can be more anxious on the subject of expense than I am. But I contend that any moderate expense by which the continuance of peace could be more firmly ensured is true economy, and the best economy this country can adopt. It is upon this principle, and after a full consideration of the state of our finances, that I think it would be wise to lay out 200,000l. in fortifications, and 80,000l. annually, the sum which the proposed augmentation of troops would cost, for the purpose of strengthening those parts of our dominions which are discovered to be weak and vulnerable, and of keeping them in such a constant posture of defence as may deter any hostile power from attempting to seize them by surprise." Fox divided the House against the proposal, but it was affirmed by 242 votes against 80.

Before Christmas there was another subject of sharp contention. The House of Lords having fixed the 13th of February for the commencement of Hastings's Trial, it became necessary for the House of Commons to appoint its Managers. The first place was by common consent allowed to the genius, the long experience, and the inexhaustible Indian knowledge of Burke. He was desirous that Pitt and Dundas should also consent to act as Managers, but from their ties of office they declined. So likewise did Lord North, whose eye-sight had become impaired, and whose health began to decline.

On the whole then, upon the refusal of Pitt and of
Dundas to serve, the conductors of the Impeachment
came to be chosen wholly from the front rank of
Opposition. Besides Burke himself as Chairman, they
comprised Fox and Fitzpatrick, Burgoyne and Windham, Sheridan and Grey. No difference of opinion was
manifested until Burke proposed the name of Philip
Francis. At his name, and considering the rancorous
hostility against Hastings which Francis had even lately
shown, there arose in the minds of many Members a
strong feeling of disapprobation. The motion was
quickly negatived, but on another day it was renewed
by Fox. "It is not a question of argument, it is a
question of feeling," said Pitt. " Ought we to appoint
as our representative in the present Impeachment the
only person in the House who has upon a former occasion been concerned in a personal contest—a duel—
with Mr. Hastings?" Moreover, it is to be observed
that only a few months before Pitt had publicly charged
Francis with " dishonourable and disgraceful " proceedings in the recent evidence of Captain Mercer. Nevertheless Dundas declared that he should vote for the appointment; which, considering his close friendship with
Pitt at this period, and the cordial concert of measures
between them on every other point, appears extraordinary, and is best explained perhaps by some previous
pledge or assurance unwarily given to Francis by Dundas. Francis himself spoke in his own case with great
ability, and, almost incredible as it may seem in him,
with great temper; but on a division he was again
rejected by a majority of two to one.

On the 17th of December the House of Commons adjourned to the last day of January. Pitt immediately availed himself of his holidays to pay a visit to his mother, but he returned to Downing Street on the last day of December.

On the re-assembling of Parliament the public expectation was most eagerly turned to the great day as it was termed—the 13th of February—the first of Hastings's Trial. At length the great day came. Westminster Hall was prepared. Thither at eleven in the morning walked the Commons, Mr. Burke leading the procession. He and the other Managers were clad in Court attire, with bag wigs and swords, but the other Members in their common dresses, and they took their seats as respectively assigned them. Then, and not till after they had mustered, the Peers began to move in established form from their own Chamber. First went the Clerks, then the Masters in Chancery, then the Judges, ready to be consulted whenever any point of law might arise, after them a Herald, then the Peers who were minors and the eldest sons of Peers, then the Usher of the Black Rod, then lastly the Lords of Parliament themselves.[1] They wore their rich robes of scarlet with rows of ermine and gold, and they walked two and two, marshalled in their right rank by Garter King of Arms, and the lowest in rank and precedency leading the way. The first in their procession as the Junior Baron was cer-

---

[1] See the rules, strictly according to former precedent, laid down in the Lords' Journals, February 5 and 11, 1788. One entry is, "that the Members of the House of Commons be there before the Lords come."

tainly one of the most conspicuous of their number, Lord Heathfield, lately raised to the peerage for his heroic defence of Gibraltar. Walking by his side was the statesman so long and bitterly denounced as the Minister of back-stairs influence—as the sole dispenser of the King's secret will—Charles Jenkinson, now Lord Hawkesbury. The stately procession closed with the Archbishops of York and Canterbury, the Duke of Norfolk as Earl Marshal, the Earl Camden as Lord President, and other high officers of ancient state; then came the Peers of the Blood Royal, the Prince of Wales the last, and the whole ending by the Chancellor, Lord Thurlow, as Chairman of the House. In passing to their seats they all uncovered and bowed to the Throne. The entire number present was of Prelates eighteen, and of lay-Peers one hundred and twenty-three.[5]

The boxes and the galleries on every side were thronged with ladies. There sat the Queen and the four Princesses, not however having come in state, nor sitting in the Royal box, but in the Duke of Newcastle's. Much as they might be gazed at, still more eager looks of curiosity perhaps were directed to another quarter of the Hall, where Mrs. Fitzherbert appeared.

Silence being first commanded, the Serjeant at Arms made proclamation in quaint old phrase: "Warren

---

[5] The number is variously stated by different writers: thus, Lord Macaulay makes it "near a hundred and seventy," and Mr. Gleig "upwards of two hundred." They had forgotten that in the Journals of the House the names of the Peers present each day are exactly recorded.

Hastings, come forth; save thee and thy Bail, or else thou
forfeits thy Recognizance." Then every eye was turned
to see the accused man enter. He was dressed in a
plain poppy-coloured suit of clothes; he seemed infirm
and ill, and moved forward slowly, with one of his
sureties at each side. He was attended also by his
Counsel, men of shining ability and high subsequent
rank: Law, afterwards Lord Ellenborough, and Chief
Justice of the King's Bench; Dallas, afterwards Chief
Justice of the Common Pleas; and Plumer, afterwards
Vice-Chancellor and Master of the Rolls. Thus did
Hastings advance to the Bar, where, as ancient form
prescribed, he dropped upon his knees until the Chancellor bade him rise. Once before in the previous
Session, when admitted to give bail, had Hastings
undergone the same humiliation. When he rose the
Chancellor next addressed him in a short speech as
opening the Trial, and Hastings replied in the following few words: "My Lords, I am come to this high
tribunal equally impressed with a confidence in my own
integrity, and in the justice of the Court before which
I stand."

We may observe that in all this trying scene it was
the humiliation of the posture that seems to have
rankled most in Hastings's mind. In a letter some
months afterwards to his friend Mr. Thompson, we find
him say: "I can with truth affirm that I have borne
with indifference all the base treatment I have had
dealt to me—all except the ignominious ceremonial of
kneeling before the House."

But the interest of this great day wholly ceased as

soon as the preliminaries ended and the business itself began. For then the Clerk at the Table was directed to read forth at length the Charges and the Answers —documents already well known to one part of the audience, and nearly unintelligible to the other. The Clerk read on so long as daylight lasted, but then he had only reached the close of the seventh article, and the remainder were reserved to consume the second day.

On the third day of the great Trial Burke rose and commenced his opening speech, designed as a general introduction to all the Charges. It extended through four days: a sustained and wonderful effort of eloquence, worthy the man, the occasion, and the audience. Even the hostile Chancellor was stirred to some cordial words of admiration.

On a subsequent day the Charge relating to Cheyte Sing was opened by Fox, with the aid of Grey. In such hands we may be well assured that the weapon of attack was brandished with shining lustre and hurled with unerring aim. Of the future Premier of King William the Fourth we find Burke write about this time to Sheridan in an almost prophetic strain: "Grey has done much, and will do everything."

The next case, that of the Begums of Oude, had been entrusted to the care of Sheridan. He made a speech, not equalling indeed his own master-piece upon the same subject in the House of Commons, yet still in a high degree beautiful and brilliant. While it was still in progress—and it took up three entire days —Burke, who stood next to Fox, turning round to him, exclaimed : "There—that is the true style—something between poetry and prose, and better than either!" [6]

The public interest which had been so keen and eager at the opening of Hastings's Trial, and during the great orations of his principal antagonists, soon afterwards ebbed, and never rose high again. In the first place the gloss of novelty had worn away. But above all, there had now to the splendours of a pageant or to the triumphs of eloquence, succeeded the dull realities of business. Instead of Heralds and Kings at Arms glittering in state-dresses, or Burke and Fox rivalling the records of Greek and Roman fame, there were now the Clerks mumbling forth tedious documents, or Counsel brow-beating reluctant witnesses. Another dispiriting circumstance was the slow progress made. Even in the Court of Chancery it could scarcely have been slower. During the Session of 1788 the Peers sat thirty-five days in Westminster Hall, yet the Managers for the Impeachment could do no more than complete their second Charge; and it was plain that years must roll away ere any decision was pronounced.

There was a wish in some quarters to urge yet another impeachment—that of Sir Elijah Impey, the first Chief Justice of India under the Act of 1773. Early in the Session Sir Gilbert Elliot had brought forward six Charges against him. Sir Elijah, now a Member of the House, spoke at great length and with no mean ability

---

[6] Life of Sheridan, by Moore, vol. i. p. 523.

in his own defence. The discussion was resumed in May, when Pitt declared that in no view could any corrupt motive be brought home to Sir Elijah Impey, and that he had never voted with a more decided conviction of mind than in giving his negative to the present motion. Yet when the House divided at past seven in the morning, the majority in Sir Elijah's favour was by no means a large one: only 73 against 55. All idea, however, of an impeachment fell to the ground.

Pitt had also been not a little busy with another Indian question in the House of Commons. The alarm of war having ceased, the East India Directors were found no longer willing, as they had been while that alarm prevailed, to send out troops in their ships to India, or to maintain them after they had landed. These gentlemen asserted that unless they had themselves made a requisition for a further military force, they were not liable to defray it under the Act of 1781, which they considered as still binding; and they supported their view of the case by the opinion of several eminent Counsel. On the other hand, Mr. Pitt, upheld by the Crown Lawyers, contended that the Act of 1784 had transferred to the Board of Control all the powers and authorities which had been formerly vested in the Court of Directors; and that those parts of the Act of 1781 inconsistent with the Act of 1784 were by the latter virtually if not expressly repealed.

It was impossible to allow any uncertainty to remain on so important a point. On the 25th of February Mr. Pitt moved for leave to bring in a Bill for removing any doubts as to the power of the Commissioners for the

Affairs of India in defraying from the Indian revenues the charge of transporting and maintaining troops. It was commonly called the India Declaratory Bill.

The Directors on their part presented a petition against the Bill, and on the 3rd of March they were heard by their Counsel at the Bar. They had sent Erskine and Rous. Erskine seems to have shown, as usual with him whenever he had not a jury to address, an entire miscalculation of the feelings of his audience. His two speeches, delivered the same day, are described in no complimentary terms in a letter addressed to the Marquis of Buckingham at Dublin Castle, by the Earl of Mornington, afterwards the Marquis Wellesley. Allowance must certainly be made for a strong bias both of party spirit and of personal regard to Mr. Pitt. Yet still we find the writer in positive terms refer as follows to the second speech: "Erskine now spoke for near two hours, and delivered the most stupid, gross, and indecent libel against Pitt that ever was imagined. The abuse was so monstrous that the House hissed him at his conclusion."

The result of this evening was by no means unfavourable to the Minister. "Pitt," says Lord Mornington, "took no sort of notice of Erskine's Billingsgate;" and the division was a very good one. "We reckon this a great triumph," so Lord Mornington continues. But the next ensuing debate took an adverse turn. Only two days later the Lord Lieutenant of Ireland received a far from satisfactory letter from his brother William. "I am very sorry," so writes Mr. Grenville on the 6th of March, "to send you in return for all your good news an account from hence of a very different nature. . . . You must often have observed that of all impressions the most difficult to be removed are those which have no reason whatever to support them, because against them no reasoning can be applied. Under one of these impressions the question of the Speaker's leaving the Chair (on the Declaratory Bill) came on last night, and after debating till seven this morning, we divided in a majority of only 57: Ayes 182, Noes 125. So many of our friends were against us in this division that I have serious apprehensions of our being beat either to-morrow on the Report, or Monday on the Third Reading. . . . What hurt us, I believe materially, last night, was that Pitt, who had reserved himself to answer Fox, was just at the close of a very able speech of Fox's taken so ill as not to be able to speak at all, so that the House went to the division with the whole impression of our adversaries' arguments in a great degree unanswered. I had spoken early in the debate, and Dundas just before Fox. I think this is the most unpleasant thing of the sort that has ever happened to us."

A few days afterwards we find another Member, Lord Bulkeley, supply Lord Buckingham with some further details. Lord Bulkeley, I may observe, unlike Lord Mornington or Mr. Grenville, was a Member of no weight and authority, and judged from his own letters may be regarded as a gossiping, shallow man; yet still he appears a fair witness as to what he may himself have seen or heard in the House of Commons. "Your brother William," so he writes to the Marquis, "suffered a mortification last Wednesday (the 5th) which I am told has

vexed him. The moment he got up to speak, the House
cleared as it used to do at one time when Burke got
up. I hope it proceeded from accident, for if it continues it must hurt him very essentially. The day after
he was in uncommon low spirits and croaked very
much. There seems a general complaint of Pitt's young
friends who never get up to speak, and I am not surprised at their timidity, for Fox, Sheridan, Burke, and
Barré are formidable opponents on the ground they now
stand upon. Young Grey has not yet spoke on either
of these last days, and he is hitherto a superior four-
year-old to any of our side.

  " But," so continues Lord Bulkeley in the same letter,
" these triumphs were, however, of short duration to the
Opposition, for on Friday (the 7th) Pitt made one of
the best and most masterly speeches he ever made, and
turned the tables effectually on Opposition by acquiescing in such shackles as they chose to put on the
article of patronage, all which they had pressed from an
idea that Pitt on that point would be inflexible. This
speech of Pitt's infused spirit into his friends. Dundas
spoke very well, and contrary to expectation so did
Scott and Macdonald. Government kept up their numbers in the division, and Opposition lost ten."[7]

  The changes made by Pitt in this Bill were, it seems,
fully sufficient to obviate the objections which it had
raised. There was no serious difficulty in any of its
further stages either in the Commons or in the Lords.

---

[7] For the letters to Lord Buckingham in Ireland see the 'Courts
and Cabinets of George the Third,'
vol. i. p. 356-363.

Pitt brought forward the Budget on the 5th of May. It was a most satisfactory statement of the national finances.   The extraordinary expenses of the year amounted to no less than 1,282,000l., which arose chiefly from the late armament and from the payment of the debts of the Prince of Wales.   Yet such was the flourishing state of the revenue that it afforded the means of defraying all these expenses without incurring either a loan or new taxes, and without any interruption to the progress of the Sinking Fund.

In this estimate, however, Pitt observed that he did not include one article of large amount and of a peculiar nature, as to which he would explain his plan on a future day—he alluded to the claims of the American Loyalists.

In considering the case of these ill-fated men, it may, I think, be asserted that the conduct of some at least of the United States since the Treaty with England, so far from being conciliatory, had not been even just. On this point we may fairly appeal to the testimony of one of their most eminent statesmen, John Adams, at this time American Minister at the Court of St. James's. Thus do we find him write in strict confidence to a kinsman of his own at Boston: " The most insuperable bar to all my negotiations here has been laid by those States which have made laws against the Treaty.   The Massachusetts is one of them.   The law for suspending execution for British debts, however coloured or disguised, I make no scruple to say to you is a direct breach of the Treaty. Did my ever dear, honoured, and beloved Massachusetts mean to break her public faith?

I cannot believe it of her.   Let her then repeal the law without delay." [8]

But these commercial obstacles, however far from just, did not weigh so heavily in England as the denial of even the most qualified forgiveness to the former adherents of the Royal cause. That some indulgence, or rather some mitigation of severity, might have been shown them soon after the peace by their victorious countrymen, was the opinion at this time of no less a man than Dr. Franklin; [9] but this the rancour of the recent conflict unhappily prevented. The recommendations on this subject to the Legislatures of the several States, as enjoined by the Treaty of Peace, had been made in the coldest terms, and merely as a matter of form. Thus it became obvious that if any provision at all was to be made for the American Loyalists, the entire weight of it must fall on England.

Under these circumstances, and the claims pouring in in great numbers and on every possible plea, Pitt had early in his administration named several Commissioners to sift and report upon the divers cases. The inquiry proved long and laborious. Three thousand applications had been sent in by heads of families, and of these no more than two-thirds could be heard and decided in England. For the remainder it was necessary to depute Commissioners both to Canada and Nova Scotia; and thus whole years elapsed; but meanwhile the sum of 500,000l. had been allotted to meet the more pressing

---

[8] Letter dated May 26, 1786, Works, vol. ix. p. 548.

[9] See a passage in his collected Works, vol. x. p. 324, ed. 1844.

cases of distress.[1] At length the inquiries having been closed, and the reports presented, Pitt took the whole subject into review; and in the comprehensive scheme which he formed upon it, sought to combine the two main objects of compassion and economy. He divided the Loyalists into three classes. The first and most deserving to consist of those who had been resident in America at the commencement of the war, and who, in consequence of their attachment to the Crown, had been driven into exile and despoiled of their estates. The second class of those who had been resident in England, but who had lost property in America. The third of those who had either held places or exercised professions in America, and had been compelled to leave that country by the war. With this division of classes, Pitt proposed that the smaller claims (those under 10,000*l.*) should be paid in full, while on the others there should be a per-centage of deduction, increasing as the claim increased, and also according to the class. Yet with all these deductions there was still one sum of 70,000*l.* awarded to a single claim—that of Mr. Harford; and the total sum to be distributed, in addition to the half million already advanced, amounted to 1,228,000*l.* Further, it was proposed that the money should be paid by instalments, to be raised by the profits of a lottery to commence in the following year.

---

[1] The most authentic history (or, as the writer prefers calling it, "historical view") of the proceedings of this Commission was published in 1815 by Mr. John Eardley Wilmot, who had been one of the Commissioners. See also an able work on the American Loyalists by Mr. Lorenzo Sabine, p. 89, &c., Boston, 1857.

This scheme, comprising also a settlement of the East
Florida claims to the further extent of 113,000*l.*, was welcomed by all parties in the House as no less generous
than prudent and well framed. Both Burke and Fox rose
to express their approbation, and it passed unanimously.
Thus was afforded to the world a great and memorable,
and it may even be said unparalleled, example of
national bounty and consideration at the close of an
unprosperous war. Seldom indeed, either in public or
in private, do we find gratitude evinced and rewards
bestowed for zeal which has proved altogether un-
availing, and for services that can never be renewed.

The Session of 1788 is further memorable for the
first steps in Parliament for the abolition of the Slave
Trade. In the earlier part of the century that traffic—
the *Asiento,* as in one word it was emphatically called—
had been by no means a matter of shame. It was
anxiously sought by commercial enterprise. It was as
anxiously secured by diplomatic treaties. The public
feeling began to be turned against it by the case of
James Somersett in 1772. Somersett was an African
slave who had been brought to England by his master,
but having there absconded was by that master seized
and sent on shipboard. The case being referred to the
Judges, it was by them at last established as a fixed
principle of law, that as soon as any slave sets his foot
upon English ground he becomes free.

A lull ensued upon the subject during the American
contest; but the Quakers especially had become alive
to the iniquity of the traffic in slaves. It is much
to their honour that when in May, 1787, a Committee

of Management was formed against it, with a benevolent gentleman, Mr. Granville Sharpe, as Chairman.
there were only two of the twelve members of that
Committee who did not belong to the Society of
" Friends."

Among those who at this early period took an active
part in the good cause may be named Sir Charles and
Lady Middleton, Mr. Bennet Langton, the Rev. James
Ramsay (who had recently published an 'Essay on the
Treatment of the Slaves,' derived from his own observation in the West India Islands), and last, not least, Mr.
Thomas Clarkson, whose great labours and services are
not to be obscured even by his own undue exaggeration
of them.   But in the arduous struggle that now commenced against the partisans of Slavery, by far the
greatest share of praise and honour belongs as of right
to the honoured name of Wilberforce.

Already had the mind of Mr. Wilberforce been
trained and moulded for this, as it proved, the main
business of his life.   In the course of the year 1785 he
had received a strong religious impulse, and determined to apply himself solely to religious objects.   He
wrote to his principal friends to explain his change of
views.   Some of them received the communication with
displeasure.   One of them angrily threw his letter into
the fire.   Still less did the Opposition in the first instance show him that reverent confidence which in
after years he so fully attained.   Thus, for instance, in
the mock Journal of Mr. Dundas, which is annexed to
some editions of the 'Rolliad,' there is an entry from
this very year 1788:—" Came home in a very melan-

choly mood—drank a glass of brandy—determined to reform, and sent to Wilberforce for a good book—a very worthy and religious young man that—like him much—always votes with us."

It was natural that with these earnest aspirations Mr. Wilberforce should now apply himself to ascertain how far the charges against the Slave Traders were or were not well founded. In his own words:—"I got together at my house, from time to time, persons who knew anything about the matter. . . . When I had acquired so much information, I began to talk the matter over with Pitt and Grenville. Pitt recommended me to undertake its conduct as a subject suited to my character and talents. At length, I well remember, after a conversation in the open air, at the root of an old tree at Holwood, just above the steep descent into the vale of Keston, I resolved to give notice, on a fit occasion, in the House of Commons, of my intention to bring the subject forward."

I may add that this very tree, conspicuous for its gnarled and projecting root, on which the two friends had sat, is still pointed out at Holwood, and is known by the name of "Wilberforce's oak."

In this concert of measures Pitt agreed that a Committee of the Privy Council should be appointed to take evidence on the African trade. Wilberforce on his part gave notice of a motion in the House of Commons. But by this time the West India merchants and planters were thoroughly alarmed. They urged the Members for Liverpool and other great ports to make a determined stand. They prepared some texts of the Old Testament which they thought convenient for their purpose. They brought forward witnesses to prove not merely the necessity, but the absolute humanity, of the Slave Trade. And even the zeal of Wilberforce could not hide from himself the probable strength and power of that great interest. Here is one entry from his journal at the commencement of 1788 : "Called at Pitt's at night: he firm about African trade, though we begin to perceive more difficulties in the way than we had hoped there would be."

It so chanced, that ere the day appointed for the motion the health of Mr. Wilberforce failed. He found himself disabled from active business, and compelled to try the waters of Bath. Before he went, however, he obtained from Pitt a promise that if his illness should continue through the spring, Pitt himself would supply his place. Accordingly, on the 9th of May, the Prime Minister rose to move a Resolution, "That this House will early in the next Session proceed to take into consideration the circumstances of the Slave Trade." With a reserve imposed upon him by official duty, he added that he should forbear from stating or even glancing at his own opinion until the moment of discussion should arrive. "I understand, however," said Fox, "that the opinion of the Right Hon. Gentleman is *primâ facie* the same as my own. . . . For myself I have no scruple to declare that the Slave Trade ought not to be regulated, but destroyed. To this opinion my mind is pretty nearly made up. . . . I have considered the subject very minutely, and did intend to have brought something forward in the House respecting it. But I rejoice that it should be in the hands of the Hon. Member for Yorkshire rather than in mine. From him I honestly think that it will come with more weight, more authority, and more probability of success." These words, which redound so highly to Mr. Fox's honour, were followed by words not less decided from Mr. Burke and from Sir William Dolben, Member for the University of Oxford.

Against an array of opinions such as these, Mr. Bamber Gascoyne and Lord Penrhyn, the Members for Liverpool, and almost officially the spokesmen for the Slave Trade, could make no effectual stand. They deemed it wisest to let the Resolution pass unopposed, and to reserve their strength for the ensuing year. And that strength was certainly far greater than at first it seemed. The opinion of Mr. Pitt had not prevailed with all his colleagues. Lord Thurlow, above all, was, and continued to be, favourable to the Slave Trade, and unhappily he found means to instil nearly the same prejudice into the mind of the King.

These differences came to light much sooner than was expected. Sir William Dolben and some of his friends had gone to see with their own eyes the actual state of a slave-ship then fitting out in the Thames. They came back deeply impressed with pity, indignation, and shame. They found, as Sir William afterwards declared in the House of Commons, that the poor slaves had not one yard square allowed them to live in. Moreover, in that narrow space they were loaded with shackles. They were fastened together hand to hand and foot to foot.[2] The suffering and the sickness that must ensue might be readily conceived, and could scarcely be exaggerated. Not a moment, said Sir William, should be lost in arresting such intolerable evils and abuses. Accordingly, while he left the general question as already voted for debate in the ensuing year, he brought in a temporary Bill providing divers precautions, and above all limiting the numbers to be conveyed—one slave to each ton of the vessel's burden.

At the introduction of this Bill the Members for Liverpool raised a piteous cry. They denounced it both as unnecessary and as ruinous. In their resentment they appear to have even taunted Sir William Dolben as unmindful of former hospitality. " I should indeed be a most ungrateful man," said Dolben, " if I forgot the merchants of Liverpool. I believe that I have eaten more turtle there than anywhere else in the course of my life ; but I would readily give up their turtle and Burgundy for mock-turtle and plain Port if they would consent to forego some part of their profits for the sake of better accommodation to the poor negroes while on ship-board."

The Bill of Sir William Dolben being moderate in its aim and supported both by Pitt and Fox, passed triumphantly through the Commons. But in the other House Lord Thurlow fell upon it with great fury. He was backed by two Peers who had gained just distinction in a better cause—Lord Heathfield and Lord

[2] See the plan of a slave-ship inserted as a print in Clarkson's | History of the Abolition, vol. ii. p. 110.

Rodney. And it was with great difficulty, and not until the last day of the Session, that there passed a measure on the subject, though curtailed of its first proportions.

The result so far, however, was encouraging to the Committee of Management under Mr. Granville Sharpe. They despatched Mr. Clarkson as their agent from place to place, partly to obtain information, and partly to diffuse their opinions. For their own seal they had chosen a design well adapted for popular effect. It represented an African in chains, kneeling with one knee upon the ground, and raising his hands in supplication, while around him the motto ran: "Am I not a man and a brother?"

Of the gross exaggerations and misstatements which were at this time put forward in defence of the Slave Trade one instance may suffice. Several of the dealers or captains had not scrupled to assert that the Middle Passage was perhaps the happiest period of the negroes' lives; that they were constantly well fed: that the close air below in the holds was congenial to their frame of body; and that when upon deck they made merry and amused themselves with their national dances. But the real facts were disclosed by the evidence before the Privy Council. It was found that the poor wretches were chained two and two together, and secured by ring-bolts to the lower decks. The allowance for each was one pint of water daily, and they had two meals of yams and horse-beans. After eating they were loosened from their rings, and allowed to jump up in their irons, as an exercise necessary for

their health; and for that reason it was not only permitted but urged on them by lashes whenever they
refused. And such, then, were the "national dances"
which had been so boldly and boastfully alleged!

In comparing the controversies on Slave Trade and
on Slavery as they once prevailed in England, and as
they still prevail in the United States, we may feel
some surprise as we observe how much they run in
opposite directions. With us the defence was based
in the first instance on such arguments as the supposed
predictions of Holy Writ, or the personal interest of
the slave-dealers to study the good health and well-
being of their slaves. By degrees these arguments
were utterly refuted and overthrown. Then the advo-
cates of the existing system, while acknowledging the
general considerations against it to be irresistible, took
their stand on what lawyers would have termed a dila-
tory plea. They contended, and certainly with great
truth, that the question was no longer a plain and
simple one, but had become interwoven with many
practical considerations; that care must be taken of
the interests which had grown up under a system which
the law had sanctioned; and that even for the sake of
the negroes themselves the great work of their Eman-
cipation should be accomplished by slow degrees. In
America the course of the discussion has been the very
reverse. We may learn from such high authorities as
the letters of Washington or the travels of Tocqueville that till within these thirty years the force of the
general arguments against Slave Trade and Slavery
was not denied, and that the planters of the south,

with few exceptions, relied, as they justly might, on the particular grounds for caution and delay. But since that time there has been taken a large step in advance. Slavery is no longer excused as an existing evil rendered necessary by especial circumstances, and to endure only for a time, but is rather vindicated as a laudable and lasting "institution." Nay, there are even found some clergymen among them so keen and thorough-going as to say—and not only to say, but to preach—that Slavery as a permanent system is perfectly consistent with, or rather enjoined by, the leading principles of the Gospel.

CHAPTER XI.

1788.

Official changes and appointments — Treaties of Defensive Alliance
with Holland and Prussia — Mental alienation of the King — Pitt's
measures — Prince of Wales consults Lord Loughborough — Mani-
festation of national sympathy — Objects of Pitt and Thurlow —
Meeting of Parliament — The King's removal to Kew — Fox's
return from Italy.

THE Session of 1788, marked both by important measures and by eloquent debates, was closed on the 11th
of July by a Speech from the Throne. Even before
its close Mr. Pitt had been much intent on some official
changes and new appointments. On the chief of these
we find him write to his mother as follows :—

"Downing Street, June 19, 1788.

" MY DEAR MOTHER,

" You have been infinitely good, as usual, in
making more allowance than could fairly be claimed
for the calls of business as well as for some necessary
intervals of idleness. I feel, however, really ashamed
of having availed myself so long of the latitude you
gave. Business is now fairly at an end in the House
of Commons, and will probably finish in the House
of Lords so as to admit of the Prorogation in the
course of next week. The Session ends most satisfactorily, and its close will be accompanied by some
events which add not a little to that satisfaction. I

feel, indeed, no small pleasure in having to communicate a piece of news which will, I believe, fully make up for my long silence, and which you will be as happy in hearing as I am in telling. It is no other than this, that a new arrangement in the Admiralty is, from various circumstances, become unavoidable, that Lord Howe must be succeeded by a landsman, and that landsman is my brother. I have had some doubts whether the public may not think this too much like monopoly, but that doubt is not sufficient to counterbalance the personal comfort which will result from it and the general advantage to the whole of our system. You will, I am sure, be happy to hear that Lord Howe does not quit without a public mark of honour by a fresh step in the peerage, without which, I own, I should feel more regret than I can pretend to do now. Another event which you will not be sorry to learn is the conclusion of a very satisfactory alliance with Russia, which will probably lead to a very secure and permanent system of Continental politics. . . . .

"I am going, the end of next week, if our arrangement is by that time completed, for a few days to Cambridge, and a fortnight or three weeks after will, I hope, bring me to Burton. Be so good as to let my news remain an *entire secret*, as it should not transpire till it takes effect.

"Ever, my dear Mother, &c.,

"W. Pitt."

The same appointment is thus referred to in a letter from Mr. Grenville to his brother in Ireland:

"Pitt's intention is to place his brother at the head of the Admiralty, giving him Sir Charles Middleton

and Hood for assistants, and prevailing with Mulgrave, if possible, to accept the Comptrollership of the
Navy. I have no doubt of this arrangement being in
general very acceptable. The great popularity of
Lord Chatham's manners and his near connexion with
Pitt are, I think, sufficient to remove the impression
of any objection in the public opinion from his being
brought forward in the first instance in so responsible
a situation. To those who know him there can be no
doubt that his abilities are fully equal to the undertaking, arduous as it is; and to those who do not, Sir
Charles Middleton's name and character will hold out a
solution."

The offer to Sir Charles Middleton was, it seems,
declined; but Lord Hood was appointed a Lord of
the Admiralty, under the Earl of Chatham as chief.
Lord Hood was a distinguished Admiral, in 1782
created an Irish Peer. In May, 1784, he had been
at the head of the poll for Westminster; but in August,
1788, on appealing to his constituents for re-election,
he was defeated by Lord John Townshend, the numbers
—after fifteen days' poll—being 6392 against 5569.
It was a considerable triumph to the Opposition, and
they extolled it as such.

The appointment of Lord Chatham himself, though
in the first instance well received by the public, did
not by any means fulfil the expectations it had raised.
As First Lord of the Admiralty the brother of Pitt
showed but little aptitude for business, and none at all
for debate; and from his want of punctuality in his
appointments he came to be often nicknamed "the late
Lord Chatham."

In June, 1788, Lord Mansfield had at last retired from the Bench, and he survived in retirement till the year 1793 and till the great age of eighty-eight. He retired perhaps a little too late for his renown, considering the infirmities which for some time past had pressed upon him. "Lord Mansfield is totally incapable of doing his duty, and is in great bodily pain." So writes Lord Sydney in January, 1787. "Lord Mansfield is at Bath, sleeps everywhere but in bed, receives his quarter's salary, and does not resign." So writes General Grant in April the same year.[1]

Sir Lloyd Kenyon now became Chief Justice, with a peerage as Lord Kenyon. The office of Master of the Rolls, left vacant by this promotion, was designed by Pitt for his early friend Pepper Arden, now Attorney-General. But Lord Thurlow offered a fierce resistance. He claimed the office of the Rolls as under his own gift, and for some time declared—no doubt with abundance of oaths—that he would sooner resign the Great Seal than put it to Arden's patent. But Pitt was resolute, and Thurlow at last, though still growling, gave way.

In due course, accordingly, Pepper Arden was appointed Master of the Rolls, and Macdonald, from Solicitor, Attorney-General. The vacant office of Solicitor-General was, to the high satisfaction of the Bar, conferred upon Scott, who had long since retrieved the discredit of his first abortive effort in the House of Commons. The King, on this occasion, laid down a

---

[1] See the Cornwallis Correspondence, vol. i. p. 256 and 287.

rule which has ever since been observed, that the
Attorney and Solicitor-General, as also the Judges, shall.
if not "Honourable" by birth, be always knighted.[2]
His Majesty's object was to keep up the reputation
of the Order of Knighthood, which at this time had
greatly declined. Accordingly, Macdonald became Sir
Archibald, and Scott Sir John. The latter, at least,
was by no means well pleased. We find him write as
follows to his brother Henry : "I kissed the King's
hand yesterday as Solicitor-General. The King, in
spite of my teeth, laid his sword upon my shoulder and
bade Sir John arise. At this last instance of his Royal
favour I have been much disconcerted; but I cannot
help myself, and so I sing—

> ' Oho the delight
>   To be a gallant knight ! '

My wife is persecuted with her new title, and we laugh
at her from morning till evening."

But the Chancellor continued full of wrath. He
was already incensed with the Prime Minister on two
other grounds—the vote of Pitt for the impeachment
of Hastings, and the motion of Pitt against the Slave
Trade. Now the fresh point of office caused his
resentment to boil over and to manifest itself without
control. On the 12th of June we find the King, in
writing to Pitt, appeal to his "good temper," which
His Majesty hoped would make him "feel for weakness" in his colleague. Pitt having carried his point,

---

[2] Lord Campbell's Lives of the Chancellors, vol. vii, p. 84.

did not desire to prosecute the quarrel; but there ceased
to be any intimacy or even any intercourse, except of
the most formal kind, between these brother Ministers.

The Treaty of Defensive Alliance with Holland
being brought to a conclusion and signed in the course
of this spring, Mr. Pitt proposed to the King to confer
a peerage on its negotiator, Sir James Harris. His
Majesty consented on condition that Sir Joseph Yorke,
for many years previous his ambassador at the Hague,
should, as an act of justice, receive the same distinction.
Accordingly Sir James became Lord Malmesbury, and
Sir Joseph Lord Dover.

The defensive alliance with Holland was speedily followed by another to the same effect with Prussia. Preliminary articles were signed at Loo on the 13th of
June, and the treaty itself at Berlin on the 13th of
August. The negotiator was Mr. Joseph Ewart, a man
of considerable ability, selected by Pitt as Minister to
the Court of Frederick William. Besides the customary
articles of mutual guarantee, England and Prussia
bound themselves to act at all times in concert for the
purpose of maintaining the security and independence
of the United Provinces. It was, therefore, in fact a
triple defensive alliance.

Thus in only four years and a half of Mr. Pitt's administration had England been extricated from her
single and defenceless state at the close of the last war.
Then, besides her old claim on Portugal, she had remained without a single ally. Now if France were
willing to remain at peace, there was a Treaty of Commerce to engage her in more friendly relations. If,

on the other hand, France desired to renew her aggressive schemes on Holland or on any other power, we had acquired the Stadtholder as restored to his just authority, and also the King of Prussia, for allies.

In this summer, as in the last, Pitt had hoped to pay a visit to his friend at the Lakes. "Pitt promises to steal down to me for a few days," so writes Wilberforce at this time. But in this summer, as in the last, the pressure of business forbade it. The affairs of Sweden now began, as I shall show hereafter, to cause some solicitude and to require a vigilant control. Even the ultimate object of Pitt, a visit to Lady Chatham, could not be accomplished without much delay. Thus he writes:

"Downing Street, August 29, 1788.

"MY DEAR MOTHER,

"I have been every day, for I know not how long, hoping to be able to tell you the day when I should have the happiness of seeing you at Burton; but, as too often has happened, every day has brought some fresh incident to put it off. This week would, I believe, have pretty nearly enabled me to speak positively, but an accidental cold (which has no other inconvenience than a swelled face and the impossibility of going to St. James's) will oblige me to defer till next week the conclusion of business which I hoped to have got rid of this. The exact time, and the interval for which I can be at liberty, must at all events depend upon news from abroad, where so many things are going on, that although we have every reason to be certain that no consequences can arise otherwise than favourable to us, a good deal of watching is necessary. My

hope was to have been able to make a pretty long stay
at once whenever I reach Burton ; but even if that
should not be the case, I can do it at twice, and I am
pretty sure of a good deal of leisure in the course of the
interval before Parliament meets.

"To-day brings no news from Paris of a fresh change.
The Archbishop has resigned, and Necker is made
Minister of Finance, which is probably the best thing
that could happen for that country, and in the manner
of it very glorious for him ; but he will have no easy
task to go through with.

" I think my brother is now really at the eve of being
able to move again. I shall probably see him established at Wimbledon before I leave this neighbourhood,
and with no other confinement but that of business,
which will be a luxury after the other. My kindest love
to Eliot, and most affectionate compliments to Mrs. Stapleton, not forgetting good Mrs. Sparry.

" Ever, my dear Mother, &c.,

" W. Pitt."

Early next month, however, the visit to Somersetshire
was duly made, and Pitt returned from it fully expecting to divide the remainder of a long Recess between
Downing Street and Holwood.

" Nescia mens hominum fati sortisque futuræ."

Never was any Prime Minister of England deemed
more secure or solidly established than Mr. Pitt in the
autumn of 1788. Never did the political horizon seem
more clear, more bright, more wholly free from clouds.
The members of the Opposition could only look on
office as a fond remembrance, and in the future as a
distant dream ; and their chief, Mr. Fox, despairing of

all present effect in England, set out with his mistress, Mrs. Armistead, for a tour in Italy. Yet at this very period was impending an event wholly without parallel in our Constitutional history, which appeared as an utter blight to the exaltation of Pitt, and as placing Fox within view, nay, almost within grasp, of the highest power. That event, so wholly unforeseen, was the mental alienation of the King.

The constitution of George the Third was by nature hardy and robust, but with a constant tendency to corpulence. To counteract this the King had from an early period adopted a system of abstemious diet and of active exercise. While his meals were of the simplest and plainest kind, the Equerries in attendance upon him might often complain of the great distances which he rode in hunting, or of his walks of three hours before breakfast. That system carried to excess, combined with never failing and anxious attention to affairs of State, was the cause of the mental malady in 1788. Such at least was the opinion of the case expressed by Dr. Willis, the ablest by far of his physicians, when examined by the Committees of the House of Lords and House of Commons.

Early in the summer of 1788 the King's health suffered from repeated bilious attacks. In a letter to Mr. Pitt he says of himself that he is certainly " a cup too low." His physicians prescribed the waters of Cheltenham, and on the 12th of July, the day after the Prorogation, he set out with the Queen for that place. A sojourn of several weeks failed, however, to yield him the expected benefit. When he returned, first to Kew,

and afterwards to Windsor, he seemed weaker in body
than before. His attendants were surprised and grieved
at seeing him, so lately the most athletic of pedestrians,
require the support of a stick. "I could not," he said,
"get on without it: my strength seems diminishing
hourly." "My dear Effy"—thus he accosted one of the
Queen's ladies, the Dowager Countess of Effingham—
"you see me all at once an old man!" [3]

Yet still in some points, at least, the King's active
habits were maintained. Mr. Rose reports that "Mr.
Pitt saw him at Kew, and was with him three hours and
forty minutes, both on their legs the whole time." [4] And
this brings us to a peculiarity in the reign of George
the Third. It was the invariable, or almost invariable,
custom of that Monarch to confer with his Ministers
standing, neither himself to sit down nor ask them to
be seated. This rule, so highly inconvenient to both
parties, was no doubt derived from some of the Continental Courts.

At this period of October, 1788, the only physician
in attendance on the King was Sir George Baker. He
states in his evidence before the subsequent Committees
that the first time when he conceived any suspicion of
a mental malady in the King was in the evening of the
22nd of October. Next morning the unfavourable symptoms which led to that suspicion had wholly disappeared.

On the 24th, however, the King made an effort beyond

---

[3] Diary of Miss Burney (Madame
d'Arblay), vol. iv. p. 275.

[4] Diaries and Correspondence of
the Right Hon. George Rose, vol. i.

p. 86, ed. 1860. See also the Edinburgh Review for April, 1856, p.
354.

his strength in going to hold a Levee at St. James's. He made that effort, as he wrote to Mr. Pitt, " to stop further lies and any fall of the Stocks." But at the Levee his manner and conversation were such as to cause the most painful uneasiness in several at least of those to whom he spoke. Mr. Pitt, in particular, could not entirely suppress his emotion when he attended the King in his closet after the Levee, which His Majesty observed and noticed with kindness in writing next day to his Minister from Kew. Probably conscious himself, at least in some degree, of his coming malady, he directed Mr. Pitt in the same letter not to allow any political papers to be sent to him before the next ensuing Levee.

On the 25th the King removed to Windsor Castle. His state appears to have fluctuated from day to day, but there was no lasting improvement in his health. His letters to Mr. Pitt, which I shall give at length in my appendix, bear no tokens of an incoherent mind. They merely manifest some reluctance and anxiety as to the measures which Pitt desired to pursue with regard to the Northern Powers. The last letter of the King before his malady is dated on the 3rd of November. In this His Majesty states that he can now sign warrants in any number without inconvenience. He adds that he attempts reading the despatches daily, but as yet without success.

Of the King's real condition at this time by far the best, and indeed, so far as published, the only good account is to be found in the private journal of Miss Frances Burney, the accomplished author of ' Evelina.' That lady was now a member of the Royal Household, and in daily attendance on the Queen as, under Mrs. Schwellenberg, Deputy Keeper of the Robes. Dull and trifling as the earlier volumes of her 'Diary,' I must confess, appear to me, the entries in it now become of lively interest and of sterling value, and are marked by not merely dutiful but warm and affectionate attachment to her Royal Mistress.

By some extracts from her journal my narrative may be best continued:

"*Sunday, November* 3.—We are all here in a most uneasy state. The King is better and worse so frequently, and changes so daily backward and forward, that everything is to be apprehended if his nerves are not some way quieted. I dreadfully fear he is on the eve of some severe fever. The Queen is almost overpowered with some secret terror. I am affected beyond all expression in her presence to see what struggles she makes to support serenity. To-day she gave up the conflict when I was alone with her, and burst into a violent fit of tears. It was very, very terrible to see!"

"*Wednesday, November* 5.—I found my poor Royal Mistress in the morning sad and sadder still; something horrible seemed impending; and I saw her whole resource was in religion. We had talked lately much upon solemn subjects; and she appeared already preparing herself to be resigned for whatever might happen.

"At noon the King went out in his chaise with the Princess Royal for an airing. I looked from my window to see him; he was all smiling benignity, but gave so many orders to the postilions, and got in and out of the carriage twice with such agitation, that

again my fear of a great fever hanging over him grew
more and more powerful. Alas! how little did I
imagine I should see him no more for so long—so
black a period!

"When I went to my poor Queen, I found her spirits
still worse and worse. . . . . The Princess Royal soon
returned. She came in cheerfully, and gave in German
a history of the airing, and one that seemed com-
forting.

"Soon after suddenly arrived the Prince of Wales.
He came into the room. He had just quitted Brighthelmstone. Something passing within seemed to
render this meeting awfully distant on both sides.
She asked if he should not return to Brighthelmstone.
He answered 'Yes; the next day.' He desired to speak
with her ; they retired together."

This day, the 5th of November, of which Miss Burney
has thus described the earlier portion, proved to be the
crisis of the King's disorder, when its real nature could
be no longer mistaken or concealed. For that afternoon the King, at dinner with the Royal Family,
broke forth into positive delirium ; and the Queen was
so overpowered as to fall into violent hysterics.

Next morning, the 6th, when Miss Burney rose, she
found that the Equerries and gentlemen in attendance
had sat up next his chamber door all night, and there
were likewise all the pages dispersed in the passages and
ante-rooms ; "and oh," she adds, "what horror in every
face I met!"

Besides Sir George Baker, who continued in close
attendance, a physician of the highest eminence—
Dr. Warren—had been sent for by express. When,

however, he came, the King positively refused to see
him. "This was terrible," writes Miss Burney. "But
the King was never so despotic; no one dared oppose
him. He would not listen to a word, though when
unopposed he was still all gentleness and benignity to
every one around him. . . . He kept talking unceas-
ingly; although his voice was so lost in hoarseness
and weakness it was rendered almost inarticulate."

Expresses had of course gone up also to Mr. Pitt.
His grief may be easily imagined. But his anxiety
was not less than his grief. He saw at once the difficulties that rose before him in the event that the
King's reason should continue clouded and yet his life
be spared. In such a case there were strong grounds
for imposing some restrictions on a Regency. Yet how
could such restrictions be imposed unless by Act of
Parliament, and how could any Act of Parliament be
passed without a King to give it his assent? Thus in
one sense a limited Regency seemed requisite, while in
another sense it seemed impossible.

Pitt, however, applied himself at once to all the
measures in his power. That same afternoon he sent
expresses to summon the Cabinet Ministers who were
absent from town. Here is his letter to the Marquis
of Stafford, Lord Privy Seal:

"Grosvenor Square, Nov. 6, 1788, 6 P.M.
"MY DEAR LORD,

"I write from Lord Carmarthen's, having just
had an account from Windsor, by which I learn that
the King's disorder, which has for some days given us

much uneasiness, has within a few hours taken so serious a turn that I think myself obliged to lose no time in apprising your Lordship of it.

"The accounts are sent under considerable alarm, and therefore do not state the symptoms very precisely; but from what I learn, there is too much reason to fear that they proceed from a fever which has settled on the brain, and which may produce immediate danger to His Majesty's life. You will easily conceive the pain I suffer in being obliged to send your Lordship this intelligence; but as you may possibly think it right, under such circumstances, to be on the spot as soon as possible, I thought no time should be lost in letting you know the situation.

"I am, with great regard, &c.,

"W. PITT."

On the same day Pitt also wrote to the Bishop of Lincoln at Buckden Palace, and here is the extract from his letter which the Bishop gives:

"The effect most to be dreaded is on the understanding. If this lasts beyond a certain time, it will produce the most difficult and delicate crisis imaginable, in making provision for the Government to go on. It must, however, be yet some weeks before that can require decision; but the interval will be a truly anxious one. You shall hear again soon; but if in the course of a few days you could spare the time to come to town, I should be very glad to talk with you, as there will be a thousand particulars you must wish to know, which I cannot write. I shall not stir from hence, except for going to inquire at Windsor."

The Bishop adds:

"I went to town immediately, and late at night

found Mr. Pitt expecting a messenger every moment
with the account of the King's death; but the intelligence, which did not arrive till two in the morning,
proved more favourable."

During the night which followed there were many
anxious watchers in the apartment next to the Royal
sufferer's. The Prince of Wales, the Duke of York,
the physicians, and the gentlemen of the Royal Household, sat on chairs and lay on sofas round the room.
All were in dead silence, and amidst the partial dark-
ness the two Princes were still to be distinguished by
their stars.

Next day, the 7th of November, towards seven in
the morning, when the Queen was already dressed,
but Miss Burney was still attending her, the
Prince of Wales came hastily into Her Majesty's
chamber, and then, in Miss Burney's presence, gave
"a very energetic history" of the preceding night.
The King had risen some hours before daylight, and
insisted on walking into the next apartment. There
he was utterly amazed at finding, instead of the mere
solitude which he expected, the large assemblage of
his family and household. With some haste he demanded what they all did there. Sir George Baker
was exhorted in whispers by the gentlemen near him,
and even, as it would seem, by the Prince of Wales,
to lead the King back to his chamber; but he had
not courage, and he seems indeed to have well deserved the character which the King presently gave
him when His Majesty penned him in a corner and

told him he was only an old woman. No one else dared approach His Majesty, and this most painful scene continued a considerable time. At length the Queen's Vice-Chamberlain, Colonel Stephen Digby, an old servant of their Majesties, resolved to act. He went boldly up, and taking the King by the arm, entreated him to go to bed; but finding entreaties in vain, began to draw His Majesty along, and to say he must go. "I will not," cried the King, "I will not! Who are you?" "I am Colonel Digby, Sir," he answered, "and your Majesty has been very good to me, and now I am going to be very good to you; for you must come to bed, Sir—it is necessary to your life." And then, continued the Prince of Wales in his narrative, the King was so surprised that he allowed himself to be drawn along as gently as a child, and thus was he brought back to his chamber.

Here, then, was the turning point. This was the precise moment when ceased the dominion of a Sovereign over his subjects, and when began, on the contrary, the dominion of sound minds over an unsound one. Here, then, let History pause. So long as the King continued a public character, it is her right and her duty to record his course; not so to explore the dismal secrets of his enforced and lonely sick room.

It may, therefore, suffice to say in general terms that during the next few days the King became greatly worse both in mind and body. Not only seemed his reason lost, but his life in imminent danger. Then, in those hours of suspense and anguish at Windsor, came to light some further revelations of his growing

malady.   The Queen had sent for Dr. Warren soon
after his first arrival, and felt it her duty to inform
him privately that for some time past she had more
than suspected the real situation of the King.   The
Duke of York had met the King on Monday the 3rd,
after His Majesty had been on horseback for some
hours, and the King, drawing his son aside, had burst
into tears and given utterance to the simple but most
affecting words, "I wish to God I might die, for I am
going to be mad!"[5]

The physicians in daily attendance—and within a
fortnight their number had been increased to four—
were of course guarded and cautious in their expressed
opinions.   But among the members of the Royal
Household the belief was most strongly prevalent that
there was little or no prospect of the King's recovery.
The Queen withdrew to her own chamber, and passed
the whole day in patient sorrow with her daughters.
The entire direction of the household devolved upon
the Prince of Wales, and nothing at Windsor was done
but by direction of His Royal Highness.

So great and awful an affliction, and so deep a
responsibility resulting from it, could not fail to impress
even the least earnest minds.

"The Prince was frightened, and was blooded yesterday." So writes one of the Grenville cousins who was
at Windsor on the 7th.

The first step of the Prince when called upon to

---

[5] See the private letters from
Captain Payne to Mr. Sheridan,
as published in Moore's Life of
the latter (vol. ii. p. 21–31). Payne
was at this time attending the
Prince of Wales at Windsor.

take the command at Windsor was to send the Duke
of York with a message to Lord Loughborough. The
Prince said that he should anxiously await the return
of Fox from Italy—that meanwhile he should look
mainly to Lord Loughborough for counsel—and that
Lord Loughborough ought at once to turn over in
his mind what steps in so unprecedented an emergency it might be best for the Prince to take. Lord
Loughborough might well consider his darling object
of ambition, the Great Seal, as close in view before
him.

Meanwhile the illness of the King and its real
nature could not be kept secret. The tidings of it
flew far and wide throughout the country, everywhere
exciting the utmost sympathy and sorrow. Then did
it become apparent how strong and deeply rooted was
in truth at this period the popularity of George the
Third, and how thoroughly had passed away from it
the clouds of earlier years. By the Queen's direction
Colonel Digby had written to the Archbishop of Canterbury, suggesting that there should be offered up
public prayers for the King's recovery. A form of
prayer was accordingly framed at Lambeth Palace and
ordered to be used in all the churches, and the manner
in which the various congregations through the kingdom joined in this act of worship clearly evinced the
sincerity and the strength of their affliction.

Other manifestations of the same feeling were not
all as commendable. Thus the physicians in attendance on the King received every day a number of
threatening letters to answer for the safety of their

Monarch with their lives. On one occasion Sir George Baker was stopped in his carriage by the mob, and required to give an account of the King's state. Poor Sir George faltered out that it was a bad one; on which there arose a furious cry: "The more shame for you!"

At this crisis the two Ministers on whom most depended were Pitt and Thurlow. But they had little intercourse, and their objects were far asunder. Pitt was thinking how best he could serve his country—Thurlow was thinking how best he could keep his place. So early as the 7th the Prince of Wales summoned to his presence the Chancellor, who went down and remained that night at Windsor. The Prince's object was a very proper one—to consult with him as to the care and safe custody of the King's jewels and private papers. On coming back to town on the morning of the 8th, the Chancellor only sent a note to Pitt, stating that the Prince desired to see him at Windsor the next morning at eleven. Pitt went to call upon his colleague, but does not seem to have obtained much further information. He learnt, however, that the immediate business for which His Royal Highness had summoned him was to inquire about a paper which the Queen imagined that the King had put into Pitt's hand respecting an arrangement for the younger Princes and Princesses. But this was a misapprehension, for Pitt had no such paper.

Pitt of course obeyed the Prince's summons. The result is related as follows by Mr. Grenville in a letter the next morning: "I need not tell you the effect

which this dreadful calamity produces. Pitt had yesterday a long conference with the Prince, but it turned
chiefly on the situation of the King, and the state and
progress of his disorder. Nothing passed from which
any conclusion can be drawn as to future measures. He
treated him with civility, but nothing more. The general idea is that *they* mean to try a negotiation. But
whether the Prince means that, and whether Pitt ought
in any case to listen to it at all, or in what degree, are
questions which it is difficult indeed to decide." [6]

The part of Pitt was promptly taken. It was, as his
part was ever, straightforward and direct. He would
listen to no terms for himself. He would consider only
his bounden duty to his afflicted King. He would, by
the authority of Parliament, impose some restrictions on
the Regency for a limited time, so that the Sovereign
might resume his power without difficulty in case his
reason were restored. What might be the just limits
or the necessary period of such restrictions he had not
yet decided, and was still revolving in his mind. But
he had never the least idea, as his opponents feared, of
a Council of Regency which might impede the Prince
in the choice of a new administration. On the contrary,
Pitt looked forward to his own immediate dismissal from
the public service, and he had determined to return to
the practice of his profession at the Bar.

Far different was the course of Thurlow. Under an
appearance of rugged honesty he concealed no small
amount of selfish craft. He was ready to grasp at an

---

[6] Letter to Lord Buckingham, November 9, 1788.

overture, and it was not long ere an overture came. Two
gentlemen in the Prince's confidence—the Comptroller
of his Household, Captain Payne, more commonly called
Jack Payne, and Richard Brinsley Sheridan—had set
their heads together. Was it not to be feared that Pitt
would attempt to fetter the coming Regency with some
restrictions? And by whom could that attempt be more
effectually prevented than by the statesman holding the
Great Seal? How important then if possible to gain
him over!

With these views, and with the Prince's sanction, a
secret negotiation with Lord Thurlow was begun. It
was proposed to him that he should do his utmost to
defeat any restrictions on the Regent, and that in return
he should become President of the Council in the new
administration. But the offer of the Presidency was
spurned by Thurlow; he insisted on still retaining the
Great Seal. This was a more difficult matter, from the
engagements of the Prince, and indeed of the whole
Fox party, to Lord Loughborough. Sheridan, however,
strongly pressed that Lord Thurlow should be secured
upon his own terms. The Prince agreed, and the negotiation was continued without Lord Loughborough.
The bargain was struck, or all but struck, awaiting only
Fox's sanction when he should arrive from Italy.

The perfidy of Thurlow in this transaction stands
little in need of comment. To this day it forms the
main blot upon his fame. Nowhere in our recent annals shall we readily find any adequate parallel to it,
except indeed in the career of his contemporary and his
rival, Loughborough.

Lord Thurlow succeeded at first in concealing all knowledge of the scheme from Pitt. In this he was much assisted by the fact that from this time forward the Cabinet Councils were frequently held at Windsor, thus affording him good opportunities for slipping round in secret to the apartments of the Prince of Wales. But a very slight incident brought to light the mystery. His cabals were detected by his own hat. Thus used the story to be told by a late survivor from these times, my lamented friend Mr. Thomas Grenville. One day when a Council was to be held at Windsor, Thurlow had been there some time before any of his colleagues arrived. He was to be brought back to London in the carriage of one of them, and the moment of departure being come, the Chancellor's hat was nowhere to be found. After long search one of the pages came running up with the hat in his hand, and saying aloud, "My Lord, I found it in the closet of His Royal Highness the Prince of Wales." The other Ministers were still in the hall waiting for their carriages, and the evident confusion of Lord Thurlow corroborated the inference which they drew.[7]

Thus might Pitt suspect, or much more than suspect, the Chancellor's double dealings. But still he had no positive proof of them; and he might feel as the younger Agrippina, that in many cases the best defence against treachery is to seem unconscious of it.[8] Thus, main-

---

[7] Lives of the Chancellors, by Lord Campbell. vol. v. p. 591. I have heard the same story told by Mr. Grenville himself.

[8] "Reputans Agrippina solum insidiarum remedium esse si non intelligerentur" (Tacit. Annal. lib. xiv. c. 6.)

taining his usual lofty calmness, he forbore from all inquiry, all expostulation.   He continued to meet Lord
Thurlow as before, but he privately determined to place
no part of the Regency business in Lord Thurlow's
hands, and to entrust to Lord Camden the conduct in
the House of Lords of all the measures consequent on
the Royal illness.

It was no slight aggravation to the embarrassment of
Mr. Pitt at this juncture that he was bound to meet
Parliament without delay.   Parliament had only been
prorogued till the 20th of November, and there remained no legal power in the State to prorogue it
further.   The two Houses met therefore on the 20th
as a matter of course, when Pitt in the Commons, and
Thurlow in the Lords, announced the King's incapacity
for business as the cause of meeting.   Pitt deprecated
any present discussion, suggesting that the House should
adjourn till the 4th of December, when he said if the
King's disorder should unhappily continue, it would be
necessary to consider what measures ought to be adopted.
Meanwhile, to give their proceedings all possible solemnity, he further proposed that the Speaker should
write circular letters to every Member, requiring his
attendance on the appointed day.   Lord Camden made
a similar proposition in the Lords, and these motions
passed both Houses without a single observation from
any side.   Mr. Fox had not yet returned, and during
his absence the Opposition were unwilling to commit
themselves by comments of any kind.

Soon afterwards a case of much difficulty arose at
Windsor.   There was a strong and just desire to re-

move His Majesty to Kew. In the first place the distance of Windsor from London was most inconvenient to the physicians in attendance; secondly. and this was the main if not the only reason put forward by themselves, it was most essential that the King should have, as he might have at Kew and could not at Windsor, a private garden, where, whenever his health permitted, he might take exercise without being overlooked or observed. But, on the other hand, the King showed the most extreme repugnance to leave Windsor. It was thought that even in his distracted state the advice of his confidential servants would have weight with him, and the necessity of compulsion be thus avoided. Accordingly on the 28th a Privy Council was held at Windsor, when the physicians were formally examined, all agreeing that the removal of His Majesty to Kew was a point of most pressing importance.

For the scene that followed, as for some of the preceding, I adopt the graphic description of Miss Burney: "Inexpressible was the alarm of every one lest the King, if he recovered, should bear a lasting resentment against the authors and promoters of this journey. To give it therefore every possible sanction, it was decreed that he should be seen both by the Chancellor and Mr. Pitt. The Chancellor went into his presence with a tremor such as before he had been only accustomed to inspire, and when he came out he was so extremely affected by the state in which he saw his Royal Master and patron that the tears ran down his cheeks, and his feet had difficulty to support him. Mr. Pitt was more composed, but expressed his grief with so much respect and attachment, that it added new weight to the universal admiration with which he is here beheld."

But whatever may have passed at these most painful interviews, it was found that they had not surmounted the morbid aversion of the King to the change required. "In what a situation was the house!" exclaims Miss Burney: "Princes, Equerries, Physicians, Pages,—all conferring, whispering, plotting, and caballing how to induce the King to set off!" Recourse was now had to a no less painful stratagem. The King had for some time been most earnestly pressing to see the Queen and the Princesses, but this the physicians had deemed it necessary to refuse him. It was then decided that the Royal ladies should proceed early next morning to Kew; that the King should be informed of their departure by the physicians; and that if, as they expected, he should doubt their assertion, he might be suffered to go through the apartments and ascertain the fact for himself. Next a promise was to be made His Majesty that on rejoining the members of his family at Kew he should be permitted to see them. On this promise George the Third did consent to the journey, and it did take place. But on coming to Kew the promise under which he had acted was not fulfilled; and the result—as might surely have been foreseen—was that same night a paroxysm of much increased severity.

Meanwhile an express had been sent to Fox in Italy with the tidings of the Royal illness, and with a pressing summons for his immediate return. The messen-

ger found the travelling statesman at Bologna, on
his way to Rome. He forthwith set out on his journey homewards, and proceeded with so much expedition as even in that wintry season to perform a
journey of more than eight hundred miles in nine days.
So great, indeed, was the despatch he used, and so
rough the roads over which he travelled, that he
severely suffered in his health for some time after his
return. With all his diligence, however, he could not
arrive in England until the 24th of this month. It is
striking to compare these details with another unlooked
for summons and another rapid return from Italy—I
mean Sir Robert Peel's, in November 1835. Each
of these statesmen came back with the expectation
of being made Prime Minister, but the hope proved
as fleeting in the one case as did the hold of office in
the other.

No sooner was Fox in London than he was apprised
of the negotiation with Lord Thurlow. Fox had no
taste at all for this underhand intrigue. But he felt
himself bound by the Prince's word which had already
passed. His own feelings of distress are best evinced
by some expressions in a note to Sheridan: " I have
swallowed the pill—a most bitter one it was—and have
written to Lord Loughborough, whose answer of course
must be consent. What is to be done next? Should
the Prince himself, you or I, or Warren, be the person
to speak to the Chancellor? Pray tell me what is to
be done. I do not remember ever feeling so uneasy
about any political thing I ever did in my life. Call if
you can."

Besides this one " political thing," another of still higher public moment was now submitted to Fox. Lord Loughborough had been devising a bold scheme, for, in fact, a *Coup d'Etat.* He had suggested that the Prince of Wales might, as next heir, seize the Regency by his own act, and without any authority from Parliament. This scheme he had embodied in a note which is written with his own hand in pencil. It still remains among the Rosslyn Papers, and it has been published by Lord Campbell in his ' Lives of the Chancellors.' [9]

But the sturdy hand of Fox brushed this cobweb aside. He was prepared, as we shall presently see, to go great lengths in asserting the inherent prerogative of the Prince of Wales. But he never dreamt of dispensing with the votes of Parliament. Under such circumstances, Lord Loughborough of course yielded to his leader ; and with his pencil note safely locked up within his desk, his Lordship a few weeks later, when speaking in the House of Peers, thought himself justified in solemnly disclaiming or denying that he held the unconstitutional doctrine which that note expressed. —Were not Loughborough and Thurlow worthy rivals ?

It appears however from some Reminiscences which Lord Carmarthen the Secretary of State drew up, and subsequently as Duke of Leeds read to a young friend,

---

[9] See vol. vi. p. 195. In the biography of Lord Loughborough are many other valuable papers. But in arranging them Lord Campbell has not always shown sufficient care. Thus, for instance, at page 205, the two notes of Fox which Lord Campbell refers to this period of 1788, belong most certainly to 1785, as is plain at once from their date of Downing Street.

that the Ministers of 1788 had soon become apprised of Lord Loughborough's perilous project. Had he persisted in it, they had designed to arrest him for High Treason and send him to the Tower.[1]

On the 3rd of December, the day before the re-assembling of Parliament, a Privy Council was held at Whitehall. By Pitt's direction a summons had been addressed to every Member, of whatever politics, the object being to impart in the most authentic form accurate intelligence on the situation of the King. Of 54 Members who came accordingly, it was calculated at the time that 24 were from the Opposition side. The five physicians who had been attending His Majesty being called in and examined upon oath, deposed as to his present incapacity for business. They added that there was a fair prospect of his recovery, but that they were wholly unable to fix or foretell the time. They had known cases of this kind last only for six weeks—they had known them last as long as two years.

Such then was the position of affairs when on the 4th of December Parliament met for business, and when the two great party rivals were again in presence of each other.

---

[1] Diary of Mr. Charles Abbot (Lord Colchester), January 24, 1796, as published in 1861.

APPENDIX.

APPENDIX.

LETTERS AND EXTRACTS OF LETTERS FROM KING GEORGE THE THIRD TO MR. PITT.

———o———

[Where in these copies the whole of the King's letter is given, " G. R.," his usual signature in this correspondence, is added at the end. Where it is omitted the reader will understand that only an extract is inserted, and that the remainder is in general of no public interest.]

Queen's House, March 23, 1783, 8·50 A.M.

Mr. Pitt is desired to come here in his morning dress as soon as convenient to him.

G. R.

St. James's, March 23, 1783, 11·55 A.M.

Mr. Pitt. I have seen Lord North, and sent him to the Duke of Portland to desire the plan of arrangements may be instantly sent to me, as I must coolly examine it before I can give any answer, and as I expect to have the whole finally decided before to-morrow's debate in the House of Commons. This seems to answer the idea I have just received from Mr. Pitt.

G. R.

I desire Mr. Pitt will be here after the Drawing Room.

Queen's House, March 24, 1783, 11·10 A.M.

Mr. Pitt's idea of having nothing announced till the debate of to-day meets with my thorough approbation. I have just seen the Lord Chancellor, who thinks that if Mr. Pitt should say, towards the close of the debate, that after such conduct as the Coalition has held, that every man attached to this Constitution must stand forth on this occasion, and that as such he is determined to keep the situation devolved on him, that he will meet with an applause that cannot fail to give him every encouragement.

I shall not expect Mr. Pitt till the Levee is over.

G. R.

Windsor, March 24, 1783, 5·12 P.M.

I am not surprised, as the debate has proved desultory, that Mr. Pitt has not been able to write more fully on this occasion. After the manner I have been personally treated by both the Duke of Portland and Lord North, it is impossible I can ever admit either of them into my service : I therefore trust that Mr. Pitt will exert himself to-morrow to plan his mode of filling up the offices that will be vacant, so as to be able on Wednesday morning to accept the situation his character and talents fit him to hold, when I shall be in town before twelve ready to receive him.

G. R.

Mr. Pitt to the King.

March 25, 1783.

Mr. Pitt received, this morning, the honour of your Majesty's gracious commands. With infinite pain he feels himself under the necessity of humbly expressing to your Majesty, that with every sentiment of dutiful attachment to your Majesty and zealous desire to contribute to the public service, it is utterly impossible for him, after the fullest consideration of the situation in which things stand, and of what passed yesterday in the House of Commons, to think of undertaking, under such circumstances, the situation which your Majesty has had the condescension and goodness to propose to him.

As what he now presumes to write is the final result of his best reflection, he should think himself criminal if, by delaying till to-morrow humbly to lay it before your Majesty, he should be the cause of your Majesty's not immediately turning your Royal mind to such a plan of arrangement as the exigency of the present circumstances may, in your Majesty's wisdom, seem to require.

Windsor, March 25, 4·35 P.M.

Mr. Pitt, I am much hurt to find you are determined to decline at an hour when those who have any regard for the Constitution as established by law ought to stand forth against the most daring and unprincipled faction that the annals of this kingdom ever produced.

G. R.

December 23, 1783, 10·46 A.M.

To one on the edge of a precipice every ray of hope must be pleasing. I therefore place confidence in the Duke of Richmond, Lord Gower, Lord Thurlow, and Mr. Pitt bringing forward some names to fill up an arrangement; which if they cannot, they already know my determination. One will be an hour perfectly agreeable to me.

G. R.

Windsor, January 13, 1784.

Mr. Pitt cannot but suppose that I received his communication of the two divisions in the long debate which
ended this morning with much uneasiness, as it shows
the House of Commons much more willing to enter into
any intemperate resolutions of desperate men than I
could have imagined. As to myself, I am perfectly
composed, as I have the self-satisfaction of feeling I
have done my duty.

Though I think Mr. Pitt's day will be fully taken up
in considering, with the other Ministers, what measures
are best to be proposed in the present crisis, yet that
no delay may arise from my absence I will dine in town,
and consequently be ready to see him in the evening, if
he shall find that will be of utility. At all events, I am
ready to take any step that may be proposed to oppose
this faction, and to struggle to the last period of my
life; but I can never submit to throw myself into its
power. If they in the end succeed, my line is a clear
one, and to which I have fortitude enough to submit.

G. R.

January 24, 1784, 9·17 A.M.

I own I cannot see any reason, if the thing is practicable, that a Dissolution should not be effected; if not,
I fear the Constitution of this country cannot subsist.

January 24, 1784, 6·25 P.M.

I desire Mr. Pitt will assemble the confidential Ministers
this evening, that he may state what has passed this day.
I should think it cannot give any reason for preventing
a Dissolution on Monday; but if it should, he must be
armed with the opinion of the other Ministers. I fear
Mr. Powys's candour has drawn him into a trap; delay

must be of the worst of consequences, and the Opposition cannot but be glad he should be the author of it. If Mr. Pitt can come after the meeting before eleven this night, I shall be ready to see him; if not, as early to-morrow morning as may suit him.

G. R.

January 25, 1784.

Though indecision is the most painful of all situations to a firm mind, I by no means wish Mr. Pitt should come to me till he has, with his brother Ministers, gone through the various objects the present crisis affords. I should hope by half an hour past nine he may be able to lay before me the result of their deliberations.

The Opposition will certainly throw every difficulty in our way, but we must be men; and if we mean to save the country, we must cut those threads that cannot be unravelled. Half-measures are ever puerile, and often destructive.

G. R.

January 26, 1784.

Mr. Pitt's language in the House of Commons this day seems to have been most proper. The idea of Ministers resigning, and consequently leaving every thing in confusion, was worthy of the mouth from whence it came, but cannot meet with the approbation of the sober-minded.

G. R.

January 30, 1784.

The account of what passed in the House of Commons yesterday, which I suppose by reading the various newspapers may be pretty nearly collected, gives every reason for commending Mr. Pitt's language and for

T 2

reprobating that of Mr. Fox and his follower, Lord North; and shows that their principles must ever prevent that kind of union to which alone I can ever consent.

I shall certainly not object to Mr. Pitt's making himself master, if possible, of what the Duke of Portland means, though I cannot suggest the mode. I cannot say the meeting of the gentlemen at the St. Alban's Tavern seem as yet to have taken the only step which ought to occur to them: the co-operating in preventing a desperate faction from completing the ruin of the most perfect of all human formations—the British Constitution.

G. R.

February 4, 1784.

I trust the House of Lords will this day feel that the hour is come for which the wisdom of our ancestors established that respectable corps in the State, to prevent either the Crown or the Commons from encroaching on the rights of each other. Indeed, should not the Lords stand boldly forth, this Constitution must soon be changed; for, if the two only remaining privileges of the Crown are infringed—that of negativing Bills which have passed both Houses of Parliament, and that of naming the Ministers to be employed—I cannot but feel, as far as regards my person, that I can be no longer of any utility to this country, nor can with honour continue in this island.

February 15, 1784.

Mr. Pitt is so well apprized of the mortification I feel at any possibility of ever again seeing the heads of Opposition in public employments, and more particularly Mr. Fox, whose conduct has not been more marked against my station in the Empire than against my person, that he must attribute my want of perspicuity in my conversation last night to that foundation; yet I should imagine it must be an ease to his mind, in conferring with the other confidential Ministers this morning, to have on paper my sentiments, which are the result of unremitted consideration since he left me last night, and which he has my consent to communicate, if he judges it right, to the above respectable persons.

My present situation is perhaps the most singular that ever occurred, either in the annals of this or any other country; for the House of Lords, by not a less majority than near two to one, have declared in my favour; and my subjects at large, in a much more considerable proportion, are not less decided; to combat which, Opposition have only a majority of twenty or at most of thirty in the House of Commons, who, I am sorry to add, seem as yet willing to prevent the public supplies. Though I certainly have never much valued popularity, yet I do not think it is to be despised when arising from a rectitude of conduct, and when it is to be retained by following the same respectable path which conviction makes me esteem that of duty, as calculated to prevent one branch of the legislature from annihilating the other two, and seizing also the executive power to which it has no claim.

I confess I have not yet seen the smallest appearance of sincerity in the leaders of Opposition, to come into the only mode by which I could tolerate them in my service, their giving up the idea of having the administration in their hands, and coming in as a respectable part of one on a broad basis; and therefore I, with a jealous eye, look on any words dropped by them, either in Parliament or to the gentlemen of the St. Alban's

Tavern, as meant only to gain those gentlemen, or, if carrying further views, to draw Mr. Pitt, by a negotiation, into some difficulty.

Should the Ministers, after discussing this, still think it advisable that an attempt should be made to try whether an administration can be formed on a real, not a nominal wide basis, and that Mr. Pitt having repeatedly and as fruitlessly found it impossible to get even an interview on what Opposition pretends to admit is a necessary measure, I will, though reluctantly, go personally so far as to authorize a message to be carried in my name to the Duke of Portland, expressing a desire that he and Mr. Pitt may meet to confer on the means of forming an administration on a wide basis, as the only means of entirely healing the divisions which stop the business of the nation. The only person I can think, from his office as well as personal character, proper to be sent by me, is Lord Sydney; but should the Duke of Portland, when required by me, refuse to meet Mr. Pitt, more especially upon the strange plea he has as yet held forth, I must here declare that I shall not deem it right for me ever to address myself again to him.

The message must be drawn on paper, as must everything in such a negotiation, as far as my name is concerned; and I trust, when I next see Mr. Pitt, if under the present circumstances the other Ministers shall agree with him in thinking such a proposition advisable, that he will bring a sketch of such a message for my inspection.

G. R.

February 18, 1784.

As Mr. Pitt's letter seems to suppose the House of Commons will this day come to some resolution either consonant to that proposed the last night, though warned

by Mr. Powys, or to an Address, I should think Mr.
Pitt, instead of coming to Court this day, had better
employ part of the time in seeing such Members of that
House who may be thought proper to take an active
part in the debate, and also consult with the Cabinet, in
case the House should come into either of those violent
measures, as to the steps then necessary to be taken.
He may depend on my being heartily ready to adopt
the most vigorous ones, as I think the struggle is really
no less than my being called upon to stand forth in defence of the Constitution against a most desperate and
unprincipled faction. Mr. Pitt being then prepared,
he may see me as soon as he pleases after this debate is
over.

G. R.

February 22, 1784.

I am not surprised that the Ministers should wish to
have all the possible time for consideration on any steps
that the Address of the House of Commons and the
answer to it may draw on, and therefore that it is
wished I should not receive the Commons till Wednesday. I very willingly consent to fixing on that day for
the reception of it; and trust that while the answer is
drawn up with civility, it will be a clear support of my
own rights, which the Addresses from all parts of the
kingdom show me the people feel essential to their
liberties.

G. R.

February 29, 1784.

I was much hurt at hearing since the Drawing Room[1]
of the outrage committed the last night under the

---

[1] Held on the same day, a Sunday, according to the custom at that
time.

auspices of Brooks's against Mr. Pitt on his return from
the City, but am very happy to find he escaped without
injury. I trust every means will be employed to find
out the abettors of this, which I should hope may be
got at.

As I suppose to-morrow will be a late day at the
House of Commons, and consequently that I cannot be
wanted on Tuesday, I mean to-morrow after Court to
go to Windsor for the sake of hunting that day.

G. R.

Windsor, March 9, 1784.

Mr. Pitt's letter is undoubtedly the most satisfactory
I have received for many months. An avowal on the
outset that the proposition held forth is not intended to
go further lengths than a kind of manifesto; and then
carrying it by the majority only of one, and the day
concluding with an avowal that all negotiation is at an
end, gives me every reason to hope that by a firm and
proper conduct this faction will by degrees be deserted
by many, and at length be forgot. I shall ever with
pleasure consider that by the prudence as well as rectitude of one person in the House of Commons this great
change has been effected, and that he will be ever able
to reflect with satisfaction that in having supported me
he has saved the Constitution, the most perfect of
human formations.

Mr. Pitt will consider of the declaration, that my
answer may meet every assertion, as I trust it will be
the last visit on this unpleasant business.

G. R.

Windsor, March 10, 1784.

It is with infinite satisfaction I learn from Mr. Pitt's note the event of the Mutiny Bill having yesterday gone through the Committee without any opposition, which may with reason be called a great victory, it having been more than once avowed in the House that it would be passed only for a month. I am sorry my time was spent in talking of so impracticable a scheme and so absurd a letter as that of the Duke of Portland; but if it has shown the impossibility of further negotiation, I hope it has proved not quite useless.

G. R.

March 23, 1784.

This instant I have received Mr. Pitt's letters, and a draft of the Speech, which entirely meets with my ideas: I therefore desire the proper copy may be prepared for to-morrow. I have, in consequence of Mr. Pitt's intimation that the Bills will be ready for my assent, sent orders for the equipages to be at St. James's to-morrow at half hour past two. I desire notice may be given that I may be expected a quarter before three at Westminster, that those necessary to attend may be there.

G. R.

March 28, 1784.

Though Mr. Pitt must agree with me that Mr. Scott would have been the fittest person for Solicitor-General, yet considering the situation of Lord Gower, and the very early decided part Mr. Macdonald has taken, the latter gentleman cannot be passed by; therefore the offering it to him without delay seems right.

T 3

April 5, 1784.

I cannot refrain from the pleasure of expressing to Mr. Pitt how much his success at Cambridge has made me rejoice, as he is the highest on the return, and that Lord Euston is his colleague. This renders his election for the University a real honour, and reconciles me to his having declined Bath.

I shall only add that as yet the returns are more favourable than the most sanguine could have expected.

G. R.

May 26, 1784.

Mr. Pitt's note on the decision of the House of Commons by so large a majority to hear the petition on the Bedfordshire election on an early day is very pleasing, as also that the petition of Mr. Fox is to be examined by the whole House on Friday. I cannot conclude without expressing my fullest approbation of the conduct of Mr. Pitt on Monday: in particular his employing only a razor against his antagonists, and never condescending to run into that rudeness which, though common in that House, certainly never becomes a gentleman. If he proceeds in this mode of oratory, he will bring debates into a shape more creditable, and correct that, and I trust many other evils, which time and temper can only effect.

G. R.

Kew, July 1, 1784.

It is with infinite satisfaction that I learn from Mr. Pitt's letter that the various Resolutions proposed yesterday to the House of Commons on the subjects of the loan, the subscription for the unfunded debt, and the taxes, were unanimously agreed to. Nothing is more natural than that, such heavy charges requiring many new taxes, those particularly affected by some will from that selfish motive, though conscious of the necessity of new burthens, attempt to place them on others rather than on themselves. Mr. Fox's moderation and candour will cease if any strong opposition to particular taxes should arise; but I trust Mr. Pitt will be able to carry all of them. It seemed to be an opinion yesterday that the brick tax was the one most likely to be opposed, but Mr. Pitt not having mentioned it, I suppose that branch of trade has not so many friends in the House as the coal pits, which are the property of more considerable persons, and therefore more clamorous, though not less able to support a new charge on their profits.

G. R.

Windsor, July 17, 1784.

It is with infinite pleasure I have received Mr. Pitt's note containing the agreeable account of the Committee on the East India Bill having been opened by the decision of so very decided a majority. I trust this will prevent much trouble being given in its farther progress, and that this measure may lay a foundation for, by degrees, correcting those shocking enormities in India that disgrace human nature, and, if not put a stop to, threaten the expulsion of the Company out of that wealthy region. I have the more confidence of success from knowing Mr. Pitt's good sense, which will make him not expect that the present experiment shall at once prove perfect; but that by an attentive eye, and an inclination to do only what is right, he will, as occasions arise, be willing to make such improvements as may by degrees bring this arduous work into some degree of perfection.

G. R.

September 10, 1784.

I am not surprised that Mr. Orde's informations on the supposed plot reach Sir Edward Newenham as well as Lord Bristol; but such heads, as Mr. Pitt very well observes, are not likely to form well-regulated plans. Yet they ought to be well watched, for they may be desperate ones.

February 18, 1785.

Great as my surprise is at the Castle having acted entirely contrary to the most direct instructions from hence in the Resolutions for finally settling the commercial regulations between Great Britain and Ireland, yet it is, if possible, exceeded by Mr. Orde in his letter to Mr. Pitt seeming to expect that Britain can consent to them so entirely changed.

G. R.

February 22, 1785.

I am glad precedents authorize the Resolutions of the Irish Parliament being communicated to the two Houses without any message on the occasion, as I could by no means show approbation to them in their present shape, and I do not see any reason for giving an opinion till the Parliament of this Kingdom has, by the enclosed draft of a Resolution, decided the line to be held, which, as it has legislative considerations, ought to commence with them.

G. R.

March 4, 1785.

From what Mr. Pitt has heard me say on the continuation of the Westminster Scrutiny, he will not be surprised that an end being put to it is not a subject of great inquietude, though I do not the less feel that it has been effected by many friends voting with the Coalition, which is not a pleasant reflection; but one must hope they will not in future allow themselves to follow so improper an example. I should hope Mr. Fox rather hurt his cause by taking so strong a step as proposing to expunge from the Journals the several Resolutions which have been made relative to the Scrutiny : he having at length postponed the consideration of it till Wednesday seems to authorize this opinion.

G. R.

March 20, 1785.

I have received Mr. Pitt's paper containing the heads of his plan for a Parliamentary Reform, which I look on as a mark of attention. I should have delayed acknowledging the receipt of it till I saw him on Monday, had not his letter expressed that there is but one issue of the business he could look upon as fatal : that is, the possibility of the measure being rejected by the weight of those who are supposed to be connected with Government. Mr. Pitt must recollect that though I have thought it unfortunate that he had early engaged himself in this measure, yet that I have ever said that as he was clear of the propriety of the measure, he ought to lay his thoughts before the House; that out of personal regard to him. I should avoid giving any opinion to any one on the opening of the door to Parliamentary Reform except to him : therefore I am certain Mr. Pitt cannot suspect my having influenced any one on the occasion ; if others choose for base ends to impute such a conduct to me, I must bear it as former false suggestions. Indeed on a question of such magnitude, I should think very ill of any man who took a part on either side without the maturest consideration, and who would suffer his civility to any one to make him vote contrary to his own opinion. The conduct of some of Mr. Pitt's most intimate friends on the Westminster Scrutiny shows there are questions men will not by friendship be biassed to adopt.

G. R.

March 24, 1785.

This morning I received the enclosed note from Lord Southampton, on which I appointed him to be at St. James's when I returned from the House of Peers. He there delivered to me the letter from the Prince of Wales. All I could collect further from him was that the idea is that I call for explanations and retrenchments as a mode of declining engaging to pay the debts ; that there are many sums that it cannot be honourable to explain ; that Lord Southampton has reason to believe they have not been incurred for political purposes ; that he thinks the going abroad is now finally resolved on ; that perhaps the champion of the Opposition has been consulted on the letter now sent. I therefore once more send all that has passed to Mr. Pitt, and hope to have in the course of to-morrow from him what answer ought to be sent to this extraordinary epistle, which, though respectful in terms, is in direct defiance of my whole correspondence. I suppose Mr. Pitt will choose to consult the Chancellor.

G. R.

March 25, 1785.

Mr. Pitt need not make any excuse for not having returned the papers this day, as his punctuality is too well known to give any room for suspicion, and the good Chancellor is rather famous for loving delay; therefore it sits on the present occasion most justly on his shoulders. Considering he had the papers so long in his hands within these three weeks, I should not have supposed they would require a fresh perusal. Not having heard anything this day, I should suppose that no inconvenience can arise from not hearing from Mr. Pitt on this subject till to-morrow.

G. R.

April 19, 1785.

Mr. Pitt's note contains so many speakers on the question that he proposed yesterday in the House of Commons, that I am not surprised the debate continued to so late an hour; I trust the adjournment till to-morrow will make him not the worse for the fatigue that it must have occasioned. I understand that Lord Camden, who never before heard Mr. Pitt in Parliament, expressed at the Ancient Concert last night great commendation at his masterly performance.

G. R.

Windsor, August 7, 1785.

I have this instant received Mr. Pitt's letter enclosing the one brought him by Count Woronzow's secretary and the paper that accompanied it, which is a copy of the one given on Friday to Lord Carmarthen. Count Woronzow also visited Lord Sydney and insisted a council was to be held the next day to give him an answer whether I would break the treaty I have in my Electoral capacity finally concluded with the King of Prussia and the Elector of Saxony to prevent all measures contrary to the Germanic Constitution. If no one has such dangerous views, this association cannot give umbrage; but the time certainly required this precaution. My only difficulty in giving any answer to the Empress of Russia is that her declaration bears so strongly the shape of a command that it requires a strong one.

St. James's, August 10, 1785.

On arriving in town I have received the three papers I proposed transmitting to Mr. Pitt. I cannot say that the time that has elapsed since last I wrote has diminished my surprise or cooled my feelings on the haughty step the Empress of Russia has taken; but I trust I have too much regard to my own dignity to wish any heat should appear in the answer that may next week be given to Count Woronzow, though she must know that when steps are taken from principle they are not to be retrograded.

G. R.

February 28, 1786.

Mr. Pitt's moving an approbation of the plan of fortifications previous to the Speaker's leaving the Chair was undoubtedly the most likely method of gaining consent to the measure; but the postponing the consideration from last Session to this, though it arose from candour, had the appearance of avoiding the decision, and certainly gave time to the enemies of the fortifications to gain more strength. I do not in the least look on the event as any want of confidence in Mr. Pitt from

the Members of the House of Commons, but their attachment to old prejudices and some disinclination to
the projector of the fortifications.

G. R.

March 30, 1786.

Considering Mr. Pitt has had the unpleasant office of
providing for the expenses incurred by the last war, it
is but just he should have the full merit he deserves of
having the public know and feel that he has now proposed a measure that will render the nation again respectable, if she has the sense to remain quiet some
years, and not by wanting to take a showy part in the
transactions of Europe again become the dupe of other
Powers, and from ideal greatness draw herself into lasting distress. The old English saying is applicable to
our situation: "England must cut her coat according to
her cloth."

June 14, 1786.

Mr. Pitt would have conducted himself yesterday very
unlike what my mind ever expects of him if, as he thinks
Mr. Hastings's conduct towards the Rajah was too severe,
he had not taken the part he did, though it made him
coincide with (the) adverse party. As to myself, I own
I do not think it possible in that country to carry on
business with the same moderation that is suitable to
an European civilized nation.

G. R.

Windsor, July 3, 1786.

The draft of a message to the Prince of Wales which
Mr. Pitt sent to me on Saturday evening met so tho-

roughly with my ideas, that I have verbatim copied it, and sent it through the channel of Lord Southampton.

I return also the two letters from Mendiola, and approve the disclaiming in the strongest manner all idea of interfering in the discontents of the inhabitants of the Spanish settlements in South America. As I ever thought the conduct of France in North America unjustifiable, I certainly can never copy so faithless an example.

G. R.

Mr. Pitt to the King.

January 22, 1787.

Mr. Pitt humbly begs leave to acquaint your Majesty that he has seen the Bishop of Peterborough, who wishes to decline the Deanery of St. Paul's, appearing at the same time very thankful for the offer, and begging to be laid at your Majesty's feet with every expression of duty and gratitude. Under these circumstances Mr. Pitt takes the liberty to submit to your Majesty his earnest wish that the Deanery of St. Paul's may still be held with the Bishopric of Lincoln, on Dr. Pretyman's giving up his prebend and living. As the preferment was held with two others in addition to it by the present Bishop, Mr. Pitt flatters himself there can be nothing objectionable in its being now given with the Bishopric, and he sees neither any arrangement of importance nor any pressing claim with which it can interfere.

Mr. Pitt will only presume to add that he can request nothing from your Majesty's goodness which he has more anxiously and personally at heart.

January 22, 1787.

Mr. Pitt, By your note which met me as I was riding to town, I find the Bishop of Peterborough declines the Deanery of St. Paul's, and that this has made you renew your application for Dr. Pretyman. I see you have it so much at heart that I cannot let my reason guide me against my inclination to oblige you. I therefore consent to his having this Deanery with the Bishopric of Lincoln, though I am confident it will be, by all but those concerned, thought very unreasonable, and I should fear will serve as a precedent to the like applications. While desires increase, the means of satisfying people have been much diminished.

G. R.

May 26, 1787.

Had Lord Carmarthen's letter, accompanied by a Minute of Cabinet, not been also by Mr. Pitt's letter, I should certainly have declined consenting to risk the advancing 70,000l. to the Stadtholder's party in the United Provinces; and though I now reluctantly consent to it from the fatal experience of having fed the Corsican cause, and Ministry never having, as they had promised, found means of its being refunded to me, which made me consequently afterwards appear in an extravagant light to Parliament, yet I trust to Mr. Pitt's honour that he will take such arrangements on this occasion as shall prevent postponing the regular payments of the Civil List, and that Parliament shall make good the payment the next winter without supposing that the demand arises from any extravagance on my part.

G. R.

July 17, 1787.

My reason for suggesting the idea that though the King of Prussia can never coincide with the Emperor's views in Germany, they might agree as to the Netherlands, arose from thinking that in politics as well as private life, when nothing but what is fair is meant, it obviates suspicion to speak clearly, and that less openness often causes mischief.

October 12, 1787.

I cannot return to the Secretary of State's Office the very material papers on the plans of France with regard to India without sending Mr. Pitt a few lines. I should hope he will acquaint the Cabinet to-morrow that I am forming four regiments for that service, and that he will push on a negotiation with M. Boers to make the two Companies understand one another, and take efficient measures to secure us against our insidious neighbour. Perhaps no part of the change in Holland is so material to this country as the gaining that Republic as an ally in India. I recommend that no time should be lost in bringing this to bear, and our Company ought to be liberal in its offers to effect it.

G. R.

March 6, 1788.

I have delayed acknowledging the receipt of Mr. Pitt's note informing me of the division in the House of Commons this morning, lest he might have been disturbed when it would have been highly inconvenient. It is amazing how, on a subject that could be reduced into so small a compass, the House would hear such long speaking. The object of Opposition was evidently to oblige the old and infirm Members to give up the attendance, which is reason sufficient for the friends of Government to speak merely to the point in future, and try to shorten debates, and bring, if possible, the present bad mode of mechanical oratory into discredit.

G. R.

March 8, 1788.

Mr. Pitt having had so long an attendance again yesterday in the House of Commons, I did not choose to acknowledge the receipt of his note this morning. I am sure Mr. Pitt has acted very properly in proposing the recommitment of the Explanatory Bill, that a clause may be added disclaiming any view of patronage; but I cannot call those gentlemen sincere friends that have harboured unjust suspicions on that head. I fear it is come of the leaven of former Oppositions, who now support Government, but are not void of sentiments more calculated for their former than present line of conduct. I own I am not quite cool on this subject; for where suggestions are unfounded, they cannot be the offspring of real friends.

G. R.

END OF VOL. I.

LONDON: PRINTED BY WILLIAM CLOWES AND SONS, STAMFORD STREET, AND CHARING CROSS.